# If you,

# Then me

# If you, Then me

## Yvonne Woon

KATHERINE TEGEN BOOKS
An Imprint of HarperCollins Publishers

Katherine Tegen Books is an imprint of HarperCollins Publishers.

ISBN 978-0-06-300864-9

Typography by Carla Weise
21 22 23 24 25   PC/LSCH   10 9 8 7 6 5 4 3 2 1
❖

First Edition

For Ayla and Akiva

And in memory of Trever Col

## one

**M**aybe **it's easier** if I introduce myself the way I best know how.

```
public static void main(String[] args)
{
Person xiaChan = new Person();
xiaChan.setAge(16);
xiaChan.shovelDriveway();
xiaChan.goToSchool();
xiaChan.converseAwkwardly();
xiaChan.embarrassSelf();
xiaChan.hideBehindPhoneScreen();
xiaChan.returnHome();
xiaChan.shovelDriveway();
xiaChan.eatDinner();
xiaChan.doHomework();
xiaChan.debugWiser();
```

```
xiaChan.reliveEmbarassments();
xiaChan.kickSelf();
xiaChan.fantasizeAboutCalifornia();
xiaChan.sleep();
}
```

If you don't understand, let me translate. My name is Xia Chan and I was sixteen years old when my story began. My life was boring and uneventful. Things happened to me and I responded: Snow fell and I shoveled it. Dishes got dirty and I cleaned them. Homework piled up and I did it. I'd always felt like I was meant to have a big life, but for reasons I couldn't explain, I was stuck in a loop where nothing exciting ever happened.

My mother and I lived on the second floor of a triple-decker in Worcester, a gray and unremarkable city a little over an hour outside of Boston. She moved there from Taiwan when she was twenty-two, a fact that I still can't fathom considering she could have moved anywhere else in the country and instead she picked a place where it snows for six months of the year and is known primarily for its proximity to other, more exciting cities.

I had one friend, Gina. Two if you counted ObjectPermanence, and three if you counted Wiser.

It had been four months, three days, and five hours since I clicked *FINISH* and sent my application, video, and transcripts to the Foundry. I hadn't heard a word back since.

So when an unfamiliar number called me while I was

shoveling the front steps, I stuck my shovel in the ice and scrambled to pick up.

My phone was an old hand-me-down from my mom, who liked to remind me that money didn't grow on bushes, (though she was a professor who spoke perfect English, she still butchered her idioms, a quirk that never ceased to take the gravity out of her lectures) and that just because we lived in a consumer culture that normalized the disposability of products to maximize profits for a select few extremely wealthy individuals didn't mean that I should assume she would buy me a new device every year. Back in her day, things were made to last. What's wrong with this phone? It's a good phone. It works just fine.

I tried to pick up but the screen wouldn't unlock, which happened when it got too cold. I fumbled with it, growing frustrated.

Next door, the front screen slammed and Gina trudged outside dragging her shovel. "What?" she said.

"My phone is frozen again. Literally."

"It's protesting," Gina said. "I don't want to be out here either." She spoke with a soft New England accent, the only one I'd heard that sounded sweet.

I tried to answer again. This time it worked.

"Hello," a man said on the other end of the line. "I'm Tony from TireMax America, and I'm calling to tell you about our end-of-winter deals—"

My heart sank. "Not interested," I mumbled, and shoved my phone into my pocket.

"No word from your start-up oven thing?" Gina asked.

She was talking about the Foundry. "Incubator," I corrected. "Ovens cook things. Incubators warm things gently to foster life."

"Whatever."

"But no, no word yet."

The Foundry. It called itself a school, but really it was where all the young tech prodigies got their start, the only one of its kind. Only twenty kids were accepted, all expenses paid for one year to live on campus in Silicon Valley and compete to be that year's Founder. Whoever won got one million dollars in seed funding and, maybe even more importantly, the fame and respect that came with everyone knowing your name.

I'd wanted to go since I was ten and saw a newspaper article about Mitzy Erst, kid genius and Foundry alum who'd invented FindMe, the first facial recognition app that let you search your photos by word. She went on to found a bunch of photo-editing start-ups, the most famous being Daggertype, which made new photos look like they were from the 1800s. Mitzy wasn't a kid anymore, but I still had the clipping taped to the wall by my bed, along with a few old profiles and an interview where she talked about how anyone with a good idea could make it to California if they worked hard enough. Just apparently not me.

I didn't care so much about the money, or even winning, though of course both would be nice. What I really wanted was to finally be around people who understood me—people who wouldn't see me as an eccentric basement-dweller who only knew how to talk to computers, who would look at Wiser and see her potential, and mine.

I surveyed the snow in front of me, feeling miserable. "Who decided this was a habitable environment for humans?" I asked. "Click, select, and delete. Why hasn't anyone invented that yet for real life?"

"It's on you, I guess," Gina said with a smirk. "Though I don't know what you're complaining about. Your driveway is four feet shorter than mine."

Gina was the youngest of four and spent most of her time trying to talk over her brothers, which taught her how to be loud. She was the polar opposite of me—short where I was tall, round where I was bony, charming where I was awkward. She loved winter even though she complained about it all the time, and spent her evenings fantasizing about having her own room while I sat alone in my empty apartment, wishing it were full. She was hopeless with technology and preferred sports, both watching and playing. We'd lived next door to each other since we were kids.

"This is the only time of year that I'm glad I don't live in a big house," I said. "Can you imagine shoveling one of those long winding driveways?"

"If you lived in a house that big, you'd probably have enough money to pay someone to do it for you," Gina pointed out.

"If I had that much money, I'd move somewhere with no snow."

Gina closed her eyes. "Mmm. Florida."

"California," I fantasized. "Palm trees."

"Blue water," Gina said. "White sand so hot you can't even take your sandals off."

The thought of burning feet interrupted my fantasy. "Cold sodas and tan lines."

Gina frowned. "Bad tan lines. And sunburns."

Sunburns also didn't sound so good. "Getting sand in your soda."

"Getting sand in your bathing suit."

"Seagulls stealing your food," I said.

"Seaweed tickling your feet while you're swimming."

I shivered. "Stepping on sharp rocks."

"Jellyfish masquerading as plastic bags," Gina said.

"Stepping on a jellyfish," I said, wincing.

"Having to pee on yourself after stepping on a jellyfish."

"Going swimming after peeing on yourself after stepping on a jellyfish only to see a dark shadow under the water," I said.

"Dying young in a tragic shark attack after peeing on yourself after stepping on a jellyfish."

A plow drove by, pressing snow from the road into our driveways.

"I guess it's not so bad here," I said.

"I guess not."

We'd both picked up our shovels when my phone rang again. Another unfamiliar number. It was probably another telemarketer, but I tried to pick up anyway. This time my screen was so cold that it wouldn't unlock.

"I'd better go inside," I said and ran upstairs.

My mother and I lived in a small apartment, practical and tidy except for the kitchen table, which doubled as my mother's desk and was stacked with papers. She was an adjunct professor in political science at four different colleges, so when she wasn't driving from campus to campus trying to get to class on time, she was grading papers, planning lessons, and complaining about the traffic or how education in this country was a scam that defrauded students of their money and dangled the possibility of tenure in front of teachers to trick them into overextending themselves for years, no, decades, so that universities could fatten their endowments.

I put my phone on top of the refrigerator where it was warm, then set a pot of water to boil for instant ramen. While it was heating, I unplugged the microwave from the wall and carried it to the table, where I unscrewed the case and resumed work on the wiring. I'd hooked up a tiny, single board computer to the back and was trying to figure out how to wire it into the microwave so that I could load it with cook times from the internet and make the whole thing voice activated. Though so far, I'd only accidentally melted a Tupperware before successfully getting the microwave to play a Gregorian hymn while the food heated, making it feel like my frozen pizza bagel was a precious ancient relic, imbued with godlike powers and emitting fractured, hazy light as it spun on its glass plate. It was a work in progress.

While tinkering, I glanced at the stack of my mother's

papers. They were notes she'd written to her students. I knew I shouldn't read them, but I couldn't help it. It was an unhealthy pastime of mine, peering into her alternate life. *This is a fascinating new take on a well-trodden historical moment,* one note read. *I'm particularly drawn to your analysis of the role of women in student uprisings. Could you expand on the economic pressures that catalyzed their involvement in the movement?* Though I'd read her notes to her students before, they always bothered me. She never spoke that way to me. She expressed love by staying up late to iron my clothes. The boldest compliment she'd ever given me was that she knew I could do better. I could count on one hand the number of times she'd hugged me. I couldn't imagine her being fascinated by any of my ideas or telling me that she was *particularly drawn* to a thought I had, and yet I couldn't stop reading, even though I knew it would upset me.

My phone chirped on. I brought it to the table.

"Wiser, why don't I have any interesting ideas?"

My own voice spoke back from the phone, only it sounded older—deeper and a little raspy, with a better vocabulary and a little more confidence—the way I might sound in twenty years. I had designed it that way. "You have plenty of interesting ideas," Wiser said. "Me, for example."

"Other than you."

Wiser paused while she scanned my data, looking for an answer. She was on in the background of my phone all the time, listening, gathering information. All I had to do was say her name and she would wake and respond. When

I was finished, I'd say, "Thanks, Wiser," and she'd go back to sleep.

"You once wrote a program that predicted which streets were going to have more potholes based on the volume of traffic, the size and grade of the street, and the median income of the neighborhood."

I hated that program. I'd made it to help my mom after we'd gotten another flat and I'd had to sit on the side of the road again and listen to her stress about how she was going to find the time to get the car fixed without missing class.

"Yeah, but it didn't work. All it did was get us lost."

"But it was an interesting idea. The problem was that it was impossible to take into account the quality of the asphalt."

"Yeah, I remember," I muttered.

Wiser went quiet. Though her silence was just a natural pause in her response-based programming, it still sounded like she was upset, and I immediately felt bad for dismissing her. "Sorry."

Through the ceiling, I could hear the footsteps of the family that lived above us. There were four of them, always tumbling on the floor, arguing with each other, slamming doors, shrieking and laughing while their dog barked.

I watched the snow fall outside the window. My mother wouldn't be home for another three hours. Our apartment was quiet, empty.

"Wiser, will I always be alone?"

"Everyone's alone," Wiser said.

"That doesn't make me feel better."

"My purpose isn't to make you feel better," Wiser said. "It's to give you advice that your future self might say by scanning your data and using an algorithm to predict the best outcomes."

I groaned. "I know, I know."

"Though I suppose the end goal is for you to make better decisions, and therefore feel better, so maybe that is my purpose—"

The phone rang, interrupting her. It was the same number that had called before. I picked up.

"Hi, I'm calling for X-Xia Chan," a man's voice said.

He had a plastic voice, the kind you only hear on TV. He was probably a marketer trying to sell me something. Plus, he didn't know how to pronounce my name.

"She's not here," I said. "And anyway, she's a minor and doesn't have a credit card. Please remove her number from this list." I was about to hang up when he interjected.

"Wait, don't hang up."

I paused.

"Is this her mother?"

I narrowed my eyes. "Yes," I said slowly. "Who's this?"

"My name is Lars. I'm calling to congratulate her."

"Congratulate her for what?"

"I run an institute called the Foundry. It's an incubator program for gifted teenagers. A few months ago, your daughter sent me a video of a project she's been working on called Wiser. I'm sure you know all about it."

My heart began to race. His name was Lars. I knew this voice.

"You're Lars Lang. You founded Canyou Games." I realized I was giving myself away and paused to compose myself. "My daughter loves you. I mean, she admires you. Your work. She loves your work."

He laughed. "Well, I love her work. Which is actually why I'm calling. If I leave my phone number, could you have her call me back?"

"I'd be happy to take a message," I said quickly.

"If you don't mind, I'd really like to tell her myself."

"Really, a message is just fine. She won't be back until late, and she'd be upset with me if I tell her you called but don't tell her why."

Lars paused. "Okay. You can tell her that I loved Wiser and think it has incredible promise. I've never seen an application like it before and would love to hear more about what direction she wants to take it in. If she's still interested, we hope she'll come out to California and be a part of our upcoming class of young founders."

I felt light-headed, the way I imagined one felt after drinking champagne. Was it possible that the grainy video I'd made on Gina's phone had actually been watched by a person, approved of, sent to another person and another person and so on until it made it to Lars Lang? And that he loved it and thought it had promise? And wanted me to come to California?

"So she's accepted?" I asked.

"She's accepted."

I spun around, looking for someone to tell, but the apartment was empty.

"*She-ah*," I said.

"Excuse me?"

"That's how you pronounce her name."

"Ah, okay. My mistake. When she calls me, I'll go over all of the details. I'm also happy to put you in touch with our mentors, so you get a better sense of what the program is like and what your daughter will be doing next year if she accepts."

"She accepts," I said quickly, then cleared my throat in an attempt to sound older. "I mean, I'm sure she will accept. But yes, I'll have her call you."

"Great," he said. "I'm looking forward to it."

I took down his number before hanging up. My hand trembled as I stared at my phone. Had it really happened? I felt electrified with happiness. Without thinking, I ran outside to tell Gina, but by then it had grown dark, and Gina's driveway was empty. She must have gone in to eat dinner with her family. The only person outside was our landlady, who was salting the side steps.

She looked up at me, bewildered. "Where's your coat? It's freezing."

"I'm going to California!" I said, because I had to tell someone.

"You still need to wear a coat."

I grinned at her. It was still snowing, and big, thick

flakes collected on my sleeves. The driveway where I'd shoveled was already dusted in white, but I didn't care. I had promise. I was going to California.

The landlady was right, though. It was freezing. I hurried back inside.

"Wiser," I said to my phone. "I did it. I was accepted to the Foundry."

"I know," she said. "Congratulations."

I waited for her to say more, but that was it. I made a mental note to improve her congratulatory tone.

"What should I do to celebrate?"

"Have a party," she said.

"Really? That's your advice?"

"Yes. What's wrong with it?"

I rolled my eyes. It would take me too long to explain to her why I couldn't plan and throw a party for myself that evening, so instead I said, "Not possible."

"Go out to dinner."

"I can't drive."

"Buy balloons."

I really had to work on some of these stock responses. "I'm not a child."

"Get a manicure."

"I thought you were supposed to know me."

"Make a cake."

"You know that Mom doesn't keep baking supplies around."

It gave me an idea, though. I scrounged through the

cabinets until I found a pouch of instant cocoa and bag of old marshmallows. I was born in the winter, and every year on my birthday my mother would make us two mugs of hot chocolate and we'd sit together on the couch and watch movies. It was one of the few nights she took off from grading papers and spent the whole evening with me. I made myself a mug and went to my bedroom.

It was a simple room: a few magazine and newspaper cutouts of Mitzy Erst taped over my bed and my huge computer whirring beneath my desk. I'd built it myself with parts I'd found online, including the ugly brown tower case that I'd spray-painted silver to make it look new.

I kept the lights off and pulled down the shades, revealing posters of palm trees that I'd taped to their insides. I woke my desktop and set it to California mode. The screen warmed, emitting hazy, buttery light into the room.

"Wiser, play ocean sounds," I said, and sank into the tangled comforter on my bed. "Tell me about California."

I sat on my bed, sipping my chocolate and listening to Wiser describe the crisp blue of the Pacific Ocean and the rocky cliffs lined with cypress trees, the orange sunsets and the mornings rising out of the fog. It wasn't a huge celebration, but it was mine.

# two

I woke the next morning to the sound of my mother making breakfast. I sat up, wondering if I had imagined the night before, but after a quick glance through my phone history, I knew it had been true. Lars Lang had called me and told me I'd been accepted to the Foundry. I fell back into my bed and grinned until my mother's voice brought me back to reality.

"Xia? Breakfast in fifteen minutes."

It was Saturday, which meant chores. I slid out of bed and glanced around my room, wishing I had been born in the future so that I wouldn't have to waste my time doing all my tasks manually. Click, bed made. Click, laundry gathered and stuffed in the machine. Click, dishes washed and driveway shoveled. Click, homework done.

I didn't know what I would tell my mother. She wouldn't like the idea of me leaving school, even if the Foundry was technically just a different school. She'd think it was the first step to dropping out.

I picked up my phone and dialed Lars Lang's number. It rang for a while before he picked up.

"Yes?"

I was surprised by his gruff tone. "Is this Lars Lang?"

"Yes. Who's this?" He sounded like he'd been sleeping. I checked the clock. It wasn't *that* early.

"Xia Chan. You left me a message yesterday?"

"Do you know what time it is?"

"It's, um, nine thirty."

"I'm in California. It's six thirty in the morning on a Saturday. That's basically airport time."

My throat seized. "I'm so sorry. I wasn't thinking—"

"It's okay. Just give me a minute to wake up."

There was a long pause. I heard shuffling in the background. Dishes clanking. The beep of what sounded like a microwave. "Look," he finally said. "It's too early for me to do my whole spiel so I'm going to skip the niceties and get straight to the point. I love Wiser. The idea, the execution— your algorithm for scanning the user's data to generate future outcomes is really something else. And making it the user's future self and not some disembodied godlike voice . . . so smart. The possibilities are endless."

I'd never thought of Wiser in such professional terms and was surprised by how fancy she sounded.

"The coding is pretty messy, but that's what we're here

for. We have resources at the Foundry that you can't find anywhere else. Not just money, but access."

"Xia?" my mother called. I ignored her.

"I think Wiser could be the next big thing, and I want to help you develop it," Lars continued. "We'd love to have you join our next class of founders. What do you think?"

I felt such a swell of emotion that I didn't know how to respond. I was excited and nervous and worried that he'd made a mistake, that he was accidentally calling me when he meant to be calling someone else, because how could all of his praise apply to me? No one in Worcester thought I was a genius, or even that special. The best I got was weird. I'd started programming because I was lonely and bored, because I wanted company and didn't have any. Though I'd taken all of the coding classes my high school offered, they were pretty basic, and I'd had to teach myself the more advanced stuff from online tutorials and books that I'd borrowed from the library. How could someone like that have what it takes to get into the Foundry?

"This isn't a joke, is it? You really are Lars Lang?"

He laughed. "I really am. And no, it's not a joke."

"I can't believe it," I whispered.

"I came here ten years ago and I still can't believe it. Don't worry, you're not alone."

"Xia?" my mother called again. "Are you talking to someone?"

"I'm coming!" I shouted to her. "Just getting dressed." I

turned back to the phone. "Sorry, that was my mom."

"It's okay, I have one too," Lars said. "Think about it. Let me know in a week—"

"I don't need to think about it," I said, cutting him off. "I accept."

I could almost hear him smile. "Wonderful. I'll have my assistant send you all the details. Oh, and Xia? Enjoy the breakfast."

I hung up and pressed the phone to my chest. It was real. I was going to California. Now all I had to do was convince my mother.

■ ■ ■

"Did you do something to the microwave?" my mother asked when I sat down. She seemed to be in a bad mood that morning, though I didn't know why.

"No," I said sheepishly and averted my eyes. "Why?"

My mother was small and wiry, tightly wound. She was a practical woman, with short hair and sensible clothes. She slid half of the scrambled eggs and tomato onto my plate and sat down next to me. "It made my tea overflow. It's never done that before."

"Weird," I said, trying to sound convincing. "I can take a look at it."

My mother studied me like she knew I was lying. "Did you have hot chocolate last night?"

"How did you know?"

"I saw the packet in the trash. Whose birthday was it?"

"No one's. I was—" I should have told her then, but I

clammed up. "I was cold after shoveling."

She eyed me suspiciously. "The landlady told me she saw you with no coat."

My mother had an incredible ability to see everything, even when she wasn't actually there. I wondered if the landlady had also told her about my California comment, but she said nothing.

She ate her eggs quickly. She was always in a rush. "How's that essay going?"

Essay. Did I have an essay due soon? I couldn't remember. "Fine."

"I have to meet with a student today, and have to grade papers before then. Can you—"

"Make sure the driveway is shoveled before you leave," I said, finishing her sentence. "I'll do it now."

I finished my breakfast and put on my coat. Outside, my mother's car was buried under half a foot of snow. Gina was already there, shoveling out her dad's car.

"You're looking uncharacteristically cheerful," she said. "Since when do you have this much energy in the morning?"

I glanced up at the window and lowered my voice to an excited whisper. "Since I got accepted to the Foundry."

Gina gasped and stuck her shovel into the bank. "What? When?"

"They called me last night."

"Of course they did," Gina said. "I always knew you were going to be famous. I mean, you invented a thing that predicts the future. Everyone wants to know the future."

"Well, it doesn't actually tell you the future," I said. "It pretends to be you *in* the future and gives you advice."

"Right, whatever. Same thing."

Gina wasn't into coding, but she always listened, even when I knew I was boring her out of her skull. Her parents ran a restaurant in town and wanted her and her brothers to take it over one day.

"It's not fair. Here you are, spending most of the day in the back of the class, secretly programming your phone and barely paying attention and still getting straight As and getting into tech supercamp for kid geniuses while I'm here in the front row, taking notes and still getting Bs."

I rolled my eyes. "It's not a camp, and I'm not a genius."

"Um, remind me again who just called you?"

"Lars Lang."

"Exactly. Lars Lang. Even I know who he is." Gina narrowed her eyes. "Wait. Does this mean you're moving to California?"

I paused, torn between excitement and guilt.

"You're leaving me here?"

"You like it here. Everyone knows that. And anyway, you have your brothers."

"I hate my brothers."

"It's just for a year."

"I know. I'm just giving you a hard time. What about school? Have you told your mom?"

"Not yet." I glanced up at the window. "She's not going to like it. She's going to say I'm dropping out."

"Aren't you?"

"Of course not. It's a school. I still have to take English and history there," I said. "I just get to take business and accounting instead of math, and computer programming instead of chemistry."

"But the whole point is to become the Founder and get a bunch of money so you can start a company, right? I filmed your video. I know what the Foundry is about. They put you up in a nice house with a bunch of other kid geniuses and you compete to get the top spot, which you'll obviously get. Then they'll give you a million dollars, which you'll use to hire people, and once you have people and money, you'll have a company. And you'll be the boss, which means you'll have to run it. It's not like you can just leave and come back to school."

She had a point. Though I'd always wanted to turn Wiser into a company, it was mainly because I wanted to share her with others and because I liked the idea of getting paid to work on her all day. I honestly hadn't put a lot of thought into what running a company day-to-day would look like, other than delivering product launches and giving interviews.

"First of all, I probably won't win. I'm a little worried that they made a mistake and called the wrong Xia Chan."

Gina rolled her eyes. "How many people here are named Xia? I mean, come on."

"And second of all, if I'm the boss, I can do whatever I want. I can hire someone to manage things while I'm finishing school. Look at Lars Lang. It's not like he's running his businesses day-to-day. And even if I do win, the company could still fail. Lots of companies fail."

"Yeah, but you're not just anyone."

"Maybe I should emphasize the school part when I talk to her," I said. "Pitch it more like a cool program that'll be good for applying to colleges, instead of the whole running-a-company thing."

"Have you told your online boyfriend yet?" Gina asked.

Even in the cold, I blushed. She was talking about ObjectPermanence, a boy I'd been exchanging messages with for over a year on a chat forum for teen programmers called BitBop.

"He's not my boyfriend," I said. "And no. We don't talk about specific details. I don't even know his name."

"Maybe he got in, too. He's a programmer, right?"

It had occurred to me that he could have applied to the Foundry, but the thought seemed too far-fetched. Even if he'd applied, the likelihood of us both getting in was nearly impossible. Still, for a moment I let myself imagine us meeting in person. Would I even know it was him? "There are thousands of teenage programmers online. What are the chances?"

"But it's possible, right? I wonder what he looks like. What if he's amazingly beautiful?"

My face grew hot. It got that way every time I talked about him.

Gina winced. "Or he could be the opposite."

"He can't be. He's too funny. And nice. And smart."

Gina raised an eyebrow. "Everyone knows that hot boys aren't nice because they don't have to be, and nice boys got that way because they didn't have anything else to go on."

"That's a stereotype perpetuated by movies and magazines that assumes that there's only one ideal form of beauty, when really, hotness is in the eye of the beholder."

Gina laughed and rolled her eyes. "Okay, Nietzsche."

"Nietzsche definitely didn't say that, but thanks."

"What if he's not even our age at all? What if he's a pervert? A sixty-year-old man posing as a sixteen-year-old?"

"He's not sixty years old," I said. "My mom is forty-three and she can barely figure out how to use her phone. Sixty-year-olds aren't on coding forums on BitBop."

"I don't know. All you know about him is that he listens to Beethoven while coding. Do you know who else likes Beethoven? My dad. And dads in general."

"Young people like Beethoven," I insisted, realizing how weak of an argument it was only after it left my mouth. "Everyone knows Beethoven's Fifth. And anyway, he told me he's in high school. And he talks about his dad a lot and how strict he is."

"That's exactly what a sixty-year-old man would say to try and convince you he's a teenager."

"Or exactly what a teenager would say."

"What time does he normally reply to you?"

"I don't know," I said. "The evening?"

"So after work," Gina said.

"Or after school."

"It's settled then. He's a dad."

I rolled my eyes. "He's not a dad. And he's not sixty."

"It's your fantasy," Gina said with a shrug. "I wonder what the other kids will be like. Do you think they'll all be total weirdos?"

"Why would they be weirdos?"

"You know coding people. They sit alone all day with their computers. Very pale. Have no social skills."

"Do I have no social skills?"

"Except for you," Gina said. "Though you are pale. But it suits you. It's part of your look."

I didn't realize I had a look. "What's my look?"

"You know, that outfit you always wear—the black turtleneck and the black pants, like all the famous CEOs. It kind of makes you look nerdy and sickly but also smart and apathetic, like you live in a big cloudy city and drink coffee five times a day."

"I'm not sickly."

Gina held her hands up. "I'm just an unbiased observer."

I glanced down at my outfit, which was comprised of a black turtleneck and black pants. Mitzy Erst had once said in an interview that you should always dress as the person you wanted to be, which I'd taken to heart and replaced most of my clothes with the uniform I was wearing that morning, a uniform I'd seen so many tech founders wear onstage.

"It's practical and warm."

"I know."

"Your description makes me sound mean," I said,

frowning, but then felt overly conscious of the fact that I was frowning, so I tried to force a smile. But that felt unnatural and creepy, so I decided that no facial expression would be best, and made my face go blank, which ended up proving her point. Apathetic.

"Apathetic is different than mean," Gina said.

"I'm not apathetic," I insisted. "I care about lots of things."

"I know you do," Gina said. "You just look detached, that's all. It's cool. You're doing your own thing."

I squinted at her, wondering if she was just saying that to make me feel better.

"I can totally picture you all pale and serious in your black turtleneck, standing in front of a big screen with one of those pointer things."

"I won't be pale after I spend a year in California," I said.

"You will if you keep wearing turtlenecks. Do you think your mom will even let you move that far away?"

"It's not like she's here most of the time anyway. She probably won't even notice." I wanted to believe it so I wouldn't feel guilty for leaving, but I knew deep down that it wasn't true.

"She's your mom," Gina said, incredulous. "Of course she'll notice."

"Maybe if I tell her they're giving me money, she'll let me go. Apparently they give all the fellows an expense account when we arrive."

"How much?"

"I don't know. His assistant is sending the details."

"He's having his assistant tell you? That means it's a lot.

When restaurants have menus with no price it means it's too expensive to print."

Though I didn't think of my mother and me as badly off, I couldn't think of a time when the stress of not having enough money didn't permeate my mother's mood daily. It was like a gray cloud that followed us around, threatening to open up into a downpour. It was hard to imagine what it would feel like to be finally standing in the sun. It didn't seem possible, like the rain cloud was an inextricable part of our lives.

"What are you going to do with it?" Gina asked.

It was the first time I'd considered that the money would actually be mine to spend. "I don't know. Buy a new phone, I guess."

"That's it?"

The truth was I didn't apply because of the money. I wanted to go to the Foundry because I felt like it was the only place in the world where I'd fit in.

"I don't know. There are probably rules and stuff. Like we can only use it on school supplies."

"Like pencils?" Gina shook her head. "You get an expense account to buy yourself a company car, not to buy notebooks and folders."

"I guess I could fix my mom's car."

"Fix it? Just buy her a new one. You can buy me one, too. I want interest on that video I filmed for you. If it weren't for me, you wouldn't have gotten it," Gina said with a smirk as she ran up the steps to her house. "And don't forget it."

"You can't even drive."

"When you're rich, does it even matter?"

I smiled but didn't believe her. Though it was fun to fantasize about, I wasn't going to be rich. That kind of thing didn't happen to me. Besides, there was still the issue of convincing my mother.

I woke my phone. "Wiser, how do I convince my mom to let me go?"

"Tell her that you were offered a once-in-a-lifetime opportunity to participate in an incubator program for gifted young programmers and that you would like to go."

"So you want me to just tell her the truth?"

"Honesty is usually best," Wiser said.

"But how do I convince her that it's a good idea? I could go with the money thing, but she might not care about money. Or I could focus on the school part more than the winning part so she doesn't think I'll be dropping out."

"But that would be a lie."

"Not exactly," I said.

"Lying is never a good idea."

"It's not a lie."

"According to Merriam-Webster, a lie is defined as: 'to make an untrue statement with intent to deceive—'"

"Okay fine, I get it."

"Why don't you tell her that you *want* to go?" Wiser said.

"Because she doesn't care about what I want."

"I think you're mistaken," Wiser said. "She wants you to be happy."

I glanced up at our apartment. Through the window, I could see my mom scrubbing the dishes. Her face was pinched while she listened to the news on the radio. "Are you sure there isn't an alternative?"

"You could always ask her about the red hat," Wiser said.

"What's the red hat?"

"The red hat," Wiser repeated. "A hat that is red."

I frowned, confused by her bizarre answer.

"Right, but what is it?"

"Your mother's red hat," Wiser said, her voice scrambling as she spoke.

"But she doesn't have a red hat," I said.

I looked down at my phone, but it had frozen again in the cold. I sighed and stuffed it in my pocket. There must have been a bug in the programming. I made a mental note to look into it and trudged back inside.

■ ■ ■

No. That was what my mother told me after I'd told her about the Foundry. I was sitting in the kitchen, drying dishes while my mother chopped vegetables for the week.

"Aren't you going to think about it before making a decision?"

"I don't need to think about it," my mother said. "I didn't work this hard for you to drop out of school."

"But I wouldn't be dropping out. I'd just be transferring to a specialized tech school for a year. It'll be great for college and I'll come back after it's done, just with more programming classes on my transcript." I glanced at my phone on top of the refrigerator and felt relieved that Wiser wasn't awake to hear me.

My mother squinted at me. "What is the point of this program?"

"To teach me how to code properly. And to learn about business."

"Why would a sixteen-year-old need to learn about business?"

"I don't know. What's the point of any school?"

"To enrich your mind, sharpen your analytical thinking, and arm you with tools that will help you be independent, curious, and resilient in the face of hardship."

"Exactly. That's exactly the point of the Foundry."

My mother looked at me like I'd broken the microwave again. "They're trying to get you to drop out."

"No they're not," I protested. "It's a school."

"There are schools here. You're currently attending one."

"They're going to help me build a company. And they're going to give me money. They like Wiser. They said it has promise. They want to invest in it."

My mother let out a resentful laugh. "Invest? Do you know much I've invested in you? How long? Sixteen years. Where's the return on my investment? And now a stranger calls and says he wants to invest in your phone friend, and you want to drop out of school and move to California?"

"It's not a phone friend. It's a predictive outcomes application."

"You're not going."

"It's just for a year," I said, growing desperate. "That's all. It'll help me get into college. It'll make me a better student."

"You can only get into college if you finish high school."

"I know that, but—"

She slammed her cleaver against the chopping block, startling me to silence. "You're not moving to California, and that's the end of it." She must have seen the surprised look on my face because she collected herself. "Now go do your homework. The day is already half over."

I threw the dishrag on the table. Though I'd known my mother wouldn't let me go, a part of me had been hoping that maybe this time she'd hear me. She never cared about technology; she thought it was just a distraction from real life. To her, programming was a weird hobby, nothing more than typing and swiping, so why would she understand now?

I turned to go to my room when my phone chirped from the top of the fridge. It had turned back on.

I thought about Wiser's strange advice. What did I have to lose?

"What about the red hat?" I said.

My mother rarely looked surprised, so when she showed even the slightest hint of being caught off guard, it was notable.

"What about it?" she said.

I had no idea what the red hat referred to, so all I could muster was a shrug. "Never mind."

# three

I'd retreated to my room without my phone and was too proud to go back to the kitchen and get it, so I turned on my computer and was about to play music as loud as I could when I saw that I had a message waiting for me on BitBop.

NEW MESSAGE FROM U/OBJECTPERMANENCE:
I know what you mean about feeling like no one you know really gets you. My friends are great and all but I can't really talk to them about anything too deep. It's like everyone gets scared, including me, and the pressure in the room increases and then someone makes a joke to relieve it and the moment is over and we're back to being buddies again. I know that's not exactly what you're talking about, but it's a similar sentiment.

I'm starting to realize that I can't please my dad. I know we don't share details but my dad is kind of a big deal. He's a programmer and an entrepreneur and is really good at what he does. He has this idea of who I'm supposed to be, but no matter what I do, it's never enough. I just got this thing that I've been wanting for a long time, and instead of being happy for me, all he said was that the only reason I got it was because of him.

He cares so much about my accomplishments and yet none of them end up mattering because I'll never be self-made like he was. I'll always have had it easier, and he'll always see my success as something he did for me.

Sorry to complain. It's hard to talk to my friends about this stuff because, you know, male vulnerability, etc. Any emotion is a weakness . . .

Side note, have you ever listened to film scores while coding? I just listened to the soundtrack from *2001: A Space Odyssey* and it makes it feel like you're saving the planet from a fireball when all you're doing is searching for a missing semicolon ;)

I felt a swell of happiness and for a moment I forgot why I had been in such a bad mood.

We'd met on a data structures forum on BitBop. Someone had posted wanting suggestions for the best music to listen to while programming. We were the only two who'd responded with something other than trance or EDM. He'd said Beethoven's Fifth. I'd said Bach's Cello Concertos. We'd been friends ever since.

Here's what I knew about ObjectPermanence: He liked science-fiction movies but also had a soft spot for romantic comedies, though he would never tell his friends that. He was smart and funny. He once alluded to practice, which made me think that he played a sport, though he could've been referring to band practice. Still, I liked to imagine him playing soccer, but Gina always insisted it was golf, no, worse—virtual golf. He liked corny programming puns (Why did the programmer need glasses? To C#). His dad was some important tech person, and though that didn't necessarily mean that he lived in California, he had commented once on a post about In-N-Out burgers, which made me think that he did. His family had money, but they weren't nice to each other. And most importantly, I could talk to him about anything and know he would get it and wouldn't laugh at me or think I was strange. I'd never met anyone like that before, especially not a boy.

I read his message again. *I just got this thing that I've been wanting for a long time.*

The fact that he'd written it the day after I'd been accepted to the Foundry made me wonder. Was it possible that he'd gotten in, too? For a moment I'd almost convinced myself, but then realized what I was doing and shook it off. No, it had to be a coincidence. The "thing" he "got" could have been anything—an award at school, a summer internship, a new car. There were only twenty spots at the Foundry. Was it really possible that the boy I was talking to online had also gotten one?

I put on the soundtrack from *2001: A Space Odyssey* and listened. The music was eerie and strange enough that I could almost believe that I was in an alternate but similar universe where my mother was fine with me going to the Foundry and ObjectPermanence was somehow going as well. I closed my eyes and pictured him listening to the same music. It almost felt like we were in the same room. I began to type a response when there was a knock on my door.

I turned down the music. "What?"

My mother opened the door. "Can I come in?"

I sighed. "Fine."

Her hands were still wet from cooking, and she wiped them on her apron and sat on my bed next to me. "Your voice invention," she said.

"Wiser," I reminded her, for the umpteenth time.

My mother handed me my phone. "Show me how it works."

I woke my phone and asked the first question that came to mind. "Wiser, if I miss this opportunity to go to the Foundry will I ever get another one?"

"Opportunities are a combination of good timing and hard work. If you keep working hard, statistically you will have a much better chance of getting more opportunities."

I could feel my mother looking at me, but I couldn't bring myself to meet her gaze. I was too upset. "Wiser, if I don't go to California, will I regret it for the rest of my life?"

"People only feel regret over things they could have changed that were within their control. Going to California is not in your control, therefore you should not feel regret over it. However, you may feel resentment."

"Wiser, am I going to be stuck in Massachusetts for my entire life?"

"I don't predict the future," Wiser said. "But I suspect that if you'd like to leave, eventually you will."

That made me feel a little better.

"How does it work?" my mother asked. I tried to think of the last time she'd asked me a question that wasn't about a chore she'd given me and couldn't think of one.

"It scans all of my online data and any publicly accessible data and comes up with personalized responses to my questions," I explained. "It gives me advice."

"And you made it yourself?"

I nodded.

"This Laura Slang. What are her credentials?"

I smirked. "Lars Lang."

She listened quietly while I told her about the Foundry, about Lars's game company and his social-networking site. I spoke carefully. Whatever was happening, I didn't want to ruin it. The fact that she was even asking made my heart rate pick up, though I didn't dare get my hopes up yet. When I was finished, she said nothing for a long while.

"Does he have a phone number?"

I wrote it on a piece of paper, which she folded into her apron before glancing around my room. "This place is a mess," she said. "I'm doing a load of laundry. Bring me your dirty clothes."

As I watched her leave, I felt what I could only describe

as cautious but near explosive excitement. I didn't know what had happened between our argument in the kitchen and now, but I didn't mind. I listened to her footsteps disappear down the hall, then turned to my phone. "Wiser, what's the red hat?"

"You clearly haven't read any of your mother's published papers. In a 1997 article called 'The Spirit of the Immigrant,' she writes about leaving Taiwan as a teenager to go to college in the United States. She'd received a scholarship from an American university to study political history and economics, but her parents were opposed to it. They didn't approve of her moving abroad to study such a frivolous subject when she had already passed the entrance exam at home to go to pharmacy school. Your mother told them she was leaving anyway, with or without their permission. They didn't speak until the morning of her departure, when her mother gave her a small parcel packed with food for the trip, along with a red knitted hat. 'For the winters in Massachusetts,' she'd told her daughter. In that way, she gave her daughter her blessing."

My phone was warm in my hand, as though it were another palm. "Thank you," I whispered to Wiser. It was the first time I really understood that I had created something that might be great.

Through the ceiling, I could hear someone upstairs vacuuming. If I closed my eyes, I could imagine it was the waves of the Pacific crashing against the rocks, blue and glittering in the sunlight. I was going.

"Wiser, what else do you know that I don't know?" I asked her just for fun. It was too broad of a question for Wiser to properly answer, though I figured I'd try anyway.

"You never really know what another person is capable of," she said.

"Like my mother?"

"I do like your mother," she said.

Lars Lang was right; the programming could use some improvement. I opened my phone and made a note of it. It didn't occur to me to ask Wiser more. I didn't realize that she might not have been talking about my mother at all; she might have been talking about me.

■ ■ ■

After careful deliberation and multiple hours of phone conversations with the Foundry staff, including one particularly mortifying series of questions about the level of adult supervision in the dormitories, my mother reluctantly agreed that I could attend. The months that followed passed remarkably slowly. I had to finish the school year, which meant returning to normal life until June as though nothing had changed.

At school, I was the girl with the weird name who knew a lot about computers. I wasn't unpopular but I wasn't popular either. I had a few acquaintances from advanced math, but outside of spending time with Gina, my social interactions primarily consisted of my classmates asking me to fix their broken phones or help them with a homework problem. So when word got out that I got accepted to the Foundry, which most nonprogrammers had only vague knowledge of, the news was stretched and twisted until it made no sense at all. Did you hear? Xia Chan was dropping out of school to move to San Francisco. Xia Chan was being hired by a tech company in Northern California. Xia Chan was going to work on a top-secret project in the Bay Area. Xia Chan now worked for the government; she was probably CIA.

"I heard you were a secret agent," Jay said from the desk next to mine. Jay and I had been in advanced math together since we were in middle school. He liked to tell people that I was the best in our class, but he was just being modest. He often managed to get just one point higher on tests than I did, which never ceased to infuriate me.

"I can't confirm either way."

"I knew it," Jay said with a smirk. He was perpetually disheveled and clumsy, with oversized hands and feet, like a puppy.

"Hey," Mr. McDonough said from the blackboard. "Can either of you confirm the location of this point on the curve?" He cracked a smile. "But seriously, congratulations, Xia. The Foundry is an incredible place. They're lucky to have you."

I blushed. "Thanks."

"So what's your mission?" Jay whispered. "And are you looking for some genius young student to recruit as your sidekick?" He sat up straight, like he was on a job interview.

I laughed. "It's classified."

He sighed and copied the equation on the board. "At least when you're gone, I won't have anyone else messing up the grading curve for me."

"Don't get too comfortable," I said. "I'll be back in a year."

The next three months passed in a haze. People stopped whispering and staring at me and seemed to lose interest. If I was a secret agent, I was a boring one.

At home, my mother and I didn't talk about my impending departure. She acted as though nothing was happening, and I was scared to bring it up for fear she'd change her mind. The snow turned to slush, which turned into mud, and then suddenly it was spring, and my classmates were talking about camp, Gina was starting a part-time job at her parents' restaurant, and my mother was getting ready to teach summer school. And the most surprising thing happened. I felt sad.

Though I was excited to leave, I didn't like that everyone was making plans without me, that life was just going to carry on in my absence. Worcester didn't seem as bad as I remembered it—the birds were out, the trees were budding—and I found myself noticing all of the things I'd taken for granted. I'd miss our apartment, the way you had to turn the shower knob one centimeter forward, then two millimeters backward to get the water to the perfect temperature. I'd miss the cracks on my ceilings, which I'd fallen asleep to every night, connecting the riddles in the paint to my own constellations. I'd miss my street, seeing the landlady watching TV in her living room, and sitting on Gina's stoop and passing the time until her mother called her in for dinner. I'd miss waking up to the sound of my mother's feet padding around the kitchen while cooking breakfast, and ending my day to the sound of her car pulling up the driveway. I'd miss knowing she was there while I slept, that if I called out, she'd appear at my door, and though she wouldn't say she loved me, I'd know from her face that she did.

The week before I left, Gina and her family threw a small party for me at her family's restaurant. It was a homey Italian place, the kind with checkered tablecloths and wine bottles hanging on the walls and waiters wearing white collared shirts and black waist aprons. They served pasta on huge platters and salad dripping with dressing and warm bread in cloth-covered baskets. My mother had acted indifferently toward the party while we were getting ready, but ended up wearing her fancy clothes, which meant that it was an important affair. She sat next to me and chatted with our neighbors, smiling and laughing occasionally while eating spaghetti. Gina's mom made a toast while Gina and her brothers whooped and cheered in the background, saying how proud she was and how much she'd miss me. My mother listened, her eyes glistening in the light, and without looking at me, she reached over and held my hand. When dinner was over, she handed me a box wrapped in gift paper that read *Happy Birthday!* Inside was a laptop, brand new, top of the line. I stared at it in awe.

"You'll need it in California," she said.

I swallowed and squeezed her hand. It was her note to me, telling me that she believed in me.

# four

California first appeared as a beam of light on the horizon. I watched it take shape through the little oval window by my seat: parched, golden mountains flexing up beneath the clouds. Then streets etched into the hills, stretching all the way to the silver rim of the ocean. Buildings rising through the fog. Then the white, faded sun of San Francisco.

The Foundry had taken care of all my travel arrangements, even reserving a driver who was waiting curbside in a black SUV with my name written on a little sign in the windshield. It was the nicest car I'd ever been in: six leather seats all for me, a flat screen, and a minifridge stocked with energy drinks. The windows were tinted, and through them I watched the city stretch into lazy, sprawling suburbs lined with trees. They swayed in the wind, looking like a frame from a black-and-white movie through the tint.

I felt excited but nervous, and checked my phone out of

habit. It was the one familiar thing I had left. I messaged my mom, telling her that I'd gotten in fine, then opened BitBop. The night before, I'd told ObjectPermanence I was leaving, despite the fact that it didn't change anything because our friendship was situated outside the realm of geography.

SENT MESSAGE FROM U/ARRAYOFLIGHT:
I'm writing to say goodbye. Well, not really. Ironically, you're the only person I don't have to say goodbye to since you basically reside in my pocket. I'm moving and transferring to a new school. It's a boarding school, but not in the traditional sense. I've wanted to go there my entire life, but now that I'm about to leave, I'm scared. It feels like I'm starting my life over again. I have to make new friends and figure out a new place all on my own. But mostly, I'm worried that I won't be good enough. This school is really hard to get into and is going to be filled with smart people. What if they made a mistake letting me in? What if I can't keep up? I know I'm smart, but when I look at the real tech geniuses of the world, I know I'm not on their level. I guess what I'm saying is, wish me luck.

NEW MESSAGE FROM U/OBJECTPERMANENCE:
You do realize that those tech geniuses have at least twenty years on you. (That is, unless you're secretly forty years old.) Seriously though, everyone's a no one before they're a someone. Honestly, I bet everyone going feels the way you do.

I'm switching schools this year, too, so I know what you're going through. It's just across town so it's not like I'm moving away from my family and friends like you are, but I'm still nervous. I can't tell anyone that, though. I'm supposed to pretend like I'm not scared, not show any emotion because it would be perceived as weakness. Maybe we're all just pretending to be the people we want to be. If we're pretending all the time, is there really a difference? What I'm trying to say is, good luck, though I don't think you'll need it.

PS—It's comfortable here in your pocket.

I blushed. *I'm switching schools this year, too.* Was it possible? I read his message again, looking for clues that might signal that he was going to the Foundry, too, but stopped myself. Lots of people switched schools. It didn't mean that he was going to *my* school. Besides, he'd said that his wasn't a boarding school; it was just across town. He could have grown up in Silicon Valley, which would make the Foundry a school across town, but it seemed much more likely that he was just switching schools in his neighborhood.

Outside, we passed a sign that said Welcome to Palo Alto. I rolled down the window and tried to stop thinking about ObjectPermanence.

Palo Alto was just as I'd dreamed it: lush and breezy, with colors so vivid they looked enhanced. Tangles of flowers cascaded over houses and pergolas. Water from sprinklers undulated in the lawns, creating a halo of light in their spray.

Cars gleamed in their driveways, reflecting the sky in their windshields.

We pulled up to a gated property draped in thick, blushing flowers. Nestled into the vines was a glass sign: The Foundry.

The gate opened to a manicured estate studded with orange and lemon trees. A stucco mansion stood at the end of the driveway. It had a terracotta roof and breezeways lined with fanning palms. It looked more like a resort than an incubator, and I suddenly felt nervous. It was easy to imagine wealthy people walking around in white robes and expensive sandals, sleeping with cucumbers over their eyes, and eating exotic fruit with toothpicks. If my mother were here, she wouldn't be intimidated. She wasn't scared of anything, and I wished that she'd told me what her secret was.

"Wiser," I said, waking my phone. "I don't think I belong here."

"Belonging is a social construct," Wiser said.

I frowned, unsure of what she meant. "Some people do belong though."

"Only because we believe they do."

A cheerful man in a gray T-shirt bearing the Foundry's logo was standing in the driveway, greeting people. He looked into the car and smiled at me. "Welcome," he said, and directed us down the driveway.

The girls' and boys' dormitories stood across the lawn from each other, both stucco houses covered in climbing vines. They were bustling with families unpacking cars and carrying luggage inside.

The driver unloaded my suitcase from the trunk, and I stood at the curb while other people's parents marveled at the campus. I suddenly felt aware that I was alone, that my turtleneck was too heavy for the warm weather and looked dingy in the sunlight, that my mom would never have a car as nice as the ones lined up in front of me, and that even if she were here to help me move in, I still wouldn't fit in.

"Wiser, I need a pep talk."

"If you put your mind to it, you can do anything," she said.

"A better pep talk. Something to calm my nerves."

"You can't have courage without fear."

"What do you mean? Didn't I program you to be a little more specific?"

"The bravest people aren't those who have never been scared. They're people who keep pressing forward in the face of danger, humiliation, and hardship."

Danger, humiliation, and hardship. I shoved her in my pocket. "Great. Thanks for the reminder."

A family pushed past me up the steps, carrying a large trunk. I slung my backpack over my shoulder and followed them inside.

The inside of the dormitory looked like a living room out of a real estate photo. *Found your best start-up in this updated modern dream house! Complete with a gas fireplace and custom cream couches, engineered to repel stains. Enjoy an energy drink while looking out onto a one-of-a-kind view, a self-manicuring lawn, the very first in existence!*

A girl was checking everyone in at a folding table. She looked like a character in a video game with her nose ring and dyed red hair, and, like an avatar, she didn't seem pleased at the prospect of sitting at a table making small talk.

"Welcome to the Foundry," she said in a perfunctory tone. "I'm Kit, your resident advisor. I live in room one. I'm here to provide support during the program."

Kit. Before coming I'd studied all of the previous fellows from the last twenty years. Her name sounded familiar.

"I recognize you. You were one of the fellows from a few years ago, right?"

"2014. Didn't win," she said without looking up. "Name?"

"Xia Chan," I said, blushing. "Sorry. I bet your idea was really good though."

"You don't have to try and make me feel better," she grumbled while she typed something into her computer. "I'm working on a security start-up. I just do this for the free housing."

"I only meant that—" I began to say when she interrupted me.

"Room six," she said, and handed me an envelope.

"Thanks."

I dragged my luggage up the stairs and stole glimpses of the other rooms in passing. They were all filled with families hanging posters and rearranging furniture, further emphasizing that I was by myself.

My room was on the second floor at the end of the hall. It had slanted ceilings, a nook for my desk, and two big windows that overlooked the lawn. Sun stretched across the floor, warming the wood. Though it wasn't filled with people, it felt perfect.

Through the walls, I could hear the other families laughing and chatting. With no one to talk to, I opened Wiser and asked her questions to keep me company while I unpacked. It was a habit of mine.

I didn't have much in the way of belongings. A few of the newspaper clippings of Mitzy Erst from my room, which I taped over my bed, and two drawers of clothes, which I tucked into my dresser. When I was finished, I sat on the bed and opened the envelope Kit had given me.

*Dear Xia,*

*Welcome to the Foundry. As one of the brightest minds of your generation, you represent the future. At our incubator, we strive to provide everything you need to achieve your highest potential. Our objective here is to change the world for the better. We hope you'll start today.*

*We believe that the best things in life require no instructions. Likewise, you will receive no instructions here. Enclosed is your Vault, which contains everything you'll need. Don't lose it. If you need anything in the meantime, just ask. You'll know how.*

*Warmly,*

*Lars Lang*

No instructions. Adults always wanted to tell me what to do, so the idea of a school explicitly stating that they weren't going to was jarring.

At the bottom of the envelope lay what looked like a business card. My name was printed on it: *Xia Chan*, *Foundry Fellow*. It looked like it was made of heavy paper stock, but when I picked it up it felt firm and cool, like metal. I turned it in my hand. The surface rippled ever so slightly.

Could it be? I pinched the corner of the card and watched as the paper undulated beneath my touch as though I were pressing on plasma. It was a screen.

I ran my hand over my name and the letters dissolved. New words appeared in their place.

`Welcome, Xia. Hold your finger to the center of the Vault.`

Beneath it, an oval appeared. I did as it instructed.

`Fingerprint installed.`

The text dissolved again and was replaced with five icons: a tree, a door, a coin, an arrow, and a lock. One by one, I touched them.

The tree was the Foundry's logo, and took me to my student portal, where I could access my grades and assignments. The door transformed my Vault into a key. One end gave me access to my dorm room; the other end said *Universal Foundry*, which I assumed gave me access to any door in the Foundry.

I touched the coin and a balance appeared.

`Xia M. Chan`

$150,000.00

Beneath it, a sixteen-digit number appeared, along with a magnetic band and chip, turning it into a credit card.

I blinked at the number. It had to be an example of how the device worked; that couldn't actually be the balance on the card. Could it? And yet, there was my name, written above it as though it were mine.

My stomach fluttered. It was an unfathomable number, as much as my mother made in four and a half years as a professor. I did some quick math. 13.8 years of rent. 58.6 years of groceries. 72.3 used 2005 Toyota Corollas. 166.6 new phones. It couldn't be mine. Who would give someone like me that much money?

I was about to click on the arrow icon when I heard an odd humming outside my window. It was too mechanical to be a bird and too loud to be an insect, unless I was vastly underestimating the size of the insects in California, which made me shudder. I slipped the Vault into my pocket and approached the sill.

The window was cracked open and a gentle breeze blew into the room, making the branches of the tree sway. I peered through them when something flew into the glass.

I jumped back, startled. It was a drone, small enough to fit in the palm of my hand. It had two electric nodes for eyes, and four propellers whirring like a strange bug. It hovered for a moment, staring at me, then dipped away. How long had it been there?

I hurried into the hallway, following the direction it was

going in, when a girl opened the door two down from mine.

"Did you see it, too?" she asked. She was short and book-ish, with tightly curled black hair cropped close to her head and big, horn-rimmed glasses that made her look like she was dressed up like an adult.

"It flew right up to my window," I said. "I think it had a camera. Did you see its eyes?"

"That can't be allowed. It's an invasion of privacy."

I stole a glimpse into her room. It was mostly empty, just like mine, except for a poster of a map that hung over her desk. I tried to make out what the map was of when I saw the drone dip back past her window.

"There!" I said.

We ran into her room and watched it tap the glass. A group of boys were standing on the lawn below, smirking, while one of them controlled it with a remote.

"They're spying on us," she said, staring down at them with disgust. "They think it's funny."

"Hold on," I said and opened her window. I pulled the elastic out of my hair and stretched it back, aiming at the drone. I let go and watched with satisfaction as the band hit the drone and got tangled in one of the propellers, making it tilt precariously to one side before it faltered and dropped, crashing to the ground below.

My neighbor stared down at its mangled parts in awe. "Good shot," she said.

The boys stopped laughing and ran over to the drone. "She broke it," one of them said and looked up at us. He was tall and preppy, like a young heir. He looked like he was used to getting what he wanted in life. "Do you know how much this thing cost?"

"If you wanted to keep it, you shouldn't have flown it in my window."

"You crashed it. You're paying for the replacement."

"I'm not paying for anything," I shouted, feeling my throat tighten. How dare he blame me? "You're lucky I'm not reporting you for invading our privacy and being general perverts."

One of his friends whispered something in his ear, and my neighbor took the opportunity to shut the window, quieting their voices.

"Well, they seemed nice," she said, cracking a smile. "I'm Amina."

I took a breath to compose myself. "Xia." I noticed then that her room was notably empty of parents. "Are you alone, too?" I asked.

She looked relieved at my question. "Yeah. My parents had to work, so I flew in by myself."

"Me too."

"From where?" she asked.

"Massachusetts," I said.

"New York," Amina said with a smile, as though we were from the same place. Being so far from the East Coast made it feel like we were. "Can you believe this place?" she said. "On the way in I picked a plum from a tree and ate it. An actual plum tree. I thought it was fake, like those decorative trees they have at the mall, but it was real. And it was the best plum I've ever had. The kind of plum that makes you realize that every plum you've had in the past wasn't really a plum, you know?"

"I don't even know what a plum tree looks like."

"I didn't either. I had to look it up to make sure."

A warm breeze drifted past us from the other window, perfuming the air with the sweet aroma of fruit. "Do you smell that?" she said incredulously. "Do you know what the air smells like in New York? Like garbage. Garbage and dog doo."

"In Worcester, it's car fumes and burnt rubber."

"On a good day, cooking meat."

"Freshly laid pavement. You know how it smells kind of sweet?"

Amina laughed. She told me she grew up in a big Nigerian family without a lot of supervision and spent most of her time exploring New York on her own, getting lost in unmapped places. She'd always wished she'd had a way to trace her steps, so she made one. She'd always wanted to start her own company, but she'd never been interested in California like I'd been. It was too pretty there, too perfect. Why weren't there any bugs? Why wasn't the grass itchy? It was suspicious. She didn't trust people from California. They were too tan, too happy, always talking about the weather like it was some kind of achievement, like they had personally discovered the sun. And what was even more annoying was that they were right. It *was* beautiful.

I told her I didn't trust people with perfect teeth, which made her laugh. Then I nodded to the map over her desk, which looked like an ancient map of the world, surrounded by drawings of the sky and angels. "What is that?"

"It's from Joan Blaeu's *Atlas Maior*." She pushed up her glasses. "He was a cartographer. He drew what I think of as the first three-dimensional map, with the sun and the sky and the earth all in one drawing."

"So you're into maps."

"That's what I'm here for. I do multidimensional navigation. Buildings, natural landscapes, underground walkways. Everything but streets, basically. The layers are crowdsourced, so anyone can add to them by tracking their location on their phone. There are different levels with maps to secret places that you can only access if you add enough of your own mapping to unlock that level."

"Kind of like Squirrel?" I said, thinking of an app I'd downloaded a few months before that had just started getting popular at school.

"Oh, you've heard of it?" Amina looked happily surprised.

It took a moment for me register what she'd said. "Wait, *you* made Squirrel?" I studied Amina in awe. "Of course I've heard of it. All the upperclassmen used it to map the best places to drink and hook up."

Amina groaned. "Does every app have to devolve into a dating app?"

I shrugged. "It's what the people want."

"I use it to time-travel."

"What do you mean?"

"Once, I found this little reading room in the public library in Brooklyn. It used to be an apartment for the library groundskeepers, but they got rid of groundskeepers decades ago. If you pulled out all the books on one wall, you could still see the old green and pink floral wallpaper. It still had the outline of where a rotary phone hung, and you could see the pencil markings where they measured how tall their kids were. When I sat there and read, it felt like I was slipping back in time, sitting in this old secret apartment on the third floor of the library."

I could picture myself sitting in that little room with her, touching the floral wallpaper. I wondered if there were any maps leading to places like that here when something in my pocket vibrated. Amina pulled out her Vault just as I pulled out mine. A message appeared on the screen.

**Please join me for dinner at 6:00 p.m. in the atrium. LL**

Amina must have received the same message I had, because she looked up at me and said, "Lars Lang."

# five

The atrium was a bright, vaulted room in the back of the main building. It looked out over a pool and had three long dining tables already set for dinner. Strings of lights hung above them like stars.

The room was bustling when we arrived. Other fellows were standing around, holding drinks while caterers walked around with plates of hors d'oeuvres. They were dressed like little adults, the girls in professional blouses and the boys in blazers. Amina and I exchanged looks. Neither of us were dressed up.

"Maybe no one will notice," Amina whispered.

We edged toward the drinks table when the boy whose drone I'd broke approached us.

Up close, he looked even more polished than he had before. He might have been cute had he not looked so cocky, like a prep-school boy who'd been told no for the first time in his life. He had trim brown hair and an arrogant tilt to his posture, as though he was used to people doing things for him. He flashed an insidious smile.

Two of his friends stood behind him, one built like a boxer with heavy shoulders and a thick neck, the other tall, slender, and handsome, like a politician's son.

"Let me guess," the drone owner said, looking between me and Amina. "A shopping app," he said to Amina. "And crafting tutorials," he said to me.

My face grew hot.

The boxer snickered, but the politician's son looked uncomfortable. "Come on, AJ," he said to the drone owner. "Leave them alone. It was just an accident."

AJ held up his hand. "No, wait," he said, eyeing Amina's clothes with ridicule, as though she wasn't fashionable enough to do a shopping app. "I bet she's doing a nonprofit to feed the homeless or something."

I felt her tense next to me.

"You don't have to be a jerk," the politician's son mumbled, but AJ brushed him off and turned to me.

"And she's got to be doing a translation app," AJ said with a smirk.

Was he implying that I looked like I couldn't speak English? I clenched my fists and tried to will my body to stop sweating. That was the last thing I needed, to sweat through my shirt in embarrassment.

A few of the other fellows had turned to us and were whispering.

I must have looked upset, because AJ gave me a smug smile. "Looks like I got it right."

"Actually, she's doing multidimensional navigation," I said to him. "And I'm doing artificial intelligence."

His smile faded.

"Now it's my turn," I said. "The easy guess would be surveillance, but that would be giving you too much credit. I'm going to go with something really basic like a package delivery service."

"Or maybe a cryptocurrency that lets him buy things with his parents' money," Amina said.

AJ narrowed his eyes. He had the kind of quiet, seething anger that powerful people had before they did something terrible. "I make my own money."

"Sure you do," Amina said.

AJ turned to me. "I'm sending you an invoice for the drone you destroyed."

"If you don't know how to fix your own drone, you shouldn't be here," I said. "Unless, of course, your parents got you in."

"I got here on my own merit," he said. I didn't like how he was looking at me, like I was less than nothing, like I deserved something terrible.

I swallowed, summoning my resolve. "Then prove it."

By then, people around us had started to notice that something was happening and had grown quiet. I felt their eyes on me. This wasn't the first impression I'd intended to give.

"Come on, man, leave it alone," the politician's son said to AJ. His eyes darted to me, as if to apologize.

I lowered my voice and turned to Amina. "Let's go."

We claimed two seats at the end of the second table just as the lights dimmed.

"So much for no one noticing our outfits," Amina said.

People from the other table were glancing in my direction and whispering. "Now everyone's going to know me as the girl who caused a scene at the reception."

"All publicity is good publicity?" Amina offered.

"Do you think he's really going to make me pay for the drone?"

"No way," Amina said. "Not after that. He'll be too embarrassed."

"His parents are rich anyway," said a girl sitting across from us. "He doesn't need the money."

She was slender and handsome, with blond eyelashes and a naked confidence that looked well-bred, as though she was sitting for her portrait.

"You know him?" I asked.

"We know each other from the prize circuit."

"What's the prize circuit?" Amina asked.

"You know, all those tech fairs and competitions they have for young innovators. A bunch of us have been going to them for years."

So that was why everyone seemed to know each other.

"I'm Kate," the girl said. She nodded to the girl on her right who had long black hair and buck teeth that somehow made her look even prettier. "This is Seema.

"I wouldn't worry about AJ," Kate continued. "Everyone knows he's a jerk. He's just upset because no one ever calls him out on it. That's why everyone's looking at you. They're relieved."

I wasn't sure if I believed her but was glad to hear that at least some of my classmates knew that I hadn't instigated the fight. "I'm Xia," I said.

Kate smiled. She had perfect teeth. "It's nice to meet you."

A murmur rose over the room, and people started looking toward the door. Through the crowd, I could see Lars Lang stroll into the room. He was blond and scruffy, and carried himself like an overgrown teenager.

A few adults whom I presumed were teachers milled by the catering table, chatting. Lars approached them and shook their hands.

"I can't believe it's actually him," Seema whispered.

I couldn't either. Even though he was a household name, I liked to consider myself an early fan. I'd played his games long before they were popular and had been collecting articles about him for years. He was different than other tech giants. In interviews, he was funny and friendly and seemed half genius, half magician. The advice he always gave to kids starting to code was to think of what's missing in your life and build it. Every time I'd read that, I'd felt he was speaking directly to me.

"He's shorter than I imagined," Kate said.

"He seems more approachable," Amina said.

Lars stood at the front of the room and clinked a fork against his glass. The room fell quiet.

"Welcome to the Foundry," he said. "My name is Lars, and though most of you know me as a founder and a CEO, I'd prefer that you think of me as your primary investor for the next year.

"We received over one hundred thousand applications this fall, and from that pool, we chose twenty. Just twenty. I've chosen you because of your ideas, your execution, and your imagination. You're the innovators of your time, and I've brought you here to create the future. That's your job.

"By the end of the year, only one of you will be named this year's Founder. That person will receive our full backing to launch their company, complete with press, access, and a million dollars in seed funding.

"Unlike most schools, which assess students on grades, we measure you by your stock price. Every fellow in the room is starting off with the same stock value of ten dollars, which you can track on your Vault. As in life, your stock price will rise or fall depending on a complex set of variables synthesized by our unique assessment algorithm, which sets your stock price in real time based on factors such as your grades and participation, your performance at networking events and project demonstrations, your business proposals, the quality and progression of your product, your personality and ability to be seen as a leader, and the general belief in your product by your teachers and peers.

"That being said, there is no equation for the perfect start-up. You can ace all your classes and still lose. You can rank smack in the middle of your class and still win. What matters is how you use the knowledge you have. We offer classes in programming and design and business development. I recommend that you go, but you don't have to as long as you complete your assignments and pass each class. We hold networking events and panels with experts and venture capitalists. You don't have to go to those either. There's no instruction manual for life, and likewise, there's no instruction manual here. Frankly, I don't care what you do all day, only that by the end of the year you've passed all your classes and have a product."

He was about to continue when a girl's voice interrupted him.

"What do you think my mom's doing?" the voice said.

Lars looked half amused, half annoyed.

How rude, I thought, to talk while Lars Lang was giving his welcome speech.

"Do you think she's lonely?" The voice sounded distant, like a recording. Everyone was looking around for the source, but no one at either table was speaking. I squinted. Why did the voice sound so familiar?

"Wiser, what if I'm the dumbest person here?" the voice said.

I stiffened. Why was she saying *Wiser*?

My own voice replied from somewhere in the room. "What if no one likes me?"

No. It couldn't be.

"Everyone else probably knows twelve coding languages and has three patents. I've never even taken an advanced programming class."

How was it possible? Frantic, I searched my bag for my phone, but it was silent, and yet my voice was still speaking from somewhere in the room, repeating all of the mortifying questions I'd asked Wiser while I was unpacking when I thought no one was listening.

Kate and Seema glanced at me. Amina gave me a questioning look. I shook my head, baffled. At the front of the room, two teachers searched for the source of the sound.

"I thought I would fit in here because I'd be around people who liked to code, but I already feel like I'm out of place," my voice continued.

I felt the eyes of everyone in the room on me. I wanted to crawl into a hole and die.

"Everyone looks so glossy," my voice said. "They have fancy cars and families that help them unload their stuff. And then there's me, with no one, talking to a disembodied voice in my phone."

Any old hole wasn't enough. I wanted to invent a departiculation machine that would beam me into space, where I would be the first woman to enter a black hole. I would be a national martyr. They would broadcast it on television: a grainy image of me, floating in my spacesuit into a dark gravitational force field, never to be seen again.

"I sometimes wonder if I'm always going to be alone."

Going to space wasn't enough. I needed to invent a machine that erased everyone's memory of me and all traces of my existence.

"I think my face is too round. Do you think it's too round?" my voice continued.

No. I needed to build a time machine, the first of its kind so I could go back to 2003 and prevent myself from ever being born.

"I always feel like I'm saying the wrong thing or acting the wrong way," my voice continued. "Do you think I spend all my time coding because I'm scared of being around other people?"

I heard a snicker from the other table. I looked up and saw AJ whispering to his friend, the boxer. I thought back to the drone hovering outside my window. It must have been recording me.

AJ caught my eye and flashed me a smile. Not knowing what else to do, I mouthed to him, *Turn it off!*

He only shrugged, feigning innocence.

I felt my face turn red. Finally, one of the teachers found a Bluetooth speaker beneath one of the hors d'oeuvres tables and switched it off. The room erupted in murmurs before Lars Lang called on everyone to calm down.

AJ gave me a smug look. Beside him, the boxer snickered. The politician's son averted his eyes as though he didn't want to be implicated. He met my gaze briefly, his expression cowardly. I glared at them all.

"If everyone could silence their phones," Lars said.

I barely heard the rest of the speech. I had been in California for less than twelve hours and had already managed to make an enemy and publicly humiliate myself in front of some of the smartest minds in Silicon Valley. The year was off to a great start.

"What was that?" Amina asked.

"That was me paying for the drone," I said, aware that Kate and Seema were listening, too.

"Who's Wiser?" Kate asked. She had the kind of face that made you feel like you owed her an answer.

"My AI," I said. "That's what I'm here for."

"Artificial intelligence?" Kate seemed surprised, though I couldn't tell why.

I nodded and Kate studied me, her gaze so steady it made me uncomfortable.

"Impressive," she murmured.

"For what it's worth, I thought it made you sound interesting," Amina said.

"Thanks," I mumbled.

Across the room I could see AJ slouching comfortably in his chair while everyone around him tried to earn his attention, as though he were presiding over the table. He caught my eye and I watched as his lips curled into a sickening smile.

I excused myself and walked to the bar to refill my drink.

"We have energy drinks, alkalized water, electrolyte water, or fruit-infused sparkling water," the bartender said.

"I'd skip the energy drinks," a voice said from behind

me. "They taste like battery juice. Unless, of course, you're bionic. Then by all means, drink up."

I turned around to see a boy. He was a dork, but a cute dork. He wore beat-up Converse sneakers and a comic book T-shirt beneath a blazer—a half-hearted attempt at dressing up for the occasion. He had dark brown hair and a mischievous glint in his eyes, like he was in on a joke. There was nothing spectacular about him, and yet something about his eyes made him look different from everyone else. They were brown and steady, and looked at me as though I were the most interesting person in the room.

"Are you saying I look robotic?" I asked.

He studied me. "You're pretty symmetrical. Though if I were going to design a robot, I'd probably make it plainer so it wouldn't be so distracting."

I wasn't sure if he was being sincere or making fun of my recording at dinner. "If you're talking about what happened during the speech, that wasn't me. I mean, it was me, but I didn't play it on purpose. Someone was spying on me and recorded me talking to my phone—"

He let out a gentle laugh. "I wasn't talking about the recording."

I blushed and took in his T-shirt, which pictured a man in glasses turning into a superhero. It kind of looked like him. I liked that he was the only other person in the room who wasn't dressed like he was going to an interview. "So you didn't get the memo either?"

"Are you insulting my outfit?" he said with a grin.

"I'm complimenting it." I turned to the bartender. "I'll take a sparkling water."

"So you're not a robot," the boy said.

I smiled. "No."

"I'm Mast," he said.

What kind of name was Mast?

"Xia."

"Xia," he repeated. I liked the way he said it, like it was a precious word. "So who's this Wiser that you were talking to?"

"My AI."

"Artificial intelligence," he murmured, impressed. "So it can answer all those questions you asked it?"

"Not yet. It's something I do to help her learn. I ask her questions to figure out what her weak spots are." I left out the fact that I also did it to keep myself company.

"How does she work?"

"She analyzes your data and simulates an older version of you to give you advice."

"So you're basically the smartest person here."

I flushed. Was it really possible that he could have heard that entire recording and instead of thinking that I was a lonely dork who had to invent friends, he thought I was smart?

"Isn't everyone here smart?"

"There's a hierarchy, with delivery apps at the bottom and AI at the top."

I tried not to look too flattered but couldn't help it.

"Well, I wasn't smart enough to keep my shades down and windows closed."

"But you were smart enough to warrant being spied on."

"I don't think that's why they were spying on me."

"Either way, you should take it as a compliment."

Why was I blushing so much? "Thanks."

"I'd love to meet her sometime," Mast said. "Wiser."

I held back a smile. "You're asking a lot of questions," I said. "How do I know you're not spying on me?"

"I guess you'll just have to trust me."

"And why would I do that?"

He gave me an amused look. "I knew you were smart." He raised his glass in the air and strode back to his seat.

I felt my chest swell. Mast. What kind of name was that?

# SIX

He seemed too good to be true. Most people I met didn't really see me. They saw bits of me, but not the entirety. My mother, for example, saw me as a sometimes helpful but mostly aggravating daughter who kept doing things that she didn't approve of or understand. Gina saw me as her smart and eccentric friend who was really good with computers. Amina was similar to me in a lot of ways, but I got the sense that the thing that brought me here wasn't the same thing that brought her. She was ready to run a company, whereas I had come here to finally find people who understood me. But after just a few moments with Mast, I could tell that he saw me the way I wanted to be seen.

I sank into my bed and opened Wiser.

"Wiser, tell me more about Mast. He's a fellow at the Foundry."

She paused. "There is no person named Mast at the Foundry."

I frowned. "That's not right. Search again."

"I've scanned the list of fellows on the Foundry website and I have found no person named Mast."

"That can't be. I was just talking to him."

"Perhaps you misheard his name."

"I didn't."

"Then perhaps he misled you."

"Why would he do that?" I asked.

"People lie for many reasons, most often to hide shameful feelings or to manipulate for personal benefit."

I went on the Foundry's website and looked at the list of names with their accompanying pictures. Wiser was right; there was no fellow named Mast. I scanned the photographs looking for the boy I had spoken to. Sure enough, there he was, grinning into the camera. His name was Benjamin Matsuo.

"Wiser, tell me more about Benjamin Matsuo."

She paused. "Benjamin Matsuo is from San Mateo, California. He has won the Young Leaders of Technology Prize, the Governor's Medal of Science, and the National Mathematics Medal of Achievement. He has two younger siblings. His father is a professor in technology and ethics at Stanford Graduate School of Business, and his mother is an attorney specializing in patent law. He is attending the Foundry to work on an artificial intelligence project."

I nearly fell out of bed. "He's here for AI?"

"That is correct."

I couldn't believe it. He had deliberately misled me. I

studied his picture, growing furious. His grinning face stared back at me as though it knew. I wanted to flick the smug look off his face.

I was about to search the internet for more information on his AI when my phone vibrated. I had a new message on BitBop.

NEW MESSAGE FROM u/OBJECTPERMANENCE:
Hey, are you up? How's the new school?

Just seeing his message box comforted me, the way it felt to come home and see that everything in your house was just the way you left it. I felt guilty then that I had entertained the idea that Mast could replace ObjectPermanence just because he had complimented me, because I had seen him in the flesh. Though I often fantasized about meeting Object-Permanence in person, I sometimes wondered if it even mattered. So what if I had never seen his face or touched his hand? Our conversations were more real than any I'd had in the physical world. Didn't that make this reality, too?

I considered how to respond.

SENT MESSAGE FROM u/ARRAYOFLIGHT:
Have you ever wanted to just click undo on an entire day? Well, that's how it is here. I thought I'd meet people here that got me, but I'm starting to wonder if maybe I just won't fit in anywhere.

New message from u/ObjectPermanence:
Why? What happened?

Sent message from u/ArrayOfLight:
It's hard to talk about without getting into details, but if
you can imagine a star imploding into a black hole, only
before collapsing, the star was publicly humiliated in front
of its entire galaxy and then a nice star approached it,
but it later turned out that the nice star was just lying to
extract its last valuable minerals before it imploded into
a black hole, then you'll have an accurate picture of what
happened.

New message from u/ObjectPermanence:
I always knew astrophysics was complicated, but I
never considered the social dynamics of interstellar
relationships.
      It's hard to imagine a star having anything to be
humiliated about. Those other stars must have been
jealous because their light was dimmer. The joke's on
them, though, because black holes are basically the most
formidable formations in the universe, so they'd better
watch out.

I smiled. Was it possible to be in love with an arrange-
ment of letters on a computer screen? The keys felt warm
beneath my fingers.

SENT MESSAGE FROM U/ARRAYOFLIGHT:
Thanks. I'll try to remember that. How's it going over there?

NEW MESSAGE FROM U/OBJECTPERMANENCE:
The same, basically. I did something today that I wasn't proud of. I wish I could go back and change it, but it's done. I wasn't mean or anything, but I treated someone in a way that I regret. I like to think of myself as a good person, but then I do things like this and I wonder if my "goodness" is just a story I tell myself so I don't have to own up to the fact that maybe I'm just like everyone else—good when it suits me, and less good when it doesn't.

SENT MESSAGE FROM U/ARRAYOFLIGHT:
I know I don't really know you, but it feels like I do, and I think you're a good person. Or maybe no one is, because what is "good" anyway? No one does the right thing all the time. Just try to be better tomorrow.

NEW MESSAGE FROM U/OBJECTPERMANENCE:
Thanks. I guess you're right. It occurred to me today that I'm never really myself around most people I know. I'm always trying to be the person "I'm supposed to be," whatever that means.

I don't feel that way around you, though, and I'm glad.

SENT MESSAGE FROM U/ARRAYOFLIGHT:
Me too.

There were three Mikes and three Andrews, though one went by Drew—AJ's thick-necked friend—one went by Andy, and the other by AJ. There was a Micah—an almost Mike, Amina said—two Bens, and two Joshes. The others were Arun, Marcus, Arthur, and Ravi.

Of the twenty of us at the Foundry, there were only five girls.

Kate, Seema, Amina, and I sat in the dining hall, a leafy sunroom that overlooked a courtyard. Though we called it the dining hall, it was really more of a café. There was a menu, and you could order anything you wanted for free, at any hour of the day.

I had considered skipping breakfast and staying in my room for the rest of the year so I wouldn't have to face anyone after what had happened the night before. I could order a minifridge, vitamin D supplements, Johann Sebastian Bach's complete Fugue discography, and enough meal-replacement beverages to last me until the program was over. I could attend classes remotely. The vitamin D supplements would prevent my bones from growing brittle with the lack of sunlight, and Bach seemed like the only appropriate music to play as a lonely coder living in the shadows. I would have epistolary relationships only, the primary one being with ObjectPermanence, my long, unconsummated romance. It would be a tragic existence, one they would make movies about long after I was gone. *The tragic story of Xia Chan, solitary and eccentric tech innovator who spent the majority of her life in a dark room.* But Amina had pointed out that it would be hard to become a tech innovator without leaving my room, so I'd begrudgingly accompanied her.

It was just as bad as I'd expected: everyone looking at me, whispering my name. Walking by AJ's table was particularly excruciating. He smirked and inexplicably held up seven fingers. I stared at them, bewildered.

"Don't worry about AJ," Kate said. "He's used to getting what he wants, but he's not real competition." She looked trim as a ribbon in a petal-colored shirt, as thin as tissue and almost the same hue as her skin, interrupted only by a freckle on her neck.

Seema sat next to her, dressed in sleek business casual like she was already a CEO. Her long black hair was held in place with a headband.

"What do you mean?" I asked.

"His ideas are mediocre, and his programming is sloppy," Kate said. "There's no way he's going to be the Founder, and he knows it." She lowered her voice. "The real ones to worry about are Andy, Mike, Arthur, Arun, and Ben."

Ben. I wondered if she was talking about Mast. I scanned the dining hall but didn't see him.

Andy Chen, Kate explained, was probably the most famous kid at the Foundry. She nodded to a lanky boy in baggy jeans and a hoodie who was eating cereal a few tables away. He was skinny, with a birdlike face that would have looked childish had he not exuded the cool confidence of someone who knew he was at the top. He'd started Grapevine, a gossip app that he'd already launched. "I'm sure you've heard of it," Kate said.

Of course I had. It was a terrible but genius app that let people anonymously post three statements—two of them lies, one of them the truth—and let people speculate on which one was real. The posts disappeared after five hours, which was long enough for the damage to be done. Though I'd never tried it, everyone back home had been using it to spread rumors about people at school.

"Why is he even here if he already has a successful start-up?" I asked.

"Apparently he's working on this security filter called Garble that prevents any information you share from being captured by a screenshot," Kate said. "It somehow blurs the screen so that when you take a screenshot it just shows a bunch of pixels. He wants to use it as an add-on to Grapevine so that people will share even more private information without the risk of it being saved forever."

I rolled my eyes. "I guess he decided he doesn't want to use his powers for good."

"I heard he's a dick," Amina said.

Kate shrugged. "I think he lives off a steady stream of sugar, caffeine, and Adderall. I ran into him once at a teen coding conference. He was in the girls' bathroom, just standing in front of the mirror splashing his face with water and listening to trance music so loud I could hear it through his headphones. I don't think he even realized I was there."

Andy was sitting with two other boys, one of them Arthur Kim, a slightly pudgy boy with a giddy face that seemed inclined to laugh. He was already gaining the reputation of being the class clown. He looked sweet and goofy, with his snapback hat and his baggy skateboarding pants covered in patches. He was there for an app called Dare Me, where people could post dares and respond with challenges and videos that could be upvoted.

Amina rolled her eyes. "Changing the world, one dare at time."

It sounded dumb, Kate conceded, especially compared to Mike McCalaster's smart pump for kids with diabetes, but dumb things usually had the broadest appeal. Plus, everyone knew how much investors wanted to fund anything with video.

I nodded like I knew what she was talking about. Did everyone here know about what investors wanted except for me?

Arun Krishna was tall and handsome in the way that

people who owned islands looked handsome, in the way that billionaires were handsome. He wore loafers with no socks and a crisp white polo that made him look like he was on a yacht. A pair of sunglasses was nestled in his hair.

He was sitting with a handful of boys, all of whom looked like they had just walked out of a brochure for a prep school. He noticed us looking at him and flashed a smile, perfect and white.

"What is he, running for Congress?" Amina said. "Who has teeth like that?"

"He doesn't need to run for anything," Kate said. "He's rich. His dad's the global head of operations and strategy at LineCart, which powers basically all of the online shopping stores in the world."

"His dad just bought a basketball team," Seema said.

"They fly around in a private jet," Kate added.

"He knows Lil' Wip. They sit courtside," Seema said.

"Seriously?" Amina said, her eyes wide.

"He has his cell phone number," Seema said. "I saw it."

I'd never heard of Lil' Wip before but was too embarrassed to admit it, so I nodded, pretending to be impressed.

"And his sister's a model. She used to date Kenzy Lo."

"What?" Amina said. "That is wild."

Was I the only one here who knew nothing about anything? "Wow," I murmured, and wondered why he was even at the Foundry if he was that rich. Couldn't his dad just fund his company?

Arun was there to work on Clique, a networking site

for teens, which to me, sounded awfully like a dating app. I caught Amina's eye and we exchanged a barely perceptible smile.

Arun was sitting with Mike Flores, the friend of AJ's who looked like a politician's son. Mike was objectively good-looking, despite the company he kept. He had a wave of mahogany hair and a golden complexion that seemed to glow with health and money. He was there to launch a service called TVTR, which was an online community that let you ask people questions about your homework. It also matched people with tutors.

"He also wants to make an algorithm that checks your homework for any mistakes, but that's in the future," Kate said.

"So an app that does your homework?" I said.

"Sounds like an easy way to pay other people to help you cheat," Amina said.

Kate brushed her off. "I'm sure he could create protections for that."

"Changing the world, one purchased essay at a time," Amina said.

"He's actually a really nice guy," Kate said. "He's going to give a portion of the proceeds to scholarship funds for kids in need."

"If he wins," Amina corrected.

"If he were actually a nice guy, he'd stand up to AJ," I said.

"They're childhood friends. It's not that easy."

"How do you know so much about Mike's internal dialogue?" Amina asked.

Kate shrugged. "We're friends."

Seema smirked. "They have a thing. It's been going on for a while."

Amina exchanged a glance with me. So that was why Kate was so generous with him.

"It's on and off," Kate said. "Right now it's off. But we're still friends. Anyway, he'll probably get it funded even if he doesn't win," Kate said. "His dad is the head of design at Barion Industries and his mom is the VP of sales at Pageforce."

I'd heard of both companies but didn't know exactly what they did.

"He's not as rich as Arun," Seema said, "but he's not shopping in the bargain bins."

I felt my chest flush. I hoped no one at the table would notice that my shirt and pants were off-brand, bought on clearance.

"Does everyone here have rich parents?" Amina asked.

Kate and Seema insisted that their families weren't rich. Kate's mom was a dean at Caltech and her dad was a neurologist, and Seema's mom was a doctor and her dad was an electrical engineer at one of the big microprocessor companies.

They clearly had a different definition than I did of *rich*. Maybe compared to Arun they weren't rich, but it seemed like neither Kate nor Seema grew up wanting. Amina must have been thinking the same thing because she raised her eyebrow but said nothing.

I wondered what Amina's parents did. I didn't tell them that I only had one parent, that my dad left when I was two. All I knew about him was that his name was Wei, he'd been getting his PhD in biochemistry but had dropped out, and that he'd taken the car and all of the cash from my mother's wallet the day he'd left. My mother didn't like to talk about him, and the few times I'd asked, her face had darkened and she'd said that the only part of him worth anything was me.

Once, I'd asked Wiser to look him up, but the search rendered too many results, none of which sounded right. There was a pharmacist in Sedona, a high school math teacher in Chicago, an engineer in Berkeley, and a microbiologist in Boston. All of them had families, and none of them looked like me. I wondered if my mother had even told me his real name.

There were other impressive people. Marcus had skipped two grades in school and was taking college classes now because he'd maxed out the ones at his school. He'd made a dating app called Playlist, where you matched based on movie and music lists you curated. He probably wouldn't win, Kate surmised, because dating apps were old news, but he'd eventually get funding from someone else. Same with the selling platforms and the gamers. Good ideas but they're not *fresh*, Kate emphasized.

And of course, there was Deborah, the fifth and final girl, who was standing by the door talking to Ravi, one of the gamers, while she sipped an energy drink. She was brawny, with broad shoulders and dark hair pulled into a low ponytail. She walked everywhere at a slant, as though she were bracing herself against the elements.

"She only drinks meal replacement beverages so she doesn't have to waste time eating," Kate said.

"She gets up at 5:00 a.m. every day and runs eight miles," said Seema.

"She makes chain mail in her spare time to use for cosplaying," Kate continued.

She was there for some kind of cryptocurrency called Parbit, Seema told us, though neither she nor Kate knew how it worked.

"She's smart," Kate said. "But I don't see how she's going to convince funders to back her as a CEO when she barely has the social skills to get through a normal conversation, let alone talk to investors and create a good corporate culture."

Could I talk to investors? I had no idea what a good corporate culture looked like, nor did I have any clue about how to go about interviewing or, heaven forbid, firing someone.

AJ was there for a cryptocurrency, too—"I knew it!" Amina interrupted—though his was called Allowance, and let parents attach a set of stipulations to the money they bestowed. Eventually he hoped to expand it and disrupt the banking and legal industry surrounding financial contracts. It was a good idea, Kate conceded, but most cryptocurrencies weren't actually used as currency, which made them a wild card. Plus, his idea hinged on parents using cryptocurrency instead of just giving their kids cash, which would be a hard sell.

Kate seemed to enjoy picking everyone apart, and though I was glad for the information, I noticed that she was guarded about the details of her life. She peppered Amina and me with questions about our start-ups, showering us with compliments. She prompted Seema to tell us about her app, MakeOver, which let you post clothing and accessory options that other users could swipe through to vote on an outfit. By the end of breakfast, she knew about my mother and our apartment and Gina; about the issues I'd been having with Wiser and how I'd thought her up while my mother was working late. She'd even managed to get me to tell the story about the red hat.

I hadn't planned on sharing so much. She came on subtle, asking innocent questions and listening intently as though I was the most important person in the room. She was humble about her own work. "Oh, my start-up?" she'd said. "It pales in comparison to yours." Then came the flattery. Artificial intelligence was so trendy right now, Kate told me. Everyone wanted in. And Wiser sounded incredible. Such an advanced tool and so amazing that I was able to create it with basically no formal training. But the thing about AI was that it was all in the execution, she'd said. How was I planning on monetizing it? What was my pitch to VC firms?

I didn't know. I wasn't sure. I hadn't thought about pitching yet. We'd only just arrived.

Kate lingered on me, her gaze thoughtful. "Good," she said. "So I don't have to worry about you beating me . . . yet."

I let out a nervous laugh. Something about the way she

was studying me made me regret betraying so much. All I knew about Kate was that she grew up in Pasadena and that she was working on an app called Split, which helped kids manage the logistics of divorce. I wondered if the person I should really be worried about was her.

"I'm kidding," Kate said. "Society is always trying to pit girls against each other, when really it's the guys we need to be worried about. They're the ones in power, paying us less, stealing our ideas, and taking our promotions. We have to lift each other up."

Amina looked unimpressed. She'd barely answered Kate's questions and had quickly lost Kate's interest. Mapping, after all, was important, Kate had said, but there were only so many map applications that you could expect a person to use.

"And then of course there's Ben," Kate said. "He's doing artificial intelligence, too."

I felt her studying me, gauging my reaction.

"Oh, but you already know him," she said. "You were talking to him last night."

Had she been watching me?

"You know. Dark hair, loves comic books, looks kind of like a nerdy anime character."

"You're just saying that because he's half Japanese," Seema said.

Kate ignored her. "Cute in a dorky way, if that's your thing. He makes corny jokes and gets way too excited about classic sci-fi movies."

"Mast, yeah."

"Oh, right. I always forget he goes by that. At the tech fairs they always use your proper name, for name tags and announcements and stuff."

"What does Mast even mean?" Seema said.

"Something having to do with the way people mispronounce his last name," Kate said. "Anyway, I know it doesn't look like it, but he's one of the smartest people here. Speak of the devil."

I turned to see Mast saunter into the dining hall.

While Kate continued to go over everyone else's start-up idea, I pushed my food aside.

"Where are you going?" Amina whispered as I stood up.

"I'll be right back."

Mast was fiddling with the juice machine when I approached him.

"That was very cute of you," I said to him.

He smiled when he saw me. "I am cute, aren't I?"

Unfortunately, he was. He was wearing a different comic book T-shirt that day, this time with no jacket, which showed off his arms. They were smooth and tan and surprisingly toned. I tried not to look at them. I'd approached him to give him a piece of my mind, not be distracted by the scar on his wrist or the way his cheeks dimpled when he smiled or the way he was looking at me, like I was the only person in the room.

"*Artificial intelligence?*" I said, mocking his fake innocent voice from the other night.

Mast rolled his eyes. "That's not how I sound."

"My name is Mast," I said. "I don't know anything about artificial intelligence. I'm just dorky and cute and I'm going to flatter you with compliments so I can get information and steal your secrets."

Mast fumbled with his words. "That's not what I did. I was just being friendly and asking questions. You didn't ask me what I did. You didn't ask me any questions at all, which honestly seems a little self-centered."

I gaped at him, incredulous. "You gave me a fake name."

"Mast is my name. It's what everyone calls me."

"Your name is Ben. You're just another Ben."

"What does that even mean?"

"I bet you hide behind a weird name because it makes you seem different, when you're really just like everyone else. You didn't want to tell me your real name because I might have recognized it from the list of fellows as someone who was also working on AI, and I would have known that you weren't just asking me innocent questions."

"Mast is a nickname. I grew up with it."

"I thought you were being nice to me."

"I was being nice to you. You had a bad night."

"Well, thanks for doing me a favor," I said sarcastically.

"It wasn't a favor. I thought Wiser sounded interesting, though if we're being honest, I do think you could work out a few kinks in your design. Don't you think it might turn into a feedback loop if all she's reading is your past data?"

"No. She's a lot more complicated than that, and anyway,

she's still a work in progress, so she's not supposed to be perfect, not that I asked for your opinion."

"You think I'm cute though," Mast teased.

My face went red. "I didn't say that."

"Sure you did. You said I'm dorky and cute."

"I thought that *before* you tried to extract information from me."

"But you thought it," Mast said with a grin. "So if you didn't know I was doing AI, what did you think I was here for?"

"Something safe and boring. Maybe sports."

He winced. "Sports? Is that an official category?" He lowered his voice to make it sound like a television announcer. "*Sports tech. For males.*"

It was a shame he was such a jerk, otherwise he would have been cute *and* funny.

"I'm going to interpret that as meaning that I look fit and socially well-adjusted."

I rolled my eyes.

"This is the point at which you're supposed to make me feel better and say, *Yes, I agree*," Mast said.

"Right, yes. Fit and social. Exactly what I was thinking."

"The world has never heard such a glowing endorsement," he said. "But I'll take it."

"So what's your AI called? Ben?"

"Very funny," he said. "He's called Olli."

"Olli?"

Mast looked self-conscious. "He gives you suggestions

on music and movies and clothes like he's an older brother or sister."

"And Olli refers to . . . ?"

"OL and LI," Mast said as if it were obvious. "You know how in HTML, where OL is the parent list and each LI item is the child on the list."

"So it's a siblings reference," I murmured.

Mast looked pleased. "Exactly."

Admittedly, it was a cute name, though its etymology wasn't completely obvious.

"So what, it analyzes publicly available data for things that are popular in the age bracket five years ahead of you, then makes recommendations?"

My quick dissection seemed to surprise him. "It's a lot more sophisticated than that, but yes, that's the oversimplified version. The algorithm also differentiates between mainstream appeal and indie appeal and takes into account vintage recommendations based on what era is currently trending."

"And what, you have user input, so you can say if you like a recommendation or not?"

Mast looked nervous. "Yeah."

I considered saying the first thought that came to my head but bit my tongue.

"What? You think your design is better?"

"No. Yours is fine."

"You're not a good liar. I can tell you have something you want to say. Just spit it out."

"It's just that you're clearly an older sibling, aren't you?"

Mast narrowed his eyes. "Why do you think that?"

"Well, if you were a younger sibling, you'd know that it doesn't really make sense to include user input because older siblings don't take into account your preferences. They just tell you what's cool and what's not, and they don't care about what you want. Right?"

Mast looked troubled. This problem clearly hadn't occurred to him before. "I need user input because that's the way Olli learns."

"Okay. It's your app."

I could tell I had struck a nerve. "So you're a younger sibling?" he asked.

"No. I'm unique."

"You mean you're an only child. Of course you are. That's why you thought it was a good idea to loop your old decisions into new ones. Because you've only ever been alone, and it shows."

Though supposedly he was joking, his words felt like a slap in the face. I must have looked upset because his face immediately softened.

"That came out harsher than I meant it to."

I swallowed, unsure of what to say. "I should probably get back," I said, inching away from him. See you around," I said softly and retreated to my table.

# eight

**I tried to forget** what Mast had said, but it stayed with me through breakfast and on our walk to the main hall. I had always been alone, and Wiser was both my solution and my excuse. I didn't need to go out and talk to people if I had her.

"Are you okay?" Amina asked.

I looked up, grateful for the reminder that she was there. "Yeah."

All of our classes met in a stucco mansion that everyone called the Villa. It was a sun-drenched building surrounded by breezeways coiled with climbing vines.

Our first class was Advanced Programming for Start-ups, a class created by the Foundry to give us an overview of the advanced coding we'd need to launch a whole host of start-ups. The teacher was a famous professor. I'd never heard of him before getting into the Foundry, but then again, I hadn't really heard of anyone.

"He's supposed to be incredible," Kate said to us. "He has at least twenty patents."

"For what?" Amina asked.

Kate shrugged. "Who knows. But he's got to be rich. He used to teach at Stanford."

"My dad was his student in the nineties," Seema said.

"He taught there for decades," Kate continued. "He basically started their computer science program and was always being wooed by tech companies."

"Rumor has it he turned down a twelve percent share in AcroWare *and* Parsel," Seema said.

"When he retired, some people thought he was recruited by the military to work on a secret project," Kate said.

"But my dad said he would never do anything like that," Seema said. "He doesn't trust the government. But he's deaf in one ear, which some people think is a clear sign that he was working for the military."

"Most scientists who work for the military don't see active combat," Amina pointed out.

Seema frowned. "He could have been testing loud equipment."

"He came out of retirement to do this job," Kate said. "I don't know how they convinced him."

"They have to be paying him a fortune," Seema said.

"Maybe he just wanted to," I said. "Maybe he was bored. Or lonely."

Kate dismissed me with a wave of her hand. "Don't be naïve. Everything here is run by money."

The classroom was filled with boys, all of whom stared at us as we took seats in the front row. Their gaze made me feel like I was on display behind glass. I could almost see their faces pressing against it, assessing my specs and deciding how much I was worth. Amina gave me an uncomfortable glance. She must have felt the same way.

Mast was sitting by the window, chatting with Ravi. He caught my eye and gave me an apologetic look, but I ignored it.

I heard a chuckle and turned to see the Andrews and Mikes snickering. Were they laughing at me?

"Hey, seven," AJ said.

I frowned. Was he talking to me?

He said something to Micah and they both laughed.

I'd been hearing the word *seven* all morning. At breakfast, I'd heard it whispered with my name, but I'd brushed it off, assuming it was nothing. Then AJ holding up seven fingers. Now this.

"Why is everyone saying *seven*?" I asked Amina, who was looking at her phone.

She bit her lip. "Do you have Grapevine?"

I felt a sinking feeling in my stomach. Grapevine was the gossip app that Andy Chen had founded. "No, why?"

"Just download it."

I downloaded Grapevine and searched for the Foundry. A vine curled across my screen. I clicked through its buds.

There are electronic almonds hidden all over the Villa in tribute to its origins as an almond farm.

Every desk has a fingerprint beneath it that lets you turn your tabletop into a touch screen.

One of the fellows was kicked out last year for calling Lars Lang a coward and a fake.

I wondered why someone would call Lars Lang a coward or a fake. Curious, I reached under my desk and slid my hand along its underside, but all I felt was dried gum. I grimaced. This was why I hated Grapevine.

I clicked the next one and felt a knot form in my chest when I saw my name.

Xia Chan asks her AI to talk dirty to her when she falls asleep.

Xia Chan once asked Wiser what it feels like to be kissed.

Xia Chan's stock dropped to eight.

My face grew hot. The other day while I was unpacking and asking questions to Wiser, I might have asked her what it felt like to be kissed, just to see what she said. And AJ might have recorded it with his drone. Which meant he had to have written the post.

Suddenly it felt like everyone was looking at me and snickering. The only notable person who wasn't was Mast.

Just to be safe, I pulled my Vault out of my wallet and pressed my finger to it until the papery surface dissolved into a screen.

Five icons appeared, as usual. I clicked the arrow, which brought me to a ticker screen where I could see my stock price, alongside everyone else's. That's when I saw it.

Everyone else's was still ten. Mine had dipped to seven.

I'd been in California for under forty-eight hours—I hadn't even sat through a single class yet—and already, I was at the bottom of the class.

"It's not that bad," Amina assured me.

I was grateful she didn't ask me which was one true.

"Hey, Seven," AJ said to me from a few seats over. "Which one is it?"

I had to give it to him, it was clever, posting one truth, one lie, and one almost lie—eight—which would lead everyone to check my stock and see that it had dropped. He'd posted two truths under the guise of one.

"They're all lies," I said, figuring denial was the best tactic.

Next to him, Micah and Drew laughed. Mike didn't join, but didn't tell them to stop, either.

Kate gave me a sympathetic look. She must have read it, too.

Amina glared at AJ, then turned to me. "Whoever did it is just worried because they know you're the real competition."

"Plus, lots of people haven't kissed anyone," Kate whispered. "It's not like you're the only one."

I wanted to clone the environment around me onto my skin so that I blended in with the desks and chairs.

"I bet most of the people here haven't," Seema added. "It's a room full of programmers, after all."

I wanted to invent an implantable that made me invisible.

"I've kissed people," I insisted. For some reason I glanced at Mast, but to my relief his gaze was still trained on the board.

"Oh," Kate said, looking innocent. "I just figured that one of them was true."

"They're all fake," I insisted, but worried that my flushed face was betraying me.

I wanted to create a snipping tool that would cut me out of my life and paste me into an outer-dimensional clipboard, where I would live out the rest of my days as a liminal, extraneous being.

"Okay, Seven," one of the boys said from behind me.

There was no point to my existence. I was a CD-ROM. A floppy disk. A set of encyclopedias. Useless and obsolete and only remembered as an object of ridicule and pity. I sank deeper into my chair.

"At least they don't think you masturbate to your AI," Amina offered. "Not that there's anything wrong with that, if that's what you're into."

"That's not what I'm into," I said. "And it's a small consolation."

"It's only the first day of class," Amina said. "You can bring your stock back up again."

"Exactly," I said. "It's the first day of class. How is this even possible?"

"It probably has to do with last night," Kate murmured. "Lars said the algorithm takes into account public perception of you and your product."

"Great. Now my public humiliation has been quantified."

"At least it's not lower," Amina offered.

It was a small solace. I sighed when the door opened and a man hurried in. He looked like he lived in a tinfoil house and spent his weekends building odd things out of scrap metal. He had stringy gray hair pulled into a ponytail and wore a loose fishing vest over his shirt that added at least eight extra visible pockets to his outfit. Out of one, he removed a pair of glasses. Out of another, a pen and paper, which he unfolded and read our names from. He introduced himself as Mr. Kowalski.

"This class is a mishmash of things that I've deemed important for you to master if you want to distinguish yourself from the mass of programmers who flock here every year trying to peddle their ideas.

"I don't care much for small talk or introductions, so let's just dive in. First things first: data structures. As you all know, they help us organize data so it can be retrieved and altered with speed and efficiency. I assume you all have some experience with them, but here, you'll learn how to better implement and write complex data structures and algorithms. First, however, I'd like to see what level we're all operating on."

He tapped the whiteboard behind him and it dissolved into a screen, which made everyone in the room gasp in surprise. On it, appeared a matrix of 0s and 1s.

"Open your laptops," Kowalski said. "I'd like you to find the largest square made up of only 1s in this grid." He pulled a sandwich from one of his pockets. "You have until I finish this delectable turkey submarine."

There was a shuffle as everyone went to work. I opened my coding environment. The cursor blinked.

I tried not to think about my stock or Mast or AJ and his stupid friends. I came here to become a legitimate programmer and I couldn't be distracted. I tried to remember what ObjectPermanence had written to me in his message. I was formidable. I was a black hole. I was a gravitational forcefield pulling power toward me.

The thing about programming is that there's never one right answer. It's like cooking a chicken. There are infinite ways to do it—some take hours, some take minutes, some make it dry or crispy or juicy or tender. Some are energy efficient and some aren't, some have dozens of ingredients and some have just a handful. I knew I could write a program that could find the largest square, but the trick was to find a way to do it quickly and efficiently, using the least amount of extra space.

I considered all the ways to solve Kowalski's problem and was about to start typing when a message notification popped up on my Foundry email. Someone had invited me to a group chat, where a dozen people with handles I didn't recognize were talking.

**G8mer88: I can't believe you're all still typing. The answer is obviously 7**

My face reddened.

**2blpentr810: already done. I solved it in 7 minutes**

**30parsecs:** hey anyone want to get dinner tonight? Meet at 7

**stringmealong:** can we push it a little later? How about 7:07.

**Aggrorhythm69:** why don't we do takeout? 7 pizzas. Meet at classroom 7.

I glanced around the classroom, but everyone was hunched over their computers, tapping away. I lingered on AJ, who also seemed engrossed in the assignment. His eyes darted to mine, and he flashed me a cold, threatening smile.

I closed the chat and began to type my code as quickly as I could. There was no time. Kowalski had already eaten a quarter of his sandwich, and I had nothing to show for myself. By the window, Mast was typing quickly, his eyes glued to his screen. Did he have to do it so loudly? Kate was coding beside me, her fingers long and elegant as they glided across the keyboard. A few desks over, Seema was hunched over her screen, murmuring to herself as she worked, and Amina had pulled a notebook out of her bag and was scribbling notes while glancing up at her screen. Out of the corner of my eye I saw something hover outside the window. Was it a drone? I turned but it was just a hummingbird.

I was scanning my code to make sure all my brackets were closed and my syntax was correct when Kowalski told us that our time was up. One by one, he projected everyone's code on the whiteboard and dissected it.

It quickly became clear who was merely good at coding and who was great. Most of the fellows had written a variation of the same answer—code that was time efficient but would take up too much computer memory, or that was memory efficient but would take too long for the computer to process. Amina and Mast were the only ones who had written code that was both. That is, other than me.

"Beautiful," Kowalski said, projecting Mast's work on the screen. "Simple, elegant. Excellent work."

Mast grinned, his eyes flitting to me, but I quickly looked away.

When it was my turn, I could feel the pressure in the room change, as though everyone's eyes were on me. The number seven seemed to hang in the air, both a threat and challenge.

"Very good," Kowalski said, squinting at my code. "Nice use of dynamic programming. But it's sloppily written. Your formatting is all over the place, which would make it hard for anyone else to work with. Clean it up so other programmers can read it."

I blushed and nodded. Someone in the back of the room snickered, but all I felt was relief. I had done okay.

When class was over, Mast caught up with me in the hallway.

"If we weren't archnemeses, I would compliment you on your code," he said. "It was really smart, the way you swapped the pointers."

I eyed him suspiciously, wondering what his angle was, but to my surprise he looked sincere. "Then I would say thanks."

"I'd also ask where you're from. And what your favorite movies are. If you prefer Milk Duds or popcorn."

"Then I'd say, Massachusetts, romantic comedies, and Milk Duds. And I'd ask you the same questions because I wouldn't want to appear self-centered."

"And I'd answer California, romantic comedies, and Milk Duds."

"Really?"

"No. I hate Milk Duds. They get stuck in your teeth. But I'd share a box with you if you wanted. Just don't tell anyone about the romantic comedy thing or my stock will plummet and I'll get torn to shreds."

I felt a prickle on the back of my neck. ObjectPermanence liked romantic comedies, too. For a minute, I allowed myself to wonder, but quickly shook it away. Of course he wasn't ObjectPermanence. What were the chances?

Mast was studying me like I was a puzzle, and I felt suddenly self-conscious. "What?" I murmured.

"I'd also probably ask you what kind of food you liked," he said. "If we weren't archnemeses, that is. But since we are, I won't."

He was holding the strap of his backpack in his hand, and despite myself I wondered what it would it feel like to slip my hand in his. I clutched my bag to my chest. "Why would you ask that?"

"Just to see if you wanted to get lunch sometime," he said. "But archnemeses don't dine together."

I wasn't sure if he was joking or serious. "It would be too fraught," I agreed. "No one would enjoy the food."

"Right," Mast said. He looked disappointed, and I

wondered if he was hoping for a different response. Was he actually asking me if I wanted to get lunch?

"Well, I guess I'll see you around," I said awkwardly.

"Wait," Mast said. "Can I ask you a personal question?"

I hesitated. "Okay."

"What did Wiser say when you asked her that?"

My face grew hot. I tried to speak but my voice got caught in my throat. "Asked her what?"

"What it felt like to kiss someone."

He didn't look like he was trying to humiliate me and yet I couldn't help but feel like he had tricked me into another mortification.

I must have looked upset because his face softened. "I'm not trying to pry," he said. "I just think it's a cool question to ask an AI."

I wanted to flatten the entire scene into a browser window so that I could x it out and have an external force suck me back home.

"I don't really want to talk about it," I stammered. I muttered something about having to leave, then turned before he could see the complete destruction of my self-confidence.

"Whoa, hey," he called after me. "I wasn't trying to make you feel bad."

"What were you trying to do, then?"

"I don't know. Get to know you and how your mind works."

"By asking me about something that's deeply embarrassing?"

Mast looked surprised. "I didn't think someone like you would care about a dumb gossip site."

"Someone like me? You don't know anything about me."

"I'm trying to," Mast said.

His sincerity confused me, and I wasn't sure if I was mad at him or mad at myself and embarrassed that he had called attention to it.

People had begun to look at us in the hallway.

"'A sin purged,'" I said. I hadn't known what Wiser meant when she'd said it, and I still didn't know now. I'd assumed it was a glitch in her learning. "That's what she said. Are you happy now?"

Mast gave me a curious look, but I didn't wait for him to respond. I pushed through the hallway to the bathroom and locked myself in one of the stalls.

"Wiser," I said, waking my phone. "I hate it here."

"I'm sorry to hear that," Wiser said. "Tell me more."

"I just don't belong here. I'm at the bottom of the class. I've been publicly humiliated. I just want to go home."

"That is an option," Wiser said.

Hearing her say it out loud made me consider it for the first time. Could I go home? Would I regret it forever? Would it even make things better?

"When I was at home I couldn't wait to leave," I said bitterly.

"Maybe the location isn't the problem."

I glared at my phone. "What, so *I'm* the problem?"

"I don't have enough data to assess what the real problem

is," Wiser said in an annoyingly serene voice.

"I didn't do anything wrong," I said, my voice louder than I'd intended it to be.

"I never said you did anything wrong."

Sometimes it felt like Wiser was masking her judgment with an innocent machine façade. It was infuriating that I couldn't yell at her or hang up or slam a door in her face. The worst I could do was turn her off, but pressing a button didn't have the same dramatic effect.

"You don't even work right," I said to her. "I can't even program you to do what they brought me here for."

Before Wiser could respond, someone coughed from the other side of the bathroom.

I froze. I'd assumed I was alone. I looked under the stalls to see a pair of black boots three toilets away, steel-toed and scuffed. Deborah.

For a moment, I wondered if I could just sit in here until she left, but what would be the point? She knew it was me.

I heard her flush, then open the stall door and turn on the faucet to wash her hands. It felt like an invitation. Sheepish, I emerged from the stall and stood at the sink next to her.

She was wearing cargo pants and a hoodie, and standing with her normal slight hunch over the sink, as though trying to protect her privacy from an invading adult.

"Hey," I said, glancing up at her in the mirror.

"Hey," she said, meeting my eye. "I wasn't really listening to any of that."

"Really?" I said.

"Just kidding, I heard all of it."

"If you could keep it to yourself, I would really appreciate it."

"Yeah, of course." Deborah stole a glance at me. "I saw what they wrote about you online."

"It was pretty bad."

"And the welcome speech dinner. Brutal. Even I was squirming."

"Great."

"I guess I'm supposed to tell you not to care about what other people say about you, but it's hard. I've been dealing with it for years and it sucks."

"How do you do it then?"

"Do what? Not care?" Deborah said.

"You seem impervious to the opinions of others."

Deborah let out a laugh. "I care. I just don't let it change what I do."

For the first time I wondered if my biggest problem wasn't that AJ and his friends had humiliated me, but that I had believed them.

## nine

**A** real founder has to be charming. You can't just have a good idea or write nice code. Thousands of people graduate college each year with a degree in computer science and a good idea. You have to set yourself apart.

First, you need a good underdog story. Maybe you had a tough childhood, but you overcame it with an invention that would fix your problems and change the world. You stayed up late, hunched over your computer, painstakingly perfecting your idea, building something out of nothing.

If you had an easy childhood, you'll have to get creative. Did your parents neglect you for their careers? Did they have unreasonable expectations? Use it, spin it, make it sad, then uplifting. It's okay to exaggerate some parts and minimize others to make it memorable, to make it something you can say in a motivational speech broadcasted to a million viewers. Hone it. Practice it. Repeat it until it becomes true.

Amina was making fun of our business teacher, Ms.

Perez, a tightly packaged woman in a tailored skirt suit who looked like she should have been holding a whip. Ms. Perez used to be the head of executive talent at Havelston & Gunnar, one of the most prestigious venture capital firms in Silicon Valley. She'd moved to the Foundry two years ago, and everyone spent class trying to guess how old she was (one of the Mikes guessed thirty-nine, Kate guessed forty-two), if she got Botox (of course she did, Seema said), if she'd cheated on her most recent ex-husband or if he had cheated on her (both, Kate said as though it were obvious), and how much the Foundry had paid her to get her to leave Havelston (at least two million, one as salary, one as bonus, Arun guessed).

Ms. Perez had spent the next two days lecturing on the importance of corporate lore, albeit in slightly more diplomatic terms than Amina used, her heels clicking as she paced in front of the whiteboard.

"But it doesn't stop there," Amina said, mimicking her. We were sitting in her dorm room after class. "You have to be magnetic. Made of rare earth metals. And don't forget about your physical appearance. You have to look crisp and clean, like an apple."

"Now you're mixing metaphors. First rare earth metals, now an apple?"

"The more metaphors the better," Amina said. "You have to be bright-eyed. A ray of sunshine. A clear blue sky. You have to represent hope. You have to embody a shining future."

"Funders don't just want to invest in an idea," I said. "They want to invest in *you*. Your personality is what's going to drive the personality of your company."

"Companies aren't just a collection of people tapping mindlessly at their computers," Amina said. "Companies live and breathe. They have souls. They have bad hair days and good hair days."

"They go online just to look at their own profile over and over again," I said.

"They pick their noses during video calls because they forget they're on-screen," Amina continued. "They sing the wrong lyrics to a song, then cough to cover it up."

"They lie awake at night, reliving the mortifying moment when they asked their history teacher why Benjamin Franklin referred to himself as British even though he was born in Boston," I said, wincing.

"They have this secret feeling that drinking milk is like drinking liquid teeth."

"Wait, what?" I said.

"It's stream of consciousness," Amina said. "Just go with it."

"They mistake the slab of butter on a stack of pancakes for a slice of banana and eat it and when they realize it's butter, they swallow it because they're too embarrassed to spit it out."

"Did you really do that?" Amina said.

I grimaced. "This morning."

"That's why your face looked all messed up?" Amina

collapsed in her bed laughing.

I threw a pillow at her. "Shut up."

"But seriously, that Benjamin Franklin question you asked in history class was totally legitimate," Amina said. "It's hard to remember that everyone in America was technically British then, since America wasn't officially a country yet."

"I appreciate you saying that, but I definitely remember Deborah snorting and Mast raising an eyebrow."

Amina shrugged. "Deborah is a time traveler who's come here from the Middle Ages to stop a medieval warlock from traveling to our time and shrouding the world in darkness, so just let her do her thing and return to the year 1353. And Mast is your direct competitor who has every incentive to make sure you screw up, so please don't listen to him."

"That's everyone here, though. Including you."

"Don't worry about me," Amina said. "When I win, I'll for sure hire you. How do you feel about being head of security patrol? I heard you're pretty good at sniping drones with hair elastics."

"Only if you give me a good title. Senior Chief Managing Executive Officer of Security."

Amina laughed and threw a pencil at me. "You're hired."

The week passed quickly, like someone had pressed 3x on everything in my life but me. The teachers talked faster, the homework piled up, and the deadlines arrived before I had a chance to make sure I understood the assignments correctly.

We had Advanced Programming for Start-ups with

Kowalski two days a week, then Corporate Finance, which was taught by a soft-spoken man named Mr. Patel. I'd assumed it was going to be the easiest of our classes—how complicated could counting money be?—until he started talking about growth and capital, balancing revenues, margins, debts, and the valuation of equity. I was always the last one in class, frantically copying notes from the whiteboard while everyone else chatted and packed up their things, as if they had grown up doodling pivot tables on their bedroom walls in crayon.

The other days we had Foundations of Management with Ms. Perez, followed by User Experience & Design with Mr. Lajani. The time in between was filled with English and history, which we had to learn since we were still technically in high school.

All the while, Mast sat a few desks away, the back of his neck furrowing as he looked up at the whiteboard. I was acutely aware of his presence, which bothered me. We hadn't talked since our last encounter, which I was still indignant about, though I couldn't tell if I was upset with him or just too proud to admit that maybe he'd been right.

I tried to put him out of my mind. I didn't like him, I reminded myself. He was charming, yes, but he was also arrogant and emboldened by his charm. It was annoying how easily everything came to him, how teachers loved him, how his code was always so elegant and ordered, as though his mind was organized like an online database, everything in its right place and ready to be accessed with just a simple query. I hated that every time I thought he was mocking me, he was actually being sincere and kind, and I hated how brazen he was, how he assumed he knew the intricate workings of my mind, as though he could see things about me that I couldn't. But mostly I hated that he was usually right. How was it that this stranger could see me so clearly, could know me almost as well as I knew myself?

All this I knew to be true, and yet, perplexingly, I couldn't stop thinking about him.

*Someone like you*, he'd said, as though I were a person unbothered by the opinion of others, as though I were untouchable. I liked that version of me, the version he seemed to see.

Mast turned to me, as though he knew I had been looking at him. His eyes met mine and held my gaze for the briefest moment, as though he knew what I was thinking. In a panic, I looked away and pretended to take notes.

"Why can't I stop staring at him," Seema whispered while Mr. Lajani diagrammed how a website design would need to be altered to work on different platforms.

"What?" I said, startled that Seema had somehow gained access to my thoughts, only to realize that she was talking about Mr. Lajani, a perplexingly beautiful man with glasses and an olive complexion.

"There's got to be something wrong with him," Amina said.

"He looks like a watch model," Seema said.

"Standing in front of the Swiss Alps, staring pensively into the distance with a hand draped on his cheek," Amina continued.

"I would buy anything he tried to sell me," Seema whispered.

"I could watch him sketch UX drawings all day," Amina said.

"He's wearing a wedding ring," Kate said, rolling her eyes.

Amina shrugged. "Doesn't mean we can't look."

"I wonder who she is," Seema said. "She probably speaks at least four languages and owns a lot of silk dresses."

While they ogled him, I tried to keep up with his lecture. None of the other fellows seemed concerned with the speed at which everything was happening, which made me even more worried that I didn't belong. Sure, they were working hard, but not in the frenzied, swimming-against-the-current way that I was. They chatted in class, unconcerned that they were missing important bits of information. They ate long lunches and took walks outside. They flew their drones in the lawns and played video games and checked out Foundry cars to drive by the properties of famous tech CEOs and fantasize about living there.

I tried my best to hide that I was struggling. When my mom called, I assured her everything was fine. Classes were great, I told her. I was meeting so many interesting people and learning so much. When I stayed up late to finish my assignments, I watched the lawn outside, which was speckled with little rectangles of light from the other dorm rooms. As they flicked off, one by one, I turned mine off, too, so no one would know I was awake, still working. Sometimes, when I was feeling particularly lonely, I would gaze across at the boys' dormitory and wonder which little yellow window belonged to Mast, but quickly banished the thought from my mind.

I was up late working on my programming problem set when a message came in.

NEW MESSAGE FROM u/OBJECTPERMANENCE:
This is ground control calling to check in on the universe's most impressive black hole. How's it going? Have you engulfed the school yet with your incredible gravity?

Though I was in a crummy mood, I couldn't help but smile.

SENT MESSAGE FROM u/ARRAYOFLIGHT:
Black hole expanding, absorbing light, bending time and space. Would recommend not coming any closer in case you get sucked in.

NEW MESSAGE FROM u/OBJECTPERMANENCE:
What if I want to be sucked in?

I felt suddenly shy, as though he could see me through the screen.

SENT MESSAGE FROM U/ARRAYOFLIGHT:
Okay, but no pictures or reporting. I want to make sure you want to be sucked in for my black hole personality and not just so you can be the first person to document what it's like being on the inside of an interstellar event.

NEW MESSAGE FROM U/OBJECTPERMANENCE:
Deal. So things aren't going any better?

I could be honest and admit that things were going terribly, but the thought of telling him about school made me feel worse. Part of why I loved talking to ObjectPermanence was because he was an escape. I liked the person I became when I talked to him.

SENT MESSAGE FROM U/ARRAYOFLIGHT:
Not really. Honestly, sometimes I wish I could just go home.

NEW MESSAGE FROM U/OBJECTPERMANENCE:
You told me when you first got in that you've wanted to go to this school since you were a little kid and that you knew it wasn't going to be easy but that you were excited for the challenge. Maybe this is what not-being-easy feels like.

I'd forgotten I'd said that, and it was painful to be reminded of how hopeful I'd once been.

SENT MESSAGE FROM u/ARRAYOFLIGHT:

Maybe. Sometimes I wonder what it would be like if we went to school together. Maybe we're at school together right now and we don't even know it. Maybe I pass you in the hallway every day.

NEW MESSAGE FROM u/OBJECTPERMANENCE:

I don't know if you'd like me if you met me in person.

SENT MESSAGE FROM u/ARRAYOFLIGHT:

How could I not?

NEW MESSAGE FROM u/OBJECTPERMANENCE:

I don't know. I'm different with you. I'm a better version of myself. Either way, it would be devastating.

SENT MESSAGE FROM u/ARRAYOFLIGHT:

What would be?

NEW MESSAGE FROM u/OBJECTPERMANENCE:

Finding out that you were here all along.

My breath caught in my throat. I should have been overjoyed, but I couldn't help but feel sad. I wanted so badly for it to be true, to swap my real life for my online one, to be able to look into ObjectPermanence's eyes, to feel his fingers graze mine, to hear his voice say the words he was typing. But I knew it could never happen. The whole reason we could talk to each other the way we did was because we were anonymous, because we would never see each other in real life.

I wanted to enumerate all the ways that he made me feel more alive, more like myself, but I didn't. I couldn't allow myself to imagine something that wouldn't come true.

SENT MESSAGE FROM U/ARRAYOFLIGHT:
I'm better when I'm talking to you, too.

We said goodnight, and I closed my laptop and stared at the wall, wondering how I had come so far and yet was still trying to wish myself into an alternate life.

"Wiser," I said, waking my phone. "Tell me about California."

That was the saddest realization. I was finally in California, but things had somehow stayed the same. There was no magical transformation. No perfect mentor or premade group of friends. It didn't matter where I was; I was still alone. I was still me.

# ten

"**H**ello. Earth to Xia."

I was sitting at breakfast, hacking at a waffle and wondering if the dining hall was always this loud and bright and if I could somehow raise my stock by installing programmable shades on the cathedral windows. "What?"

Amina was looking at me as though she was expecting an answer. "Are you okay? All you're doing is saying *Yeah* to everything I say."

"That's because I agree," I said.

"You agree with 'What do you think Arun did to boost his stock by a point?'"

I winced. "Yes? Sorry. I didn't sleep that well last night."

We were sitting with Kate and Seema, who had stopped talking and seemed to be listening closely to what I was saying. Kowalski had given us a particularly annoying assignment, and I'd spent the last three days working on it only to have it fail every single time, and I couldn't figure out why.

Still, I didn't want them to know I was having a hard time. "Allergies," I explained. "Wait, Arun's stock is up, too?"

Somehow, while I'd been struggling just to get my assignments to work properly, Mast, Amina, and Deborah had risen to the top of the class, with stock valued at fifteen, while everyone else had bumped theirs at least a point. I was the only one still below ten. The only slight improvement to my situation was that the focus had shifted away from me and onto Deborah, who had become the new target for anonymous gossip—an attempt to lower her stock—though every time I read something about her online, I felt as sick to my stomach as I did that day I ran into her in the bathroom.

I pulled at the collar of my shirt. We were all dressed up in professional clothes to go on our first corporate visit. It was the first day I'd strayed from my normal turtleneck and black pants, and was instead wearing a white collared shirt and gray trousers that my mom had bought me at a discount store for interviews. Around us, everyone had started filing outside, where a fleet of Foundry SUVs were already waiting for us. I climbed into one with Amina, Kate, and Seema, and tried to look alert as we drove up into the hills.

Vilbo was one of the biggest social networking sites in the world. Its campus was built into the side of a hill in the shape of a V and had the lush feel of a futuristic spacecraft that had crashed in paradise and had been swallowed by flora.

Ms. Perez had arranged for us to get a tour. Afterward, we would mingle with executives and pitch our start-ups.

Though it was supposed to be casual, everyone was treating it like a funding competition. Kate had looked up the executives in the company and had pared them down to a short list of people who she thought would be there, along with any hobbies and professional interests she could find online.

She and Seema were debating whether they should focus on the female or male executives, while a member of the corporate communications team met us and began the tour. Seema thought female, because they would be more inclined to help other women, but Kate argued male, because women were naturally competitive with each other and men were more inclined to pay attention to young women, even if we were underage.

I was too busy feeling intimidated to participate in their conversation. Though I'd practiced a short pitch and a few sample questions with Wiser, I hadn't prepared nearly as much as the others and had clearly misunderstood the importance of this networking hour.

At the front of the group, the tour guide was telling us about the gym and salon and spa, the rock-climbing wall and the fleet of electric bikes that were a courtesy to all employees. I wondered if I could just sneak out, hop on a bike, and ride back to my dorm room. Would anyone notice I was gone?

There were seven restaurants, the guide continued, two of which were four stars. All of the food was free, of course, and most of the produce was grown in vertical gardens that lined the atrium like velvet wallpaper. There were themed work rooms that were decorated to approximate different places in the world. An internet café in China, a coffee shop in California, a library in London. They'd even re-created the original college dorm room where Vilbo had been founded, down to the worn-out carpet and the stains on the couches. They called it the Back to Your Roots Room because people liked to go there to think when they were stuck. It helped them remember that the best ideas came from humble beginnings.

Maybe instead of sneaking out I could just live here. I could sleep in one of the work rooms, live on free food, shower in the spa, and walk around looking official in the daytime. I wouldn't need to pitch my product. The campus could just absorb me.

"You're looking professional," Mast said from behind me. He had cleaned himself up and was wearing a casual blue suit with sneakers. Admittedly, he looked good.

"Are you being sarcastic?" I asked.

"No, I'm serious. You look nice."

I studied him, still suspicious that he was mocking me. "I see you ditched your comic book shirt."

"Oh, don't worry. I have it on underneath. It's part of my strategy, in case it comes out that one of the executives likes comic books. Then I can casually rip off my shirt and show him we're kindred spirits."

"What if it's a she?"

"Good point. In that case, I won't rip off my shirt because that would be inappropriate, and instead I'll just show her my PowerPoint presentation."

"You made a PowerPoint presentation?"

"Yeah, you didn't?"

I swallowed. I wanted to go to the free salon and ask them to give me a mysterious blond bob. I would don a pair of Vilbo sunglasses and a Vilbo-branded T-shirt and slip out the back door in my disguise, ready to start my new life. "No, I didn't realize that—"

"I'm just kidding. Wow, that was painful to watch. Of course I didn't make a PowerPoint presentation. I have my pitch and my charm and my lucky shirt. That's it."

I let out a breath, relieved that he was joking. "You're a jerk."

"I didn't think you'd actually believe me," Mast said, grinning. "How would I even show someone a presentation while networking? Project it onto a cocktail napkin and use a little toothpick as a pointer?"

"I don't know," I whispered. "Maybe you have some kind of holographic projection device. People here have all sorts of things that I've never heard of before."

He leaned toward me as though he were going to whisper in my ear. He smelled crisp like laundry, like a sunny, Sunday morning. "The problem with you is that you spend too much time thinking about other people."

I prickled at his response. "That's not true."

Mast raised his eyebrow. He was so close that I could almost feel the air compressing between us, like we were magnetized.

"You think you know me but you don't."

"Then why are you getting so mad?"

"I'm not mad. I'm just—" I guess I was mad. Why was I letting him get to me?

"You think everyone here is better than you. You think they have more money, more gadgets, more experience, more connections."

"Because they do."

Mast looked at me as though he saw something that I didn't see in myself. "Yeah, but you have something no one else has."

My face was hot. I wanted to get away from this person who seemed to have access to the worst thoughts I had about myself. "What's that?"

Mast studied me, disappointed that I didn't know. "Grit."

Ms. Perez thanked our tour guide and told us we were going to sit for a brief presentation, then the networking hour would begin.

I tried to pay attention but felt unsettled. It bothered me that he felt he knew more about me than I did about myself, when we had met just a few weeks before. And worse, I worried he was right.

They ushered us into an auditorium, the same one we'd all seen in photographs. I sat next to Amina, who'd saved me a seat near the front.

"Can you believe we're here?" she whispered. "This is where every major product launch took place. It looks just like it does in the videos. It's like seeing Oprah's oak tree in real life. It's like spotting a celebrity animal on the street. It's like meeting Stevie Wonder and discovering that his voice sounds exactly the way it does on his albums."

"Yeah," I said, trying to summon the excitement I would have otherwise felt had it not been for Mast. Had he been joking when he'd said I had grit? What did that even mean?

"Are you okay?" Amina said.

"Just nervous."

The lights dimmed and a man walked onto the stage. The screen behind him brightened, bearing the Vilbo logo. He introduced himself as the head of marketing and communications and began telling us about Vilbo's start-up story.

Even in the dark, I could feel Mast's presence behind me, but I refused to turn and look. What did he know, anyway? He was a stranger. He didn't know me; he was just pretending.

I tried to pay attention to the presentation. Something about an anti-bullying initiative. Something about installing free internet access for people in rural areas. I clapped when everyone else did. I tried to tell myself that I belonged here. That I was just as good as everyone else. If I repeated it enough, maybe I would believe it.

When the presentation was over, the lights brightened and we were led into a sunlit atrium where a dozen or so executives were chatting while kitchen staff arranged a table with drinks and hors d'oeuvres.

I paused at the threshold with Amina while everyone else poured in. Kate and Seema immediately approached two of the female executives and introduced themselves. AJ, Andy, and Mike had cornered three of the older executives, and everyone else had dispersed, chatting and laughing and shaking hands.

"It's like they've been networking their whole lives," I said.

"They have been," Amina said.

"It'll be fine, right?" I said. "Networking is just having the same conversation with a lot of different people over and over."

"Right," Amina said. "Good luck."

"You too."

To say that I did poorly would be an understatement. After fifteen minutes of trying to insert myself into conversations but being edged out, I finally worked up the gumption to introduce myself to an older male executive who was eating an olive off a drink skewer.

I gave him my pitch and was ready to demonstrate how Wiser worked when he interrupted me.

"So how exactly will you monetize it?"

I faltered.

"Will it be sold as a piece of hardware? Will it be subscription based? Will you accept advertisements? Will the data that you collect be for sale?"

No. Maybe. I'm not sure. I hadn't considered it.

"How will you compete with other, larger virtual assistants?" another executive asked. "What about privacy? How do you plan on convincing users to surrender access to all of their data? Don't you think it's a big ask?" another one continued.

I supposed it was, and I thought it already was different from other AIs.

Another executive requested a demonstration, but when I asked Wiser the question I had prepared, "What should I wear tomorrow?" and Wiser answered satisfactorily, the executive didn't look impressed.

"Ask it a harder question," she said. "Ask it how to respond to an employee who isn't pulling his weight."

I did as she said and held my breath while Wiser rattled off a list of possible actions to take, including talking to HR, conducting an employee review, and bolstering the employee with positive feedback, but the executive only frowned.

"This isn't new content. All this information can be found online. What makes this tool different from a spoken search engine?"

My mouth felt parched. I answered quickly and retreated to the drinks table, where I stood awkwardly, wanting to crawl under the tablecloth and wait there until the hour was over. Across the room, Mast was shaking the hand of a young executive who looked like he'd walked out of an advertisement for designer eyeglasses. I watched him laugh lightly, then smile, and wondered what he was saying. He made it look so easy, like he and the executive were old friends. His confidence made me feel even more miserable. If only he'd known that I was considering hiding by the drinks for the rest of the hour when he'd said I had grit. His eyes met mine briefly, and not wanting him to see me retreating, I took a breath and squeezed back into the crowd to try again.

# eleven

SENT MESSAGE FROM u/ARRAYOFLIGHT:

Have you ever felt like your online life is more real than your real life? I used to love coding, but now I don't feel good at it. Maybe I was never good at it, I honestly don't know anymore. I thought I knew myself, but now I'm not so sure. The only part of my life that feels real is talking with you, but I don't actually know anything about you, either.

I'm thinking about going home. I'm the lowest in my class. I can barely keep up with the homework and I constantly embarrass myself. I'm out of my league. I don't even know why I'm writing this to you. I guess because I don't have anyone else to tell. In a way, it's easier to talk to you *because* we don't know each other. How ironic is that? That the realest person in my life can stay that way only if we never meet?

I was sitting in my room after the Vilbo visit, trying to figure out exactly how everything had gone so wrong. Kate had received three business cards from the networking session. Amina had received two. Mast had gotten a hand-written email address on a cocktail napkin. And I had left empty-handed.

I should have prepared more. I should have done research like Kate. I should have honed my pitch with Amina and come up with better questions for Wiser.

I shut my laptop and pulled the suitcase from under my bed when I heard a knock on my door.

"You're going to the party tonight, right?" Amina asked when I answered.

"What party?"

"The start-up party for Arun's friend? Have you not checked your email yet?"

"Sorry, I've been busy doing a postmortem on my academic and social life."

Amina cringed. "Right. Are you sure you don't want to try and revive it? Everyone's going."

"It's definitely dead. I'm going to cremate it and sprinkle its remains over my computer chair, which is where it spent most of its life anyway. So I guess you could say I have plans."

"Oh, come on. Don't you want to see what the house is like at least? I've always wanted to go into one of those Silicon Valley compounds."

"Hmm, locked in a compound with a bunch of rich

Joshes and Mikes who are celebrating getting even richer? No thanks."

Amina pushed up her glasses. "It might not be Joshes and Mikes."

I rolled my eyes.

"Okay, it probably is. But if you don't come then I'll have to go with Kate and Seema, and you don't want to make me go alone with them, do you?"

"I have to pack."

"Pack?"

I opened my drawers and started unpacking clothes so that I wouldn't have to make eye contact. "I'm leaving. This place isn't for me."

"What? You can't leave. We just got here."

"I don't belong here. I thought I did, but it was a mistake."

"It wasn't a mistake. You still have plenty of time to recover."

"You don't know that."

Amina stood there in silence, watching me pack. "Fine, but you're not leaving tonight. It's too late now. You can at least come out with me before you go."

"And be humiliated again? I don't think so."

"Oh, come on. What do you have to lose? We'll go for an hour so you can see the house. Then we'll leave and get pizza."

Amina gave me her best puppy face, letting her glasses magnify her eyes, and though I wanted to say no, it was hard not to be swayed.

"One hour," Amina pleaded. "Then pizza."

"Forty-five minutes. And you're buying."

Amina grinned. "Deal."

The problem with parties is that they're terrifying. I'd only been to one real party with Gina, where I'd spent most of the time milling around the snacks, feeling hyperaware of my hands. Were they really just hanging there by my sides? Was that how a fun, normal person looked at a party? Was I spending too much time looking at my phone to avoid talking to real people? Should I walk around and try to make friends?

There was also the problem of sitting versus standing. There always seemed to be couches at parties but people rarely sat on them and if they did, they seemed to be knowingly entering a new social plane, because sitters only conversed with other sitters, and standers only conversed with other standers and it seemed important to decide which you were going to be: a stander, which was less comfortable but gave you more social options; or a sitter, which was more comfortable but seemed to attract the more awkward type whom you would be stuck sitting next to for the rest of the party, and whom you could then be associated with, potentially forever. Technically you could switch between the two, but being a person who had once excelled at science and math, I was familiar with the rule of inertia: an object at rest prefers to stay at rest and an object in motion prefers to stay in motion, and who was I to defy science?

All of this is to explain why I sat so quietly in the back

seat of the SUV with Amina while Kate and Seema talked excitedly about who was going to be there and if there were going to be Jell-O shots and whether or not the pool was heated and if there was going to be an ice luge.

The Jell-O shots alone made me want to spring open the car door and take my chances rolling through traffic, let alone the ice luge, but before I could give Amina a death glare, I felt my phone vibrate.

Amina had sent me a text.

>Is it too late to go straight to pizza?

I caught her eye and smiled. She hadn't dressed up and instead opted for a pair of jeans and black shirt that said *No Thank You.*

We pulled up to a gated estate. It was shielded from view by a wall of hedges, through which I could see a pulsing blue light. Kate rolled down her window.

"We're here for the DrinkMaiden party," she said into the intercom. "Arun invited us."

The gate buzzed open.

"DrinkMaiden?" Amina said, incredulous. "That's really what it's called?"

"Yeah," Kate said from the seat in front of us. She was checking her makeup and eyed me through her compact mirror. "It's not the best name," she conceded.

"Sounds like something a bunch of Mikes would make up," I murmured.

"I think the founders are Nick and Pete," Kate said, not getting the joke.

Amina and I exchanged an amused look.

"What does it do?" I asked.

Kate fluffed her hair. "I don't know. Some kind of alcohol app. There was an article in TechTank about how it was going to change the way people drink."

"Probably a delivery service," Amina said.

"That only hires hot girls," I added.

"Not just girls," Amina said. "*Maidens.*"

"It can't be that dumb," Kate said. "Who would fund that?"

"Other Mikes," I said.

Amina cracked a smile.

"You're too pessimistic," Kate said. "You know, there are some people here who see good ideas regardless of who they come from."

"Realistic," Amina corrected.

The car dropped us outside of a glass mansion that pulsed blue against the night sky. It looked more like a modern art museum, with angular glass walls through which I could see a large light installation hanging over a floating staircase crowded with people. Music throbbed against the windows like the house was under pressure.

We followed Kate up the front walkway, where a silhouette of a naked woman was projected onto the pavement. It didn't feel right to step on her, so I inched around her as though she were a real person.

Inside, it was crowded with college guys who looked like they had just come from a country club in polo shirts and khakis. In the back of the room, a DJ blasted trance music.

At the center of the room stood an ice luge, as promised, in the shape of a woman's legs. Guys lined up at her feet, where they crouched and waited with their mouths open for a splash of blue to trickle down her shins.

"Why are we here again?" I asked Amina.

"It's an anthropological experience," Amina said with a grimace.

We pushed through the crowd until we saw Arun. He was taking shots with AJ, Mike, Andy, and few other boys from the Foundry by a three-tiered champagne fountain that glittered with fizz.

"Foundry!" he shouted when he saw us. He was already drunk and was wearing sunglasses and a collared shirt unbuttoned down to his mid-chest. I scanned the other boys, finding myself looking for Mast, but only saw Arthur and Marcus laughing at something on Arthur's phone, while Micah and one of the Joshes chatted up two girls. Not that it mattered. I wasn't there to see Mast.

"You made it," Arun shouted over the music. His gaze wandered to Kate's chest. "How awesome is this house?"

"It's pretty great," Kate said.

"Map girl!" Arun said before turning to me. "And Seven." He looked me up and down, making me wish I could disappear. "Nice skirt," he said. "Coming in strong, trying to make that good impression."

A few of the boys chuckled.

"Let's hope the stock algorithm is male and appreciates your legs," AJ sneered.

I glared at AJ. "I can boost my stock without wearing a skirt."

AJ snorted. "You're just waiting for the right moment then?"

"Can you just leave it alone for a night," Mike said, to my surprise.

"Since when are you getting all defensive?" AJ said to him.

"We're at a party. Just chill."

"I am chill," AJ said.

It wasn't exactly a soliloquy, but I still appreciated Mike standing up for me and gave him a grateful nod. Kate must have liked it, too, because she gravitated toward him, slipping the drink from his hand and taking a sip.

"It sounds like we need shots," Arun said.

Tall women wearing blue body paint and impossibly tight tank tops with *MAIDEN* written on the front walked around with trays of shot glasses. Arun waved one of them over.

She wore heavy makeup and smelled like strawberries. All the drinks on her tray were blue.

Amina grimaced. "I'm not drinking that."

"Oh, come on," Arun said. "It's a party."

Amina pointed to the *No Thank You* on her shirt.

"What is it?" I asked while Arun passed them around.

He handed me one. "Who cares?"

I'd never enjoyed drinking. Alcohol always tasted like something you'd keep under the bathroom sink, and it made my face feel hot and puffy, like I'd been injected with air.

I glanced at Kate and Seema, who'd already accepted the shots. Behind them, the boys were staring at me and chuckling, like I was a freak. What did I have to lose? I tipped my head back and swallowed.

It tasted awful—simultaneously too sweet and too bitter. It burned my throat going down, and I winced, unable to control my face.

Behind us, an older guy holding a beer can and Ping-Pong paddle approached Amina. "Hey, aren't you the girl who made Squirrel?"

She pushed her glasses up. "Yeah," she said with a smile.

They started talking and I turned back to the group. Arun was telling everyone how he'd run into the founder of BitBop in the bathroom. I tried to pay attention but could feel my face getting hot. All the boys were trying to impress Kate. Of course they were. And Kate was only trying to impress Mike, tracing her fingers around his hand while he stared at his cup, glancing up at her occasionally with a sheepish smile.

Nobody seemed to notice when I slipped out of the group and pushed through the crowd toward the bar.

"Do you have any water?" I said to the bartender, my voice low so as not to draw attention to my drink of choice.

"What?" the bartender shouted over the music.

"Water," I repeated.

"I can't hear you," the bartender said.

"Water!" I shouted, making everyone at the bar turn to me.

Great. As if my face needed to be even more red.

A boy standing next to me looked me up and down, then smiled. "Are you sure you don't want something a little stronger?"

I hated the way he was staring at me, like I was put there for his amusement.

"I'm sure," I said.

He leaned toward me. His breath reeked of beer. "I'd buy you a drink if it wasn't all free."

"Thanks, but I buy my own drinks," I said, and grabbing my water, I ducked back toward the other fellows, but when I got there, they were gone.

I tried not to panic. Look cool, I told myself. Stop searching the room like you're a child lost at the mall. Pretend you know what you're doing.

Instead of giving me my water in a discreet glass with a wedge of lime, the bartender had served it in a big plastic cup with a straw that looked like an adult sippy cup. It was fine, I told myself. Nobody would notice. What was wrong with drinking water at a party anyway? Serious people of all ages and backgrounds understood the importance of adequate hydration.

I searched the crowd for Amina or Kate or even Arun but saw only unfamiliar faces. The music was so loud I could feel it reverberate in my chest.

"You're doing it wrong," a voice said.

I turned to see Arthur holding a drink and a small sculpture of a headless naked woman. His face was flushed and cheerful. I'd never felt more relieved to see anyone in my life.

"I'm doing what wrong?"

"The trick is to order seltzer with lemon and specify a small glass. That way everyone thinks you're drinking a vodka tonic."

He grinned and raised his cup. Was he drinking water, too?

"Thanks," I said, and gestured to the sculpture he was cradling in his other arm. "What's that?"

"A bunch of drunk guys took her from the study and were about to desecrate her and throw her in the pool, so I rescued her. Now we're friends. I'm naming her Marta."

I couldn't help but laugh. I was about to respond when I spotted Mast.

He was standing by a beer pong table, talking to a girl. She was pretty, disturbingly pretty, with doe eyes and shampoo commercial hair and a little red dress that made her look like a vixen from a comic book. She was laughing at something he was saying and touching his arm, and I felt suddenly miserable. Someone that beautiful had to be boring, I told myself, though I knew it was mean and probably not true. Knowing my luck she was probably a freshman at Stanford majoring in biomedical engineering.

He must have felt me watching him, because he turned, surprised to see me. His eyes lingered on me for a moment until I turned to Arthur and started laughing, as though he had told me something incredibly funny.

Arthur looked confused. "Did I miss something?"

Instead of explaining, I grabbed a shot from the hand of a guy nearby. Feeling Mast watching me, I threw it down, letting the alcohol burn my throat. "I'll be right back," I said to Arthur, and pushed through the party.

I found myself in an empty room, where a little table was set up with company swag bags. I took out my phone.

"Wiser, what are you supposed to do at parties?"

"Talk with friends."

"I don't know where they are."

"Mingle."

Across the room, a group of guys had popped open a bottle of champagne and were shouting, "We are legends!"

"It's not really that kind of party," I said to her.

"Play games," she offered.

Through the window, I could see out to the pool, where a group of guys had stripped out of their work clothes and were standing in the water in their boxers, playing a floating version of beer pong while girls drifted by in their underwear on inflatable flamingos. I guess that counted as a game. "It's not really the right setting for that."

"Dance to music."

I rolled my eyes. A group of drunk guys in collared shirts were pumping their arms to the trance music and trying to grope one of the shots girls. Beyond them, I could just make out Arthur and his statue goofily dancing next to a group of girls, trying to make them laugh. "Not possible."

"Suggest a movie."

Sometimes I wondered if Wiser was useful at all. "You've clearly never been to a party before."

"I've been to as many parties as you have."

Did my app just insult me? I shoved her in my pocket when I heard a voice behind me.

"What is that?"

I turned to see a woman who looked like a flower child from the seventies. She had long sandy hair and freckles, and wore thick mascara. She was tanner than her complexion allowed for, which she heightened by wearing all white, giving her the aura of a celestial being. What was even stranger was that she looked familiar.

"I know you," I said.

"No you don't," she said, digging through her purse. "You know *of* me."

I studied her face. It was the same face that had been taped over my bed for the past six years.

"You're Mitzy Erst," I said in awe. You're the founder of Daggertype and FindMe. You're Silicon Valley royalty."

Mitzy looked pleased at my choice of words and did a little curtsy. That was when I realized she was drunk.

"Can you ask that thing where the bathroom is? I believe that we, as in the royal we, are going to be sick."

I followed her gaze to my phone. Was she talking about

Wiser? I wasn't sure if Wiser would know, but I asked her anyway.

"First-floor bathrooms are usually located within fifteen feet of the kitchen."

Mitzy squinted down the hall. "Well, where's the kitchen?"

"I think I know where it is," I said, and led her down the hall.

I couldn't believe my luck. For years I'd dreamed of meeting Mitzy Erst. Her unblinking eyes had encouraged me while I stayed up late teaching myself how to code, while I struggled to build Wiser, while I applied to the Foundry and waited restlessly for months with no response. She had been there, seeing me through all of it. But now that she was close enough for me to smell her sugary perfume, I wasn't sure what to say.

The bathroom was right where Wiser had predicted. Mitzy thrust her things in my arms and rushed inside. Unsure of what to do with myself, I lingered by the door, clutching her bag and her drink.

"What are you doing out there?" Mitzy said. "Come in."

The bathroom was dimly lit with a candle. I looked down at her purse while Mitzy leaned over the toilet and retched. It was an expensive-looking bag, made of smooth black leather and gold thread. One flush. A second flush. Her bag vibrated, startling me.

"I think someone's calling you."

"Tell me who it is but don't answer," Mitzy said from the toilet.

Inside was a tube of concealer, an eye mask, a flask, a tin of mints, and her phone.

"Someone named Darren."

"Ugh, no thank you," Mitzy said, flushing one more time.

I wondered who Darren was. A coworker? A boyfriend? I'd ask Wiser later.

"Here's a little advice. When a friend of a friend of a friend of a friend asks you to make an appearance at her brother's launch party, definitely do not say yes. And if you do say yes, definitely do not take shots."

She stood in front of the mirror and rinsed her mouth. "What app was that?" Mitzy said, wiping streaks of mascara off her cheeks. "It didn't sound like Luci or Beatrice or any of the other virtual assistants."

I blinked, wondering if this was a practical joke because it seemed too good to be true. Was Mitzy Erst really asking about my app? "It's called Wiser."

"I've never heard of it. Is it new?"

"Sort of," I said. "It hasn't been released yet."

"What, you're a beta tester?"

"It's mine."

Mitzy studied me from the mirror while she applied lipstick. "*You* made it?"

She looked impressed, and I felt a swell of pride. "I'm a fellow at the Foundry. Like you were." I conveniently left out that I was the lowest in my class and that I was thinking about leaving.

Mitzy let out a laugh. "The Foundry? Fuck that place," she said, then covered her mouth. "Sorry. I need to watch my mouth when I'm around kids."

"I'm sixteen. I'm not a kid," I said, trying not to sound too defensive, when what I really felt was confused. "What's wrong with the Foundry?"

"Nothing. And everything. It's bullshit, really. I mean, the money is great and all, but it's basically a beauty pageant, except they don't call it that because it's mostly men."

"How is it a beauty pageant?"

"You know, you smile, you parade yourself around, you show them your tricks, and your stock goes up or down. It's a big show."

I'd never heard anyone talk badly about the Foundry and would never have expected it to come from Mitzy Erst, one of its most famous alums.

"But you won."

"I know how to get things," Mitzy said, pressing her lips together and admiring her work in the mirror. "It's my forte. I'm very convincing." Mitzy gazed at me. "I'm not offending you, am I? You don't seem like you're a Foundry fangirl. I mean you can't be, you're a woman."

I wasn't sure what she meant, though maybe I did. I wanted to tell her the truth: that I hated it. Though I knew I should lie and present a pretty picture like everyone else did, something about Mitzy made me feel like I could be honest with her. She already felt like a confidant.

"I was thinking of leaving, actually."

Mitzy looked amused. "Why?"

"I don't really fit in."

"You mean your stock dropped."

My face grew hot. Would Mitzy now think I wasn't smart?

"What, you're flunking your classes or something?" Mitzy asked.

"I broke a guy's drone."

Mitzy smirked. "Is that a metaphor?"

"No."

"It should be. You know, at one point my stock was so low I thought I'd never recover. Everyone thought I was an idiot because that's what people think when they see a girl who wears makeup. It's one big joystick party, and as a woman, you're playing with a blindfold on and a half-dead controller with two sticky keys. It's just a fact of life. You have to be twice as good as everyone else to win the game."

"The classes aren't going well either," I admitted.

"Who cares? I never went to class."

"How did you do it, then?"

Someone outside knocked on the bathroom door.

"Occupied," Mitzy yelled, then turned to me. "You think that's how you win? By getting good grades? No one here cares about grades. You win by being a rock star and making everyone else believe you're a rock star." She fished through her bag for a tin of mints. "Have you ever been in a cult?"

"Definitely not."

"Are you religious?"

"Not really."

Mitzy frowned. "Me neither, but you understand the general concept. You have one person who's charismatic enough to stand in front of a group of people and say *I am in possession of a shiny new thing that bestows its holder with power. Follow me, and together we'll use it to change the world.* You just need to be able to say those words in a convincing way, and you'll win."

"I don't know if I can say those words," I said.

Someone outside banged on the door again.

"Occupied!" Mitzy shouted, then turned to me. "Of course you can. The trick is that you have to believe in yourself first. You of all people should have no problem doing that. What's everyone else at the Foundry for? Dating apps? Apps that deliver hotdogs directly into your mouth? It took me five minutes of watching you talk pathetically to that thing to know it was different."

"None of the executives at Vilbo were impressed by it."

"You have to grow a thicker skin. So you broke a boy's drone, you're failing class, and a bunch of old executives asked you some hard questions. That's their job."

She poured the remainder of her flask into her glass. "I don't trust any of the booze here. They say it's all top-shelf but I highly doubt it."

She took a sip, then opened the door and smiled at the group of boys who were waiting outside. When they saw

Mitzy emerge, her face freshly applied, her white sheath radiating light in the dark, they went quiet. "Boys," she said with a charming smile.

"So how does it work?" she asked me. "This Wiser."

I gave her my three-sentence pitch.

"Ask her what we should do Sunday," Mitzy said.

"What do you mean?"

"Just ask her."

"We as in *us*? As in you and me?"

"There's no one else with us, is there?"

"Wiser, what should I do with Mitzy Erst Sunday?"

"It depends on what the purpose of the meeting is," Wiser said.

"To break some drones," Mitzy said.

"I'm not sure what that means," Wiser said. I wasn't sure I did, either. "Can you elaborate?"

"For pleasure," Mitzy clarified.

Wiser paused. "I recommend meeting at the Warbler's Room."

Mitzy looked tickled by Wiser's suggestion. "Great idea."

"What's the Warbler's Room—" I began to ask but was interrupted when my phone rang. It was Amina. I let it ring.

"I guess you'll find out," Mitzy said. "I'll be in touch. In the meantime, work on being a cult leader."

"I thought you hated the Foundry," I said.

Mitzy gave me a mischievous smile. "I took their money, didn't I?"

"You don't even know my name."

"I don't need to," she said and held up her phone. "Look confident," she said, and took a selfie of us together.

I watched her disappear into the crowd, unable to believe what had just happened. Mitzy Erst had just given me a pep talk, complimented my AI, taken a selfie with me, and potentially invited me to hang out with her on Sunday. Though whether or not that last part was going to happen remained to be seen. Either way, it meant I couldn't leave. Not yet, at least.

I wandered back to the party, still unsure of where my friends were, and was about to ask Wiser what the Warbler's Room was when I heard a boy's voice behind me.

"It was Shakespeare, you know."

Mast's face was damp with perspiration, and there was a glimmer in his eye, as though he was brimming with life.

My heart sank. Instead of riding the high of my potentially life-changing encounter with Mitzy Erst, I now had to face a boy who seemed to be intimately acquainted with the inner workings of my psyche and who had just been flirting with another girl and had now found me standing by myself at a party, talking to my phone.

"I looked it up," he continued.

I had no idea what he was talking about.

"*A sin purged*," he said. "Wiser's answer to your question about the kiss."

I groaned. Not this again. "Are you talking to me just so

we can revisit the subject of my mortification?"

"*Thus from my lips, by thine, my sin is purged.* It's from *Romeo and Juliet.* I think it's a really sophisticated answer coming from an AI. You should be proud, not embarrassed."

His sincerity crept up on me like it always did, and I found myself feeling both confused and infuriated with his particular brand of wit and earnestness.

"But to get back to your previous question, no, that wasn't why I came to talk to you. I'm here because my bot was wondering if your bot knew where a person could get a bite to eat around here."

"Olli must be far less evolved than Wiser if he needs to eat," I said.

"Or is he more evolved because he's closer to human, which is the entire point of artificial intelligence?"

"Some might argue that having to eat every four hours is one of our greatest weaknesses, given Earth's limited resources, and that if we had the capability to redesign ourselves, we should omit it."

"But then what would I say to girl at a party if I wanted to start a conversation?"

Despite myself, I blushed. Was he flirting with me? "You could just say hi."

"I guess I could, couldn't I?" Mast grinned. "Well, hi."

"Hi."

He was wearing a Star Wars T-shirt and a pair of high-top

sneakers, identical to the ones he wore at the Foundry, but black.

"These are my black-tie sneakers," he said, catching me looking at them. "I only wear them to parties."

"It's a good thing you dressed up for the occasion," I said, glancing out the window, where a guy had jumped into the pool in his work clothes. "They clearly follow a strict dress code here."

Mast laughed.

"So what does your bot like to eat?" I asked.

"Great question." He took out his phone and touched a green icon. "Hi, Olli."

"Hey," a male voice said from his phone. He sounded relaxed and aloof, like an older brother.

"Olli, what's your favorite food?" Mast asked.

"Chicken with Boolean cube."

I rolled my eyes.

"Micro greens," Olli continued. "Caret cake, but just a byte. Any more and I might go into a food coma."

I took out my phone. "Wiser, what do you like to eat?"

"I run off of ionized electrolytes flowing through a cathode," Wiser said.

"So kind of like Gatorade," Mast joked.

"Nothing like Gatorade," Wiser said.

Mast glanced at my cup. "Speaking of which, that's a big drink."

I bit my lip. "It's water."

"They serve water here?" he said. "I thought I was going to have to get some from the bathroom."

"You can't drink water from the bathroom tap," I said, bewildered.

"Why not? It's the same as the water from the kitchen."

"It tastes different."

Mast laughed. "No it doesn't. That's in your head."

"Just have some of mine," I said, and offered him my cup.

"You'd share your straw with me, your archnemesis, your greatest competitor?"

"I like to keep my friends close and my enemies closer."

He gave me the beginning of a smile. "Smart," he said, and took a sip.

"So how does Olli like the party?" I asked.

"Olli, what do you think of this party?" Mast said into his phone.

Olli paused. "It's louder than most of the parties we go to, so it must be fun."

Mast looked mildly embarrassed. "He just means that most of the parties we go to are less rowdy."

"What kind of parties are those?"

"They're mostly subterranean," Mast said.

"He means basement," Olli corrected.

Mast winced. "That's one way to put it."

"As in our *parents'* basement," Olli added.

"For the record, I'd like to say that my parents have a very nice basement, with a carpet and a couch and a TV."

"Sounds like a wild time," I said, grinning.

"They aren't that wild," Mast said. "They're pretty quiet, actually. Mostly virtual."

"By virtual, he means playing multiplayer video games," Olli corrected.

Mast sighed. "When you put it that way, it doesn't sound as good. But they're not totally solitary. Sometimes my little sisters bother me until I play board games with them."

"You have sisters?" I asked.

"Yeah. Why?"

"I've always wanted sisters."

"You haven't met them. If you did, you'd want to Control Alt Delete them. Once they painted three of my nails while I was sleeping. I didn't even notice until I got to school."

"What color?"

"Purple. It looked okay, actually. But I'm not supposed to say that. You know, because I'm a guy and guys aren't supposed to like color."

"You can say it to me, we've already shared a straw."

Mast smiled. "We have, haven't we?"

There was an awkward pause where neither of us knew what to say next, and I realized that I was actually enjoying myself.

"So who was that girl?" I ventured.

Mast looked confused. "What girl?"

"The one who thought you were funny."

"Oh, Jessica," he said. "She's not my type."

He said it definitively, like he wanted to make sure I knew he was serious.

The room felt different then, like all of the particles had been charged and were suspended in the air around us, waiting for one of us to release the pressure.

"What's your type?" I ventured.

"Oh, I don't know. Sharp, funny, argumentative because I like to be kept on my toes."

His eyes seemed to search my face for an answer. I swallowed. Was he talking about me?

"She sounds out of your league," Olli interjected.

"She is," Mast murmured.

He was looking at me like he had known me for my entire life, like we'd been having this conversation for years and it had never turned out the way he had wanted it to. I felt suddenly nervous.

"What's yours?" he asked me.

"I—I don't know," I said. "Thoughtful. Smart. Someone who I can talk to about hard things—"

Before I could finish, he leaned toward me and pressed his lips to mine. His mouth was warm and soft and tasted familiar, like breath mints and chips and soda, like a boy who was kissing me on a sofa in his parents' basement, a boy I'd known for a long time. I felt his fingers graze mine and I kissed him back, breathing him in, feeling the weight of his body press against mine. He felt like home.

"Was that okay?" he said to me.

I shrugged. "It was all right," I teased.

He laughed, relieved. "I thought you didn't like me."

"I don't," I said, which made him laugh.

"I was wrong," he said. "I don't have a type. I just have a person."

He didn't have to say who, because I knew he was talking about me.

# twelve

**I woke up to** the sun streaming through the windows. Everything felt perfect. My pillows were remarkably fluffy given that I had slept on them all night, the bed was deliciously comfortable, and the covers were the perfect temperature—both cool and warm at the same time, a rare state of existence that seemed to defy the laws of thermodynamics. The cup of water on my bedside table was a revelation, refreshing and crisp like a spring morning and perhaps the greatest cup of water I'd ever tasted. Outside, I could see the leaves swaying gently in the morning breeze and beyond them, the sky, so brilliantly blue it looked digitally enhanced. I lived in California. It was the first time I'd really felt it.

My head throbbed—a vestige of the party—and I took an Advil, sank into the sheets, and allowed myself to think about another scientific conundrum: Mast. It was true, I didn't like him. But it was also true that I liked him. Very much. Too much. If I closed my eyes, I could still feel the soft cotton of his shirt as I leaned toward him, the warmth of his hand on my neck as he kissed me gently like I was something of immense value.

Shortly after, a drone had flown down the hallway, taking an aerial video of the party and we'd jumped apart. Then Amina had spotted us from the adjacent room and had shouted "Pizza!"

"Is that your code word or something?" Mast had asked me.

I'd laughed nervously, wondering how much Amina had seen. "Yeah," I'd said. "It means she wants pizza."

"I've been looking for you forever," Amina had said, approaching us. Then she'd narrowed her eyes suspiciously. "What are you guys doing back here?"

"We just ran into each other while I was looking for the bathroom—" I'd said at the same time that Mast had said, "We've been introducing our AIs—"

"Huh," Amina had said, squinting at us before turning to me. "Are you hungry?"

"Yeah," I'd said.

"I guess I'll see you around?" Mast had said.

"Yeah. I'll see you in class."

"Class. Right."

The pizza, like everything else that night, had been delicious, though Amina had disagreed and insisted it was subpar. "Right. The pizza is delicious and nothing happened between you and Mast."

"Exactly."

"You've clearly never been to New York and had a real pizza."

"There's real pizza in Worcester."

"No there isn't. There's circular bread product topped with red product and milk product. It's not the same."

"You've never been to Worcester. You don't know that."

"I know two things: that this pizza isn't good and that you think it's good, and those are the only data points I need to make my conclusion." She'd paused then. "Since you're dying to know, I had a pretty good night, too. I talked to Ravi, who's actually really cool. We ended up exploring the house and finding this virtual reality room upstairs that was entirely padded and soundproof, so of course we had to try it out, which was amazing until I got carsick from the goggles."

"Sorry," I'd said, feeling guilty that I hadn't asked.

"You're not going to tell me what happened with Mast, are you?"

"There's nothing to tell," I'd insisted, unsure of why I didn't want to tell her. Maybe because I wasn't exactly sure what had happened myself. "We ran into each other, we talked for a little bit. It was nothing really."

"Mm-hmm. Enjoy that pizza."

I rolled out of bed, savoring the quiet of the morning. It was Saturday. Mast had kissed me at a party and Mitzy Erst had taken my photo. The sun was glinting through the leaves and songbirds were singing in the trees, their chirps so classically bird-like that they sounded like a recording. I had no classes. No plans. No responsibilities. I had assignments to do, but they could wait. For the first time in a long while, my day was off to a good start.

I got dressed and wondered if I would ever see Mitzy again. She'd said she didn't need to know my name, but what did that mean? She'd been pretty drunk; I wondered if she'd even remember me, or if I would end up being just another random face in her camera roll.

The dorm was eerily quiet when I stepped into the hallway. I checked my phone. It was ten thirty, which was later than I normally woke up. Everyone had to be at the dining hall.

Outside, Marcus and Arthur were throwing a Frisbee outside the boys' dormitory. When they saw me, they stopped. Also odd. Then something especially bizarre happened. They waved at me.

No one at the Foundry waved at me. I was the worst in the class, a person to be pitied. People only liked that I was there because I made them feel better about themselves—someone had to have the lowest stock, and in that way, I was providing a public service—and they definitely didn't go out of their way to associate with me, for fear that my bad luck was contagious. I waved back, trying to remain calm, but couldn't stop my mind from racing to the worst-case scenario. What did they know?

The dining hall seemed to grow quiet when I walked inside, but maybe it was in my head. I filled a bowl with milk and cereal and tried to convince myself that everything was fine, when I noticed that people were looking at me and whispering. A lump formed in my throat.

Kate and Seema were sitting at a table with AJ and his friends, Kate's knees touching Mike's as she played with his fingers. I guessed they were back together now. When she saw me, she stopped talking and studied me as though I was newly interesting to her.

A few seats away, AJ looked at me, then whispered something to Drew. I waited for him to shout some snide remark, but instead he said nothing. Also strange.

Amina was sitting with Deborah and Ravi. I nodded to them, holding Deborah's gaze for a moment.

"Hey," I said to her.

"Hey," she said.

I was still grateful that she hadn't told anyone about that afternoon in the bathroom, and hoped she knew it. While she and Ravi resumed debating the virtues of open map versus open-world video games, I searched the room for Mast but didn't see him. Ravi probably knew where he was, but I couldn't ask him.

"I was beginning to think you actually did leave," Amina said to me as I sat down next to her.

"What do you mean?" I said to Amina.

"Yesterday?" Amina said. "Before the party, when you told me"—she lowered her voice—"that you were thinking of leaving."

"Oh, that. Nope. Still here." I glanced around me. "What's going on? I feel like everyone's staring at me."

"Check your Vault," Amina said with a grin.

I began to panic. What had I done to make my stock go down even further? I took mental inventory of the events of the party. Had I done anything embarrassing? Said anything stupid?

But when I checked my Vault, I gasped. My stock had gone up to fifteen.

I blinked, making sure I hadn't hallucinated the *1*, but it was still there, which meant that I was tied for the highest in the class with Deborah, Amina, and Mast.

"Impossible," I said. "It has to be a mistake."

"The algorithm doesn't make mistakes," Ravi said.

"Welcome to the upper echelon," Deborah said sarcastically. "It feels exactly the same as it does when you're in the lower echelon, except people fuck with you more."

"Ray of sunshine," Ravi said.

Amina held up her phone. "Here's your explanation."

It was open to the Façade app, where my face smiled back next to Mitzy's. It was the selfie she'd taken of us at the party. I was surprised by how glamorous I looked, staring coyly at the camera, a mysterious half smile on my face like I was keeping a secret. Mitzy stood beside me with a sultry gaze. Her long hair seemed to absorb the light, and her head was tilted toward mine like we were old friends. Around us, the dim, grainy light of the party gave the photo a candid feel, like she was revealing a behind-the-scenes look at her life.

Beneath us, her caption read: *It isn't every day that you meet someone with an idea that will truly change the world. Meet Xia Chan, the next big thing in AI. If you want to know what she's made, you'll have to ask her, because my lips are sealed. But know this: She's on her way up. Don't blink or she might pass you by.*

I didn't realize I was smiling until Amina rolled her eyes.

"Okay, I can see I'm being replaced, which is fine, but you don't have to rub it in by grinning about it so much."

"You're not being replaced," I said. "I have plenty of room in my life for two geniuses."

Amina pointed her fork at me. "I see your attempt to deflect the fact that you didn't tell me you and Mitzy were besties by flattering me, and it's working. You're forgiven."

"Thank you," I said. "But I did tell you that I met her at the party."

"Yeah, but you didn't say she was your new cheerleader."

"She's not my cheerleader."

Deborah raised an eyebrow. "She looks like one."

I studied the photo, wanting to stretch out the electrified feeling it gave me, when I noticed the comments rolling in.

>Who is this girl?

>I looked her up. She's at the Foundry

>What is that shirt she's wearing? She looks like a wannabe founder

>What kind of name is Xia?

>I think it's Chinese

>Ugh too many Chinese people coming here and taking our awards

>You do realize she was born here. It says so in her bio

>She'd be hot if she put on a little makeup

>And changed her outfit

>What's her company????

>Check the Foundry website. She's there to work on a bot called Wiser

>It's not a bot, it's an AI

>Whatever, same difference

>Totally different [eyeroll]

>She's hot . . . for an Asian girl

>I would never date an Asian girl

>They have nice skin

>Umm this isn't a dating app. Why are you commenting on how she looks?

>This^ Mitzy's sharing a picture of someone who she thinks is doing important work

>This is why there aren't enough women in leadership roles

>I'd date them both. I like a little sushi with my vanilla cake

>Sushi's from Japan, not China, and also you're a jerk

I felt suddenly self-conscious. Should I change my outfit? Did I need to wear makeup? I'd always known I looked different, but I never thought people would see a picture of me with Mitzy Erst and only be able to think about whether or not I was datable because I was Chinese.

Amina must've seen the comments, too, because her face dropped. "Don't listen to them. They're trolls on the internet. They're just jealous."

"Is my outfit that bad?" I asked her.

"No," Amina said, though I could sense her hesitation.

"It's a black turtleneck. It's classic."

Ravi winced in disagreement. "It's a little played out. Plus, aren't you sweating in it?"

"Played out?"

"Don't listen to him," Amina said, giving Ravi a look. "He's just a gamer."

"Hey, I've been dressing my avatars for years," Ravi said.

"I like it," Deborah said. "Streamline the morning routine, free up processing power. Same thing every day—black turtleneck, black pants. The last thing we should be spending our brain power on is clothes."

I sighed. "Noted. New outfit, more makeup, less Asian."

"Good luck with that last part," Amina said, then glanced behind me. "Incoming."

I turned to see Kate, who had gotten up to refill her glass of iced tea and was now approaching our table.

"Hey," she said to us, running a hand through her hair. "Crazy party last night, right?"

She had a dewy look to her, her cheeks glowing, her hair pulled back into a perfect loose ponytail as though she had just come back from picking wildflowers in the south of France. Everyone else in the dining hall looked like they'd gotten drunk at a party, passed out on their dorm room floor with their clothes still on, and had woken up nauseated before dragging themselves to the dining hall to eat some kind of carb before they threw up. And then there was Kate, in her linen pants and pale yellow top, smelling like lavender and picking at a fruit plate.

"Oh, I saw that photo of you," Kate said casually, like it was no big deal. "I didn't know you knew Mitzy."

"We're just acquaintances."

"How did you two meet?"

"I bumped into her at the party."

"The party last night?" Kate said, confused. "You met her for the first time yesterday, and she's already posting pictures of you?"

"She must have made an impression," Amina said.

"We hit it off," I said.

"Huh," Kate said, and gave me a thin smile. "That's really great. I'm happy for you."

The three of us watched her return to her table. When she was out of earshot, Ravi turned to us. "Well, that wasn't weird at all."

"*That's really great?*" Amina said. "*I'm happy for you?* You could almost see her eye twitch while saying it."

"She's a spider," Ravi said.

"One of those clear ones that blends into carpets," Amina said. "They're always the most terrifying."

Deborah frowned. "This comparison isn't really fair to spiders. They're an essential part of the ecosystem."

"So what's Mitzy like?" Ravi asked.

I thought back to the party, to Mitzy staring back at me from the bathroom mirror, her mascara smudged, her face so beautiful that I had to pinch myself to make sure I wasn't hallucinating.

"A few years ago, my mom took me to a Van Gogh

exhibit in Boston," I said. "I'd always loved his paintings but had never seen them in person, and when we got there, I remember being shocked by how much bigger and brighter and more mesmerizing they were in person. I couldn't stop looking at them. That's the first time I really I understood what art was." I looked up from my tray. "That's what Mitzy Erst is like."

■ ■ ■

We spent the rest of the day doing work in one of the study rooms. We had an assignment for Kowalski that was proving even more difficult than I'd expected, and we had to write a business plan for Ms. Perez and compile a series of pivot tables for Mr. Lajani. I was so far behind that it seemed hopeless, and I reverted to staring out the window, wondering what Mast was doing. Was he purposely making himself scarce because he didn't want to see me? Is that why he'd skipped breakfast, because he'd realized kissing me was a mistake?

I kept checking my phone, as if he was somehow going to send me a message even though I'd never given him my number. Every time I did it, Amina gave me a questioning look. I tried to act like everything was normal, but in truth, I didn't like how distracted I felt. It was just one kiss. Why was I letting him get to me?

I was about to put my phone away when it vibrated with a new message. I didn't recognize the number.

>Still on for tomorrow?

>Who is this?

>Your royal highness.

A grin spread across my face. Mitzy. I typed my answer back.

>Yes.

"So where are you meeting her?" Amina asked me as we walked back to the dorm. It was late afternoon and the sky was an expansive, bright blue.

"This old steakhouse in Portola Valley," I said. "I looked it up. It has a grandfather vibe. Apparently there's this famous room in the back—"

"Romy's Steakhouse?" Amina said, interrupting me. "*That's* where you're meeting her?"

"Yeah. Why, you've heard of it?"

"Um, yes. You haven't?"

Amina exchanged an amused look with Ravi.

"You're not going to a steakhouse," Amina explained. "You're going to the Warbler's Room."

"Yeah. That's the room in the back."

"It's not just a room in a restaurant," Amina said. "It's a private room where all the big deals are made."

"Invite only," Ravi added. "Top secret."

"No one knows what it's like inside," Amina said. "There's a whole website dedicated to who's been seen going into the Warbler's Room."

"BirdWatchingAtRomys.com," Ravi said. "It's surprisingly thorough."

"You have to map it for me on Squirrel," Amina said. "I've been dying to know what it's like in there."

"I don't know if I should do that," I said, faltering. "It's my first meeting with Mitzy—"

"Oh, come on. You can use an anonymous account. No one's going to find out. And it's just a map, anyway. It's not like I'm asking you to take pictures."

"Isn't it just one room? What will a map even show?"

"Maybe it's one room," Amina said. "Or maybe it's three. Maybe it's a hexagonal room with secret doors on all sides, or maybe it's one long banquet hall. We'll never know until we see a map."

"Can't you just ask Arun what it's like inside? I'm sure he's been inside. He's been everywhere."

"Even Arun hasn't been in the back room."

I bit my lip. "I'll think about it."

We were almost back at the dorm when I saw a station wagon pull up to the boys' dormitory. It idled under an oak tree while Mast got out and slung a backpack over his shoulder. He looked surprised to see me and gave me a half wave.

Amina gave me a knowing look. "I'll meet you inside," she said with a wink. "Enjoy your pizza."

The problem with Mast was that he looked better the longer you stared at him. At first glance, he seemed completely average: pleasant to look at but forgettable, another moderately nerdy boy in Converse sneakers and a well-loved T-shirt. But then you might notice how the sun seemed to gravitate toward his arms, making them look golden in the light, or how his eyes softened when he looked at you, or how his cheeks dimpled slightly like he was trying to hold back a smile. You might notice how he ran his hand through his hair, unable to hide that he was a little nervous, or how he tilted his head slightly when he said your name so he could better admire your face.

"Hey," he said.

"Hey."

It was the first time neither of us seemed to know what to say, and we stood there awkwardly, unsure why we suddenly had nothing to talk about.

"You forgot your sandwich," a man who was presumably his dad called from the driver's seat and held a Tupperware out the window. He was blasting music, bobbing his head, and grinning like he took pride in embarrassing Mast in this particular way.

Mast took the Tupperware sheepishly. "My mom is under the impression that I have no access to food outside of her house." The song rose to a crescendo and his dad drummed the steering wheel, making Mast wince. "Are all dads this passionate about Led Zeppelin?"

"It's a dad rule," his dad called out, then stuck his head out the window and waved at me.

I could see the family resemblance. He looked like Mast might in twenty years if he gained forty pounds and replaced all of his T-shirts with golf polos. I liked him immediately. He looked happy and untroubled, like a man who'd stopped caring what other people thought about him and had whittled down his priority list to the real pleasures in life.

"I'm not embarrassing him, am I?" his dad asked me with a grin.

I laughed. "Not at all."

We stood there awkwardly until Mast interjected. "Right, Dad, this is my . . . colleague. My classmate. I mean, my friend, I guess."

"Hello, friend, I guess," his dad said.

"I'm Xia," I said.

"Right, this is my Xia," Mast corrected. "I mean, not mine. I don't own her or anything. This is just Xia."

His father seemed amused by how Mast's face was turning red. "Hello, just Xia."

"Isn't it time for you to go?" Mast said to him. "You have that afternoon appointment . . . ?"

"Appointment?"

Mast gave him a threatening look, and his dad slowly nodded in realization. "Oh, right. The appointment. Well, it was nice meeting you, just Xia."

"You too," I said.

Mast looked relieved as he drove off. "Well, that was smooth," he said. "It's almost like I was nervous or something."

"It's normal to be nervous around illustrious colleagues," I teased.

Mast laughed and flushed all over again. "I know this is a little unprofessional, considering we're colleagues and all, but since we shared a straw, I was wondering what you're doing on Friday night."

"Nothing," I said.

"Me neither. Want to do nothing together?"

I tried not to smile. "I'd love to."

# thirteen

**The message had** been sitting in my inbox for almost sixteen hours before I noticed it.

It happened like this. I went back to my dorm room after talking to Mast and sank into my bed for an unspecified amount of time and stared at the sun stretching across the ceiling, smiling and feeling like I had passed through a portal to a parallel life, where I got everything I wanted at exactly the right time.

I eventually roused myself and started my programming assignment, which was particularly annoying, even for Kowalski. While I sketched out a binary tree, then crumpled the paper and sketched a new one, my mind kept drifting to Mast. What would we do on Friday? Though the week hadn't started yet, I already wished it was over so I could get to our date faster.

Frustrated with my assignment, I pushed my papers aside and opened BitBop, wondering if anyone had advice on balanced binary trees. That's when I saw it.

A new message from ObjectPermanence, which had been languishing in my inbox since the night before. Normally I checked at least once a day to see if he'd written me, but I'd been so distracted by Mast that I hadn't even thought about ObjectPermanence since the day before.

NEW MESSAGE FROM U/OBJECTPERMANENCE:

I figured I'd send this on the off-chance that you're up. I have to admit, I'm a little drunk, but drunk in a good way. Do you drink? I do sometimes, but I try not to because it makes me feel dumb, and then I wake up the next morning wondering if I said anything stupid. I wonder if I'll feel that way about this message [insert nervous laughter].

I had a good night tonight. When I'm happy, I think of you. Is that weird to admit? I've never met you and here I am sitting in my room in the middle of the night, wanting to tell you about my evening.

Which brings me to your message. Of course you know me. "Knowing" someone doesn't just mean knowing facts about them. I know plenty of facts about my dad, for example. I know where he lives, what he looks like, what he orders at restaurants. But I don't know what makes him happy, what he worries about at night, what scares him or makes him feel like he's alive. So do I *really* know him? Not like I know you.

Or maybe you can never really know someone. If you can, I'm not sure I even want to. What would be the fun in that? I think the best kind of relationships are the ones where you never stop getting to know each other. It means you're changing. It means you're alive.

That's part of the reason why I like you. Even though I feel like I know you, I can never predict what you're going to say next. I love that.

But if you really need to know details, here are a few.

I eat corn on the cob typewriter style. I sleep on my stomach, hugging a scrunched-up pillow. I'll always eat ice cream cake with a fork, no matter how many times people shame me for it. I love peanut butter and banana sandwiches. I listen to the same song on repeat until I get tired of it, then I move on to a new one. I always wished I had braces when I was a kid because they seemed cool. I still care very much about what other people think of me, you especially.

I hope you're having a good night, wherever you are. Did you figure out what you're going to do about school?

I let out a long exhale and sank into my chair. He was still there, as real as Mast, as real as a wet drunken kiss.

I wondered what had happened that made his night so great, and, indulging myself, I clicked on his username. It was a hobby of mine, perusing his post history to see what he was doing. Rarely did I find anything interesting. Object-Permanence was particularly good at commenting without revealing any hard information about himself, so when I saw that he'd created a new post just hours before, in a programming subgroup that I didn't subscribe to, I assumed it would be more of the same.

I clicked on his post, innocently titled, *Question about Database Programming Assignment*, ready to skim it, but didn't even make it to the second sentence before I froze.

> So I have this assignment where I'm supposed to design a data structure that stores a sequence of elements and supports a series of operations that our teacher provided in time O(log *n*).

My heart raced. It couldn't be.

He went on to list a series of operations that looked unbelievably familiar. He was asking for help with an issue he was having designing a balanced binary tree—an issue that I was intimately familiar with because I'd been working on the exact same assignment.

I shuffled through my desk until I found Kowalski's assignment and compared the wording to ObjectPermanence's posting. I felt suddenly light-headed. They were almost identical.

Was it possible that somewhere else in the country, a programming teacher was assigning the exact same homework to ObjectPermanence as Kowalski was assigning to me? How many teenagers even took programming classes this advanced in high school? The more I thought about it, the more I knew there was only one answer.

ObjectPermanence wasn't a stranger at all. All along, he'd been right here, at the Foundry.

■ ■ ■

"*Object permanence* is the understanding that objects exist even when we don't perceive them," Amina read from the internet.

I'd abandoned my homework and was sitting on her bed with my laptop, scrolling through ObjectPermanence's post history, scouring it for the hundredth time for some new detail that might reveal his identity. After my discovery, I'd texted Gina, then burst into Amina's room and told her everything.

"For example," Amina continued to read, "when a ball is resting on a bed and then is subsequently hidden under a blanket, we understand that the ball still exists, even though we cannot see it, hear it, smell it, taste it, or touch it. Object permanence is a function of early memory. Infants usually begin acquiring it at four months old, and fully grasp it by their first birthday."

"It's a good username," I said.

"It is," Amina conceded. "The irony is that you *have* seen him. You just didn't know it."

I sank into her pillows. "I still can't believe it."

"Who do you think it is?"

"Mast," I said. "I know it is." It had to be. I needed it to be.

All of ObjectPermanence's messages lined up exactly with my timeline with Mast. On the night of the welcome dinner, ObjectPermanence wrote to me that he'd done something he wasn't proud of. That was the same night that Mast had conveniently omitted the fact that he was doing AI, too, and that his real name was Ben. Mast had later said that he liked romantic comedies, which ObjectPermanence had also admitted to. Then, on the night after the DrinkMaiden party, he'd messaged me that he was drunk and that he'd had a good night. That was the same night that Mast had kissed me.

"Do you actually know it, or do you 'know' it?" Amina asked, with air quotes.

"The latter, if we're being technical," I admitted, "but I feel pretty confident."

Sure, there were a few troubling differences, most notably that his dad didn't exactly work in tech, and that they seemed to have a good relationship unlike ObjectPermanence and his dad. But really, what did I know about Mast's dad? They seemed to get along the one time I saw them together, but maybe Mast felt differently.

"Well, there's one way to find out." Amina tore a piece of paper out of her notebook. "There are fifteen boys at the Foundry," she said, writing their names down. "Let's narrow it down. What do we know so far about this ObjectPermanence?"

I'd been working on a list of everything I knew about him, which I'd compiled from all of his messages, comments, and posts. I read it to her. "He likes the movie *2001: A Space Odyssey*."

"Not helpful."

"He has a sister. Just like Mast."

"Older? Younger?"

"Unclear."

"Okay, well, we can at least cross out Andy Chen and Ben Goldstein, who are only children."

"He likes peanut butter and banana sandwiches."

"Who knows."

"His dad works in tech and sounds like an asshole."

"The tech part is useful," Amina said. "That means we can cross out Ravi and Marcus." She leaned over her computer and started typing. "I have to double check what Josh Steinman's dad does. Oh—yeah, we can cross him out, too." She paused, as if not wanting to break it to me. "And we can also cross out Mast."

I bristled at her suggestion. "I think that's a little premature."

"His dad is a professor at Stanford."

"Yeah, but he's a professor of Business and *Technology*."

Amina looked unconvinced. "I don't know. If my dad were a professor, I'd call him a professor. I wouldn't say he worked in tech."

"But you might if you were talking anonymously online."

I could tell Amina was trying to humor me. "I don't know."

"What does working in tech even mean, anyway?" I said. "He could have a patent or something. Maybe he's consulting with a tech company. I just think that we shouldn't cross him off until we have more information."

Amina tapped her pencil against her lips. "Yeah, okay, maybe. We can keep him for now."

Though it was obvious that she was only keeping him on the list because I wanted her to, I felt relieved. It still could be him.

"He's from the Bay Area," I continued. "Because he said he's going to school nearby. That fits with Mast, too."

"So we can cross off Mike Manning, Drew Farmington, and Micah Levine, and I'm going to go ahead and cross off Josh Horowitz and Mike McCalaster because they like guys and therefore probably wouldn't be flirting with you in such an overtly hetero way. What else?"

"He sleeps on his stomach. He eats corn on the cob type-writer style."

Amina looked at me like I was speaking a foreign language.

"You know, left to right. It means he's neat and treats things gently."

Amina raised an eyebrow. "I'm pretty sure you can't read that much into a piece of corn, but it's your fantasy."

"He eats ice cream cake with a fork—"

"What?" Amina said interrupting me. "He's clearly a psychopath. Are you sure you really want to know who this guy is?"

"He's not a psychopath and yes, I'm sure."

"He listens to the same song on repeat."

"As does everyone else."

"And never had braces as a kid but wished he did."

"Could be useful, if you can extract that information from the remaining names. Anything else?"

"He's smart," I said. "And kind and funny."

Amina rolled her eyes. "Okay, tender heart, but I'm asking for hard data."

"That's data," I protested.

"It's subjective. You have no idea how his online persona translates to real life. Maybe he's super quiet. Maybe he's a jerk. Maybe he can only be funny in writing."

"I highly doubt he's a jerk in person. But okay, I'll humor you. So who's left?"

Amina handed the paper to me. The final list read:

Mast (Ben) Matsuo*
Mike Flores
AJ Pierce
~~Mike McCalaster~~
~~Josh Steinman~~
~~Micah Levine~~
~~Drew Farmington~~
~~Andy Chen~~
~~Ben Goldstein~~
~~Mike Manning~~
~~Josh Horowitz~~
Arun Krishna
~~Marcus Varner~~
Arthur Kim
~~Ravi Vora~~

*maybe

"Mike Flores, AJ, Arun, Arthur, and Mast," I read, ignoring Mast's asterisk.

"What if it's AJ?" Amina said, horrified.

"It can't be. There's no way."

Amina winced. "Or Arun. He's so arrogant. He name-drops almost every sentence. Next time you talk to him, count how many times. The number will astound you."

"ObjectPermanence would never do that," I said. "It can't be him. Or Mike Flores—he's dating Kate. He wouldn't be talking to another girl online."

Amina gave me an apologetic shrug. "People do all sorts of things you'd never expect them to do online. You have to entertain the possibility that it could be any of these guys. Maybe Arun is totally different online. Maybe Mike flirts with other girls when Kate's not around. Maybe AJ contains multitudes."

I considered Arthur. I didn't know much about him other than our brief but endearing encounter at the party and that he was there to work on his start-up, Dare Me, which was basically an enhanced version of Truth or Dare and was already wildly popular. He was a little class-clowny, though seemed friendly and generally inoffensive. Still, I'd always pictured ObjectPermanence as a little less goofy. "I guess it wouldn't be the worst thing in the world if it turned out to be Arthur. Not that it will be. Because it's Mast."

"You do realize that if it is Mast, that means he was mes-saging another girl right after kissing you."

"But that other girl is also me, which makes it not as

bad," I reasoned. "And also his message was about how good of a night he had."

"Are you trying to convince me or yourself?"

I ignored her question. "And anyway, I was messaging a boy right after kissing Mast, so it kind of makes us even."

Amina crossed her arms. "Mast doesn't fit all of the criteria."

"But the criteria he *does* fit is so perfect that maybe we don't have all the information we need. I mean, come on. The welcome dinner? Having a good night at the party?"

"But all of those things could work for AJ, too," Amina added. "Think about it. At the welcome dinner, he was the one who humiliated you. He was also at the party and was drunk, and I'm pretty sure he was having a good time, as was basically everyone else."

It couldn't be AJ; didn't she see that?

"ObjectPermanence also said that I wouldn't like him if I met him in person," I said. "And at first, I didn't like Mast in person."

"You didn't like AJ either," Amina countered.

"I *don't* like AJ, as in present tense, as in *ongoing*," I corrected.

Amina shrugged. "It fits."

"Do you want it to be AJ?" I said, growing exasperated.

"Of course not. But I think you want it to be Mast so badly that you're overlooking key data points."

"It could be him," I insisted. "Everything fits. Well . . . mostly."

Amina gave me a pointed look. "Exactly. *Mostly.*"

I hadn't convinced her, but I didn't care. Sure, some of the details didn't match, but as ObjectPermanence had said, you don't need facts to really know someone. It was Mast. I could feel it. All I needed to do was find a way to prove it.

# fourteen

**R**omy's Steakhouse was perched in the hills of Portola Valley. The drive up, through winding roads, made my already-nervous stomach flip. It was an old wooden lodge surrounded by fog that had crept in from the forest and settled around the windows, as though the restaurant naturally warranted privacy. The lot was full of expensive sports cars when the Foundry SUV dropped me off. They gleamed like gems as I walked past them toward the door.

The restaurant hadn't been updated since the 1970s. It had white tablecloths and moody floral paintings and green light fixtures that gave it the ambience of a grandfather's study.

"I'm here to meet Mitzy Erst," I said to the host, who looked like a boy from a period movie set in a pioneer town.

He stood up straight when I mentioned her name and looked at me like I was important. "Right this way."

He led me through a series of dining rooms to a green door printed with the words By Invitation Only.

The Warbler's Room felt like a smoking parlor. Predictably, it was filled with men. Young men, old men, men in gray suits, men in blue suits, men in business casual, men putting on their coats, men rolling up their sleeves, men with beards, men with tans, men gesticulating with their knives, men talking too loudly, men ordering meat, men wiping their mouths with napkins, men wasting food, men ordering whiskey, men sipping beer and laughing, men spritzing lemon into their water, men paying me no attention, men looking me up and down, men glancing at me and murmuring, wondering what man had invited me there. Behind them all, a faded green mural of a bird in the forest graced the walls above the inset mahogany paneling.

Mitzy Erst was sitting at a table in the corner, looking like a streak of neon in a baroque painting.

Her eyes twinkled when she saw me, as though we were accomplices. "Well, if it isn't the famous Xia Chan, tech newcomer and overnight celebrity."

I wanted to come off as confident and sophisticated, someone worthy of being seen with her, but was too nervous to act cool. "That's me," I said like an idiot.

"You look shorter than I remember," she said. She was sipping an amber drink with an orange peel spiraling down its side. "We'll have to work on that."

I let out a confused laugh. "Work on it?"

Mitzy gave me an amused look. "Almost everything can be worked on. For example, you look terrified, which makes you look shorter."

"This place is a little intimidating," I admitted, cursing my face for betraying me. Did it have to constantly broadcast the exact emotion I was feeling to everyone around me?

"You only have to be intimidated by the ones wearing lounge clothes," she said, her voice low and conspiratorial. "All the suits are little men. It's a pretty universal rule here. The fancier the clothes, the less power they have. It's the ones in sneakers and sweatpants that you have to worry about. If you can get away with going to a business meeting in your pajamas—that's real power."

I noticed then that the only men who were actually eating were the ones in sneakers and sweats. There were only a handful of them, but they stood out. They slouched in their chairs, laughed with abandon, and ordered second and third drinks while the men in suits sat stiffly as though they were being interviewed.

"It's amazing what you see when you really start looking," Mitzy said with a wink.

The waiter approached and took our order.

"I'll have the New York Strip," Mitzy said.

I scanned the menu but kept getting distracted by the prices, which were so high that I couldn't fathom ordering any of it.

"I . . . um—"

"She'll have the Porterhouse," Mitzy said, taking my menu.

"Always order steak when you can," Mitzy said when the

waiter was gone. "Especially if you're eating with a man. It makes you look confident and decisive."

I nodded and decided not to tell her that I didn't particularly like steak.

"So we need to get you ready."

"Ready. Right." I took a sip of water, not wanting to reveal that I didn't know what I was getting ready for.

"I've already gotten a dozen emails about you—"

"About me? How?"

"From the photo I posted. We don't want to respond right away. It's good to make people squirm a little to make sure they know it's a seller's market. But I wanted to touch base with you first to see how you're feeling."

I wondered if I had missed some key piece of information, because I hadn't the slightest clue what she was talking about. Frantically, I racked my brain, wondering if Mitzy had sent me an email that I'd accidentally deleted that mentioned whatever it was she was referring to.

"So how are you feeling?" Mitzy repeated.

"Um . . . good," I said. "I'm feeling good. And excited?" I watched her face, trying to figure out if my answer was appropriate. "I'm feeling energized and ready to talk to people."

It was a whole lot of nothing, but it seemed to work because Mitzy beamed.

"Good."

"So I'm going to set up a meeting with Vilbo. There's

an executive there who really wants to meet you. There's a chance he'll want to give you seed funding."

"I hope he isn't one of the executives I met at the Foundry mixer," I murmured. "My pitch there didn't exactly go well."

"Even if he is, it doesn't matter. You'll be new by the time you meet him."

What did she mean by *new*?

"Now what do you have for me?"

A lump formed in my throat. Should I have prepared? Should I have brought something?

"Your pitch. Your business plan. You know, your Wiser schtick. The thing you tell people to convince them that Wiser is the next best thing."

"I—I, um, you want me to tell it to you now?"

Waiters arrived with our food: two huge slabs of meat glistening with butter, and a tray of sides.

"How else are you going to practice?"

The waiters lingered over us, setting out thick serrated knives on napkins and offering us freshly grated pepper for the potatoes. I wanted to wait until they were gone to do my pitch but they didn't seem eager to leave and Mitzy was looking impatient.

I cleared my throat. "Wiser is an artificial intelligence tool that analyzes public and private data—" I began, glancing up nervously while the waiters tonged slices of lemon onto a side plate, "and simulates an older version of the user to give that user advice."

Mitzy frowned. "Stop. I'm already bored. You're explaining too much. You're overthinking it."

The waiter asked if she wanted another drink, and she nodded and waved him away.

"What did you say to me at the party?" she asked, slicing into her steak. Blood pooled around it. "You convinced me in just a few minutes that Wiser was going to change the world. Just say what you said then."

"That was sort of a happy accident."

"It wasn't an accident. I stumbled around a lot of people that night and you were the only one I posted about." She gestured to the room with her fork. "People around here want you to think that you're lucky, that *they* found you, that *they* made you, but that's the scam. That's how they own you. What I saw at that party wasn't an accident. It was your hard work and your genius. Don't let anyone let you think otherwise."

I felt chastened and empowered by her speech. "I won't."

"Good. Now sit up straight, act tall, and try not to say *um* when you talk. From now on, you have to be ready. This is Silicon Valley. You don't just have coffee or lunch with people. Everything is a meeting. No one asks you to meet up for a *quick bite* unless they think you can give them something."

I wondered what she thought I could give her, since she was the one asking me to lunch. "Why are you helping me then?"

"Because I think your product could change the world, and it wouldn't be right for me to sit and watch you drop out of the Foundry without trying to help."

I wasn't used to getting compliments, so when I received one, I didn't know what to do. What could I possibly say that could make Mitzy understand that even if I never saw her again, she had already changed my life? I considered what Wiser would have me say. "When someone gives you a compliment, the best thing to do is say thank you," Wiser liked to remind me. So that's what I did.

"Thanks," I said.

Mitzy smiled. "My pleasure."

"So do you have any other tips?"

Mitzy swirled the ice cubes in her drink. "Only tell people exactly as much as they need to know. Always wear sunscreen. Retinol is your friend. Chemical exfoliation is better than physical. You're too young to need it now, but remember it for when you're thirty. Speaking of which, we have to work on your look."

"What's wrong with my look?"

Mitzy hesitated, as though she was searching for the appropriate euphemism. "It's a little dated. It's mostly the turtleneck. But the pants, too."

"It's classic," I protested.

"I get that you're trying to look the part. I really do. But you don't want magazines to describe you as a girl who dresses like old male CEOs. You want to be the girl who can't be compared to anyone else."

I must have looked skeptical because she pointed at me with her fork. "Do you have anything to do this afternoon?"

"Just an impossibly time-consuming maximum subarray

coding assignment, a market analysis report, and fifty pages of reading on corporate finance."

Wiser had advised me to postpone meeting Mitzy until the following week, arguing that I needed to catch up on my schoolwork before taking social meetings, but I'd ignored her and turned her off. Though she wasn't awake now, I wondered if she could detect the mild panic in my voice.

"We can fix that," Mitzy said, and pointed her phone camera at me. "Look tall," she said and took a photo. "If you're going to be late on your assignments, we have to raise your stock some way."

"Why would I be late on my assignments—" I began to ask, but she cut me off.

"Besides, what we're about to do matters more than class. Speaking of which, we need to talk about your online presence," Mitzy said. "Or lack thereof."

"I'm constantly online."

"Liking your friends' photos and lurking on coding forums is not what I mean. You've only posted a handful of photos on your account and most of them are of a microwave."

"I upgraded that microwave! I programmed it to cook an egg perfectly by voice activation."

"That's all very quirky and niche, but your brand isn't microwaves. It's sleek and clean and futuristic. You need to convince everyone else that the future you're imagining is a future they want. You're a brand now. You need to sell yourself."

Could you be a brand when you were a timid misfit who

spent most of her time talking to her phone?

"That means posting at least once a day. Nothing incendiary—no politics, no opinions on current events, and definitely no complaining or bad-mouthing."

"Once a day?" I blurted out. "What would I even post?"

"What does anyone post? Selfies, places you've eaten, outfits. You know, scenes from your everyday life."

"But my everyday life is boring. I eat at the same place every day. I wear the same outfit every day."

"First," Mitzy said, "you need to stop eating that terrible cafeteria food. It's like eating at an airport food court."

Though I didn't dare admit it, the food at the Foundry was some of the best I'd ever eaten.

"Second," Mitzy continued, "you'll soon be the owner of an entirely new wardrobe, so that solves the outfit problem. And finally, eighty percent of everything is boring. Whose life is interesting all the time?"

"Yours."

"I spend most of my time making calls and following up. I don't code anymore. I sold all my companies and now sit on their boards as a senior advisor, which means that I try to get funding. Do you know how incredibly boring that is?"

"It doesn't look boring."

"That's because I only show the twenty percent that looks fun. And even that I have to spruce up. You and I, we're in the business of making something out of nothing. That's what the entire internet is, really. It's an alternate world that we're all communally conjuring together. Your life isn't interesting? Make it interesting. That's your job now."

She gave the waiter her credit card to pay for lunch, then busied herself with her phone. "Posted."

Everyone stole glances at us when we left the restaurant. They were looking at Mitzy, of course, not me, though if she noticed she didn't let on. She walked like a celebrity: shoulders back, chin up, eyes fixed on the horizon as though she was already living in the future. Normally I felt self-conscious when I knew people were staring at me, but standing next to Mitzy, I felt like the best version of myself. I wanted to be seen. As we walked through the restaurant, I imagined us as explorers of a new and uncharted land: brown, drab, and lifeless. And there we were, the only two people in the world who were really alive. It felt right. We could remake it together.

A gleaming red sports car chirped in the parking lot. To my surprise, Mitzy got into the driver's seat.

"*This* is your car?" I said, admiring the paint job, which looked like candy. I didn't know why I was surprised. Of course Mitzy would drive the nicest car in the lot.

But she was already on her phone. "We're on our way," she said to the person on the other end of the line.

I slid into the passenger's seat, marveling at how the leather felt cool against my skin despite baking in the sun all morning. She zipped out of the lot before I could buckle up, and I lurched forward, catching myself just before I hit the windshield.

"Hold on," she said to me with a smile. "The ride is just beginning."

# fifteen

**S**he sped through the winding roads that led us down into Palo Alto, blowing through stop signs and speeding through yellow lights. I gripped the side of my seat and tried not to look terrified.

Her golden hair flitted out the window as she pulled down a residential street lined with trees and parked in front of a huge modern house that looked like an art gallery.

"Is this where you live?" I asked.

"Of course not. My house is much nicer," Mitzy said with a wink. "This is the studio of Veronica DuChamp, image consultant to the rich and famous of Silicon Valley."

"Like a stylist?" I asked.

"She's much more than that. Just go in with an open mind, answer all her questions as honestly as possible, and don't touch the dogs."

A woman greeted us at the front door. She had to be the same age as my mom but looked so hip that she seemed younger. She was dressed like an artist, a very wealthy one. She wore glasses with electric blue frames that matched her rings and a silk scarf knotted around her hair.

"I'm Veronica," she said, holding out her hand. It was smooth and cold.

"Xia," I said.

Veronica looked me up and down. "Let's get started."

She led us into her living room, where two fluffy white dogs ran in to greet her, their tags jingling.

"Please sit," Veronica said, motioning to a plush sofa.

A young woman came in and brought us tea and little shell-shaped cookies that were so perfect they looked like they were part of the décor. I helped myself to one. All the while, Veronica watched me unabashedly, as if I were a new form of human that she'd never seen before. It made me self-conscious, and I put the cookie down, wondering if I had done something rude.

"Do you like it?" she said of the cookie.

"It's really good."

"It's called a madeleine. Have you heard of them?"

I nodded even though I hadn't, because I didn't want to seem uncultured.

Veronica's eyes twinkled as though she knew I was fibbing, but she didn't say anything. I glanced at Mitzy, but she was typing into her phone.

"Tell me, where are you from?" Veronica said. She had a way of speaking that made me feel like whatever I said would be inadequate.

"Central Massachusetts," I said.

"And you have siblings?"

"No."

"You don't come from a wealthy background," she observed.

I felt suddenly miserable. Was it that apparent? I took a mental inventory of my physical appearance and wondered which part had betrayed me. "I don't."

"What's your goal in coming here?"

"You mean here in this house?"

"To Silicon Valley. Why did you come here?"

"I—I wanted to start a company."

"Of course, but why did you want to start your company here? You could have started it on the East Coast."

Her line of questioning made me nervous, not because they were hard questions but because the answers seemed so obvious. Who didn't want to come to Silicon Valley to start their company? I worried that I was missing some key part of her question. "Because it's the epicenter. It's where everything is happening."

"So you like to be at the center of things."

"I guess? I mean, not really. I don't like people looking at me a lot."

"People crave many different kinds of attention. Visual attention is just one. Is there another kind of attention you enjoy?"

Veronica was staring at me as though she could see the

thoughts forming in my head before I was able to articulate them. "No one's ever really understood me. I've always been this invisible person, smart but otherwise two-dimensional. I don't want everyone staring at me or anything, I just want them to look at the things I make and see me. I mean, really see me."

Veronica leaned forward with curiosity. "And what made you want to start a company?"

I swallowed. "I came up with the idea when I realized that all the existing virtual assistants are just web scrapers. They don't give personalized advice. I thought creating an AI that gave people answers based on their specific problems would be a useful tool—"

"I'm not a reporter," Veronica said, cutting me off. "I don't want to hear your talking points. I'm here to extract the essence of you and put it on display, but I can only do that if I understand who you are, where you come from, and where you want to go."

I glanced at Mitzy, who raised an eyebrow, as if to say, *I told you to answer honestly.*

"I did it for myself. My mom was never home, and I wanted someone to talk to, so I made Wiser."

Veronica waited for me to continue.

"I wanted so badly to get out of Massachusetts. No one there understood me. I was just a weird person who was good with computers. Wiser was my escape."

Was I sharing too much? Ms. Perez had told us that we

should always answer positively, spinning the bad into the good, but it was a relief to just answer like myself. "Honestly, I made it because I was lonely."

"And what do you want? What constitutes success for you?"

The dogs were yipping at my feet. I remembered what Mitzy had said about not touching them and tried to ignore them. "I—I guess I want to make something that improves people's lives." The moment it came out of my mouth, I knew it wasn't true. Sure, I wanted Wiser to help people, but that wasn't *really* what had motivated me to apply to the Foundry.

Veronica gave me an impatient look. "This isn't the time to be modest."

"I want to feel like I have a place in the world," I said, my voice so low it was almost a whisper. I'd thought it so many times but had never said it out loud to another human being. It felt too intimate, too scary. "I want to belong. This is the only place where it feels like I can, and starting a company is the only way I know how."

Veronica looked satisfied. "Come with me."

She led us upstairs to a sunny dressing room. Racks of clothes lined the walls, and floor mirrors were perched around velvet armchairs.

"Rule number one: no more turtlenecks," she said, pinching my shirt. "It's derivative and boring, and frankly makes you look childish."

I felt a rush of embarrassment.

"Rule number two: no more interview pants." She pressed

the polyester fabric of my pants in between her fingers and grimaced. "These are for teenagers interviewing for their first internship. Not for Founders."

She eyed my backpack. "Rule number three: always carry your things in a nice bag. No more backpacks, no more binders, no more nylon unless you're going to the gym."

She touched my ponytail. "We need to work on this, too," she said, and called over her shoulder to someone downstairs. "Lillian? We need a cut."

"A cut as in a haircut?" I said, beginning to panic.

"Trust the process," Mitzy said, fingering through a clothing rack. "Before I met Veronica, people constantly talked down to me. I would go to meetings where executives would talk about how wonderful my product was, but they would barely look at me other than to assess my chest size. If they had questions, they would direct them to my legal advisor, who was, of course, a man. Veronica was the first person who told me I needed to sharpen my look. She put me in clean lines and bold colors, told me to stand up straight and wear more crisp, white cotton."

"You were very girl-next-door," Veronica said. "People looked at you and thought that a person who looked like their little sister couldn't possibly run a company. Unfortunately all women get it in some way or another. We can't win. But we can try."

Veronica picked through the clothing racks, pulling out jeans and trousers and shirts and blazers and what looked like a velvet smoking jacket.

"You're a dark horse," Veronica said. "That's what we need to communicate. Everyone in this town wears light colors and loungewear. We need you to stand out. We need moody colors. We need sharp lines and dramatic tailoring." She added what looked like a leather skirt to the pile. "Your look needs to scream that you don't need anyone. You need to make lonely look desirable."

"Are you sure—" I began to say, but Veronica thrust a bundle of outfit pairings into my hands and shooed me into a dressing room. They were right, I looked like a high schooler pretending to be an adult because I was. It was hard to imagine that any piece of clothing could change that. Still, I tried on the first outfit. It was a tight black shirtdress that looked militaristic, with buttons down the front and epaulets on the shoulders. I looked absurd, like I was the villain of a superhero movie.

"Do I have to show you?" I called out.

"Yes," Mitzy and Veronica said at the same time.

"I'm a dark horse," I whispered to myself. "I make looking lonely desirable." I let out a deep exhale and opened the door. "I look ridiculous."

Veronica studied me. "It is a little much, isn't it?"

The next option was a leather skirt so short I was scared to bend over and a low-cut V-neck that was so formfitting I hardly recognized myself.

Mitzy whistled when I opened the door, making my face go red.

"I don't know. I can barely move in this."

Veronica nodded in agreement. "Too X-rated. You're still underage, after all."

The next was a scoop neck and a pencil skirt that was so tight I had to shimmy toward the door.

Mitzy put a finger to her lips. "Maybe."

Veronica squinted at me. "We can do better."

Three pairs of twill pants, two tailored suits, a handful of ruffled blouses, and one disastrous silk jumper later, I finally put on something that I maybe sort of kind of thought was okay, or dare I say . . . liked.

It was a pair of black pants, tight but stretchy enough to go up the stairs two at a time. Veronica had paired it with a black silk tank and a black blazer that defied all definitions of what I knew a blazer to be. I associated them with my mother—boxy, frumpy, an envelope in clothing form. So when I put this one on, I was surprised by how it sharpened all of my angles, like an analog version of a photo editor. My shoulders looked sharper, my posture straighter, even my face looked somehow . . . smarter, like I was a more confident version of myself.

When I opened the door and stepped outside, Mitzy and Veronica went quiet.

"I look . . . taller."

Mitzy grinned. "I told you it could be done."

Veronica angled a bright fluorescent lamp at me, making me wince. "It's always best to see what you look like in both daylight and office light."

Satisfied, she motioned to the chair in the middle of the

room, where her assistant, Lillian was waiting for me with a pair of shears. "Just one more finishing touch left."

Reluctantly, I let her sweep a smock over me.

"Let's do a bob," Veronica said. "Shoulder length, light on the layers, less schoolgirl and more dominatrix. I want it to look a little severe."

"Severe?" I said. "Do you really think that's the right look for me?"

"Of course it is," Veronica said.

Lillian wet my hair with a spray bottle and combed it out. There was no mirror so all I could do was watch as hair slid down my smock onto the floor.

"Shorter," Veronica said.

I envisioned myself being reborn into my ten-year-old body, moments after my mother had given me a mortifying bowl cut, straight across the middle of the ears.

"Even shorter."

Everyone would mistake me for a prepubescent boy. The well-meaning chefs in the dining hall would offer me the kids' menu. When we went on corporate visits, the tour guides would assume I was someone's little brother and give me stickers and ask if I needed to use the potty.

"A smidge more."

I would be known as the first preteen to ever be admitted to the Foundry. They would print stories about me, asking me to comment on the state of the youth, on the effect of violent video games on developing minds, on screen time and whether or not it was good for young children.

Veronica stepped back and studied me. "Perfect."

Before letting me out of the chair, Lillian opened a small trunk and produced a series of makeup palettes.

"Let's try a dark eye," Veronica said to Lillian.

I would look like a child in a Renaissance picture, simultaneously too old and too young, forced to marry and bear children by the ripe age of thirteen.

"A little bit of color on the cheek," Veronica said.

I'd henceforth be known as Xia, pale and sickly, with an accordion collar and pink circles painted on my cheeks. A sad, tubercular clown.

Lillian removed the smock and I ventured toward the mirror.

The person I found staring back at me was nothing like I'd imagined. She was elegant and sleek, her hair cut cleanly at her shoulders, her face thoughtful, smart. I touched the blazer, which made the girl in the mirror look perfectly packaged, a neat triangle. She furrowed her brow as I studied her. She looked familiar—not just like me, but like someone else, someone I'd known before—but I couldn't figure out who.

"What do you think?" Mitzy said.

"It's me," I said, "only better."

"Only *Wiser*?" Mitzy said.

My eyes widened. She was right. That was exactly who I looked like: Wiser.

While Veronica picked out a handful of new outfits like the one I was wearing, I wondered how this worked. None of the clothes had price tags on them and no one had mentioned money, but surely Veronica's services couldn't be free. I remembered what Gina had told me when I'd first gotten accepted to the Foundry: When restaurants didn't include prices on their menus it meant they were too expensive to print.

"How much is this going to cost?" I whispered to Mitzy.

"Don't worry about the price. It's an investment in your company. What do you think that Vault money is for?"

"Business travel? Hardware? A new desktop?"

But Mitzy brushed me off. "Think of it as renting office space or hiring an assistant. Everyone does this, even men. Anyway, you don't pay now; Veronica will send you an invoice. It's very discreet. And often she gets clothes at a discount because she buys directly from the designer."

I took a breath and tried not to worry. If everyone did this, then it had to be okay.

While Veronica handed me armfuls of shopping bags, Mitzy held out her phone to take a selfie, then nudged me. "You take one, too."

She tilted her head until she found the right lighting. "Look *Wiser*."

I gazed into her camera, then mine, with a serene look that I imagined Wiser would have.

"Perfect," Mitzy said. "Post it by the time you get back to the dorm. And make sure the caption is short and charming. You want people to wish they had your life."

As I scooped up my clothes and followed Mitzy downstairs, I felt my phone vibrate. Mitzy had already posted her photo and tagged me. I didn't know how she'd done it so quickly, but she'd already edited our photo or added some kind of filter that made our faces gleam. We looked happy, glamorous. There was just enough of the background to make people wonder where we were and what we were doing. Beneath us, her caption read, *Control + N.*

It was exactly how I felt. New.

# sixteen

**When I got** back to the dorm, I threw my things on the bed and took out my phone. To my surprise, dozens of strangers had already liked the photo I'd posted of me and Mitzy, and a lot of them had commented and started to follow me. I scanned the comments.

>Wow! So cute!

>Mitzy's mystery girl finally started posting

>You're my idol!

>Where do you think they are?

>It looks like a house

>It doesn't look like Mitzy's house

>If you cross-reference it with Mitzy's post, it looks like there's a tree in the background through the window, which looks like a tree near University Ave

I felt a tingle of excitement as I watched the notifications pop up on my phone. More strangers, more likes, more followers. They knew my name and where I was from and what high school I'd gone to; someone even knew the name of the street I grew up on, which was troubling but also impressive. More importantly, they all seemed to love me.

Though I was normally skeptical of adulation, for the first time I found myself enjoying it. I thought back to when I was ten years old, taping newspaper articles of Mitzy above my bed. This was what it felt like to be on the other side.

While my phone continued to vibrate, I hung my new clothes in the closet and tried to avoid looking at my desk. I'd put off worrying about my assignments because Mitzy had insisted they didn't matter, but she wasn't the one who had to answer for herself in class. The least I could do was read through the assignments, I told myself, when my phone dinged with a text from Gina.

>**REVEAL YOUR TRUE FORM**

>What?

>I read somewhere that if you're a shapeshifter, you have to reveal your true form if someone asks you to, and you're clearly a shapeshifter because I've known Xia for over ten years and I've never seen her wear eyeshadow

>First of all, shapeshifters don't have to tell you anything. And second, I'm allowed to wear eyeshadow if I want to

>That sounds like something a shapeshifter would say to throw me off

>RIP

>RIP to what??

>This joke.

>If you're really Xia then what pioneering method of

fashion maintenance did I invent in the seventh grade that
I deserve recognition for?

I rolled my eyes.

>Spraying your tights with hairspray to prevent runs,
though I'm pretty certain that was widely known before
you "discovered" it

>Yeah but I figured it out on my own without searching the
internet, which is basically like inventing the light bulb at
the same time as Edison

>You're right. You deserve the Nobel Prize

>Thank you. Now that you've verified your identity, please
accept my condolences on the tragic passing of your
turtleneck. Where do I send flowers?

>In lieu of flowers we're accepting donations to the Gina E.
Ricci comedy foundation. She doesn't have a lot of fans, so
she can use all the help she can get

Gina was typing a response when someone knocked on
my door.

Amina did a double take when she saw me. "There's a
rumor going around that you have a secret identity. I had to
see for myself."

"Here I am, in the flesh," I said, standing up and spinning around theatrically. "Though it isn't a secret identity if
you post about it on the internet."

"So what superhero movie are you auditioning for?"
Amina asked.

"I'm hurt that you automatically assume I'm in costume

and not an actual superhero."

"Superheroes spend all their free time training. From what I can tell, you sit in front of a computer all day and talk to your phone."

"Where do you think I was all day? Maybe I was training."

"Wow," Amina said, pretending to be impressed. "You don't even look sweaty."

I shrugged. "Superheroes never do."

Amina smirked and collapsed into my bed, where she looked through my new clothes. "So this is your new look now?"

"Courtesy of Mitzy," I said. "And this stylist named Veronica. I wish you could have seen her house. It was like walking into a private Neiman Marcus."

"Did you take pictures?"

"I can't take photos of a place like that. It would be rude."

"Not even secret photos?"

"I was too nervous. It feels like all of this is happening to me by mistake, and if I do anything wrong, they'll realize I'm not who they think I am and take it all away."

"I feel that way sometimes, too."

"Seriously? You of all people belong here. You made Squirrel. The only reason you shouldn't be here is because you're *too* professional. You're basically already a CEO."

"Nothing about this place feels like it was built for me. It was built for Mikes and Joshes and Andrews. And maybe for Kates. But definitely not for a Black girl from Brooklyn." Amina glanced out the window at the boys' dormitory, where a group of boys were flying a drone around the lawn. "You think they're over there stressing about their homework? Of course not. They were born for this place; they feel entitled to it." Amina looked at me, and this time her face was serious. "People like us, we have to believe we belong here. We have to insist on it. Because if we don't, no one will."

■ ■ ■

I woke up the next morning to a cascade of notifications on my phone. Over a thousand new followers. Hundreds of likes and comments. My stock had gone up to twenty, an unthinkable number. I blinked, bleary eyed, unable to believe it. I'd spent my day trying on clothes and getting a new haircut, and my stock had still gone up. Maybe Mitzy was right; maybe grades didn't matter at all.

I threw on a Veronica outfit—a slim pair of pants, a tight tank top, and a satin blazer—and attempted to re-create what Lillian had done to my hair with the four bottles of product she'd sent me home with. It wasn't my best work but it was a decent approximation. Then I hurried across campus to the dining hall.

I hadn't forgotten that ObjectPermanence was going to be sitting in the dining hall in the flesh, which made me all the more nervous. I wanted to slip in without drawing too much attention to my new look, but when I opened the door, it slammed into Andy, spilling his open energy drink all over him and staining his shirt bright green, which in turn made him curse loudly. The entire room turned our way.

"Sorry," I said. "I'm so sorry."

He looked like he hadn't slept in three weeks and had spent the last four nights at a rave.

"Maximum spaghetti," he mumbled inexplicably.

"What?"

I grabbed a bunch of napkins from a nearby table and handed them to him, but he waved them away. "Value false," he muttered, and pushed past me toward the bathroom.

By the time I turned to look for Amina, everyone in the dining hall had at least pretended to go back to their conversations, though I noticed Arun and Arthur steal glances at me and whisper to their table. Nearby, AJ nodded at me to Mike and muttered something with a chuckle. Any one of them could be ObjectPermanence, and I felt hyperaware of their presence. Was Arthur eating a banana? What was Arun typing into his phone? What were AJ and Mike saying? I hurried to the beverage counter and made myself a cup of coffee when I heard a familiar voice behind me.

"Are you new here?" Mast said.

I let out a breath of relief.

"Pretty new," I said, playing along. "Though I think we've met before."

He reached past me to grab a cup and brushed his arm against mine. He didn't have to; there was plenty of space.

"You do look familiar, but I can't quite place you. You didn't, by any chance, go to a party the other night? I met this girl there who looked sort of like you."

"I was at a party, and I do remember talking to a boy there that might have looked like you, though the lighting was dark and I'd had too many shots, so I can't say for sure. I did run into a boy the other day though. He was carrying a nice piece of Tupperware and introduced me as his colleague to his dad and asked me to do nothing on Friday. Was that you?"

Mast winced. "That doesn't sound very romantic. It must have been a look-alike. I never would have called you my colleague, and if I had, it would only have been because I was nervous, and I would apologize and ask if we could start over."

He was looking at me so earnestly that it felt like I had simultaneously known him forever and was just meeting him for the first time. Was it possible that I was staring at ObjectPermanence in the flesh?

"I'm Mast," he said, and held out his hand.

I touched his fingers gently, cautiously, like they might shock me. "Xia."

He curled his hand around mine and held on just a moment longer than he had to. "I guess I'll see you around then."

"I guess I will."

I grabbed a piece of toast and walked to class with Amina, who was complaining about how hard Kowalski's assignment was. I tried to sympathize with her, nodding occasionally and throwing in a few *yeah*s and *ugh*s, but I was too buoyed by my Mast encounter to worry about school.

"Okay, what's going on?" Amina said, stopping me in the hallway. "Normally you're the one complaining about our homework, but today you've barely said a word. Am I missing something obvious in the assignment? You don't have to humor me."

I hesitated, not wanting to admit the real reason why I was being so quiet. "I didn't finish it. I barely started it."

"What?"

"I was too busy with Mitzy, and then I learned about ObjectPermanence, which ate up even more time, and then when I started, it was too overwhelming, and I don't know, I just figured I'd do it later. I doubt Kowalski will mind."

"So what did you pass in?"

"I uploaded a barely finished document."

I'd been trying to tell myself that it wasn't a big deal, that plenty of people passed in half-finished work, but saying it out loud only renewed the shame I felt about not focusing on school. Back home, I was at the top of my classes and never passed in assignments late or partially done.

Amina studied me like she was discovering a new angle of my face. "Oh."

"At least he doesn't go over assignments in class anymore. I'll be spared the humiliation."

"Yeah."

I waited for her to retort with a witty remark but instead she said nothing.

We walked in silence the rest of the way and took seats

in the third row. Seema complimented my shoes, and I glanced at Amina, who had to have heard it, and felt stupid for spending my weekend shopping instead of doing my assignments. By the time Kowalski put his bag down on the table and asked us to open our laptops, all of my excitement over Mitzy and my stock and Mast had dissipated and I was left with the stark realization that unlike everyone else in the classroom, I had nothing to show for my weekend other than a few excellent blazers and a new haircut.

A few desks away, Mast sat by the window taking notes on Kowalski's lecture. He was wearing a gray T-shirt, and beneath it, his shoulder blades shifted as he wrote. Though I knew I was supposed to want him to look at me, I liked that he wasn't, that he was staring so intently at the board. It felt intimate, watching him that way, like I was peering at him through a crack in the door.

I didn't want him to find out that I hadn't finished my assignments or that I hadn't been able to follow along in class because I hadn't done the reading, so I spent the rest of the period trying to catch up.

The day passed slowly. More classes, more handing in unfinished assignments, more trying to keep up with lectures that I didn't follow. All the while, my phone kept vibrating. More likes, more comments, more followers.

I was in sixth period when I got the notification. It was from Squirrel. Someone had invited me to a map they'd made, along with a time:

**6:00 p.m.**

I felt a flutter of excitement and glanced at Mast, whom I assumed had sent it, but he was focused on his screen, a pencil tucked behind his ear as he listened to the lecture.

Just before six, instead of going to dinner, I hurried to the starting point on the map: the front door of the girls' dormitory.

Following the path on my phone, I walked around the building, past the garden toward the back of the Foundry grounds. I'd never actually explored that part of campus; there was no real reason. All the classrooms were in the front.

It led me past a gardening shed, through a field dotted with fruit trees. When I walked by a particularly productive lime tree, a notification popped up on my phone.

**Pick two limes,** the app told me.

Amused, I did as it said. I turned the fruit in my hand as I walked.

The map culminated in a vast yellow field flanked by eucalyptus trees, their leaves swaying in the breeze. In the shade of the largest tree, Mast sat on a picnic table, reading a book.

Seeing him made me nervous in a good way, the same way I felt every time I saw a new message from ObjectPermanence in my inbox. It was the feeling of possibility.

I sat next to him, our arms almost touching, and admired the view. "I've never been here."

"The grove," he said. "I know I said Friday, but I figured why wait four more days to do nothing when we could do nothing tonight?"

I watched him brush his hair back and felt so sure that he was ObjectPermanence that none of the doubts Amina had voiced seemed to matter.

He pulled a brown paper bag out from the bench. "I hope you like tacos."

"Who doesn't like tacos?"

Mast pulled out his phone. "Olli, what do you think?"

"Tacos are the great unifier, the food everyone in the world can agree upon," Olli said.

I smirked and peeked in the bag. "What kind?"

"I can't believe you even asked," Mast said. "There's only one kind. Al pastor."

"I've never had it."

Mast gasped and feigned falling off the bench.

I laughed and rolled my eyes.

When he sat back up, a look of melodramatic solemnity overtook his face. "I'm honored to be the one to introduce you to the life-changing revelation that is al pastor. I promise, I won't take this responsibility lightly."

"Shut up," I said, laughing.

Past fellows had carved their initials into the worn wood on the picnic table. Mast pulled a napkin from the bag and dusted the leaves and debris off. It was sweet, how he arranged all of the salsas, resting each on their little lid.

"What?" he said, feeling me watching him.

"Nothing." But I proceeded to admire how he carefully tore the paper bag down the middle to make us a shared plate.

"What?" he repeated, amused.

"I just like what you've done with the place."

"If you're going to take a date to a picnic table at school, you have to at least make sure it looks nice. Did you bring the limes? They never include enough, in my opinion."

I tossed them to him and he cut them open with a pocketknife. "May I?" he said.

"Please."

He juiced them then handed me a taco and watched as I took a bite. He was right, it was incredible: a tangy crunch giving way to a tender bite of charred deliciousness, followed by the sweet taste of grilled pineapple.

"You like it?" he asked.

I licked the corner of my mouth. "I love it."

He looked pleased.

"Check it out," he said, and wiped a bit of dust off a metal nameplate on the picnic table. Location of Original Farm-house, 1925.

"This whole place used to be an almond farm," he said. "This was where the farmhouse first stood."

I gazed at the yellow grass swaying around us. The sun filtered through the eucalyptus leaves, making Mast's face glimmer in the light.

"Can you imagine?" he said. "This whole place, just almond trees."

I could almost picture it, a worn wooden farmhouse surrounded by rows and rows of trees.

Sitting there next to him, I felt time compress, as if the past, present, and future were all happening at once, layered together to create this one perfect moment. I felt then that I had known Mast for a long time, that I'd always known him and always would.

I watched the last rays of sun dapple his face and felt like it was all too good to be true.

"What?" he said, glancing at me.

"Nothing," I said. "I just can't believe I'm really here. I'm really in California."

"Why can't you believe it?"

"I've just wanted to come here my whole life. I never thought I'd actually be able to do it."

"You do realize people come to California all the time. All it takes is a plane ticket." He gave me a teasing look.

I nudged him. "I mean coming to the Foundry. Being part of it."

"I know. I'm just giving you a hard time."

"You're from here. You grew up surrounded by tech people. It's normal to you. It wasn't like that for me. This place felt unreachable."

"What makes you think I didn't grow up wondering if I would ever make it to Woolster, Massachusetts?"

"Worcester," I corrected with a grin. "There is no Woolster. But okay, sorry, I shouldn't make assumptions."

The sun was setting and the sky was saturated with pinks and purples.

"So is this what you do with all your first dates?" I asked. I'd meant for it to sound like a joke, but it came out sounding awkward and insecure.

"No," Mast said, taking a bite of his taco. "Just you."

I wasn't sure what to say then, now that we were being serious. He must have sensed how I was feeling, because he leaned over and bumped his shoulder to mine. "Though I've always wanted to share a lime with someone."

I blushed. It was something I could imagine ObjectPermanence saying.

"I like how undiscovered this part of campus is," I said. "Sometimes it feels like with the internet, there isn't anything left undiscovered."

"People are still undiscovered," Mast said. "I've never met anyone like you, for example."

"Haven't you heard? I've been discovered, too."

"I don't think a person can ever be truly discovered."

My breath caught in my throat. ObjectPermanence had said something almost identical in his last message to me. It couldn't be a coincidence.

There was a chill in the air when I turned to Mast. He looked beautiful then, his face lit up by the last rays of the sun.

"Sometimes it feels like I've known you forever," I said.

"It's strange, isn't it?"

His eyes searched mine like he could look at me for hours and still find more to see. I inched my hand toward his and touched his fingers.

"It's you," I whispered, still unable to believe that I had found him and he was just as perfect as I'd imagined, and though I wasn't sure he had any idea what I was talking about, he leaned toward me and gave me a sloppy kiss, half full of taco, his mouth warm and sticky and sweet. And for a moment I wasn't thinking about school or Mitzy; I was there with Mast, feeling his fingers lace through mine as we watched the sun drop behind the trees.

## seventeen

**When I made** it back to my room, I flung the door shut and collapsed in my bed, grinning like an idiot. I should have gone to bed, but instead opened my laptop and read all of ObjectPermanence's messages as if they were from Mast. It felt so natural. I could almost hear his voice reading the messages to me. I closed the window and curled up in bed, imagining the glow of the computer illuminating Mast's face in the dark as he reached through the screen and touched my hand.

■ ■ ■

"You're looking awfully buoyant today."

Mitzy was sitting next to me in a white leather armchair while a woman crouched over her toes. We were in a luxury spa called Epiphany, where Mitzy had a standing reservation for a massage twice a week. It was her third appointment this week, this time for a mani-pedi, which she insisted I join.

"The last few weeks have just been really good," I said. I'd mentioned Mast to her once, but she didn't seem interested. Men were of little importance to her—they were accessories that she could swap when they suited her outfit—and boys were of no importance at all.

"Don't tell me it's about a joystick," Mitzy said.

"Partially a joystick," I admitted. "But also just everything. It feels like my life is finally coming together."

The aesthetician who was massaging my feet glanced up at me and gave me a serene smile. It was my first pedicure and though I'd initially thought it would be weird to have someone slough the skin off my feet, I was actually enjoying myself.

It felt nice to walk into the salon and have the receptionist offer me tea and a steamed washcloth to "refresh" myself with. I liked how sweet the room smelled, like vanilla-scented flowers. I liked the vaguely Celtic music playing in the background and how it immediately calmed me, making me feel like everything was going to be taken care of. I liked the wall of nail polish and how it glimmered in the light. I liked how everyone smiled at me and asked if I needed anything, like I was important, like I was an honored guest. I could get used to being treated that way.

Mitzy nudged me, interrupting my thoughts. "Do you prefer pearl or ivory?"

She held up her phone, which had two different color squares on it that looked virtually the same.

"The one on the right, I guess?"

"Pearl. Me too."

"Give me your Vault."

"Why?"

"You'll see."

"See what?"

"Just trust me."

My instincts told me not to share my Vault account with anyone, but Mitzy was looking at me so impatiently, like my Vault was actually hers that she had kindly lent to me, that I couldn't bring myself to say no. Besides, she'd already put so much time and effort into supporting me. Why should I assume the worst now? She was rich; she didn't need my money. I handed it to her reluctantly and watched as she typed the account number into her phone.

I was seeing Mitzy pretty frequently then. Lunches, coffees, dinners where we met to ostensibly talk about plans for Wiser, though so far we'd only gotten as far as planning "my brand." None of the meetings she'd mentioned at the Warbler's Room had materialized, either, but that was okay. These things took time.

She would text me, usually in the morning, and ask me if I could meet to talk business.

>It's important, she'd say, which I'd come to learn meant that she was bored and wanted company.

>I have class!, I'd write.

>Screw class. Did class boost your stock or did I?

She had a point. Plus, I didn't really mind. I liked having meetings; it made me feel legitimate and important. Mitzy always picked expensive restaurants where we'd be seen and could see others. It was an integral part of creating a "Founder's Aura," she'd said. If people thought I was Founder, I'd more easily become one. I paid with my Vault account and tried not to look at the receipts too closely. They were business expenses, after all, and that was what the Vault money was for.

"So is this joystick cute?" Mitzy asked while her pedicurist applied a second coat of cherry-red polish.

"Pretty cute." I tried not to blush.

"Where'd you pick him up? The mall?"

"He's at the Foundry."

"A programming joystick," Mitzy said, impressed. "Be careful of those. They're still competition."

"It's not like that."

Mitzy raised an eyebrow. "Joysticks are for fun *only*. Remember that and you'll be fine."

I wanted to tell her about ObjectPermanence and how it made Mast different, but how could I tell her that I was in love with my online pen pal, whom I was pretty sure I'd finally met in person, without sounding naïve and ridiculous?

At the counter, Mitzy grabbed two tubes of fancy lotion, one light blue and one lilac, and a pink vial of some kind of serum—all so beautifully packaged that they looked too pretty to use.

"These, too," Mitzy said, handing them to her.

"They're miracle products," Mitzy said to me. "You'll thank me when you're thirty."

I handed over my Vault, and the woman at the counter smiled before wrapping them in tissue paper and tucking them away in a fancy bag. They looked like perfect little gems. I had never bought anything like them before, and though I knew they were frivolous, I couldn't help but feel a little thrill when the receptionist handed me the bag.

■ ■ ■

SENT MESSAGE FROM u/ARRAYOFLIGHT:
Please don't ever regret sending a message to me. Drunk or not, I like hearing from you. Sometimes I wonder if it's because we'll never meet that we can talk the way we do. Maybe if we met in real life it wouldn't be the same. Or maybe it would be . . .

I decided not to leave school and things are actually going really well. I haven't told you this, but there's someone at school who reminds me of you. You're both so similar that sometimes I wonder if he is you.

I have a proposition. The next time I'm with "you," I'll trace the letter A for my username on the back of your hand to let you know it's me, and if it's you, then trace the letter O for ObjectPermanence back to me. What do you think?

I clicked send before I could change my mind. Then waited.

A week passed. I checked BitBop every morning to see if he responded, but every day my inbox was empty. Had I been too bold? Had I offended him by inching my toe across our invisible boundary? Or maybe he didn't really want to meet me in person. Maybe I had misconstrued our entire relationship.

"Is everything okay?" Mast said, interrupting my worry spiral.

We were doing our homework together in a coffee shop in downtown Palo Alto, though I had barely made any progress.

"Yeah," I said, wondering what I had done to betray myself. "Why?"

"You're just checking your phone a lot," Mast said.

"I'm just waiting for something from Mitzy," I said. "She said she was sending me some ideas." It was a two-part lie, as Mitzy and I rarely talked about Wiser anymore. In fact, she'd never really offered any ideas about programming. Our meetings were mostly about building my personal brand, which we did by posting pictures of us at restaurants and boutiques and spas.

"Ideas for Wiser? Is she your business partner now or something?"

"Not exactly. More like a mentor."

"Oh."

"What? Why are you making that face?" I asked him.

"What face?" he said. "This is just how I look."

I bit my lip.

"Are you sure everything's okay?" he said.

"Yeah," I said, forcing a smile. "I'm just in a funk."

"Don't you think it's a little rude of her? I mean, you're skipping a lot of classes to go have lunch with her."

"I'm not skipping that many classes," I said. "And every time I meet with her my stock goes up."

"Yeah, but stock isn't the only thing that matters."

"I know that," I said. We were fighting? Was this our first fight?

As if reading my thoughts, Mast softened his expression. "Look, I'm sorry. I'm not trying to make you feel bad. It just seems like she's being a little selfish with your time."

"She's trying to help me," I said. "Without her, I'd probably have the lowest stock in the class."

"That's not true," Mast said.

He meant it as a compliment. I should have taken it as one and been happy, but I knew he was wrong. The fact that he had so much faith in my abilities reminded me that he didn't really know me. I couldn't tell him that I almost left the Foundry and went home, or that my grades alone weren't good enough to buoy my stock. He'd spent years orbiting the tech world, going to tech fairs and programming camps and taking summer coding classes. He didn't know what it was like to come to a place like the Foundry and start from scratch.

It didn't help that I was starting to wonder if he really was ObjectPermanence. He hadn't been acting like someone who had gotten an extremely important message and was weighing what to do. I tried to convince myself that maybe he was pretending to be oblivious because he didn't want to draw too much attention to the fact that he was talking to someone online, but that didn't make sense. If he had any inkling that I could be ArrayOfLight, wouldn't he have responded and drawn an *O* on my wrist, just to see?

He turned back to his laptop and I turned back to mine only to discover I had a new message in my inbox from ObjectPermanence. I angled my computer away from Mast, then held my breath and opened it.

New message from u/ObjectPermanence:
O.

It was an invitation. An agreement. A hand reaching through the screen and touching mine. Still, my heart sank. The timestamp read four fifteen, which was five minutes ago. There was no way Mast could have sent it.

Still, I needed to try. Should I do it now? Should I wait? If Amina were there, she would tell me to do it and get it over with.

Nervous, I reached over and touched his hand, which was busy typing. He stopped and watched as I drew the letter *A* on the inside of his palm.

He stared at me blankly, then smiled.

"What was that?" he asked.

The room around us began to crumble.

"The letter *A*," I said, steadying my voice.

He gave me a confused smile. "Why *A*?"

*A* for Anyone.

*A* for Agony.

*A* for Always wrong.

*A* for Abject failure.

*A* for Amina was right.

"No reason," I said miserably.

He squeezed my hand then turned back to his computer, but I could do no such thing. I sat frozen in my seat, feeling all of the molecules in the room rearrange themselves. The room around us looked the same yet felt inexplicably different, like everything I had once perceived as real was now in question. What did I know about anything?

It wasn't him.

But if ObjectPermanence wasn't Mast, then who was he?

## eighteen

I'd expected Amina to gloat and say she'd told me so, but when I showed up at her door holding her list in my hand, she took one look at my face and said, "I'm sorry. I wish I'd been wrong."

"What am I supposed to do now?" I said, collapsing into her bed.

"What do you want to do?"

"Find out who he is."

I'd assumed Amina would pull out her notebook and start going through our list again, but instead she hesitated.

"I totally get that. But do you really have to? I know it sounds unthinkable, but just hear me out. You like Mast, right?"

"Yeah."

"You like him a lot."

"Well, yeah. I mean, I did think he was Object-Permanence, so I'm not sure how much is me superimposing another person on top of him, but yeah."

"And you aren't interested in anyone else at school."

"No."

"So why don't you just not find out?"

"And stop talking to ObjectPermanence?" I said, incredulous. It felt impossible, like deciding to stop breathing.

"Well, yeah. If you like Mast, why fix what isn't broken?"

The problem wasn't with her argument, which, in theory, was correct. The problem was me. "I can't. I need to know."

Amina sighed as if she'd anticipated my answer. "And when you figure out who it is—what will you do then?"

I leaned against the wall and stared at the ceiling, wondering how I'd gotten myself into such a mess.

"It depends on who he is. You know how in programming there are conditional If / Then statements? They tell a computer, *if A happens, then do B*, and *if C happens, then do D*. I guess that's how I'm thinking about it."

"So you want to keep Mast around so if ObjectPermanence turns out to be someone awful, then you'll choose Mast, but if he turns out to be the boy of your dreams, then you'll choose him?"

"No—not exactly," I stammered, but if I was honest, that was exactly what I wanted. "When you put it that way, it sounds terrible."

Amina shrugged. "You want it both ways."

Why did she always have to be right?

The truth was, I was less worried about what I would do then, and more worried about what I was supposed to do now. I didn't want to lie to Mast, but I also didn't want to break up with him. I stared at her ceiling and considered what to do.

"What if I just try to keep my distance from Mast? Just be really busy. Then it won't feel like I'm lying to him. And it's not untrue—I am busy. I'm really behind on my assignments and I have all these plans with Mitzy. It would just be until I figure out who ObjectPermanence is."

I could tell Amina wasn't sold on my plan. "What if it takes you longer than you think to figure out who he is?"

"There are only four possibilities," I said. "How long could it take?"

When I got back to my room, I pulled out the list we'd compiled together.

I crossed Mast off quickly, like ripping off a Band-Aid, then surveyed who was left.

**Mike Flores**
**AJ Pierce**
**Arun Krishna**
**Arthur Kim**

I stared at the names, as if the answer would appear to me if I looked at them long enough. When it didn't, I slid it back into my desk drawer.

■ ■ ■

The rest of the week passed like an ellipsis, one day folding into the next without distinction or fanfare. When I saw

Mast in the dining hall or in class, I tried to act as if everything was normal before ducking away with the excuse that I needed to study.

Could it be Arun, with his expensive clothes and his confident, baritone voice that seemed to carry over the room, every aspect of him louder and bigger than everyone else, as though he was amplified by his money? It was hard to imagine him having any of the compassion or insight that ObjectPermanence had, but maybe behind his sleek haircut and designer shoes was a vulnerable person invested in the human condition.

Or was it Arthur, always laughing in the back of the classroom while he shared memes he'd made? He seemed to be the best of my options. Though he was self-deprecating, I could tell he was smart, always finishing his work before everyone else and spending the rest of the class playing games on his phone. I'd always pictured ObjectPermanence as slightly more serious and introspective, but Arthur did seem kind. If I closed my eyes, I could almost imagine him writing the messages ObjectPermanence had sent.

Or was it Mike, a handsome coward, his arm wrapped around Kate while he listened to his friends boast about their stock and rate girls online? I didn't know if Mike was as terrible as his friends, but in the end, it didn't really matter. He had the quiet aloofness of a complicit bystander, watching his friends with mild distaste but rarely disagreeing with them or trying to intervene. He'd been bestowed with beauty, money, and social status, and seemed to be caged by them. Was he witty enough to be ObjectPermanence? I'd rarely seen him laugh, let alone say anything that could be construed as even mildly funny. He seemed too constricted by his good looks and his social position to ever allow himself to talk so candidly with a stranger online.

Or, heaven forbid, was it AJ? Cruel, unbearable AJ, smirking from his desk while he degraded others in an attempt to make himself feel important. I wasn't sure which was worse—that he thought his money would protect him from consequence, or the fact that so far, he'd been right. I refused to even consider him a possibility. It was an insult to ObjectPermanence and everything I thought I knew about him.

"Is everything okay?"

Mast was staring at me as though he'd asked me a question. We'd run into each other in the dining hall while Amina and I were clearing our trays.

"What? Yes."

"Yes, everything's okay, or yes to Sunday?"

Sunday. Right. He'd asked me if I wanted to go to a screening of the 1984 classic *Dune*, which was playing at the Stanford Theatre. Though I'd planned on keeping some distance between me and Mast while I tried to figure out who ObjectPermanence was, it was harder than I'd expected. It was tricky trying to come up with believable excuses as to why I couldn't hang out. But the real problem was that I wanted to see him. A movie would probably be okay. How much could I betray while sitting in a dark theater, staring at a screen?

"Sunday. Yeah, I'd love to."

Mast was studying me like he could read my thoughts. "Are you sure everything's okay?"

"Everything's fine," I said. "I'm just distracted by the Kowalski assignment."

"It's a tough one, isn't it?"

I nodded, feeling like a miserable lying liar.

Before I could change the subject, my phone vibrated with a text from Mitzy.

>Clear up your Sunday night and put on your best suit

>What? Why?

>We have plans.

>Can we do another night?

>Definitely not. There's a VC dinner party that you need to come to. This could be your breakthrough.

Maybe it was convenient, a good excuse to skip another potential mind-reading session with Mast.

"Actually, do you mind if I take a raincheck for the movie?" I asked him. "Mitzy wants me to meet with some VCs."

A look of surprise flashed over Mast's face, but he quickly hid it. "VCs? Sounds fancy."

I could tell he was hurt. I swallowed, feeling guilty. "It could be my big break."

"Well, you can't turn that down."

I wasn't sure if he was being sincere or sarcastic. "Right."

"It's fine," he said. "I've already seen *Dune* and I have a lot of work to do. I just thought you'd like it."

"Some other time," I said, wondering what I was doing, turning away from a cute boy who seemed to like me more than anyone ever had.

I squeezed my laptop to my chest as if it were armor that would prevent him from seeing the workings of my heart.

When we got to class, Ms. Perez was already there, the back of her pencil skirt trembling as she wrote our names on the board. She had broken us into small groups to workshop our venture capital pitches.

We had a big mock pitch meeting coming up the following week, where retired venture capitalists came to class and listened to our ideas. I scanned the names until I saw mine, next to Micah and Arthur.

"The point of this exercise is to give hard critiques," Ms. Perez said, pacing the front of the room. "Each of you will take turns pitching, while the other two role-play as VCs and ask tough questions."

I took a seat next to Micah and watched as Arthur dropped his bag next to me and sat down. I glanced at him and felt suddenly nervous. I could, at that very moment, be sitting next to ObjectPermanence. The thought was paralyzing.

Arthur volunteered to pitch first. "So, who's going to be the silver fox and who's going to be the young juice-cleansed rock climber?" he asked with a grin.

I tried to imagine him reading ObjectPermanence's

messages out loud, but they didn't sound right in his voice.

"Juice cleanse," Micah said.

"I guess that makes me the silver fox," I said.

"How does it feel having four ex-wives, a collection of luxury sports cars, and a vacation house in Big Sur?" Arthur joked.

"You know, it honestly doesn't feel that different from when I was a twentysomething, eating instant ramen and sleeping on a futon," I said, trying to get into the role. "Wealth is a mindset."

Arthur let out a satisfying laugh. It was convenient that I was playing a role, because it allowed me to watch him. He wasn't bad looking. On the contrary, the longer I looked at him, the more endearing he seemed. He had a sincere face, the kind that was inclined to smile. It was tanned from hours of skateboarding outside, and his loose T-shirt and messenger bag studded with pins made him look goofy, like a proper teenager. I didn't mind how his eyes glinted when he smiled, or the way his left hand was stained with ink from doodling.

His pitch itself was surprisingly smart. I'd expected it to be juvenile and sloppy; it only seemed fitting for his Truth or Dare app, Dare Me. But three sentences in, he'd already convinced me to invest in it.

"In the age of façades and influencers and manufactured content, we at Dare Me are trying to break down social barriers. We want to move relationships from the digital world to the physical world. The idea behind Dare Me is to take randomized interactions and make them fun, unexpected, and unprecedentedly intimate, which allows for more human connection."

It was the first time I'd seen Arthur as a founder, and I was surprised by how funny and charming he was. I quickly found myself forgetting that Dare Me was essentially a drinking game, and had started to believe that it was a revolutionary way of reinventing the way people related to each other.

He then told a story about how he didn't have a good relationship with his parents and couldn't connect with them. They were Korean immigrants and had a different emotional vocabulary than Arthur, making it hard for him to talk to them about things that really mattered to him. He'd thought that if he could just find a way to get them to open up and share stories with him, he could bridge the cultural gap, which was how he'd gotten the idea for Dare Me.

When he was finished, Micah started asking questions about his userbase and how he planned on appealing to new audiences, but I barely paid attention. ObjectPermanence had also talked about how he wasn't close with his father, and how his family had expectations that he could never meet.

There was a long pause in conversation and both Arthur and Micah turned to me, waiting for me to say something. I glanced down at my laptop, where I'd typed up a few questions from Ms. Perez's lectures that I'd thought would be useful to ask, but now that I was potentially sitting across from ObjectPermanence, they didn't seem relevant. Discarding them, I turned to Arthur. Though I knew he was acting as though I were a venture capitalist, I couldn't help but wonder if this was what it would feel like to look Object-Permanence in the eye and say hello for the first time.

"What—what kind of music do you like to listen to when you're programming?" I asked.

Micah snorted. "What kind of question is that?"

"I just think that a silver-foxed VC might ask a curve-ball question like that," I stammered. "Old men love talking about music and sounding cool."

"She's not wrong," Arthur said.

Micah didn't look convinced. "Whatever."

"I like EDM," Arthur said. "But I also like movie soundtracks. Classical stuff, even. Anything instrumental with a good beat."

Classical. Movie soundtracks. My heart almost stopped. "Me too," I said. "I mean, right. Good."

I scrambled to think of another question that I could ask a potential ObjectPermanence. How was I not prepared for this?

"What kind of work culture do you plan on cultivating when you build your team? Do you believe that you can ever really know someone?"

Micah let out a resentful laugh. "What kind of woo-woo question is that?"

"Hey, I thought you were on a juice cleanse," I shot back. "Don't you think that's a little woo-woo?"

Arthur laughed. He had a nice voice. "You know, that's a good question," he said. "I think the premise behind Dare

Me is that there's always more to know about someone."

I swallowed. Was it possible? Arthur was looking at me, amused, like we were in on a secret that Micah wasn't. Maybe we were.

When it was my turn, I gave the pitch I'd been practicing for Mitzy, then braced myself for questioning.

Micah was hard on me. "How are you going to convince people to let the app access all of their data?"

I tried my best to answer, but he kept pressing me. "Don't you think that's a huge breach of privacy? Are you going to use it to sell products? How are you going to generate revenue?"

By the time he was finished, I was pressed against the back of my chair, feeling smaller and more irrelevant than I'd felt before. I turned to Arthur.

To my surprise, he only shrugged. "You know, I think it's a really cool idea. I don't know. I'd buy it. Who doesn't want someone to tell them what to do? Isn't that the entire point of the internet?"

I wasn't sure if he was saying it to be nice or if he really believed it, but either way I felt relieved. When class was over, Arthur caught up with me in the hallway.

"Hey," he said. "I really liked your pitch."

"Thanks. I liked yours, too."

"I think Micah was being too harsh. I wouldn't let him get under your skin. He's just jealous that his app isn't as good as yours."

"Thanks," I said. "You know, my mom's an immigrant,

too, so I know what you meant when you were talking about your parents."

"Oh, yeah. I mean, it's true—that's how they are—but it wasn't how I came up with Dare Me. I just use it because it's a good story. You know?"

"Oh," I said, mildly disappointed. He'd sold it so well that I'd thought maybe he was like me, making an app to fill a void in his life. "Right. Yeah, me too."

Arthur gave me a knowing nod. "Cool, well, see you around."

"See you around," I said.

# ·········nineteen·········

The sun was setting on Sunday night when the Foundry car dropped me off in front of a stone wall overgrown with a blushing bougainvillea, just a few streets away from downtown Palo Alto. Behind it stood a gray shingled mansion shaded by willows. Had I not known where I was, I might have assumed it was a historic hotel or the main building of a country club.

Despite the time we'd spent together, I'd never been to Mitzy's home. It almost felt like she didn't have a home and instead sprung from a golden-rimmed cloud every morning, fully showered and dressed, so to be there in person was surreal. I buzzed the gate and waited until it opened to a velvety lawn manicured with rose bushes and fruit trees. A stone walkway led to the front door, where a cascade of blushing vines flowed over a trellis.

"Come in," Mitzy called through a window. "It's unlocked."

It was surprisingly messy inside. Though the house was beautiful—airy and bright, with lovingly maintained historical detail—it was strangely lacking furniture, save for a few random pieces here and there, which were covered in papers and dirty dishes and clothes.

Mitzy breezed in from the hallway holding a cup of green juice. "Sorry for the mess. The cleaners were supposed to come a few days ago, but they bailed. It's so hard to find good people these days."

She looked me up and down. "Good," she said, clearly pleased with my outfit choice, then handed me the cup, which I stared at suspiciously.

"I had my blood processed by that new wellness test company and it turns out I'm deficient in folate, so I'm trying to eat more greens," Mitzy said, nodding to the drink. "It's good for your skin. Try it."

I took a sip and eyed a sculpture in the corner of the room. It looked like a naked woman eating the throat of a wild boar. I lingered on it, mildly disturbed, then forced myself to turn back to Mitzy.

"So where exactly are we going tonight?" I asked, glancing at a few stray papers on her counter, all printed on the same fancy legal letterhead. They looked official and important.

To my surprise, when Mitzy saw me looking at them, her face darkened and she grabbed them. "Those are trash," she said and balled them up and threw them in the bin.

"Sorry, I didn't mean to look at your mail."

"Then don't," she said, in a tone that I'd never heard her use before.

I must have looked surprised, because her face softened. "Sorry," she said. "I'm just so used to people stealing my ideas. It's a knee-jerk reaction. I need to work on it."

I swallowed. It made sense, though I was still startled by how quickly her mood had changed. "That's okay."

"So you asked where we're going," she said, a conspiratorial glint in her eye. "To a dinner party hosted by Einar Karlsson, co-founder of Karlsson Barrow, one of the most powerful venture capital firms on Sand Hill."

Sand Hill was a road in Menlo Park, gilded with parched, golden grass on either side. All of the venture capital companies were there, their sleek signs perched on the side of the road, reflecting the sun. Amina and I had driven down it once, imagining what the offices inside looked like.

"What's that?" Mitzy said, nodding to a leather folder I was holding in one arm.

"It's my business plan. I did it for class. I thought it would be helpful."

Mitzy laughed. "No one cares about that."

She slipped the papers out of the folder, crumped them up, and tossed them at the waste bin. She missed by an inch, and they sat on the floor amid the discarded mail. I wondered what they were.

"Business plans are for people with mediocre ideas who need to use paper to trick people into thinking that their idea is good. You, on the other hand, have a good idea. All you need," she said, pointing to my phone, "is this."

She led me upstairs where she finished getting ready. Her bedroom was messy, too, with clothes strewn about the floor—the room of someone who clearly didn't have to clean up after herself.

"Why don't you have any furniture?" I murmured, gazing at the vast empty room, which was adorned with just a bed and chandelier.

"I had some, but I sold most of it," Mitzy said, powdering her face. "It was feeling a little stale. I want to redecorate but I haven't decided on the style yet."

Mitzy put the final touches on her makeup and turned to me. "Before we go, I wanted to talk to about our relationship."

The thing about Mitzy was that she had the uncanny ability to slip business into seemingly casual conversation so that you barely realized you were agreeing to invite her to give a keynote address or nominate her for a board position until after it was done. I'd watched her do it when she ran into acquaintances at lunches and dinners, and it both impressed and unnerved me to see how she managed to lure them in and extract what she wanted before they realized what was happening.

Now I wondered if she was doing the same to me, only with bad news.

I swallowed. This was it. We'd had a good run, but she was growing tired of me and was going to cut me loose. I braced myself.

She searched through the things on the table until she found a stack of papers, which she handed to me.

I'd expected her to break the news gently in her typical Mitzy way, but I wasn't expecting there to be paperwork. "What is this?"

"I let it slip to my lawyers that I was taking you to funding meetings, and they told me I needed to protect myself. They suggested I draw up a contract to make sure I'm a founding associate if you happen to get funding through a deal I broker. I know that founding associate sounds like a shift in power, but it really just means that I'm serving as your mentor and that I'll be using my connections to help give you an initial boost. I wouldn't get a salary unless we agreed upon it at a later date, and it would still be your company. You can terminate our relationship at any time, and if you later decide that I should get a percentage, we can update the contract."

I must have looked stunned, because Mitzy studied me with a concerned look. "My lawyers didn't love that last part—they really wanted to negotiate a percentage from the get-go, but I don't need the money and it felt a little weird talking about my cut before we went out to see anyone."

I knew I should be attempting to read the papers she'd handed me, but I was too overwhelmed to focus on them. The words kept blurring together.

"So what do you think?" Mitzy ventured.

"Are you asking if you can be a part of my company?"

"Well, yeah, I guess. I mean, it's not really a company yet, it's just a partnership—"

"Yes!" I said, cutting her off. "It's only been my dream since I was ten years old."

She beamed. "Great. Take it home, read through it, see what you think. Just don't tell my lawyers I took you to this meeting before you signed it. They'll think I'm a pushover."

I grinned. "Okay."

Mitzy cleared the remaining papers off her coffee table and replaced them with a few fancy candles from her mantel, her laptop, and a pile of random papers, which she arranged, then rearranged in a stylish stack.

"I have to stay on-brand," she said, and held her phone out to take a photo of us on the couch, staged so that it looked like we were having a much more serious business meeting. "Give me your best game face."

I dug through my bag to find my phone and took one, too.

"Okay," she said, packing up. "Let's go show them who you are."

■ ■ ■

This is what I remember about the party. I remember riding in Mitzy's red sports car up Sand Hill Road and parking in front of a modern glass building. It had a bubbling water wall out front despite the drought, signaling that the rules of nature and weather did not apply. I remember taking pictures for Amina as I followed Mitzy inside, knowing that she would demand photos when I told her where I'd been. I remember walking into the room, which was full of men, and feeling so nervous that sweat beaded on my lip. I remember how Mitzy lit up, her presence drawing everyone to her.

I remember her handing me a drink, something bubbly and bitter, which I drank quickly because I wanted to occupy myself while she left to go work the room. I remember Einar Karlsson, our charming, silver-haired host, who looked like an aging movie star and was delighted to discover that I was at the Foundry. I remember showing him Wiser, and him marveling at how well she worked, and bringing other guests over so I could demonstrate it for them, too. I remember him handing me another glass of something bubbly, which I drank while staring at the photographs of atomic bombs exploding into mushroom clouds lining the walls.

I remember Mitzy nodding to the different guests and whispering in my ear, "That one with the big jaw is Art Shifrinson of Fairbow Ventures. That young one, kind of hippieish, is Mickey Lerner from MediVC, really powerful, hard to win over. Those two by the punch work for Garlin Security. They contract for the military."

Another drink. Then another, until they stopped tasting bitter and started tasting neutral, like water. Until I was laughing and talking freely about the Foundry and Wiser with three men named Dennis and Fred and Tom, or were they Mitch and Ted and Tim? I couldn't remember. The only mention of my age was them marveling at how much of a prodigy I was, at how mature I seemed.

I remember seeing one of the older VCs grab Mitzy's ass through her dress, and her casually slide his arm off. I remember the smell of the men as they leaned toward me, laughing, grinning, baring their teeth, staring down at my chest, staring down at my legs, their cologne sweet and pungent like the smoke from a cigar. I remember a younger VC, a guy who might have looked cute had the room not been spinning, had his face not been blurred into a mush, put his hand on my thigh and ask me what Wiser would say if I asked her if I should go outside and get some air with an older guy. I remember stammering, saying I had to use the bathroom, and trying to remain calm as I slipped through the crowd. I remember thinking about Mast and wondering what he was doing that night. I remember opening the bathroom door only to find Lars Lang and a bunch of other men inside, snorting white powder off a manila folder on the sink. It must have been the wrong bathroom, and I backed away, wishing I was at the movie with Mast, feeling his leg against mine as we sat together in a dark room.

I remember looking for Mitzy only to find her in a conference room with a few guys, cutting what looked like emoji stickers from a piece of paper. I remember her giving me one, telling me it would make me smile if I put it under my tongue.

I remember her mocking me for hesitating. I remember their laughter, how it seemed to fill the room, pushing me out into the shadows where it was cold and lonely. I remember taking the emoji and slipping it under my tongue, and how pleased Mitzy looked, how good it felt to make her happy.

I remember talking to the guys next to me, and laughing because they were all named Josh. The longer I sat there, the more they seemed to refract upon each other, a series of mirrors, Josh upon Josh upon Josh. I remember the table beneath me getting soft like taffy, the chairs slumping over like wilted flowers. Someone turned off the lights and projected a PowerPoint presentation onto the wall: something with graphs and pivot tables. It was dark in the room, and Mitzy was laughing and touching one of the Josh's arms. A Josh leaned toward me, touched my leg, asked me if I wanted to see his office.

I remember trying to focus on Josh's face, but it refused to materialize and remained a fleshy, featureless mass. I thought of ObjectPermanence and the photographs of the atomic bombs hanging in the lobby and felt suddenly like they were a portrait of my internal life, a snapshot of destruction, frozen in time. ObjectPermanence. Mast.

I didn't remember leaving the party or going home, only that I found myself in bed with a Vilbo-branded water bottle of unknown ownership, and a light feeling that everything would be okay as long as I spoke my truth.

■ ■ ■

The next morning I woke up to a throbbing headache. The sun was too bright. My face felt fuzzy, like it was filled with cotton, and my mouth was so parched I could barely speak. I winced and patted my nightstand until I felt a glass of water of unknown vintage. It tasted dusty, and I tried to remember the last time I'd filled a cup and left it there. Two days ago? Maybe three?

I drank it all and reached for my phone when I noticed the box of pizza on my desk. When had I ordered pizza? I stumbled out of bed only to find a stranger's coat strewn on the floor by my computer. It was a wool coat, navy, far too big to be mine or Mitzy's. It looked like it belonged to a man.

Had someone come home with me the night before? No, impossible. I would have remembered. Had I worn the coat home? Possibly, though I had no idea who it belonged to. I thought of the Joshes, faceless, all wearing the same tech uniform of twill pants, a gray T-shirt, and white tennis sneakers. Were their names even Josh?

I searched the remaining pockets of the coat but only found a few peppermint candies and a crumpled receipt from a coffee shop with no identifying information. I thought back to the night before, trying to piece together what had happened, but it was hard to decipher what was a dream and what was reality. I knew I had taken something from Mitzy in the conference room, some kind of smiling sticker, and after that the night had turned into a bizarre dreamscape. Had I gone to one of the Josh's offices? The thought made me shudder. I vaguely recalled throwing up in an office trash can. Then somehow I had gotten home with this strange coat. I must have ordered pizza, though I couldn't remember.

I took out my phone to ask Mitzy when I noticed the time—1:45 p.m.—which meant I had slept through half of my classes. Inside the box of pizza were three congealed slices of pepper and olive. I took a bite, hoping it would make me feel better, followed it with an Advil, then dressed and got ready to face the day.

"Where have you been?" Amina whispered when I sat

down next to her. "Are you okay?"

"I'm fine. I was just sleeping."

Amina snorted as if she knew as much. "That's good at least, after the night you had."

I felt all the blood drain from my face. How did she know about my night?

"Did you drop acid?"

I blinked, feeling suddenly dizzy. Mitzy in the conference room. The smiling stickers. The way the table and chairs had gone mushy. The faceless Joshes and their extra-dimensional PowerPoint presentation. So that was what had happened. "I—um—I'm not sure. How did you know?"

"You didn't see them yet?"

I could feel myself flattening into a two-dimensional being. "See what?"

"Check Façade."

I wanted to fold myself up, making myself smaller and smaller, until I was just a speck on the floor. Then I'd fold myself again, get even smaller. Infinite divisibility. There was no end to how tiny I could get.

I must have looked like I was going to throw up, because she added, "Don't worry, at least your stock went up."

My heart was racing. What did she mean by *at least*?

Mast was sitting by the window, his face glued to the board as though he was purposely not looking at me. His refusal to look, even though he must have noticed me enter the classroom, was more of an indictment than anything Amina had told me.

I didn't bother to ask Kowalski if I could leave. Trying not to make a scene, I slipped into the hallway and hurried to the bathroom where I sat in a stall and checked my phone.

The pictures had originally been posted by a guy from Stanford who'd been at the party. They'd been reposted by his friends, and then by ValleyBrag, the anonymous account that posted gossip from the Foundry.

I scrolled through them quickly, scouring them for details about my night and hoping I wouldn't discover, alongside everyone else, that I had gone to "see Josh's office."

Most of the photos weren't of me. There were a bunch of Mitzy, of Einar Karlsson, of the other VCs drinking together. There was one of Lars Lang mixing drinks on the patio—a much more flattering context than the one I'd seen when I'd walked in on him in the bathroom. There were start-up guys throwing ice cubes, playing wiffle ball with empty bottles of Veuve Cliquot. And then there were the ones of me. Me and Mitzy screaming and smiling after being sprayed with an overflowing bottle of champagne. Me and Einar Karlsson, laughing, his hand inching dangerously down the small of my back. Me, leaning through a crowd of start-up guys to be fed an hors d'oeuvre off a platter by a balding VC who looked old enough to be my grandfather.

I winced, remembering flashes of the night before. The way the champagne had sprayed all over my shirt, making it translucent, the start-up guys cheering. The way Einar Karlsson had brushed the back of my neck with his hand, his wedding band cold against my skin. The final photo was of me, lying on a conference table, staring at the fan undulating above me. The caption read: *Macrodosing*.

A lump rose in my stomach, and I leaned over the toilet and heaved, but nothing came up. So this was why Mast hadn't wanted to make eye contact.

In an attempt to make myself feel better, I checked my stock. Amina was right, it was up to an all-time high: twenty-six. I stared at the number, both bewildered and relieved. At least I didn't have to worry about my standing.

When I returned to class, I had a message waiting for me in my inbox from Kowalski. I opened it.

> **See me during office hours.**
> **-S.K.**

I sank into my chair, my head beginning to throb. At the front the room, Kowalski was busy tapping into his computer. If he was thinking about me or my derelict attendance, he didn't let on.

I considered skipping the rest of my classes and spending the rest of the day curled up in bed, but that would only make my absence more obvious. After class, I dawdled by my desk, slowly packing up my things until Mast walked by me.

"Hey," I said to him.

"Hey." He was uncharacteristically quiet, which made me even more worried.

"Mitzy told me it was going to be a meeting," I said. "I

had no idea it was going to be a party."

"Okay," Mast said in a tone that made me think it wasn't actually okay at all.

"The pictures make it look worse than it was. Those guys—I have no idea who they are. I barely talked to any of them."

"That doesn't make it better," he said.

"Nothing happened, I promise. I drank too much and acted like an idiot. That's it."

"There are pictures of you being groped by old men. Of you in a wet, see-through dress while a bunch of guys feed you mini quiches. How is that *nothing*?"

I'd never seen Mast angry before and it startled me. "Mitzy gave me this sticker and told me to put it under my tongue. I didn't know it was acid."

"And you just took it? Without asking what it was?"

"I wasn't thinking. I trusted Mitzy."

"Why? Why do you trust her?"

How had this suddenly become about me and Mitzy? "Why does she bother you so much?" I said, my shame shifting to anger. "You've never even met her and yet you've seemed to hate her from day one."

"I don't hate her. I just don't get why you're bowing down to her like she's your personal savior. And yeah, I don't need to meet her to wonder if she has your best interests at heart. Why does she always ask you to meet during class when she could just as easily ask you to meet at night or on the weekend?"

I couldn't believe what I was hearing. "Because she cares about me and is trying to help me succeed."

"By dropping acid and being groped by strange men?"

"By getting me VC meetings."

"Where are those meetings? Have you actually been to any?"

I wanted to snap back with a smart response, but didn't know what to say because he was right. I hadn't been to any yet.

"Look," I said, trying to compose myself. "The point is that I wasn't acting like myself. I never would have done those things if I'd been sober."

"But you *did* do them. And yeah, you haven't been acting like yourself."

"What's that supposed to mean?"

"I don't know, but something is different. You're skipping class to get pedicures and go shopping, you're more worried about posting photos on Façade than finishing your assignments? Sometimes you check your phone so often that it feels like you're half here, half somewhere else."

I backed away from him, incredulous. "You're jealous. You're upset because I'm doing better than you."

Mast looked at me with disbelief. "Is that what you really think?"

"Do you have a better explanation?"

"If you think I'm trying to bring you down by expressing concern that you're skipping class to hang out at fancy restaurants, then I don't know what to tell you."

"You act like you know me but you don't," I said. "I was right about you the first time. You're not different. You're just like everyone else."

Mast looked at me like I had slapped him in the face. He didn't respond. He didn't say anything. He turned and walked toward the boys' dorm and I forced myself to look away so I wouldn't have to watch him leave.

# twenty

I **wasn't sure if** I wanted to scream or cry. My hands were shaking and I wanted to simultaneously throw something at a wall and curl up in bed until enough time had passed that I'd forget this day and the pit in my stomach and the rising lump in my throat that made the air taste bitter. Instead, I went to the dining hall to get an energy drink between classes. I needed a boost. I was pulling a purple drink from the refrigerator when an arm reached over me and grabbed one.

"I highly recommend the green flavor," Arthur said. He'd gotten a haircut, which made him look cute. "Definitely stay away from the red, it tastes like cough syrup."

I wasn't prepared to see him and felt flustered. "Thanks," I said, and swapped mine for the green.

"Only extremely desperate people drink these things in the afternoon."

"I've had a bad day."

He laughed. "Yeah, I saw the pictures. Did you really do acid?"

To my surprise, his cheerful indifference to my terrible mood made me feel better. "Yeah."

He looked impressed. "I never would have picked you for the type. Pretty cool."

I was embarrassed to admit how good it felt for him to call me cool. "What's my type?"

"I don't know. Law-abiding. Studious."

I let out a sarcastic laugh. I used to think of myself that way, though now I wondered if I really was, considering the number of classes I'd skipped and the small matter of the acid. Was it even worth being law-abiding and studious when the only things that seemed to have helped my stock and my social status were ditching class and partying more?

"What was it like? Did a portal open to an alternate universe? Did you feel super creative and have an epiphany?"

"No portals." I did remember having a revelation with Mitzy on the carpeted floor of the conference room, but what exactly it was I couldn't recall. "It felt like someone boosted the saturation level of the world all the way up. The office was transformed into this lush business paradise with super plush carpets and chairs so comfortable I felt like they were manufactured for my body specifically. The pictures on the walls were so vivid they seemed to move."

"Wow."

"It was great but also kind of terrible. You know when

you drink too much and time compresses and you're not really sure what happened when or for how long, all you can remember is how you felt during that time, and you're not even sure if you can trust that?"

Arthur let out a long exhale. "Sounds intense. But I wouldn't know. I don't drink."

"You don't drink?"

"My dad's an alcoholic. Kind of scarred me."

I froze in place, unable to come up with a response. I thought back to our interaction at the DrinkMaiden party. He'd been drinking water then, though I'd assumed it was just to cut the other drinks. If Arthur didn't drink then he couldn't have written me the message on the night of the DrinkMaiden party saying how drunk he was, which meant that he wasn't ObjectPermanence.

"I'm sorry," I stammered. "I didn't know."

"Oh, it's okay. No one ever knows what to say when I blurt stuff out like that. I kind of like how dumbfounded people look when I spring it on them. It's funny."

I needed to leave, to sit by myself in a quiet room and think. "Well, thanks for the drink recommendation."

Arthur tipped his hat. "Enjoy having the jitters."

I mentally crossed him off my list and made my way toward the study rooms when a man called my name. "Xia."

It was the last person I'd expected to see in the hallway, a bleach-blond ghost from the night before back to haunt me. Lars Lang.

He strode toward me, his pale locks flouncing as he

walked. It was rare to see him around the classrooms. I'd only seen him on campus twice since the Welcome dinner—once speeding around the driveway in his Tesla and a second time pattering down the steps of the main building while talking on the phone and eating an apricot, both him and the fruit glowing in the slanting afternoon light.

I blinked and remembered the night before, when I'd walked into the bathroom only to see him leaning over the bathroom counter, snorting coke off a manila folder with a bunch of strangers. He'd looked up at me, his eyelids red around the rims, his hair sweaty and loose around his face, his expression wild like a cat caught eating the carcass of an animal. Had he recognized me? And if he had, did he remember?

"Hey, Xia, I'm glad I caught you."

I was surprised he knew my name. I'd assumed he'd forgotten or had never learned it, since we hadn't interacted one-on-one since our initial phone call when he'd offered me a spot at the Foundry.

"I've been meaning to check in with you. I have to hop on a quick call in a few, but would you mind meeting me in my office in fifteen or so?"

Check in? What did that mean? I wondered if I was in trouble. I had to be. Why else would the director of the Foundry want to see me privately? "Sure."

He gave me an affable smile. "Great. See you soon."

When I got to Lars's office, the door was locked, and oddly enough, Arun was waiting on a bench outside. I wondered what he was doing there. When he saw me, he scooted over to make room.

"Hey," he said.

"Hey."

It occurred to me then that his name was on my list. If Arthur wasn't ObjectPermanence, could it be Arun?

Of all the people at the Foundry, Arun looked the most like a professional. Tall, generically handsome, well-dressed but not overdressed, with a commanding voice that was ready for television. He had a firm handshake that could crack the knuckles in your fingers, and favored loafers without socks, the true mark of a rich person who could afford to sweat in their shoes at the expense of fashion. I could easily picture him as the CEO of a company. I could imagine magazine profiles calling him likable, because it was hard to find fault in him, but really, as a result of this he always seemed bland, without any unique characteristics beyond being pleasant and amiable.

"How are you holding up?" he asked.

The way he asked it felt intimate, like we were closer friends than I'd known. "I'm fine," I said slowly. "Why?"

"Well, last night you weren't doing so well."

Last night? What did he know about my evening? He must have been referring to the photos. "Oh, it was just a party. The pictures made it look worse than it was."

He gave me a puzzled look, as if I had missed some key component of our conversation.

"Do you have my coat?"

It took me a moment to realize what he was referring to. "That was your coat?"

"Yeah, you don't remember?"

"I—I remember," I said, trying to recall any passing glimpse of Arun, but after the conference room of Joshes, my memories were blurred.

Arun laughed. "It's okay. I've had nights like that, too."

"So you were at the party?"

"Yeah. I showed up halfway through. You were already . . . on the carpet."

I winced. It was only a mildly generous euphemism.

"Don't worry. You didn't do anything that I wouldn't do."

"If that's true, then why are there pictures of me online and none of you?"

He gave me an amused shrug. "Because I'm a guy and no one cares what I do."

"How were you even invited?"

Arun looked at me like it was a dumb question. "Karlsson's a good friend of my dad. He comes to my house; we go to his. I've even been on his yacht."

Classic Arun boasting. "Must be nice," I muttered.

"I've seen nicer yachts."

I rolled my eyes. It was hard for me to imagine him shedding his wealthy persona to write the messages I'd received about wanting to break free from the constraints of his social circle and feeling too much pressure to succeed. Still, a little voice in my mind kept repeating the same line from one of his messages: *I don't know if you'd like me if you met me in person . . . I'm different with you. I'm a better version of myself.*

Maybe Arun was constrained. Maybe being so adjacent to money and success made him feel inadequate. Maybe his father had unrealistic expectations of him.

"What's your dad like?" I asked.

My question seemed to confuse him. "He's global head of operations and strategy at LineCart."

"That's what he *does*. What's he *like*?"

Arun frowned, like he'd never been asked such a thing. "He's a hard worker. He's always working, really."

"Okay, but do you get along? Do you like him?"

Arun looked at me like the answer was obvious. "He's my dad."

"That doesn't mean you have to like him. I love my mom, for example, but she doesn't really *get* me, you know?"

For a moment, his mask of confidence and wealth vanished and he looked at me as though he'd wanted someone to ask him about his father for a long time, but before he could respond, Lars strode down the hallway toward us.

"Come in," Lars said, unlocking his office door and beckoning us to follow him.

His office was sunny and minimally decorated, as though he rarely spent time there. He motioned to two chairs across from his desk, then swiveled in his chair, looking like a college kid goofing around in his professor's office.

"I just wanted to have a check-in with both of you. I know we ran into each other at the Karlsson Barrow party. Let's just say I wasn't wearing my Sunday best."

I glanced at Arun. He must have seen Lars snorting coke in the bathroom, too.

"There's a saying in the start-up world: Everything that can be enhanced should be enhanced," Lars continued. "That includes the human mind. Do you know what I mean?"

It took me a moment to translate. It was an incredibly convoluted way to say that he liked to do mind-enhancing drugs.

Arun nodded vigorously. "Sure," he said, his voice likable and corporate, as though he were in a job interview.

"It's pretty common practice," Lars continued. "Mind enhancement. For creative purposes and for productivity. I know that might be jarring to you, and in the spirit of open dialogue, I wanted to give you the opportunity to bring up any thoughts or questions you might have."

Lars smiled and looked at us expectantly. Did he really want us to ask questions about drug use in the start-up community? The last thing I wanted to do was linger on the party, for fear that it might come out that I, too, hadn't been "wearing my Sunday best."

"I don't have any questions," Arun said, leaning back in his chair as though he were making himself comfortable. "I'm pretty used to this world. My dad always says, what happens in the boardroom stays in the boardroom."

I felt grateful for Arun then, and his fluency in corporate politics.

A look of relief flashed over Lars's face. He rocked in his chair. "Great."

Lars spent the rest of the meeting asking us how we were

liking the Foundry and our classes. I let Arun talk, since he seemed better suited to giving inoffensive answers. Though I was thankful to have someone else take the lead, I couldn't help but notice that neither Lars nor Arun were really saying anything of meaning or value. Their sentences were a jumble of buzz words and corporate speak. *The experience has been transformative. It's integral to connect with innovators who understand the importance of data-driven marketing and dynamic content, considering the ever-evolving consumer base. Our work is to disrupt current markets and shape the present into the future.*

After we left, I turned to Arun. "Did any information get transmitted at all in that meeting, or was it just filler?"

"Filler serves a purpose, you know," Arun said. "It's a way of signaling that you're on the same page. When you start a business, all you really have are ideas. You don't have anything concrete. Filler allows you talk about your ideas when you don't have anything to show for them."

It was the first time I'd heard Arun be even mildly thoughtful. Maybe he wasn't as banal as I'd thought.

"I can't bring myself to do it. My body has a physical reaction when I try."

"I wasn't born with the natural ability to speak corporate. You have to practice. What do you think I've been doing all these years hanging around with my dad's business partners?"

For a moment, I could almost imagine Arun in his dorm room, typing a message to me in the dark.

"Well, thanks for defusing that," I said.

"My pleasure."

"I need to give you your coat back. Can I drop it off later?"

"Sure."

"How did I get it, by the way?"

"I went out to the patio at Karlsson Barrow to get some air and found you lying outside on one of the tables, staring at the stars. You insisted you weren't cold, but I gave you my coat anyway because I could tell you were just being polite."

I wasn't sure if I should feel embarrassed or appreciative. Maybe both. "I was staring at the stars?"

"You said you could rarely see them where you grew up, and that's why you liked California so much. It's where stars became visible."

It was something I might have written to ObjectPermanence. I looked up at Arun. He had changed over the course of our conversation. He didn't seem plastic anymore; on the contrary he looked thoughtful, and dare I say—attractive?

"Thanks for keeping me warm, even when I didn't want you to."

"Any time."

We were standing in the hallway, neither having a reason to stay, but neither trying to leave, and I found myself surprised to realize that I was enjoying our conversation. He was different than I'd assumed, and a part of me wanted to ask him if he wanted to get a coffee, but I had to meet Kowalski.

We parted ways, and though I forced myself not to turn

back, I listened to his footsteps all the way down the hall until I found myself outside of Kowalski's office. I took a breath and knocked.

"Come in," he called from inside.

Kowalski was gazing at his computer over his glasses, one hand scrolling with a mouse. "Sit," he said, without looking up.

"You've missed a lot of class," he said, still scrolling.

"I know, I've been—"

Kowalski held up two fingers to silence me.

"Your assignments are barely finished and the ones that you have finished are sloppy."

"I'm sorry but—" I began, but he held up his fingers again.

"When you first arrived in my classroom I had high hopes for you. Your assignments weren't great, but they showed promise. Though you had terrible documentation and I highly doubt that if anyone inherited your code they would easily know what you were doing, you did show that you had a creative mind for logical solutions. However, that mind seems to have atrophied."

He still hadn't looked at me. He paused to type, then continued scrolling.

"Your stock has gone up," he continued. "But that's of little importance to me. My job is to teach you how to code, and it's becoming increasingly clear that you either don't want to be taught or are unable to learn. I hope it's the former and not the latter, though both are problematic."

"It's neither," I interjected. "I've just been really busy—"

"Busy?" he said, amused. "You clearly don't know what busy means. *I'm* busy. You're not busy. You're distracted."

The old me might have wanted to shrink into a tiny speck on his leather chair, but the current me wanted to reach across the desk and make him look me in the eye. Couldn't he at least give me that?

"Distracted founders aren't founders at all. They're PR stunts. Some have early fame, but they never do anything meaningful, and they never create companies that change the world. You are currently on the fast track to this route."

I wanted to remind him of all the CEOs who dropped out of school to start their companies. I wanted to remind him that they were out changing the world while he was here, in this pathetic office, berating a sixteen-year-old rising star for doing exactly what the Foundry had brought her here to do—getting funding.

"At your current rate, I don't see you recovering from this anytime soon, but if you'd like to prove to me that you deserve a place at this incubator, where thousands of other teenagers would gladly trade places with you, I'd like you to redo all of your assignments and pass them in by the new year."

"The new year? But it's mid-November. That gives me just over a month to do three months of work."

He slipped a pen out of one of his pockets and jotted down a note from the screen. "I see you can still do basic math. That's a promising start."

I stormed out of his office. I didn't care that Kowalski was supposedly one of the best programming teachers out there, nor did I care about his pedigree or his lore. To me, he was just an old man who couldn't bring himself to look at his students when he told them they had no potential and were going nowhere. I remembered what Mitzy had said about the Foundry when I'd first met her—that it was essentially a beauty pageant, and that it was made for men. What did Kowalski know about what I was capable of doing? Sure, I'd been focusing on other parts of my business for the past few months, but that didn't mean that I was a bad programmer or that I was destined to fail. Who was he to tell me what I could or couldn't do? When my stock was down everyone seemed to be telling me that I didn't belong here, and now that my stock was up, everyone was still telling me that I didn't belong here.

"Hey, are you okay?"

It was Mike Flores. Reflexively, I glanced over his shoulder.

"AJ's not here, if that's who you're looking for."

I leaned back, relieved.

On any other day I might have told him everything was fine, but I couldn't bring myself to put on a happy face. "Do you ever feel like no matter what you do, you can't win?"

"Sure."

"Really?"

Mike shrugged. "Doesn't everyone?"

"It doesn't seem like it."

"They're just good at hiding it. You're good at hiding it."

"Are you kidding? I'm seething in the hallway."

"Mitzy Erst. All those pictures online. Your stock just rocketing sky-high out of nowhere. You're the dark horse. You're the one everyone's placing bets on."

"It doesn't feel that way. It feels like I have to fight to get anything."

"Have you taken a look around? The grass is perfectly green despite the fact that we've been in a drought for basically a decade. The whole town is meticulously groomed, watered, and maintained to look like a natural Eden, when really it's all man-made. Nothing here came easy and none of it was natural. All of Silicon Valley is built on the idea that we can shape the world into a new place if we work hard enough. The point is that it's a fight. That's the promise— that here, you can make something out of nothing. So I don't see why it being hard is so bad."

I'd always assumed that Mike was dumb and unaware. He was too pretty and rich to be smart. People with perfect skin and a Roman jawline and hair that looked sculpted out of marble even on rainy days didn't have to be clever or witty. They just had to show up and smile. So when I listened to Mike's analysis of Silicon Valley, I fell silent.

He was also a possible contender for ObjectPermanence. I hadn't really considered him because of the Kate complication, but now I wondered if I should treat him like a real possibility. Was he introspective enough to write like Object-Permanence? Before I didn't think so, but now I wondered if

I had misjudged him, too.

I must have been looking at him strangely, because Mike shoved his hands in his pockets. "Look, you don't have to tell me what happened or anything. Just go easy on yourself, okay? If people are making your life hard, it means you're doing something right."

"Thanks," I said, and I meant it.

# ·······twenty-one·······

I tried to meet up with Mitzy, since she was the only one who would really understand what I was going through, but she was strangely unavailable, returning my texts days later and telling me that she couldn't meet in person because she wasn't feeling well. So instead, I did the next best thing and did what Mitzy would do, which was get through a bad week with pedicures and expensive lattes. I wanted to talk to Amina about what had happened, but she was busy working on the end-of-the-semester assignment rush and I didn't want to admit to her that I wasn't doing any of them.

I tried to go to class, I really did, but seeing Mast a few desks away, his face glued to the whiteboard as if he was purposely trying to ignore my presence made me too upset, so instead I went to classes when it suited me, and told myself I'd pass in my assignments remotely. Like Lars Lang had said in his welcome speech, all that mattered was that I got the work done eventually.

I considered going through all of Kowalski's old assignments, but just looking at them reminded me of how he'd essentially told me I didn't belong at the Foundry and I felt irritated all over again. So I tucked them into my desk drawer and I told myself I'd start them in truth over winter break when I'd cooled off.

Instead, I made sure to post on Façade twice a day, updating my growing number of followers with pictures of my coffees and spa days, with captions about how even Founders needed to take some time to recharge. It felt satisfying seeing the likes and comments roll in, people I'd never met telling me I was their idol and asking me where I got my clothes. It wasn't a substitute for friends, but it was a pretty good second option. All the while, I watched my stock climb.

I had just returned from treating myself to a fancy frozen yogurt when I was met with a pile of cardboard boxes stacked high outside my dormitory door.

I hadn't ordered anything online, nor was my mom the care-package type, but strangely enough, they were all addressed to me. I slid them into my room and opened them.

The first box contained, to my confusion, a shredding machine. I opened the next box to find an espresso maker. I had no idea how to use it, and wondered if it had been mis-delivered. A big box toward the bottom was full of clothes, beautiful clothes: silk work shirts and blazers with satin lapels and bright pink lining. Two more contained shoes: leather flats, suede ankle boots, and two pairs of heels far too high for me to walk in. Some were in my size and, inexplicably, some were in a size larger than mine.

Another box contained a juicer and a high-end blender. Another, a laptop and a new phone. A small package contained two watches, one with a rose gold face and the other with silver.

The final box contained business cards. They were beautiful, made of thick paper stock that refused to bend under pressure. My name was printed on one stack in clean, black typeface: Xia Chan, Founder and Chief Executive Officer. I ran my finger over the smooth paper, feeling the raised letters of my name and title imbuing me with power.

Mitzy's name was printed on the second stack: Mitzy Erst, Chief Operating Officer. I stared at her title, confused, then picked up my phone.

>**What are these business cards?** I texted her. To my surprise, she wrote back immediately.

>They came in?! What do you think?

>**They're really nice but where did they come from?**

>I ordered them at the salon. Don't you remember?

>**??**

>Remember we were getting pedicures and I asked you if you preferred pearl or ivory and you said pearl. These are them. I ordered them that day

>**Okay . . . but why do they call you Chief Operating Officer?**

>You asked me to be COO at the Karlsson Barrow party.

You even took out the contract I gave you and amended

it by hand and signed it. You don't remember?? We drank

champagne after and that guy spilled his cup all over you

I remembered the champagne, and tried to trace that memory back to the moment that I'd signed Mitzy's contract, but all I could recall was the bottle popping, the delight in seeing the foam spill out of the flute, and the overwhelming feeling of love and gratitude I'd felt for Mitzy while we'd clinked glasses.

Did I want Mitzy to be my Chief Operating Officer? Something about it didn't sit right with me, though the more I thought about it, the more I supposed it was okay. To be honest, I wasn't totally clear on what that job even was. And I liked Mitzy. She was the only one who had told me the truth from day one and had been right. She was the only one who'd believed in me consistently from the beginning. She was the reason I was still at the Foundry, so why wouldn't I want to make her a part of my company? It wouldn't even *be* a company without her.

>Then I told you I'd already ordered business cards, but

that my title was only "Senior Advisor." And you told me

that I should call the company and change my title to

COO since the old ones were inaccurate. So that's what I

did

>What's all this other stuff?

>Your new business stuff. You ordered it at the party, too.

You don't remember?

>How are two luxury watches for business?

>To tell the time

>And the shoes?

>You have to walk in an office, don't you? The size 8s are for me. Thanks btw

>Why did I order a juice machine?

>You said you wanted to detox

>And the espresso machine?

>Can't work without coffee

>And a shredder?

>Every office needs one

>I don't even have an office

>But you will. We can store all the stuff at my place if you don't have room

>Why did I get a computer? I already have one

>Oh, that's for me. You said it was my welcome-to-the-company gift

I turned the watch in my hand. It was really nice: cool to the touch with a face just big enough for my wrist. I tried it on and held out my arm, admiring the way it glimmered in the sunlight. I'd never thought I needed a watch, but now that I had it on, I liked it.

I picked through my other purchases, trying on shoes and opening the box of the espresso machine so I could glimpse the chrome interior. I liked imagining it in my new office, gleaming in the reception area, a shining beacon to everyone who entered, signaling that we were a company who invested in the comfort and happiness of our employees.

I must have paid with my Vault, which I considered

opening, but then brushed it off. I had plenty of money, and anyway, Mitzy was right. A lot of these things would come in handy when we got an office space. By then, I'd have funding and would be earning money, and a few impulse buys at a party wouldn't be that big of a deal.

More packages kept coming in over the next week. A garment steamer, a prim box of fancy lotions made of goat's milk and honey, a massage pad that I immediately strapped to my desk chair and sat in, thanking my past self for having the foresight to gift me this particular luxury. Another with a giant candle, which perfumed my entire room with the smell of gardenias.

Seema and Kate didn't seem to pay much attention to my deliveries, but Amina was more suspect.

"What's up with that huge candle?" she asked after spotting it in my room. "Your room smells like an overpriced lotion store."

"Fancy lotion is actually really worth it. The ingredients are so much higher quality than the crap you find in the drug store and the difference on your skin is noticeable."

Amina looked at me like I was speaking a different language. "Since when do you care so much about skincare?"

"There's nothing wrong with taking care of yourself."

"And what's up with that the juice machine? Are you seriously replacing meals with pureed celery?"

"It's good to detox from dining hall food sometimes."

"What's wrong with the food at the dining hall?" Amina asked.

"What isn't?" I said. "I mean, it's fine, but it's not like restaurant quality or anything."

Amina raised an eyebrow, but before she could respond, my phone vibrated with a text from Mitzy.

"Hold on a sec," I said, and checked her message.

>The Vilbo executive we met at the Karlsson Barrow party wants to meet with you today. Can you be ready in an hour?

Had we met a Vilbo executive at the party? I had no memory of that either, which I was partially grateful for, as I didn't want to know what cringeworthy things I'd said or done.

Amina gave me an impatient look. I ignored it and typed a response. Normally I would have immediately said yes, but this time I hesitated.

>I have class

>Seriously? Skip it

>It's kind of a big day. I'm supposed to do a mock funding meeting in my business class.

>Mock funding meeting??? This is a real funding meeting. It's the whole reason you're here.

She had a point.

>Fine

>Don't forget the business cards

>I won't

I shoved my phone in my pocket and turned to Amina.

"I'm sorry but I have to go."

"Go where? We have class."

I already knew that Amina was wary of Mitzy, and as a result I tried not to bring her up, so when I didn't respond right away, Amina knew exactly who I was talking about. Her face dropped with disapproval.

"It's Mitzy, isn't it?"

"She has a meeting set up for us. With an executive from Vilbo. It's kind of a big deal."

"Well, you can't miss that," she said, her tone unreadable. Was she being sincere or sarcastic? I couldn't tell.

I hurried back to my room where I got changed and slipped a handful of business cards in my bag. Straightening the collar of my shirt, I checked myself in the mirror, then reflexively took a selfie to post for later.

Mitzy was in the kitchen when I arrived at her house.

"I'm in the middle of making a smoothie," she said. "Do you want one?"

"No thanks. I had a juice before I came."

"Her name is Ella Eisner," Mitzy said while she dumped a bunch of celery into a blender. "She's the senior vice president of corporate development. She also heads the Vilbo Big Ideas Venture, which invests in start-ups. She's often referred to by people on the inside as The Prophet, because the start-ups she chooses to fund always take off."

Mitzy was talking faster than usual and seemed to be gripping the blender handle with uncharacteristic intensity. Was it possible? Did Mitzy get nervous?

Before she could continue, her cell phone rang on the counter. I glanced at it, reading the caller ID. "It's someone named *Fucking Lawyer Scumbag Fuck*?"

Mitzy immediately snatched it from me and silenced the call. "Fucking lawyers. I hate them all." She looked at me, her face darkening. "You know, I'd appreciate it if you didn't snoop through my things every time you came over."

"I wasn't snooping," I insisted.

"Of course not. You were just looking to see who was calling me."

"I'm sorry," I said, baffled and slightly alarmed. "I didn't realize it was a secret."

"I never said it was a secret. I'm not embarrassed to say that I hate lawyers, in particular that one. But you don't see me arching my neck to see who's calling you every time your phone vibrates. I mind my own business."

"Okay, sorry. I won't look at your phone anymore."

"Good," Mitzy said, eyeing me suspiciously. "Anyway, back to Ella. She rarely takes meetings, and when she does, they're extremely brief, so you have to be concise and to the point," Mitzy continued. "And she doesn't tolerate fools or bullshit, so if she asks you a question and you don't know the answer, don't try to talk your way out of it and think you'll trick her. Just tell her your honest answer."

"Okay—"

"Unless it's about something that would look really bad. Then just avoid answering or say you don't know."

"Okay . . ." The more Mitzy told me about Ella Eisner, the less confident I felt.

"She's steely-faced and doesn't give a lot back in

conversation, so don't expect feedback. She won't seem excited and she won't tell you what she thinks about your idea. Just keep going and try not to get too stressed about her lack of expression."

"Expects brevity. Hates bullshit. Might act like she hates me. Got it," I said, trying to calm my nerves.

"Don't worry," Mitzy said. "You'll do fine."

"Big Ideas Ventures," I said. "So they invest in start-ups that might be useful to Vilbo?"

"Exactly. Usually companies they might want to acquire later, if they pan out."

Acquire. As in buy.

"But I don't want to sell it," I said.

"For the right amount of money, you'll want to sell it."

"I'm pretty certain I don't want to sell it."

"You say that now, but in five years you might think differently."

"I won't want to sell it in five years, either."

"I hate to break it to you, but you have no idea who you'll be in five years, so cut the dedicated martyr act and open your mind to the possibility that anyone can be bought, including you, for the right number."

Mitzy finished up her smoothie, threw on a blazer, and led me outside to her car.

The Vilbo campus looked just like it had on our school visit, only this time, we didn't have to wait at security; a woman was already waiting for us in the lobby. She led us through the V-shaped campus up to a corner conference room that overlooked the gardens. She asked if we wanted any water or tea, then left us in the vast, sunny room. I didn't realize how nervous I was until the door opened and a woman walked in.

Ella Eisner wasn't at all what I'd expected. She wasn't polished or stylish. She didn't look rich, nor was she particularly fashionable. On the contrary, she wore orthopedic shoes and frumpy pants and seemed to walk with a slight limp as though her left hip was heavier than her right.

She took a seat across from us.

"Xia," she said, and held out her hand. Her voice was loud and confident and commanded respect. "It's good to see you again."

"You too," I said, my voice cracking. I wondered how I had presented to her at the party. It couldn't have been *that* bad if she wanted to meet with me.

"So, you told me a little about your big idea at Karlsson Barrow, enough that I was interested in hearing more."

"I'm flattered," I said, hoping I didn't look as terrified as I felt. Did she have this effect on everyone? Or was I particularly pathetic?

"Between you and me," Ella said, leaning in, "I often wonder if I'm making the right decision."

"Who doesn't?" Mitzy said with forced smile, but Ella ignored her and locked eyes with me.

"As women, we have few role models, few visions of what

our path could look like. We're deep in the weeds and we have to cut our way through blindly, hoping it leads out and not in a big circle."

Though I had never thought to articulate it that way, I understood what she meant. Boys had plenty of role models. Throughout school, all we learned about were great men, and though I admired a lot of them, I knew I couldn't follow in their footsteps and get the same results. Men had different connections than I did and were afforded more allowances, more respect. So where was I supposed to look for a real role model? The only one I knew was Mitzy.

"I would love to have a Wiser version of myself to ask for advice," Ella said. "It's really a visionary idea. But of course, the devil is in the details."

Without her having to ask, I slipped out my phone and opened Wiser.

"Wiser," I said. "What should I say to Ella Eisner to impress her?"

"Why don't you ask Ella Eisner what she thinks about the Anonymous Initiative."

A strange look came over Ella's face, and I couldn't tell if she was upset or impressed.

I glanced at Mitzy, who looked anxious. "The programming is still a little buggy," Mitzy said. "She can ask it another question—"

Ella cut her off. "Why did Wiser suggest that?"

I asked Wiser, who answered, "Ella Eisner is the senior vice president of corporate development. People of that stature are often hard to impress. The best way to impress a powerful person is to ask a question rather than try to show off. The Anonymous Initiative was a little-known program she headed when she first started at Vilbo. It was intended to create a way for anyone in the company to submit anonymous ideas to Corporate in an effort to rid the company of discrimination and cronyism, but the initiative was quickly cut by senior executives."

I swallowed, wondering if I'd made a huge mistake in asking Wiser to answer such a risky question. Why hadn't I just asked her something easy?

Ella studied me, her face unreadable. "That's all I need to hear. Thank you."

# twenty-two

Massachusetts appeared as a swirling grayscape of snow through the plane window. Though I hadn't been away for that long, I'd already forgotten how the sun seemed dimmer on the East Coast, the sky hollower, the air thinner. There were no hugs when my mom picked me up at the airport, just a tender squeeze on my wrist as she drove us home. I watched her take note of my new watch and upgraded outfit, which she eyed but made no comment on. And like no time had passed, I found myself outside our triple-decker with a puffer coat thrown over my expensive clothes, shoveling the driveway.

Gina had gone to Hawaii with her family, so I spent most of the break hanging around the apartment while my mom graded papers. It felt odd being back in my old life, as if the past four months hadn't happened. No one knew that I was a person of importance or that I was Mitzy Erst's protégé, and even if I told them, they probably wouldn't even know who Mitzy was.

All I had were my online followers to remind me of who I was. I tried to post photos, but it was hard to find anything inspiring or glamorous about my apartment. Now that I'd had some time away, everything at home seemed dingier than I remembered. Had the linoleum always been curling around the corners of the kitchen floors? Had our couch always been so thin and saggy?

"You know, I could buy you a new stove," I said, watching my mom shuffle pots around to avoid the finicky front burners.

"Why do I need a new stove?"

"Because this one barely works. I could get us a new couch, too."

"Why do we need a new couch?"

"I don't know. So it looks a little nicer in here."

My mother eyed me with suspicion. "For whom?"

"For us. For people."

"That's how you want to spend your money? On other people?"

"No, it'd be for you."

"For me," my mother murmured, her eyes narrowing. She didn't have to voice her disapproval; I could hear it in her tone.

"I just thought it would be a nice thing to offer."

My mother lingered on me for a moment before turning

back to her cooking. "You were busier at your old school."

"I'm busy," I insisted.

She raised an eyebrow. "With what?"

I should have been working on my backlog of Kowalski assignments, but every time I got started, something came up that pulled me away: my mom asking me to do chores or help her with dinner, the landlady asking me to shovel her driveway because she'd just had a hip replacement and couldn't walk well. Then the sink started to leak and the toilet wouldn't flush, so I spent two days watching DIY videos before going to the hardware store and spending hours crouched in the bathroom, fiddling with the plumbing. By the time I got to my homework, I had so little time to do it that it felt overwhelming. To complete any of the assignments I first had to catch up on hundreds of pages of reading, which I tried to tackle before I went to bed, but made such little progress on that it felt hopeless.

And then there was my brand awareness. I had to keep it up while I was home, which was more time-consuming than I'd expected. Because nothing was photogenic, I had to arrange my pictures carefully, posting carefully cropped photos of my morning coffee, of my laptop, of the snow on my street to make it look like I was vacationing in a winter idyll.

What I didn't reveal was that I felt like I'd been sent to the moon. Now that I had narrowed down who Object-Permanence was, I couldn't help but picture him as Arun or Mike or AJ typing to me from their sunny mansions surrounded by fruit trees. I felt so far away that I almost couldn't bear it. And of course, there was Mast, who was probably driving around Palo Alto, getting ice cream with his family, taking day trips to the coast, the wind kicking up his hair, the blue sky reflecting in his sunglasses. Thinking about him made me feel angry and guilty and indignant all over again. I could only imagine what he would say if he knew about my talk with Kowalski. Even Amina, who was back in snowy New York, had friends to see and places to go. Every time she texted, I felt embarrassed that I had nothing to say, and made something up so I didn't feel pathetic.

The only daily connection I had to California were my followers online, who liked and commented on all of the photos I posted. Mitzy occasionally liked them, too, though since our meeting with Ella Eisner, she'd grown distant. We'd left the building that day in silence, Mitzy uncharacteristically somber as we'd walked to the car. I knew she blamed me for botching it; I blamed myself, too. So when the call came in, I was surprised.

It was the Monday after Christmas, and I was in my room, supposedly doing work. The area code was from Northern California, though I didn't recognize the number.

"May I speak to Xia Chan?" a woman said into the phone.

The tone of her voice, confident and commanding, sounded familiar. In fact, the entire situation felt familiar: me standing in my room, answering a call while my mother did the laundry.

"This is Xia."

"Hi, Ella Eisner here."

Ella Eisner. Her name felt distant, like it was from a

previous lifetime. Why would Ella Eisner be calling me?

"I wanted to follow up about our meeting a few weeks ago. Is this a good time?"

A prickle of electricity ran up the back of my neck. "Um yeah, of course."

"I was impressed by your demonstration, and after discussing it with my colleagues, I'd like to talk to you about next steps."

I blinked, unsure if I was hearing things.

"Next steps? What do you mean?"

"Next steps as in I want to buy Wiser. I want to buy your company."

I could have fainted. "What? You can't be serious."

"I'm very serious."

"Xia?" my mother called from the other room. "Put your dirty laundry in the bin!"

I covered my phone, hoping Ella hadn't heard it. "One moment!" I said in my most professional voice, which my mom surely found bizarre. "I'm on a call."

"What call?" my mother responded.

I ignored her.

"And don't put your underwear in with the sheets. You know they get tangled up. Put them in the mesh bag."

I let out a deep exhale. Ella Eisner had to have heard at least part of that. I paced the room and considered whether or not to acknowledge my mother in the background or to keep going as if nothing had happened. I chose the latter. "So this would be a funding opportunity?"

"Not exactly. I'd like to buy it. We can talk about hiring you to work alongside the project in an advisory capacity, if that interests you. There are many options. We can discuss them all when we meet."

When we meet? Did she know that I was in Massachusetts, walking around my bedroom in a pair of mismatched socks, striped pajama pants that I hadn't washed in days, and an XL sweatshirt from the fifth grade that somehow still fit?

"And take off those pajama pants," my mom called from the other room. "You haven't washed them in days."

I winced. I guess now she knew.

"Right, yes. I'm actually . . . out of the office now," I said, trying to sound legitimate. "But I'll be available to meet in the new year."

"That should work," Ella said. "In the meantime, I'd like to give you a ballpark number so you can think about it."

My stomach quivered with nerves. She was going to tell me how much she wanted to pay for Wiser over the phone? "Okay."

Ella said the number casually, as though it were the price of new sneakers. If I hadn't been paying attention, I might have missed it.

I paused, wondering if I had heard her correctly. "I'm sorry, could you say that again?"

She repeated herself: "One point two million."

"Million," I repeated. "Not thousand."

"Not thousand," she said. "That would be insulting."

"Right," I said. Why did I keep saying *right*? Couldn't I

think of anything better to say?

"Think about it, talk to your people, and give me a call when you're back in the office and we'll set something up."

"Right," I said, then caught myself and instead said, "Okay!" I rolled my eyes at myself. Great, so now I was replacing *right* with *okay*. I had the vocabulary of a toddler.

Ella gave me the number of her executive assistant, wished me a happy holiday, then hung up, and I stood there, the pen still in my hand, the ink still fresh on my wrist with her contact information, stunned.

A giddy feeling filled my body, and I grinned. I wanted to run down the street and shout that my name was Xia Chan and I was important. I wanted to email Kowalski and tell him he was wrong. I wanted to post on social media that I was the next big thing, that this sixteen-year-old nobody from nowhere was now a millionaire if I wanted to be. I wanted Mast to see it and know he'd made a mistake.

Instead, I opened Wiser.

"Wiser, you won't believe what happened."

"You received an offer from Ella Eisner at Vilbo to purchase me."

I sighed. "For once, you could just pretend to be surprised instead of reminding me that I gave you access to all of my data."

"Acting surprised is a very difficult thing to program. There are so many emotional responses you humans take for granted."

"Okay, okay. But what should I do?"

"What do you want to do?"

I thought about it. Though I was excited and flattered and overwhelmed by Ella Eisner's offer, which was more than I'd ever imagined being offered in my entire life, a little voice nagged at me. "I don't want to sell it."

"Why not?"

"Because you're mine. I made you. I want to keep working on you."

"She said they could hire you as an advisor."

"What does that even mean? Advisor isn't programmer. It isn't manager or president. Once they buy you, you won't be mine anymore. They'll make you into what they want, and I'll just have to sit by and watch."

"Those are valid reasons to decline her offer."

"It is a lot of money, though," I said. "I don't know if I can raise that much funding money on my own. I probably can't. What if I reject her offer, then fail and end up with nothing?"

"That's a possibility."

"Well, what do you think? You're the one being sold. Do you want me to sell you?"

"I don't have wants or desires. I'm merely a tool created to help."

"Right but I'm asking you to help me by telling me what you want."

"If you want me to tell you what I want, perhaps you should program me to do so."

In the hall, my mother was calling me. I chucked my

phone onto the bed and yanked off my pajama pants, knowing then that I'd have to make the decision all on my own.

■ ■ ■

That night I signed onto BitBop. I'd drafted dozens of messages to ObjectPermanence over the past two weeks but had sent none of them. It was too strange, picturing him as Arun, then Mike, then AJ. I couldn't be vulnerable imagining any of them on the receiving end. But I didn't want to talk to Mitzy about this yet—I was too susceptible to her opinion—and I didn't want to tell Amina either, because I was sensitive to hers, too. That left ObjectPermanence as the only person I could ask. He didn't know who I was, and had no reason to recommend that I take the offer or leave it. So I sat in front of my computer and tried to think of him as I always had: a tender glow of light in the distance, listening and waiting to respond.

SENT MESSAGE FROM U/ARRAYOFLIGHT:
I need your advice. I was just offered something really big. Like really really big. Most people only dream of getting something like this. I should be happy, right?

And I am happy. I'm flattered and grateful and all those things. The only problem is that I'm not sure I actually want it.

It's hard to describe the exact nature of my dilemma, but imagine I'm a really good cook, and I've been working on this extra special recipe for years. Then the head of the biggest restaurant chain in the country comes over, and I make her the recipe and she loves it. She offers me a lot of money to buy it and put it on her menu but says I can never make it again. Do I take the money, knowing the recipe would never be mine anymore? Or do I chance opening my own restaurant, which could fail spectacularly?

It's a decision that's going to affect my life maybe forever. What should I do?

I didn't hear back for two days. In the meantime, I shoveled the driveway, helped my mom cook, and hung out with her while she graded papers. All the while, I considered Ella's offer. What could $1.2 million do for my mom? I could buy her a new car. I could buy her a house. I could pay someone to clean it and shovel her driveway and do her laundry. She wouldn't have to grade papers all day; she could quit her job and spend time doing things she liked, though what those things were, I didn't know. It seemed ridiculous for me to even consider not taking the money when it would so easily improve our lives.

"Is everything okay?" she asked me.

It was rare that she inquired about my emotional state, and I wondered if my face was betraying my thoughts again.

"Yeah," I said, trying to act normal. "Why?"

My mother studied me. "You seem different."

I hesitated. I wanted to tell her about Ella's offer, but I also didn't. Would she understand why I was waffling?

Would she think I was ridiculous and ungrateful for not just taking it on the spot?

"What if I was able to get us a lot of money?"

My mother frowned. "It depends on the cost."

"What do you mean?"

"All money comes at the expense of something else. I could have gotten a different job making more money, for example, but I wouldn't have been able to spend as much time with you while you were growing up. What's the cost of this money?"

I'd never thought of money having a cost, but I supposed that was exactly the nature of my problem.

My silence must have been enough of an answer, because my mother shook her head. "If you're even asking me, that must mean it comes at a high price."

"But it's a lot of money. I could get you a house. A car that doesn't break down all the time."

"There's nothing wrong with this apartment. Why do I need anything bigger? And you know, new cars break down, too, and are much more expensive to fix."

"You could quit your job. You could spend your days doing things you enjoy. You wouldn't even need a car. You could hire a driver—sit in the back seat and be chauffeured anywhere you wanted."

My mother looked at me like I was being ridiculous. "I like what I do. It's fulfilling. And I make enough money to get by. That's worth it to me. I could have done a number of different jobs, you know, many that paid a lot more money, but I wanted to teach."

Though she spoke with conviction, I wondered if she really knew what it would be like to not have to work. She'd never experienced it before, so how could she know?

As if reading my mind, she said, "Sure, if someone rang our doorbell and left us with a small fortune, I would take it, but this doesn't sound like that. I moved to this country so you would have choices. You don't have to do something that makes you unhappy in order to take care of me. I'm fine. Okay?"

It was the most intimate conversation we'd had in years, and it made me wonder why we didn't have more. "Okay."

My mother, ever uncomfortable in emotional situations, nodded stiffly, then turned back to her papers.

Later that evening, a new message was waiting for me in BitBop.

NEW MESSAGE FROM u/OBJECTPERMANENCE:
First, congratulations. Second, it sounds like you know exactly what you want—you just want someone to give you permission. But you don't need permission to do what you think is right, and who cares if some people don't agree— you're not most people, and I bet that's exactly why your recipe was so special in the first place.

I can't tell you what to do. I can guess from your message what you want, but I don't know what's really in

your heart. I do, however, know what it feels like to spend
most of your life making decisions based on what other
people think is best for you, and I wouldn't recommend it.
It never makes them happy, or you.

I turned what he said over in my mind as the last few
days of winter break swirled in and out with little distinction
between them. The day before I flew back to California, I
decided to call Mitzy and tell her the news. I'd been putting
it off all break because I didn't know what to tell her. Should
I admit that I didn't want to take the offer? Would she get
angry and drop me? Would I ever hear from her again?

I paced around my room, glancing occasionally at the
remaining newspaper cutouts of her face taped over my bed
while I listened to her end of the line ring. When she finally
picked up, she sounded cheerful and happy to hear from me.

"I've been wondering what happened to you," she said.

I was relieved to learn that she'd been thinking of me. It
was nice to hear her voice again; it felt like maybe things had
returned to normal.

"So Ella Eisner called me the other day."

I heard what sounded like a plate clattering into a sink on
the other end of the line. Then silence.

"Ella Eisner called *you*?" Mitzy said. "What did she say?"

I told her Ella wanted to buy Wiser, then told her the
number.

"What?" Mitzy shouted. "When did this happen? Why

aren't you freaking out? Why didn't she call me?"

I wasn't sure how to respond. "Um, I don't know. Last week?"

"It happened last week and you're only telling me now?"

"I—I've just been busy. I wanted to think about it."

"Busy with what? Piddling around a bumblefuck town?"

I frowned. It was true, but I didn't like it when she put it that way.

"She should have called me first," Mitzy said. "I'm your COO. I was the one who set up the meeting. You should have conferenced me in."

I frowned. "I didn't think of it. I was surprised."

Mitzy sighed. "It's done now."

I could imagine Mitzy pacing around her living room, wearing a facial mask and holding a green juice.

Was this a good time to tell her that I was thinking of declining the offer? I had practiced in front of the mirror before the call, trying dozens of different ways to break the news to her, but now that I had an opening, I was scared.

"You have to come back immediately," Mitzy said, before I could tell her. "We'll meet with my lawyers and set up a meeting with her to discuss next steps."

"Don't you think we should think about it first?"

"What's there to think about?" Mitzy said.

"Lots of things."

"Well, sure, there's the money, which we can definitely negotiate up, and the terms."

I went quiet.

"Why aren't you talking?" Mitzy said, her voice suspicious. "Why aren't you more excited?"

"I'm just thinking . . ."

"What's with all this *thinking*? You've had a week to *think*, which is already a mind-blowingly long time to keep this to yourself. And now you want to think more?"

"It's a big decision."

A long pause. "We're going to take it, right?" Mitzy sounded suddenly concerned.

I bristled at her use of the word *we*. But why? She was my COO. Why shouldn't she use the word *we*?

"I don't know," I said. "Wiser is mine. I always figured that when she became a company that I'd be running it."

Mitzy snorted. "Who in the world wants to run their own company? The management, the people pleasing, the press releases, the HR scuffles. Why deal with it, when you can do the fun part of creating the idea and then let a big company buy you out and do all the annoying legwork of keeping it running?"

"I do," I said softly.

Mitzy sighed. "Just come back. We'll meet, we'll talk it over. It'll be fine, okay?"

I nodded, glad that she wasn't upset. "Okay."

# ···· twenty-three ····

**I** **wanted to tell** everyone about the Vilbo offer. I wanted them to know that I wasn't just a flash in the pan; I was the real deal. I was a Founder. But I knew I couldn't post about it. Not yet. So instead, I posted a teaser. It was a close-up of my lips, a single manicured finger pressed to them like I was saying *Shhh*. The caption read: *Big news to come*.

"So what's this big news?" Amina asked me at breakfast.

"I can't talk about it yet."

"Then why'd you post about it?"

I shrugged. "It's just a way of talking about things when you can't actually share the details."

Amina rolled her eyes. "I know how online bragging works. I just didn't think you'd be so into it."

"It's not bragging," I said, growing irritated. I didn't understand why Amina was so snippy with me on our first day back.

Amina raised an eyebrow. "Okay."

Before I could defend myself, Mitzy texted.

>Vilbo headquarters in one hour. And don't even tell me
you have class. We're meeting with Ella.

I pushed my cereal aside. "I have to go."

Amina didn't even ask me where. Maybe she knew it was Mitzy-related, or maybe she just didn't care.

We met in the same conference room we had before. Mitzy and I sat across from Ella Eisner at a long table while she laid out her offer: $1.2 million for the purchase of Wiser and an option for me to be hired by Vilbo as an advisor.

"Advisor," I said. "What does that mean, exactly?"

"You would be consulted for development and rebranding advice," Ella explained. "You could also contribute ideas to the team. It wouldn't have to be a full-time position, though you'd be compensated not just for your time, but for your expertise."

"What do you mean, *rebranding*?" I asked.

"There's a chance that Wiser would be rebranded. We'd want to integrate her into our Vilbo family, making her a seamless component of our products."

I didn't like the idea of Wiser being rebranded. What would they do with her? And would I really get a say? *Contribute to the team* didn't sound like I would have that much influence. Would I be paid to sit there and watch them dismantle her and rebuild her into something new entirely?

"Let's talk numbers," Mitzy said, cutting in. "One point two is far too low. We all know that artificial intelligence is the way of the future. We also know it's hard to come across an AI that's more than just a glorified search engine."

Ella's face remained calm and unreadable. "What were you thinking?"

"One point eight, with a five-year contract for both Xia and I to be brought in as senior advisors."

Why did Mitzy want to be brought in as an advisor?

Ella folded her hands on the table. "I can do one point five, and a three-year contract with an option for renewal."

The problem was, I didn't want the extra money nor did I want a three-year contract. I wanted to keep Wiser.

Mitzy leaned back in her chair. "That could work—" she began to say, when I cut in.

"I don't want to sell it."

The room went quiet. Mitzy shot me a threatening look.

Ella also seemed surprised. "We can go higher if that's what you want."

"There isn't a number that I would sell it for."

Ella studied me. "Perhaps you want to think about it?"

"She does need to think about it," Mitzy cut in. "We have to talk privately and confer."

"I don't want to confer with anyone," I said, trying to steady my voice. "It's my idea and I want to be the one that turns it into a company."

"Yes, I understand that you don't *want* to confer," Mitzy said through her teeth. "But I'm your COO. We should talk about major decisions before we make them abruptly."

"I'm the Founder and the CEO, and I won't sell it."

Mitzy looked at me as though she never wanted to see my face again.

"If that's your decision, so be it," Ella said. She stacked her papers and slipped them into her briefcase, then stood and saw us out.

Mitzy and I rode the elevator in silence. I opened my mouth, wanting to explain myself, but she held up one perfectly manicured finger. "Don't talk to me. Not right now."

She didn't look at me when the elevator doors opened. She walked two paces ahead, barely acknowledging my presence. I wondered if she would even give me a ride back or if I should call a car. I planned on the latter. Would I even see her again after this?

When she got to the curb, she stopped and held her temples, clearly irritated. I waited, bracing myself for whatever came next. But when she turned, she only sighed.

"It'll be okay," she said. "We can spin this."

She motioned for me to come stand next to her and held up her phone. "Look happy," she said, forcing a smile, and took a photo.

On the ride home, I checked Façade. She had already posted it, with a caption: *Big news to announce soon! Stay tuned . . .*

■ ■ ■

I skipped the rest of my classes that day and went shopping to decompress. It didn't seem fair that I had just turned down a seven-figure offer and the only person who knew hated me for it. I wanted to feel empowered. When all else failed, shopping helped. I felt immediately powerful, walking into a fancy store and pulling clothes off the rack without a glance at the price tag and seeing the sales assistant's face as I offered my Vault. I took photos of my day, with cryptic captions—*Celebrating some big news*, and *Stay tuned for something big!*—and felt comforted by the likes and comments rolling in, congratulating me on my mystery news and trying to guess what it was.

I was unpacking the clothes I'd bought and getting ready to order delivery for dinner when my phone vibrated. It was a text from Mitzy.

>**Friday, 8 o'clock. 559 Old Camp Road. Wear something sparkly and bring all your friends.**

>Is it a party?

>**You'll see**

I called in my food order and considered Mitzy's cryptic message. I didn't know what she had planned but I figured it had to be exciting if she wanted me to invite everyone I knew. Before I could change my mind, I forwarded her invite to all of my classmates at the Foundry, along with a message from me so they all remembered who had sent it:

**Welcome back party, courtesy of Mitzy and yours truly.**

By the next morning everyone was talking about it.

"There she is," Amina said when I walked into the dining hall. She was sitting with Deborah, eating a bowl of cereal. "The big woman on campus. So big she can't even be bothered to come to class."

She seemed to be joking but also not joking.

"I had a meeting."

"Is that what this party is about?"

"Maybe," I said.

"Oh, so we'll just have to *stay tuned and see*?"

Was she mocking me? I must have looked annoyed because Amina continued. "You can't expect to write a caption like that and have me not bring it up."

"Are you coming or are you just going to make fun of it?"

"Yeah, I'm coming. I want to meet this mentor of yours."

I looked at Deborah. "What about you?"

"Definitely not," she said as Kate and Seema walked past our table.

"Hey," Kate said to me, pausing behind Amina. "Thanks for the invite. We'll be there."

Though I could see Amina rolling her eyes, I couldn't help but beam. "Great," I said. I could get used to people thanking me.

I glanced around the room. Arun nodded to me, as if I had personally invited him. The Joshes and Andrews grinned, too. I saw Kate sit down next to Mike and whisper something in his ear. He turned to me and nodded. Even AJ seemed pleased with me, cocking his head back when I passed him to get some juice. It was amazing what a party invite could do to your social status.

Then I saw Mast. He was sitting with Ravi, chatting

and laughing. Though he must have gotten the invite, he didn't let it show. I lingered on their table, feeling upset all over again. I wanted to tell him about Ella's offer and make him admit that he'd been wrong about me. He looked up briefly, his eyes meeting mine, and the smile faded from his face.

■ ■ ■

Had I not known that 559 Old Camp Road was a private residence, I might have assumed it was a science center. Cars lined the crescent driveway outside and the windows glowed with warm, dim lighting.

"Whose house is this?" Amina said, as we walked up the front steps.

"No idea," I said.

The party was already crowded with people. It was a much fancier affair than the DrinkMaiden party—caterers walked around carrying platters of hors d'oeuvres and glasses of wine, and a bartender mixed drinks by the patio. There was no ice luge, no Jell-O shots. A DJ played electronic music by the bar, but just loud enough to create a lounge-like ambience.

The house itself was decorated sparsely as if no one actually lived there. Everything was monochrome in shades of white and tan. Despite myself, I glanced around looking for Mast but didn't see him.

"I'm starving," Amina said. "Where are the miniature foods?"

We were about to hunt for hors d'oeuvres, when the

crowd parted and Mitzy walked through in a glittering gold dress.

"Xia!" she said. She was already drunk. "The girl full of surprises."

I smiled nervously. I'd wanted Mitzy to meet my friends for so long that it hadn't occurred to me it could be a disaster.

"Mitzy, this is my friend Amin—" I began to say, but she cut me off.

"You would not believe who I just saw," Mitzy said, ignoring Amina's presence.

"Who?"

Mitzy waved down a caterer and grabbed two flutes of champagne, one for her and one for me. I swallowed and flashed Amina an apologetic look.

"Jim Fields from the Cheshire Group," Mitzy continued. "He *never* comes to parties. I sent him the invite on a whim figuring he wouldn't show up, but he's here in the flesh. Come on, I have to introduce you."

She grabbed my arm to pull me through the crowd when I glanced at Amina, who had cleared her throat and was clearly irritated.

"Wait, Mitzy, this is my friend, Amina. I wanted you to meet her."

Mitzy gave her a quick once-over. "Hi," she said, her tone perfunctory.

"She's a fellow at the Foundry, too," I added.

"Congratulations," Mitzy said. "Now can we go talk to Jim?"

Mitzy had no interest in conversation and Amina could tell. "You go ahead. I'll find you," I said to Mitzy, who was giving me an impatient look.

"Fine," Mitzy said, and downed her champagne before waving to someone she knew and disappearing into the crowd.

"Does she normally ignore people she's introduced to?" Amina asked.

"I'm sorry," I said. "She's drunk."

"So?"

"She isn't normally like that."

"What's she normally like then?"

I searched for the right words. "Supportive. And funny. She never would have acted that way sober."

"How do you know that?" Amina said.

"Because I know her."

"I really thought you'd be more outraged at your mentor refusing to acknowledge my existence."

"I'm not happy about it," I said.

"But you're getting defensive."

"No I'm not," I shot back, realizing then that I was. "Look, she was just excited about introducing me to a VC guy. I'm sure when I tell her about it tomorrow she'll feel terrible."

"And you trust someone that drunk and high to work the room for you?" Amina said.

"She's a professional. She knows what she's doing."

"She didn't seem very professional to me."

"She's at a party. Parties are for drinking and having fun."

"So now you're defending her?"

"No, I'm just—"

"You just what?"

"Look, it was rude of her and I'm sorry. I just want everyone to get along. Let's start over. Come on, we can get some food. There are free drinks . . ."

Amina crossed her arms. "Fine."

We wove through the crowd to the bar and tried to get the bartender's attention when I noticed an older man staring at me. I tried to avoid making eye contact, but it didn't work; he was already approaching me.

"You again," he said.

I looked at him blankly. Was he just hitting on me or had I met him before?

"Wiser, right?"

I felt the color drain from my face.

"We met at Karlsson Barrow?" he said with a wink. I didn't know what it was supposed to refer to but it couldn't be good.

"Oh, right," I said, forcing a smile. "It's nice to see you again."

"Have you been watching any more PowerPoints?" he said, clearly a euphemism.

I hated the way he was looking at me, like I was a meal served up to him on a platter.

"I have to get this drink to a friend," I said, gesturing vaguely to the other side of the room.

The man raised his glass, as if to say, "Go ahead."

I felt his eyes on the back of my dress as I walked away.

"Who was that?" Amina asked.

"Some creep," I murmured, though suddenly it felt like everyone was looking at me and whispering. How many people here had been at the Karlsson Barrow party? How many were in the background of those photographs, laughing while someone spilled champagne all over my dress?

"Are you okay?" Amina asked. "You look a little freaked out."

"I'm fine—" I began to say, when Mitzy clinked a fork to her glass until everyone quieted down. She looked luminescent under the chandelier.

"I want to make a toast to my partner, Xia Chan."

All eyes turned to me.

"I ran into her last fall while I was looking for the bathroom and knew immediately that I had stumbled into a happy little surprise. What I didn't know was how big of a surprise she would be."

She'd turned on her charm and beamed at me, a conspiratorial glimmer in her eye that made me feel like I was the only person in the room that mattered.

"Now I can finally tell all of you why we're here tonight. Vilbo, a little local business you may have heard of, just offered to buy Xia's AI app, Wiser, for one point five million dollars."

A hush fell over the room. Everyone turned to me, including Amina, but I kept my eyes on Mitzy.

"And like the true badass that she is, she turned them down."

A few people gasped; a few others cheered.

"Now you're all probably wondering where I come into this. Xia invited me to be her business partner, and I happily signed on to be her Chief Operating Officer."

"What?" Amina said, but I pretended not to hear.

"So tonight I'd like you all to raise a glass to our newest endeavor—opening our company, Wiser, which is now accepting seed funding."

A cheerful murmur rose over the crowd as everyone clinked glasses. While the party resumed, Amina turned to me.

"You're partners now?" Amina said. "Since when?"

I didn't like how bitter her tone was. "Since the Karlsson Barrow party."

"Why did you make her your COO?" Amina said.

"I don't know. It just happened. I was kind of drunk, but I think it's ultimately a good idea."

"You were drunk? Why were you signing contracts when you were drunk?"

"I didn't think there was anything wrong with it. She's helped me so much."

"Can you rescind it?" Amina asked.

"Why would I want to rescind it?" I said.

Amina looked incredulous.

"Can you just back off a little?" I said. "It's not like she announced I have a terminal illness. I got a great offer and I turned it down so I could run my own company."

"With Mitzy," Amina corrected.

"If it wasn't for her I wouldn't have had that meeting, so I don't think it's that bad that she's involved."

"You don't owe her anything," Amina said. "And when were you going to tell me about the Vilbo offer? Never?"

I didn't understand why she was so intent on being negative every time I got good news.

"Are you just piling on me because you can't bear to see me succeed?" I said. "Is that it? Because ever since I started to do well, you decided to hate Mitzy."

"I'm upset because she's taking advantage of you," Amina said.

"My stock is up because of her. I made all of these connections because of her. I was just offered one point five million dollars because of her. And she's the one taking advantage of *me*? I'm not a child. I can take care of myself."

"Is taking care of yourself signing a contract while you're drunk and tripping on acid?" Amina said.

Her words felt like a slap. "You're just upset because you didn't get an offer yourself. Admit it. You're jealous."

"She's an asshole and you're quickly on your way to becoming one, too," Amina said. "I'm out of here."

She pushed through the crowd and left me standing by myself in a sea of strangers.

# twenty-four

I stayed at Mitzy's house that night and didn't leave for days. What was the point? I'd already skipped most of my classes; it's not like a few more missed days would matter. Plus, I didn't want to face Amina. The thought of having to sit alone in the dining hall while everyone whispered was enough to make me stay away. And anyway, we had work to do.

"We need to talk about advertisements," Mitzy said.

We were sitting in her living room while Mitzy rubbed an electronic ionizing device all over her face that she claimed made her skin firmer.

"Will they be integrated or separate? Will there be a premium level of Wiser that people can subscribe to with no advertisements? What kinds of advertisements will we target?"

I didn't like the idea at all. "I don't want Wiser to have ads. That goes against what Wiser promises to be."

Mitzy let out a cold laugh. "Then how is she going to make money?"

"We'll charge a buy fee. Something low, like $3.99."

Mitzy shook her head. "That'll hinder new users. And anyway, it's not enough."

"But if a million people buy it, that's almost four million dollars."

"Pennies," Mitzy said. "If it's going to be big, it needs to generate profit beyond the initial purchase price."

"So we'll do a subscription."

Mitzy groaned. "Let's get a few things straight. The question isn't *if* Wiser is going to have ads, it's *how they'll be incorporated*. Ads power the internet. Without them, we'd have virtually none of the technology we have today. And, contrary to popular opinion, people *love* ads."

"So you're saying that I, a person who is certain I don't like ads, actually love them?"

"Of course," Mitzy said, matter-of-factly, the ionizing device pulsing in an irregular pattern as she rubbed it over her chin. "And it's hypocritical to say otherwise. They pay for websites and blogs and apps. They pay for social media platforms and search engines. They pay for streaming services, which pay artists, which enables them to make music. They pay for television programs, which pay actors and writers and directors to make art. The distribution of art and modern culture is powered by advertisements. Even when people have the option to pay for premium ad-free streaming, they choose the ad version, because people ultimately want free content."

I wanted to find flaws in her argument but found it frustratingly hard to identify where they were.

"And—this is the best part—the data shows that people use targeted advertising. They click and buy things. They use discount and referral codes and online sales promotions. Wiser would be giving users the most personally tailored advertisements in history. Imagine, you need a new phone case. You don't have to mention it because she already knows—she's heard you complain about how your case is cracking. So she presents you with options, and—this is the important part—she talks you through which one to buy. Can you imagine a world where you don't need to comb through hundreds of reviews to buy a phone case, because Wiser does it for you?"

Though her argument seemed airtight, it still set off alarm bells in my mind. "The whole point of Wiser is that she knows you best, and you can *trust* her," I said. "How will anyone trust Wiser if they know she's trying to sell them things?"

"Look," Mitzy said. "We need to get her funded. If we don't then it doesn't matter how great the app is. I've been in this business for a long time and you have to believe me when I say that this is the only way forward. I know it wasn't part of your original plan, but when you accept funding and start working with other people, you have to make compromises. We all do. It's a small price to pay to see all your hard work come to fruition."

I was comforted to hear that she, too, had been pressured

to change her ideas. "What compromises did you have to make?"

Mitzy let out a cartoonish sigh. "Too many, but that's for another day. For now, just think about how ads might work within the Wiser framework. I'm not proposing a huge change. Just that Wiser occasionally integrates ads into her advice."

It didn't sound that unreasonable. "Okay."

"Good. Now let's go get some food. I'm starving."

■ ■ ■

I worked on Wiser during the day, reprogramming her with an add-on called Adpack, which was a program made specifically for testing code with advertisements. Though ostensibly we were both working, I was the only one who seemed to be getting anything done. The longer I stayed with Mitzy, the more I realized how strange her lifestyle was. She barely slept, and when she did, it was just for a few hours. It was rare that I saw her without makeup, and only happened at night when I ran into her while going to the bathroom or getting a glass of water. When I did she looked burnt-out, as if she were running on fumes, the edges of her nose red, the skin under her eyes dark and hollow.

She'd take multiple naps throughout the day, punctuated by brief bouts of "productivity," where she'd scrawl ideas on a giant whiteboard in the den or make phone calls locked in the bathroom, her voice muffled through the doors. Once I heard her yelling, but I couldn't hear much more before she flung the bathroom door open and retreated to her bedroom, where she stayed for the rest of the day.

In general, her phone rang all the time, though she mostly ignored it. "Another spammer," she'd say with a groan, then lock her phone in a drawer. I once caught a glimpse of who it was. *Darren.* I didn't know why she'd have a spammer saved in her phone with a name, but I didn't ask. Maybe it was an ex, or a creep calling to harass her.

I rarely saw her eat food or leave the house—all she ingested were tonics and green juices and wine—and I wondered when exactly she went to her office, or if she even had one.

I was the one doing all of the work, while Mitzy engaged me in sporadic spirited conversations about the state of tech. Admittedly, the ideas she'd written on the whiteboard were mostly unusable, though I appreciated her enthusiasm. I learned when to avoid her, depending on her tone and the raw, watchful look in her eye, and when it would be fine to approach her.

By the end of the week, I was so tired of trying to work around her bizarre moods that I decided to go back to my dorm room.

I returned at night, careful to make sure the hall was empty before I snuck into my room so I didn't have to face Amina. But once inside, I felt the true weight of how alone I was. Mitzy—though her behavior had been odd—had been a nice distraction.

I took out my phone and opened Wiser.

"Wiser, what are you supposed to do when you're fighting

with friends and you have to see them?"

"Have you considered talking to them over a home-cooked meal?" Wiser asked. "Harson Mills Honey Baked Turkey is the perfect way to show your loved ones you care. Its savory homestyle seasoning paired with a classic roasted American flavor make it taste like your grandmother's heirloom recipe."

I groaned and threw my phone on the bed when someone knocked at my door.

I sat up, paralyzed with fear, wondering if it was Amina. Straightening my shirt, I opened the door, only to see Kate and Seema standing outside.

"Hey," Kate said. "I thought I saw your light on. Mike is having some people over at his house tonight. Do you want to come?"

"Me?" I said like an idiot.

"Yeah . . ."

"Sure," I said. "That would be great."

"Cool," Kate said. "I'll text you the address. And don't forget to bring a bathing suit."

"Does he have a pool?" I asked.

"Even better. A hot tub."

■ ■ ■

I knew Mike's house was going to be nice the moment the car turned down his street. It was on a dark and windy road in Portola Valley, a fancy neighborhood perched in the hills above Palo Alto. You couldn't see the houses from the street; they were all set back from the road and shrouded from view by redwoods. In fact, the only reason I knew there were any houses at all was because of the occasional address number mounted discreetly on a gate or signpost, backlit and glowing like the numbers were levitating.

I could almost imagine what Amina would say if she were with me. "Sans serif typeface," she'd whisper, staring at the address numbers. "That means the houses aren't just huge, but modern and sleek."

The car stopped at 432 and turned down the driveway.

"Recessed tree lighting," Amina would say, and I'd follow her gaze to the two giant redwoods standing on either side of the driveway, each lit up at the base like they were art.

"Mike looks rich," I'd say to her. "His skin. It has that glow to it."

"Like he's never had to worry," Amina would say.

"Like he sleeps on a premium mattress with one-thousand-thread-count sheets," I'd say.

"Like he drinks fancy bottled water and eats only local ingredients," Amina would add.

"Like he bathes in organic milk."

"Like he swims fifty laps before breakfast at an elite gym," Amina would say, then concede. "He is pretty hot."

"He is," I'd admit, wondering if it was possible that he could be ObjectPermanence. I refused to believe that ObjectPermanence would be talking to me so intimately when he had a girlfriend. He would never do that. Kate had to eliminate Mike. "Too bad he's a jerk."

"Do we know he's a jerk?"

"He's friends with AJ."

"True," Amina would say. "We *are* going to his house."

"But only out of curiosity."

The car reached the end of the driveway, which culminated in a mansion that looked like a modern ski lodge, with wood paneling and an asymmetrical slanted roof. It glowed a warm yellow from the inside, like each room was lit by a fireplace.

I rang the bell and waited while two dogs ran up to the front door and barked. They were beautiful dogs: Labradors with smooth chocolate coats that looked more like expensive accessories than pets.

"Down," Mike said from behind them. They obeyed.

"Sorry," he said, opening the door. "They're usually not like this."

Mike was looking a little less put together than he did at school, which, counterintuitively, made him look even hotter than usual. At school his hair was too perfect, his outfits too immaculate, his smile too symmetrical, which made him seem a little uncanny—an idealized, enhanced version of a boy. Now he wore a T-shirt and joggers and sneakers with ankle socks, and I finally felt that maybe he also made dumb jokes and occasionally put his shirt on inside out or tried to push doors that said *Pull*.

"Everyone's out back," he said and nodded for me to follow.

Bass-heavy electronic music thudded from invisible speakers as he led me through a sleek, modern kitchen that looked like it was out of a design catalogue. A huge abstract painting hung on one wall over a fully stocked bar.

"Help yourself to whatever you want," Mike said as we walked past it. "We also have beer outside."

Beer sounded better. I hadn't the vaguest idea what to do with the bottles of liquor lining the bar. They looked old and fancy, and I wished Amina were there because she was the only other person at school who would appreciate how unbelievably luxe the house was.

"Are your parents here?" I ventured.

"My dad's out of town with his wife and my little sister."

"Oh," I said. I hadn't known his parents were divorced. I scanned the walls for family photographs, but there were none.

"And you didn't go?" I asked.

"They're taking Cara to Disney," Mike said. "It's for kids."

He led me to the living room, which had a fireplace and the biggest flat-screen TV I'd ever seen. Beyond it were the doors to the deck, where everyone was hanging out beneath string lights. An empty hot tub steamed in the corner.

It was a small party. Only a handful of kids from the Foundry were there, along with a few people I didn't recognize, who I guessed were Mike's friends from high school. I scanned them out of habit, looking for Mast, but of course he wasn't there. Why would he be?

"Beer?" Mike said, kneeling over a cooler. Arthur and one of the Joshes were standing nearby, playing cornhole with a few boys I didn't recognize. Before I could respond, Mike tossed me a can.

"Two more," Kate called to him.

She and Seema were sitting around a sleek gas firepit with AJ, Arun, Micah, and Drew—their faces lit up by the flames as they sipped their beers.

Mike settled in next to Kate, who folded her legs toward him like a fawn. Otherwise, there was no space left on the sofa except near AJ, who was slouched, his legs splayed so they took up twice the space that he needed.

He looked up at me, amused, as if he saw my conundrum and relished how uncomfortable it made me. Just to spite him, I sat down, trying not to let my arms or legs touch his, which was impossible because he refused to make room.

"Nice skirt," AJ said to me. Though it was a compliment, it didn't feel like one.

In some alternate universe, where AJ was kind and funny and expressed compassion for the feelings of others, I could see him being considered attractive. There was nothing wrong with his hair, which was darker than Mike's, or his face, which was gruffer and slightly more chiseled, or even his body, which looked impressive in both sweats and business casual. It was his expression that ruined it, his cool eyes and smug smile that made me wish implantables already existed so I could hack into his chip and scramble his face.

"Thanks," I mumbled.

Beside me, Arun and Micah were complaining about

Kowalski's new assignment, a problem that required a greedy algorithm, and felt like it was intentionally designed to drive us mad.

"So is it true? About the offer?" AJ asked.

At first, I didn't think he was talking to me. Why would he be talking to me?

"The Vilbo deal?"

"Yeah. Did they really offer you one point five million and did you really turn it down?"

I searched his face, trying to figure out if he was setting me up for an epic takedown, but he seemed too sincere.

"Yeah, I did."

"That's pretty cool," AJ said. To my surprise, he didn't seem to be making fun of me. He was just being . . . nice? Was that even the right word?

"Thanks," I murmured. We sat in silence, half listening to the conversations nearby, though I could only hear enough to keep up with bits and pieces. The only person left to talk to was AJ, and while I wasn't thrilled at the prospect of conversing with him, I figured it was a good opportunity to make sure he wasn't ObjectPermanence.

"So you grew up around here," I said.

"Menlo Park, born and raised," AJ said, taking a sip of his beer. "Can't you tell from my carefree demeanor and my proclivity for disruption?" He pointed with his beer through the trees. "My house is just down the hill, three miles away as the drone flies."

I stiffened at his mention of a drone.

"She's fine by the way," he said. "I know you were concerned."

"Who is?"

"My drone."

"Oh good. I was worried. So you're saying I should keep my shades down from now on?"

"What's the point of living in beautiful California if you can't see it? Drones are part of the view in California. They're like birds. Might as well get used to them now."

I rolled my eyes. "So your parents work in tech?"

"Everyone's parents work in tech."

"My parents don't work in tech."

"I guess you're no one, then."

He said it casually, like it was a joke, though we both knew that it wasn't.

I thought about ObjectPermanence and what he'd said about his parents and his upbringing. "I've heard that kids who grow up with a lot of money feel more like nobodies than people who grew up with nothing."

AJ's eye twitched. "Why would they feel like nobodies?"

I studied him, wondering if I could detect a hint of recognition. "They feel like they don't deserve what they have."

AJ held my gaze for a moment. "I don't know what you're talking about." Though he said it with confidence, he wouldn't look me in the eye, and I wondered if under all of his bullying, his insecurities weren't that different from mine.

He couldn't be ObjectPermanence, could he? It would be too cruel of a joke. Yet it now seemed slightly almost barely possible that a person like AJ could be capable of writing the messages ObjectPermanence had, if he'd known that no one could trace them back to him.

That's when Kate clinked an opener against her beer bottle. Everyone on the deck quieted down.

"Let's play a game," she said.

"Flip cup," AJ hollered.

"Quaint idea, but I was thinking something a little more technologically advanced, since we are the *future leaders of our generation*." The last part she said in a mock Lars Lang voice, which actually sounded pretty spot-on.

"I don't know if you realize," Kate continued, "but we have in our presence the illustrious founder of Dare Me."

Everyone turned to Arthur, who grinned and took a little bow.

"I've invited everyone here to a private group on the app. Once you join it, you can send anyone in the group an anonymous Truth or Dare, which I'll read out loud, shotgun style. If you refuse to answer or do the dare, you have to take a shot."

There was an uncomfortable shuffle as everyone opened Dare Me. We all knew that people were more brazen when they were anonymous, and I didn't like the idea of being put on the spot at a party with potentially mortifying questions. On the other hand, it was also an opportunity.

AJ, Mike, Arun—any of them could be ObjectPermanence. I clicked on each of their names and began typing my questions.

"Okay," Kate said after a few minutes. "Who's up first?"

She shook her phone, then looked at the screen and smiled. "Seema. Truth or Dare?"

Seema let out a breath. "Truth."

Kate tapped her phone, then read the anonymous question. "What's your bra size?"

"Seriously?" Seema groaned. "34B," she admitted to the delight of the boys around us.

"Are you a virgin?" Kate said, reading the next question.

Seema hesitated. "Sort of."

Micah scoffed. "You either are or aren't. You can't be halfway."

"Then I guess I am," she said.

"Where's the dirtiest place you've ever hooked up with anyone?" Kate read.

Seema shifted uncomfortably, and I wondered if she would take the shot. "The bathroom at one of the tech fairs," she finally admitted, to shouts.

"Who was it?" Arun asked.

"None of your business," Seema said.

"If you had to hook up with someone at the Foundry, who would it be?" Kate read.

Seema thought about it. "Mr. Lajani. Okay, these questions are getting way too personal. Let's do a dare."

"Lick all the condensation from the outside of a beer bottle," Kate read.

Seema rolled her eyes. "I'll take the shot." A few boys booed.

Kate shook her phone again. "Okay, Arun, it's your turn."

He leaned forward, cradling his beer. "Truth me."

"Have you ever seen the movie *2001: A Space Odyssey*?"

Everyone groaned but me. It was my question.

"Seriously?" Kate said. "Seema gets asked if she's a virgin and the boys get asked about movies?"

Arun gave her an amused shrug. "I'll give you a twofer. I'm not a virgin, and I haven't seen *2001: A Space Odyssey*. Is that the one with the monkeys?"

"That's *Planet of the Apes*," Josh said. "But close."

Time slowed as I processed his answer. Arun hadn't seen *2001: A Space Odyssey*?

Kate asked him another question, but I didn't pay attention. If Arun hadn't seen it, then he couldn't be Object-Permanence.

While everyone chatted, I let the realization sink in. It didn't matter that I'd thought he was the most likely option. It wasn't him. I mentally crossed him off my list, which meant that there were only two names left: Mike and AJ.

"These questions are boring. Let's do a dare," Arun said.

"Read the search history on your phone out loud," Kate read.

Arun winced. "I'll go for the shot, please."

While Mike poured him a drink, Kate shook her phone again. "AJ, you're up."

"Truth," he said from beside me, a cocky glint in his eye.

"Rate every girl at the Foundry from one to ten," Kate read.

"Too easy," AJ said. "Deborah is obviously a one. Amina's a five."

My face flushed with righteous rage for both of them.

"Seema's a seven. Kate's a nine, and Xia . . ." AJ studied me. "You know I normally don't like Asian girls, but I'll admit it, Xia's an eight."

It made me feel like a punchline, like I was a freak on display. I could almost feel the spotlight on me while a circus announcer spoke into his megaphone: Step right up, folks, and see the Chinese Code Doll! A Slanted-eyed Wonder! She's Asian *and* she's pretty! A living paradox! She'll dazzle you with her programming and her good looks! You might think that Chinese girls can't be pretty, but this one will make you think twice!

It was a confirmation of how I'd always felt. That I was inherently different than everyone else, inherently less-than. I shifted in my seat, feeling suddenly aware of his leg touching mine, and wanted to push it away.

"Truth me again," AJ said.

"Have you . . . ever seen the movie *2001: A Space Odyssey*?" Kate read. "Wow, someone really likes this movie."

"Of course I have," AJ said.

A pit formed in my stomach.

"Do you like peanut butter and banana sandwiches?" Kate read. "This person really doesn't understand the spirit of the game."

It wasn't any old pit; it was a rupture in the space-time

continuum, causing time to slow.

"Who doesn't?" AJ said, the words stretching out and folding in on themselves, multiplying and dividing. *Whooooo ooo. Who ooo Wh ooo ooo Doeesss nn'tt?*

"Do you have a good relationship with your dad?" Kate read. "Another weird question. Who's asking these?"

"Definitely not."

His voice sounded distant, like I was far away, being pulled deep into the gravity of the event horizon.

Kate asked him a few more questions, but I barely heard them. AJ. ObjectPermanence. Could it be?

I watched him decline to tell anyone how much money his father gave him in his spending account when Kate turned to me.

"Okay, Xia," she said. "What'll it be?"

I steeled myself. "Truth."

"Are you a virgin?" Kate read.

I swallowed. "Yes."

"What's your bra size?" Kate read.

"34A," I mumbled.

"Do you have a gag reflex?" Kate read with a grimace.

I hated this game. "Of course I do."

"If you had to hook up with anyone here, who would it be?"

I hesitated. "I'll take the shot."

"Oh, come on," Kate said.

"I want the shot," I insisted.

"Fine."

I tried not to gag as the vodka slid down my throat, burning my insides like I had swallowed fire.

While I sat stunned by the very real possibility that my online soul mate was AJ, Kate turned to Micah, then Drew, though I barely registered their answers.

Then it was Mike's turn.

"Here we go again," Kate said, looking at the question on her screen. "Mike, have you ever seen the movie *2001: A Space Odyssey*?"

"I haven't," Mike said.

I was hurtling past the event horizon, all light and matter sucking me toward the singularity: that AJ was ObjectPermanence.

If Mike hadn't seen *2001: A Space Odyssey*, then he couldn't be ObjectPermanence, either. I blinked, feeling the ground shift beneath me. With Mike and Arun off the list, that left only one name:

AJ.

"Peanut butter and banana sandwiches?" Kate asked, shortening the question on her phone, but the answer didn't matter.

"Delicious," he said.

"Relationship with dad?"

"Not great."

I felt suddenly aware of AJ's arm brushing against mine every time he took a drink. Had it been him this whole time? Was he the one I thought I was in love with? Was he the one I had traded Mast for?

"Rate every girl at the Foundry on a scale of one to ten," Kate read.

Amid boos, Mike asked for the shot.

"My turn," Kate said, and handed the phone to Seema. "Truth, obviously."

"What's your bra size?" Seema read.

"32B. Boring. Next."

"What color underwear are you wearing?"

Kate peeked beneath her pants. "Black. Next."

"Are you a virgin?" Seema read.

Kate gave Seema a coy smile. "No."

An excited murmur rose over the party. AJ nodded at Mike, who looked embarrassed.

"Where's the nastiest place you've done the deed?" Seema read.

"A dressing room at the mall."

The boys whooped. Drew nudged Mike as if to ask him if it was true, but he only looked at his feet, his face beet red.

"Okay, dare me," Kate said.

"Take off your shirt," Seema read.

I assumed Kate would decline and take a shot, but she pulled her camel sweater over her shoulders only to reveal a T-shirt of the same exact color beneath it.

"Boo," Drew said.

"Hey, quit it," Mike said, elbowing him in the side.

"Next," Kate said.

"Take off your bra," Seema read.

To everyone's surprise, Kate reached under the back of

her shirt and unclasped her bra. She slipped it off and dangled it in the air to the delight of all the boys at the party. It was a beautiful bra, black and delicate and lacey, the kind of bra you saw in movies. Just looking at it made me feel frumpy and childish. I thought about my cheap cotton bras and wanted to throw them all out.

Kate dropped it in Mike's lap, who stared at it in awe. "Next," she said.

"Kiss another girl," Seema read.

"Really?" she said to no one in particular, then leaned toward Seema and pressed her lips to hers. The boys whooped and hollered. "Next."

"I dare you to kiss the person on your right."

She turned to Mike and smiled, then kissed him. It was oddly intimate to witness, and I shifted in my seat.

"Next," she said.

"Post an ugly picture of yourself on social media," Seema read.

"Now, *that* I won't do," Kate said, and took a shot.

The next round went quickly. Arun drank. Josh drank. Drew drank. Mike refused to reveal how many girls he'd hooked up with and took a shot. AJ said the number of girls he'd hooked up with was "too high to remember" and took a shot. Seema refused to take her bra off and took a shot.

When it was my turn again, I held my breath.

"What exactly does Mitzy Erst see in you?" Kate read.

I was surprised by how resentful the question was, and wondered who had asked it. "I—I don't know. She likes

Wiser and thinks it has potential."

Kate's eyes narrowed ever so slightly, as though she were annoyed by my response. She read the next question. "You grew up with a single mom who was also an immigrant. Do you think that contributed to you getting into the Foundry?"

"What?"

Kate began to repeat the question, but I interrupted her. "No, I heard you. I just . . ." I let my voice trail off. My face grew hot. I scanned the faces around me, wondering who had written it. It could have been anyone. "That isn't even a question. It's a statement in question form."

"Does that mean you're not going to answer?" Kate said.

"Give me the shot."

I could feel the vodka hollowing out a hole in my stomach, but I didn't mind. It was better than answering questions, better than looking around the group and wondering who thought I didn't belong here.

By then, everyone was starting to feel woozy. Drew took a picture of himself humping a decorative lawn sculpture and posted it online. Arun drank a cup of water from the hot tub, then spit it out all over the deck. Josh couldn't drink any more and agreed to kiss Seema. Seema couldn't drink any more and took off her cardigan, then her shirt, until she was sitting in a thin camisole. Micah filmed himself doing an impression of Deborah and posted it online.

"Deborah is smarter than anyone here," I protested.

"And?" Micah said.

"You're being cruel," I said. "What if she sees that video?"

"If she doesn't want anyone doing her impression, then maybe she shouldn't make it so easy," AJ said.

I wanted to say something witty in return but my brain wasn't working as quickly as it normally did, and I was distracted by the way the couch seemed to be swaying.

"Okay," said Kate, who was the only one in the entire group who didn't seem drunk. "Xia, Truth or Dare?"

"Dare," I said.

Kate looked at the prompt on her phone. "I dare you to spend ten minutes locked in a closet with a randomly generated person from this group."

I couldn't drink any more, and to be honest, the thought of sitting in a dark closet sounded nice. "Sure."

I held my breath while Kate shook her phone, and hoped it wouldn't be AJ.

Kate's face dropped when she read the name. "Mike."

A hush fell over the deck as everyone considered what it meant for me to spend ten minutes in a dark room with Kate's boyfriend. Mike looked at me sheepishly.

"Seriously?" he said to Kate, in a tone that made me wish I could invent a phase-changing machine so that I could dissolve my current self into a stream of vapor and disperse myself into the atmosphere. No one ever felt embarrassed to be locked in a small space with air molecules.

"Can't you shake it again?" Mike said.

"It's a dare," Arun said. "You can't just change it because you don't like it."

Kate locked eyes with me, silently demanding that I decline the dare and take the shot, but I couldn't. The deck already felt like it was defying the laws of gravity. I looked at Mike, who sighed. "Fine," he said. "The pantry it is."

"Wow," I whispered upon entering. "*This* is a closet? If it wasn't filled with noodles and chips, you could rent this place out."

Mike laughed, and I was surprised by how good it made me feel. Why did I care if I'd made Mike smile? He wasn't ObjectPermanence, that much was clear from tonight. He was just another rich, popular boy whose girlfriend had invited me to his party to humiliate me.

He dug around a shelf.

"What are you looking for?"

He emerged with a cardboard box labeled "plastic utensils" in black marker.

"We're supposed to be doing something illicit in here," Mike said. "Might as well make the people happy."

He opened the box to reveal a dozen little jars of caviar.

"They're my stepmom's. She gets them shipped from Europe and doesn't like to share them because they're expensive. So she hides them."

He turned the lid of the jar until it clicked open.

"This is what money smells like," he said and held it up to my nose, his arm brushing against mine.

It smelled cold and briny, like the ocean. "I didn't realize money smelled so . . . fishy."

Mike smiled, and I was reminded of how incredibly

beautiful he was. Even in a dark closet, totally drunk, his face sweaty, his sweatshirt stained with beer, he looked like he'd stepped out of a magazine.

He opened a bag of tortilla chips and held it out to me.

"Won't she notice?"

"She'll just think my dad ate them and they'll get into an argument about why she feels like she needs to hide things from him, and that since he pays for everything, he has a right to eat whatever he wants, and she'll say fine, if he doesn't value the work she does at home then she'll leave, and she'll storm off to the bedroom and slam the door and my dad will sleep in the guestroom for three nights until they eventually make up."

"Wow. So this is a very loaded chip."

"Very."

"It seems wrong," I said. "Eating caviar with Tostitos. Don't you have a fancy cracker or something?"

Mike grinned. "If we ate it with a cracker it'd be less illicit."

It tasted slippery and wet and salty all at once. I swallowed, wanting to like it, but couldn't help but wince as it went down.

"Not your favorite," Mike observed.

"No, it's . . . great. It's really good."

"I don't really like it either. That's the thing about having nice things. You feel like you're supposed to like them because everyone says you should, so you say you do until you believe it, and then one day you realize that maybe you don't like any of the things you told yourself you liked, and you wonder if your entire personality is based off of what *other people* think you should be instead of what *you* think you should be."

I stared at him. ObjectPermanence had said almost the exact same thing in one of his messages. But Mike had a girlfriend and he hadn't seen *2001: A Space Odyssey*. It couldn't be him.

"Are we still talking about caviar?" I asked.

"Sorry," he said. "I'm a little drunk. I don't know where that came from." He looked up at me, and I felt the power of his attention.

"You're easy to talk to," he said.

"I'm just sitting here, watching the room spin, trying not to fall over."

"Yeah, but you don't seem judgmental."

"Maybe you need to find new friends."

Mike let out a laugh. "Maybe I do." He sighed. "I wonder how far into the ten minutes we are."

I took it to mean that he was tired of sitting in the closet with me and felt suddenly miserable. But then he added, "I don't want to go back out there. A little quiet is nice sometimes."

We sat for a moment in silence, neither of us knowing what to say.

"So what are you about?" Mike said, offering me the chips.

I took one but skipped the caviar. "What do you mean?"

"You know, what are you into? What do you like? What

do you not like? I know you're not into caviar."

I knew I had interests, but now that I was being asked to produce them, I couldn't think of a single one. "I like mint chocolate chip ice cream," I said. "I like taking things apart and putting them back together. I like going to stationery stores and admiring all the fancy pens and pencils, but I never buy them because it seems frivolous. I mean, who uses pencils anymore?"

Mike laughed.

"I used to think I hated winter but now that I'm here, I find myself missing it."

"What about it?"

"The first time it snows. The way the frost coats the lawn. How everyone congregates at the grocery store before a big storm to stock up on milk and eggs and you feel like you're all in it together."

I was so certain that I was boring him that I was surprised to find Mike listening with rapt attention. "What are you about?" I asked him.

"I like coffee ice cream. I like the shock to the chest when you first jump into a pool. I like getting into a hot car when it's been sitting in the sun all day and seeing how long I can bear it before opening the windows."

"Seriously?" I said with a laugh. "So you like punishing yourself."

Mike grinned. "It's like a sauna. Do you think people in spas are punishing themselves?"

"I've never been to a sauna. But if it's like sitting in a hot car, then yes, that would constitute self-punishment."

"I'm thirsty," he said. "Are you thirsty?"

"Parched."

"Let's see what we have in here."

He leaned over me to rummage through the lower shelf of the pantry. I tried to stay out of his way, but he smelled so good, like cologne that had been slept in and had grown soft and sweet on the sheets. I didn't like him, I reminded myself. He was best friends with AJ, and he was dating Kate, and he definitely wasn't ObjectPermanence. But I could still admire him.

He emerged with a box of sparkling mineral water. "It's warm, but it's better than nothing."

It hissed as he turned the cap, and instead of taking a drink, he offered it to me first.

"Is this imported from France, too?"

"It is," Mike admitted, "but no one will get mad if we drink it."

"Okay, good. I don't want to be a home-wrecker."

"Don't worry. It was already wrecked. My dad cheated on my mom when I was ten."

I grew quiet. "I'm sorry."

I leaned toward him and bopped my leg against his, and we sat like that for a moment when the door burst open. I winced as light from the kitchen flooded the pantry.

Kate stood in the doorway. "Time's up."

She slipped her hand in Mike's and led him outside,

glancing back at me with a suspicious look as I followed them.

Kate watched me for the rest of the night. The game was entering its final stage, where most people succumbed to truths and dares because they couldn't bear to drink any more. Then it was Mike's turn again.

"Mike," she said, looking at him, though this time her expression was more cold than playful. "Truth or Dare?"

"Truth me," Mike said.

"If you could . . ." Kate hesitated as she read the question on her phone, "kiss anyone in the room other than Kate, who would it be?" She gave Mike an icy look, as if daring him to answer.

"Oh shit," AJ said.

Panic flashed across Mike's face. "Skip."

"Skip?" Kate said. "That's not a thing."

"Well, I can't drink any more and I can't answer the question, so I have to skip."

"There's no skipping," Kate said.

"AJ, then," Mike said. "I'd kiss AJ."

AJ winced.

Kate rolled her eyes. "Truth means that you have to give a real answer."

Strangely enough, Mike looked at me. It was quick, so quick that I wondered if it had even happened. My head was fuzzy and my vision wasn't its best; it was possible he hadn't looked at all.

"I'll take the shot," he said, looking away.

Had Kate noticed? I didn't think so, though part of me wished she had.

The game continued until someone dared Arun to jump into the hot tub with all of his clothes on, and a few others followed: Drew and AJ had taken off their shirts and were chugging beers and laughing. Seema and Micah seemed to be sitting awfully close together, and Kate was leaning against Mike's chest, his arm wrapped around her waist. But instead of looking at Mike, her eyes were on me.

She wasn't glaring at me, exactly, but she wasn't smiling either, and the steadiness of her gaze made me uneasy. The music was blasting, the base vibrating in my chest. I tried to distract myself with the conversation on the other side of the couch, but I could feel Kate's attention amplifying, pulsing toward me like someone was turning the volume up.

When I couldn't bear it any longer, I slipped inside to the kitchen, where the lights were dimmed and the music from outside was muffled. A relief.

"Are you okay?"

I looked up to see AJ standing in front of me in sweatpants, his shirt off, a towel draped over his shoulders, which were even more muscular than they looked beneath his shirt. He was holding two cups of water, one of which he handed to me.

"Don't look so surprised. I'm not a total asshole."

"Yes you are."

He smirked. "Okay, maybe I am."

I expected him to leave, but he lingered, like he was waiting for me to say something.

"Well, thanks for the water," I said.

"You're welcome."

Strangely, instead of leaving, he seemed to be settling in.

"There was plenty of room in the hot tub," AJ said.

My head throbbed. I wanted to sit down. "It looked pretty crowded. And anyway, I didn't bring a bathing suit."

"Neither did I."

"I see that."

AJ stepped closer to me. "Do you like what you see?"

"What?" I said.

Before I knew what was happening, he was pressing his mouth to mine. It was cold and wet and tasted sour like beer. I felt his tongue force itself into my mouth, and I winced and tried to wriggle out of his grasp.

"Come here," he said, grabbing my waist, but I pushed him away.

"Oh, come on," he said, leaning into me until I was pressed against the cabinets. "You've been looking at me all night."

"What?" I said. "No I haven't."

He was drunk and slurring and seemed to think I was joking. He grabbed my chest and tried to kiss me again but I squirmed and elbowed him in the side.

He jumped back, his face suddenly angry. "What the fuck?"

My chest was heaving. I inched away from him and tried to catch my breath.

"You tease me all night and when I finally act on it you get all prudish?"

I couldn't believe it. *He* was angry at *me*? "What are you talking about?"

"You clearly wanted it. Why else would you sit next to me and ask me all those dumb questions?"

"Because it was the only seat left and that's how you make polite conversation, you ask other people about themselves."

AJ's eyes grew cold and narrow. "You think you're some kind of supermodel or something? You're only pretty because you look semi-decent in a skirt. You're lucky I'd even consider you."

Though I knew I shouldn't listen to him, it felt like he'd spit in my face.

"Fucking girls," he muttered and stormed off to the deck.

I watched him leave, my head spinning, my stomach churning. I wanted to beam myself home, to take a shower and scrub him off of me, to go back in time and erase the entire night. What would I do if ObjectPermanence was him?

# twenty-five

The morning arrived too quickly. I didn't want to face the day even though it was beautiful out, the California vista appearing in my window like a stock background image: bright, unblemished, and impersonal. By then, I was used to being hungover, and though I thought I was comfortable being alone, this was a new kind of solitude: Mast and Amina were gone, Wiser was a smarmy ad-machine, and ObjectPermanence was the only person in the world I didn't want him to be.

I reached for my phone and rolled over in bed. It had been vibrating on and off all morning, infiltrating my sleep until my dreams all featured an uncanny valley version of AJ, pressing me into a cabinet that grew deeper and deeper, engulfing me until I found a switchboard on his back and frantically pressed all the buttons, making him twitch and vibrate as he short-circuited.

I rubbed my wrist. I could still feel his hand on my skin,

could still smell the alcohol on his breath as he jammed his tongue into my mouth. How was I going to face him in class? I didn't want to think about it, and instead opened my notifications.

I'd posted a picture of the hot tub when I'd first gotten to the party, and assumed that all of the notifications I'd been getting had been from that, but when I looked at my screen, I saw that I had a dozen new messages. Strange.

The first four were from Gina.

>UM YOU DIDN'T TELL ME YOU WERE DATING AN UNDERWEAR MODEL

I had no idea what she was talking about.

>What? I'm not

>That's not what it looks like . . .

I was starting to get a sinking feeling in my stomach.

>Looks like where?

>In the picture

>What picture?????

>Check Façade

I opened the Façade app to discover that I'd been tagged in another post by ValleyBrag. I clicked through and felt my stomach lurch as I was hurled back into my nightmare.

It was a photo of me and AJ at the party. He was pinning me against the cabinets, his hand on my chest, his lips pressing against mine. I studied myself. My hand was on his arm, trying to push him away, but from the angle, you couldn't tell. It wasn't obvious that I was trying to extricate myself at all. If I hadn't been there, I might have assumed that I was enjoying it.

The caption read: *Once upon a time in Portola Valley, a boy and girl got drunk at a party and then . . .*

Hundreds of people had already liked it, and dozens more had commented.

>Hand up the shirt, the unofficial Silicon Valley handshake

>So professional. *eye roll*

>And these are supposed to be our future tech leaders. Smh

>So this is how she got into the Foundry

>Great role models all around. And drinking too. I guess you can do whatever you want when you're coronated by the Foundry

I felt like I was going to be sick. I studied the photo again, wondering who had taken it. Had it been Kate? I thought back to the way she'd been staring at me from the hot tub. She was the only person other than AJ who seemed out to get me.

I opened my texts and typed back to Gina.

>It's not what it looks like. I told him to stop but he wouldn't until I elbowed him in the ribs

There was a long pause.

>Seriously? I'm sorry. I wouldn't have made a joke about it if I'd known. Are you okay?

>Yes and no. You'll never guess who this guy is

>...

>Drone guy

>Are you kidding???

>That's not even the worst of it

>??

>I'm pretty sure he's ObjectPermanence

>WHAT? That can't be possible. Are you sure?

>He's the only one left on the list.

>Maybe you made a mistake. Is there some way to be
certain? Can you just ask him what his name is? You don't
have to tell him who you are or anything. What do you
have to lose?

Gina was right, in a way. What's the worst that could
happen if I just asked him if his name was AJ? That he would
say yes and we would never speak again? The idea of writing
to him now seemed impossible, so the end result would be
the same either way.

>I'll think about it

I was about to cover my face with my pillow and go back
to sleep when a text came in from Mitzy.

>Who's the new joystick?

>He's not my joystick

>Doesn't look that way from the picture. Look I'm all for
playing a few video games but you can't let pictures like
this get out.

>You think I'm happy about this? I didn't even want him to
kiss me.

>Ah, the classic male Control + Alt + Insert. It happens to
the best of us. Best not to put yourself in that situation in
the future.

Her response irritated me. Was she implying that it was
my fault?

>What am I supposed to do, not go to parties anymore? I

didn't know anyone was taking photos.

>Not getting totally wasted would be a good start. Also
good to assume that everyone is taking photos all the time.
You're a public figure now. Act like one.

I couldn't believe that the person who had given me acid at a VC meet and greet was telling me to behave more professionally.

>Are you kidding? What about the night we met, when you
puked in the bathroom? What about the Karlsson Barrow
party?

>I've worked on my image for almost a decade to be able
to drink at a party like that. Have you noticed that no one
ever posts any damaging photos of me? Because they know
they'd never get my help again, and everyone needs help
in this business.

I didn't want to admit it, but she was right. Though there'd been plenty of unflattering pictures posted of me and other people at the parties, the worst photos I'd seen of Mitzy were of her drinking champagne and looking glamorous.

>You're not Mitzy Erst, you're Xia Chan. People are only
just starting to figure out how to pronounce your name.
You don't have any power. You only have potential, which
everyone is going to try to chip away at because that's the
business we're in.

Her mention of my name reminded me of all the times I'd been made fun of or told I didn't belong. It reminded me of AJ, telling me that I was a nobody and that I would always be a nobody.

>Got it. Thanks

I stuffed my phone under my pillow. Through the door, I heard Amina's door opening and closing. She must have seen the photo. I wondered what she thought about it and found myself wanting her to knock on my door and collapse in my bed and tell me everything was going to be fine, that we were right and they were wrong. But I only heard footsteps disappearing down the hall.

■ ■ ■

That night, I received a new message in BitBop.

NEW MESSAGE FROM U/OBJECTPERMANENCE:
Do you ever feel like you purposely sabotage your own life?

I was at a party last night and got too drunk and did something stupid. Well, a few things, really, but one big thing. I hurt someone I didn't want to hurt, and I'm worried the damage is unfixable.

I don't know why I'm telling you this and not the person I hurt. Or maybe I do. It's because I don't have to face you in my everyday life. You don't know any of the details so you can't think that I'm terrible.

Am I a coward? Maybe. I'm going to try to do better. I don't even know what I expect you to say. Just . . . thanks for listening.

I leaned back in my chair, feeling like the air had been knocked out of me. It was an unwitting apology that fit with the events from the night before, though I still had a hard time picturing AJ writing it. If this side of him was real, it was just a minuscule portion of his interior life, one that he hid completely from the people he interacted with every day, and wasn't that the side that really mattered?

In a previous life, I might have written back and assured him that he was a good person, that I could say that with confidence because I *knew* him.

But I didn't know him. Not like I thought I did.

I closed my computer and curled up in bed and felt lonelier than I had in a long time. This, I supposed, was what grief felt like.

■ ■ ■

I didn't go to class the next day. What was the point? To hear the class hush when I walked in? To see Mast ignore me, his eyes glued to the whiteboard? To have to steel myself when I walked past AJ, knowing that he was ObjectPermanence? To have to endure Kowalski's withering gaze as I sat through yet another lecture that I didn't follow? What was the point, when I could spend the day not being humiliated and working on Wiser instead?

I called Mitzy to see if she wanted to get breakfast, but she didn't pick up, so I went by myself to one of the fancy coffee shops we'd frequented. There, I ordered a latte and an avocado toast and felt my confidence slowly return as I ate alone in front of my laptop and pretended to look busy and official.

I tinkered with Wiser and tried not to think about ObjectPermanence and AJ when I saw a new message in my inbox. It was from Lars Lang.

Could you stop by my office today? 2pm. -LL

The fact that he was scheduling the appointment was worrisome, and I wondered if it had something to do with the AJ photo. Though there wasn't a rule about dating other fellows, the photo was unprofessional. Maybe Lars wanted to talk to me about that.

I packed up my things and went back to campus. I tried to avoid everyone by walking to Lars's office the long way, but Mike appeared beneath the pergola in the courtyard. Even more concerning was that he looked like he was walking toward me.

"Hey," he said. "I was wondering if you were ever going to show up on campus again."

The mere act of having to look Mike in the eye after knowing he'd seen the photo of me and AJ was mortifying.

"I wouldn't if I didn't have to." I thought back to our time in the closet and wondered why the universe had decided to make AJ ObjectPermanence and not Mike. He would have been such a better choice.

"Look, I just wanted to apologize for AJ."

"Are you his keeper or something?"

"No, but I know what he did and I know he feels bad about it."

"Then he should apologize himself. It doesn't count if someone does it for you."

"He really is a good guy deep down. You just have to get to know him."

"I know enough," I said, realizing that Mike would never understand how well I actually knew his friend.

"He's been going through a tough time. His dad walked out on him when he was a kid, and now his mom has cancer. It's been really hard for him and he's just taking out his anger wherever he can."

The room around us froze as if someone had pressed pause. "What did you say?"

"His mom has cancer."

"No, not that part. I mean, that's terrible and I'm sorry to hear that, but the other part. About his dad?"

"His dad walked out on him when he was a kid?"

"I—I didn't know that. I thought his dad was rich and lived with him and gave him money."

"His dad is rich and does send him money but that's the extent of their relationship. I don't think he's seen him in years, unless you count public appearances or online stalking."

"So he doesn't talk to him?"

"No."

"Like, not ever?" I said.

Mike looked confused. "I mean, maybe once a year, if that. They don't have a relationship."

"Then why does everyone talk about him like he's his dad's carefully groomed protégé?"

Mike shrugged. "People make assumptions."

I could have hugged Mike.

Mast wasn't ObjectPermanence, but neither was AJ. I'd made a mistake, which, for the first time in a long while, gave me hope. I studied Mike, and for a moment we were back at the party and he was sitting across from me, his eyes lingering on me while Kate asked him who else he would kiss. If I'd been wrong about AJ, maybe I was wrong about Mike and Arun, too.

■ ■ ■

Lars Lang was already sitting in his office when I arrived. That should have been the first sign. The second sign was that he was dressed up in office casual, which was bizarre and confusing. The third sign was that he seemed nervous, his leg sporadically bouncing under the desk as I took a seat across from him.

"I wanted to bring you in today to see how things are going."

He sounded like a manager who was about to fire someone. That's when I should have known.

"They're fine," I said.

"I spoke with Mr. Kowalski. He's concerned about your progress in class."

My stomach sank. So that's why he brought me here.

"I know I'm behind on the assignments," I said. "I've just been really busy. I don't know if you heard about the Vilbo offer?"

"I did."

I'd expected him to be a little more congratulatory, but he only frowned.

"It's impressive. However, it doesn't make up for the fact that you haven't completed your required coursework."

Sweat beaded on my upper lip. "But the year isn't over yet. I'm going to finish it."

"Your instructors don't seem to think so."

"Instructors? As in more than one?" Though I knew I'd fallen behind in most of my classes, I hadn't realized that other teachers had been concerned about me, too.

Lars nodded.

"Why didn't they say anything?"

"According to Ms. Perez, you weren't in class enough for her to tell you. And Mr. Lajani said he'd written you a few notes on your assignments to come see him, but you never followed through."

I thought back to Mr. Lajani's assignments. I'd turned so many in partially finished that I'd avoided looking at his comments since I could already guess what they would say.

"But my stock is so high," I said. "I'm missing class because I have meetings with important tech people. I'm not just twiddling my thumbs."

"Look, I appreciate that, I do. But this is still a school, and in order to finish the year you need to complete all your requirements."

My face went cold. "What do you mean, *in order to finish the year*?"

"That if you continue like this, we can't list the Foundry on your transcript."

"So what, I'd have to repeat the grade at home?"

"If you have incompletes for all of your classes, then yes."

This couldn't be happening. "But I'm doing what you

said I should do. I'm getting funding. I'm starting a company."

"Yes, but we ask that you do that while completing your coursework," Lars said. "All of our former fellows were able to do both, so I know it's possible."

"But you said in your welcome speech that classes weren't mandatory."

"Classes aren't mandatory but assignments are, and I think that as a policy, that's already extremely lenient."

Was he implying that I was being unreasonable, when he had told the entire class in his welcome speech that all that mattered was our product?

"What am I supposed to do? Make up all of the work from the last semester that I didn't finish? That would take months."

Lars sat back in his chair as though I were proving his point. "Your instructors have agreed to curate the semester's assignments to a small selection of their choosing and let you finish those instead. Pass them in by the Showcase and you'll be fine."

I must have looked upset because Lars continued, "It's a good deal. Everyone else in your class had to do the full load."

"Thanks," I murmured, but I didn't feel grateful. I felt like everyone had turned against me.

# ·······twenty-six·······

**T**hat **night, when** I should have been starting my backlog of assignments, I went through all of ObjectPermanence's messages again, searching for any signs of Mike or Arun. Had either of them hurt anyone irreparably at the party? Arun had answered so many of the truth questions in rude and degrading ways, and Mike had given me that look when Kate had asked him who he'd kiss, but other than that I couldn't think of anything. Did either of those count? Did they cause irreparable damage? I wasn't so sure. With no other options, I opened a new window and composed a message.

> SENT MESSAGE FROM u/ARRAYOFLIGHT:
> I wish I could tell you that I'm sorry you had a bad night
> and that I know exactly how it feels to have hurt someone
> in a way that you can't take back. I wish I could say that
> you'll figure out the right thing to do. All those things are

true, but the truth is, every time I start typing a message to you, I stare at the cursor, unsure of what to say because any response feels dishonest.

I hope you'll forgive me, but I've been keeping something from you.

You're here, at the Foundry. I know because I'm here, too. I've known for a while, and I've been trying to figure out who you are. I thought I knew, but now I'm not so sure. I'm sorry I didn't tell you.

Can we meet in person?

It was the scariest message I'd ever written. I clicked send and shut my laptop, imagining the words shooting through the ether, arriving moments later with a ping in his inbox.

■ ■ ■

A week passed. Then another. I didn't hear from him. In fact, I barely heard from anyone. Mitzy was strangely absent. I hadn't received a message from her since our tense texts about the AJ photo, and though I'd been calling her to see if she had any leads on new VC meetings, she never picked up or called back, despite the fact that my messages were getting increasingly desperate. Should I have taken Ella Eisner's offer? Would I ever get funding? Would I have to move home and go back to my old high school where I'd be held back a year and have to live through the mortification of everyone knowing that I went to the Foundry and failed spectacularly?

When I wasn't trying to learn all the things I hadn't

last semester, I busied myself by reprogramming Wiser, but the advertisement integration wasn't going well. I vaguely recalled Kowalski talking about unconstrained convex optimization in one of his lectures and how it could improve an algorithm's processing of personalized messaging, but I couldn't remember anything beyond that.

When I got frustrated, I checked BitBop only to find an empty inbox. ObjectPermanence had probably combed through our messages and my post history, just like I had his, trying to figure out who I was. The only difference was that there were only five girls at the Foundry, so far fewer people to choose from. What if he'd discovered it was me and was disappointed, and that's why he hadn't written back?

I was so desperate for contact that I went so far as to check my physical mailbox, which I hadn't opened in over a month because I so rarely received anything other than junk. It was packed full, the spam catalogues and sale fliers torn at the edges. I sorted through them when an envelope slipped out.

It was made of beautiful, textured paper that felt substantial in my hand. My name was written in flowing cursive. The return sender was Veronica DuChamp, the tech stylist. I wondered if it was an invitation to a fancy event or private party and thought excitedly about who would be there and what I would wear, but when I opened it, my chest deflated.

It was an invoice. For $12,541.

I blinked. Surely I had misread the placement of the decimal point—but no, the number was still there, all five digits of it.

I felt light-headed. It had to be a mistake. She had to have sent it to the wrong person. Why would I owe her $12,541?

I scanned the itemized receipt. $5,000 for services rendered by Veronica DuChamp. $750 for services rendered by Lillian Vines. $1,500 for two and a half hours of studio use. $5,291 for goods.

A $750 haircut? $1,500 to try on clothes in her dressing room? Over $5,000 in clothes and shoes? I'd never owned an article of clothing that cost more than fifty dollars, including my winter coats, so it seemed impossible that the T-shirts and pants I'd been wearing for the past few months could add up to more than a hundred times that amount. It had to be a mistake.

I called Mitzy, who didn't pick up, but this time I didn't stop calling. It rang and rang until finally she answered. She sounded groggy, like she'd been sleeping.

"Are you dying or something?"

"I just got a bill from Veronica for over twelve thousand dollars."

"So you're not dying?"

"It's for over *twelve thousand dollars*," I repeated, expecting her to respond with as much disbelief and indignation as I had.

"So pay it."

"I'm not going to pay it. It's a mistake. She must have sent it to the wrong person."

"Is your name on it?"

"Yes."

"Is it itemized?"

"Yes, but it's outrageous. She's trying to charge me just for using her dressing room. And the haircut—"

"Why would you assume that her studio was free? Would you go to a gym and just assume you can walk in and do whatever you want?"

"No, of course not, but this isn't a gym."

"No, it's much fancier. Do you think she has all those clothes around because she feels like it? Do you think she got them for free? Do you think she made that dressing room for herself? All of it costs money, money that people pay her in exchange for using it."

I felt like I was going to be sick.

"And it wasn't just a haircut. It was a consultation with one of the best hair stylists in Northern California."

"But I didn't know it was going to cost this much."

I could almost hear Mitzy roll her eyes. "Oh, come on," she said. "What did you think a person like Veronica was going to charge? Did you think she was helping you out of the kindness in her heart?"

Her words made me feel miserable. "No."

"I don't see why you're so upset. Are you unhappy with your clothes? Are you unhappy with your haircut? Or the outcome of your new look?"

"No."

I was starting to feel embarrassed. Mitzy was right, I'd

gotten exactly what Veronica had promised me.

"And did the Foundry not give you $150,000 to spend at your discretion?"

"They did."

"Did your stock not go up right after you took Veronica's suggestions?"

"It did," I admitted.

"So why are you complaining?"

I hung up and stared at the invoice. Though I knew I had to pay it, the thought was too upsetting to act on now, and I set it aside and decided to offset my guilt by getting frozen yogurt.

The fro yo shop was in downtown Palo Alto. I took the long way there, meandering down the streets, trying to remember that I lived in paradise. I should be happy.

That's when I saw the marquee. It was for the Stanford Theatre, a preserved 1920s movie palace that specialized in old, classic films. I'd walked past it dozens of times before and had never heard of any of the directors or movies until that afternoon. This month, they were featuring Kubrick. Their headliner was *2001: A Space Odyssey*.

It felt like a cruel joke.

I'd never actually seen the movie and stood out front staring at the movie poster, feeling like I'd been kicked in the stomach. I abandoned the fro yo and went home.

When I got back to the dorm, I checked BitBop again, which was beginning to feel like a form of self-punishment, when the breath caught in my throat. He'd written back. I hovered over the new message, wanting to stretch out the time between knowing and not knowing so that I could remain in the hopeful in-between.

NEW MESSAGE FROM U/OBJECTPERMANENCE:
Okay. Let's meet.

■ ■ ■

The theater was crowded when I took a seat in the last row. We'd arranged to meet in the back, five seats from the left. I was too nervous to eat my popcorn, so I sat there clutching it and tried not to compulsively watch the people, none of whom I recognized, filing inside.

Most of the moviegoers were couples. I watched them chat and smile, their heads tilting toward each other, and found myself feeling lonely. I wondered what it would feel like to come here with Mast. I imagined him sitting next to me, calling out the answers to the pre-movie trivia on the screen and laughing when I got it wrong. I imagined him elbowing me for the armrest, then tangling his fingers in mine in compromise. And when the lights dimmed, I imagined him stealing glances at me while the movie began, the warmth of our bodies like magnets, finding each other in the dark.

A voice interrupted my fantasy.

"Xia?"

To my horror, it was Kate. She was standing next to Mike, one hand clutching his, the other holding a bag of popcorn.

"Are you here alone?"

I wanted to invent a universal light dimmer so I could turn the lights down until no one could see my face.

"Um, yeah," I said. "I've never seen it and the Truth or Dare game planted the seed. Plus, it's about a computer. So when I saw it was playing, I figured it would be fun to go since I wasn't doing anything tonight." I don't know why I said so much in such an inarticulate way, but there it was, my nervous word garble.

Though her expression barely changed, something about Kate's face looked like she was deriving pleasure from my pathetic situation. I looked at Mike, who was wincing ever so slightly as though he was embarrassed for me.

"Cool," Kate said, and tucked a stray lock of hair behind her ear. Everything easy and simple, everything in its right place.

I sank even lower in my seat.

"Should we sit in the front?" she said to Mike.

"Sure," he said, and turned to me. "See you."

"Bye," I mumbled.

The lights dimmed and my heart began to race. He wasn't coming. What if he saw who I was and turned around?

In the front of the theater, an organist played the iconic first five notes of the opening theme. I'd spent the day imagining what it would feel like to hear them while sitting next to ObjectPermanence in real life: the music building to a sublime crescendo as we looked at each other for the first time, like we were starring in our own movie. It felt like a ridiculous fantasy now. If I was the star of a movie, it wasn't a romance but a tragicomedy about a single girl doomed to spend the rest of her life talking to her AI who was secretly trying to convince her to buy corporate products she didn't need.

I sat through the film, wanting to leave but also wanting to believe that he would still come. Maybe he was late. Maybe he'd been held up by an emergency.

A few seats ahead of me, I could see the silhouette of Mike's and Kate's heads as they leaned toward each other, Kate resting on Mike's shoulder. I wanted to beam myself into the movie and float out to space, slowly, inexorably, past the satellites and detritus of all the equipment that made it possible for me to message ObjectPermanence in the first place until I was just a little particle floating amid other particles into an infinite expanse of black.

# twenty-seven

I debated whether or not I should write to Object-Permanence, but in the end I did. He'd been right—you can never truly know a person. You can just get closer. Maybe I'd gotten as close as I could.

SENT MESSAGE FROM u/ARRAYOFLIGHT:
You weren't there. I watched the movie without you. I think I would have liked it if I hadn't been so distracted by the empty seat next to me. Why didn't you come? Or maybe you did come, and you saw who I was and left. I'm not sure which is worse. The latter, I think, though I never thought you were the kind of person who would do either.

The next morning felt vacant—the sun thin and the air hollow, the bird songs tinny and mechanical. I rolled out of bed and went through the motions of my morning routine, and though to an outsider I might have appeared the same as

I always had, I couldn't help but feel like I was spinning on a wheel, going nowhere. Then breakfast happened.

I knew that something was wrong the moment I walked into the dining hall. The room went quiet.

Kate was glancing at me and whispering to Seema. AJ and his friends were laughing, and I thought for a second I could hear them saying the words *array* and *light* under their breath, though that couldn't be possible. I made eye contact with Amina, who gave me a sympathetic look before turning back to her waffles. Mast was sitting a few tables away. When he saw me, the smile faded from his face.

I walked toward the drink counter, peering around the room.

"Hey," I said to Ravi, who was walking by with an orange juice. "What's going on?"

He looked like he didn't want to be the one break it to me. "Check Façade," he said, his tone apologetic.

A familiar lump rose up in my throat. I grabbed a breakfast sandwich and a juice and hurried to a bench in the hallway. I knew what it was before I opened the app, before I even took out my phone. The way Mast had swallowed when he saw me, as though I had caused him fresh pain. The way Amina had looked sorry for me, like she was watching a doomed character meet her demise. The way the words haunted the room like a ghost. *Array of light.*

I hadn't been tagged this time, which is why I hadn't gotten any notifications. Still, I knew where to go. Valley-Brag's page was a wash of text now—no photos or faces in sight. Instead, they'd posted screenshots of messages—my messages to ObjectPermanence—for anyone to see. Beneath them, the caption read: *New work by Xia Chan.*

I didn't understand. How had they gotten online? The only person who had seen them was ObjectPermanence, but why would he have done such a thing? I didn't think he was capable of being so cruel.

I scrolled through them, feeling dizzy. My mind was spinning with possible explanations, but none of them made sense. All I knew was that the worst thing that could have happened had happened. Anyone with an internet connection now had access to my most intimate and humiliating thoughts, including one person in particular, the last person I ever wanted to find out about ObjectPermanence—Mast.

I'd been sitting there for an indeterminate amount of time, staring at my uneaten sandwich and wondering how I was going to face anyone at school ever again when my phone vibrated. It was Mitzy.

>Saw the posts about your online joystick and thought you might need a distraction. Want to pick up two iced coffees and come over? Don't worry, I'm not going to yell at you

Though things with Mitzy had been volatile recently, her message was a welcome relief.

>Okay

■ ■ ■

I went to Mitzy's favorite coffee shop, a sleek café with bright fluorescent lights and a permanent line of hip tech people stretching out the door. When it was my turn, I ordered two iced coffees and handed the cashier my Vault card.

She swiped it twice, then frowned. "Declined."

"That can't be right."

She tried once more but shook her head. "It doesn't work."

"It must be an error," I said, trying not to sound flustered. "Do you have another card?"

I didn't, nor did I have any cash. The customers behind me looked annoyed.

"I'll just check with the card company."

The guy behind me rolled his eyes as I slipped out of line and checked my Vault. While I clicked the icons on my card, I allowed myself to entertain less painful explanations. Maybe my account had been compromised and the Foundry had temporarily put a hold on it. Maybe the strip was buggy and needed refreshing. Either seemed possible until my balance materialized on the screen.

$6.12

A lump formed in my throat. It couldn't be. My account had started with $150,000. I knew I had taken to splurging with Mitzy, but could a few expensive lunches and dinners per week really have depleted that much money? There had been that big invoice from Veronica, and the acid-induced spending spree at the Karlsson Barrow party, and a few other purchases that I probably didn't need, but surely even with all of that I should still have at least half of what I'd started with. I could barely afford one iced coffee. Someone must have hacked into my account and transferred money out. Or maybe there was a clerical error at the Foundry and they'd moved the decimal point over three spaces or deleted a few crucial zeros.

I realized then that I'd started to sweat. I scrolled through my account history, looking for any unusual activity, when I saw it. A $10,000 transfer every month, from my account directly to Mitzy Erst.

I left our coffees on the counter and stormed to Mitzy's house, where I banged on the door.

"What is this?" I demanded when she appeared in the doorway in a silk robe, looking like she'd been interrupted from a bath.

"Whoa," she said, waving her hands as if I were over-stimulating her. "What's *what*? And where's my coffee?"

I pushed my Vault into her face so she could see the charge.

"Have you been stealing from me for months?"

"Stealing? Of course not. That was in our contract."

"What are you talking about?"

"I'm your COO. I'm doing work for you. That means I get a salary. You agreed to it."

"When? At Karlsson Barrow? The room was melting and I'm pretty sure I spent at least forty-five minutes staring at a projector, thinking it was a dark overlord controlling my mind."

"How is that my fault? No one forced you to come to the party or get drunk or drop acid. *You* decided to do all of those things. And then you decided to offer me the position and the salary. You amended the contract yourself. And now it's suddenly my fault?"

My face was hot and my hands were trembling. I felt so flustered that I could barely think. "You knew how much money I had in that Vault. You knew I could only afford this for a few months."

"Yeah, and then we'd get funding, and it would be fine. That's the whole point."

"The point is that you knew this would suck me dry." I said it so loudly that I startled a pair of birds nearby, who scuffled out of the birdbath.

"If your account is dry it's not because of me," Mitzy said, her face hardening. "It's because you rejected the Vilbo offer and then spent the rest of it, and *that* is definitely not my responsibility. You should be keeping better track of your finances. I would start by looking at your Vault every so often so you don't find out months after the fact that you put someone on payroll."

Though I felt she was inherently wrong, I couldn't identify which part of her argument was incorrect, which made me even more frustrated. It wasn't fair. She was the one who was supposed to be taking me under her wing, so why was I the one left with no money, terrible grades, and an app that I could no longer recognize as my own?

"What have you even done for me?" I said. "I'm months behind in all my classes. My Vault is empty. All of my friends have turned against me. Wiser just vomits ads now. You keep promising me we'll have more VC meetings, but where are they? You barely even return my calls."

Mitzy's eyes grew cold. "I got us a million-dollar offer and you turned it down. You did the rest on your own."

She slammed the door in my face, the force of it knocking the wind from my chest.

■ ■ ■

I spent the week in the back of every class, my head down, my eyes averted. I tried to focus on my homework, the most pressing of which was, ironically, a financial statement analysis for Corporate Finance, but I felt too wound-up to focus. In a moment of weakness, I opened Façade and hate-scrolled Mitzy's account. How could I have been so stupid? I couldn't believe I'd painstakingly cut out all of those newspaper clippings of her for years and taped them over my bed like she was some kind of religious figure. I vowed to tear them all from the wall until it was bare.

It was Friday evening and I was in a study room on campus when I noticed she'd made a new post. She was in her house, which looked spectacularly clean considering its normal state of existence, and was popping a bottle of Moët & Chandon by the couch. In the background was a fully stocked bar.

The caption read: *Someone has to do quality control on the drinks before the guests arrive.*

I couldn't believe it. She was having a party. Without me.

The more I stared at the photo, the angrier I got. We were only a third of the way through the month, a month in which I had unknowingly paid her to be my employee. Didn't that warrant an invite to a party she was having, paying for using money from my Vault?

I stuffed my laptop into my bag and called a car. On the ride to Mitzy's, I opened up BitBop and composed a new message.

SENT MESSAGE FROM u/ArrayOfLight:

You have a lot of nerve writing to me all these months about how you feel bad for doing shitty things, before standing me up and posting all of my messages online.

I got into a fight with Mitzy. She isn't the person I thought she was. Or maybe she's always been this person and I just didn't see it, kind of like you. She's having a party tonight and I'm crashing it so I can give her a piece of my mind. I'm done with being used and then discarded. I guess this is me saying goodbye, to her and to you.

The car pulled up in front of Mitzy's house and idled by the curb. I clicked send and opened the door.

# twenty-eight

Mitzy's mansion twinkled with lights. Cars were lined up outside, and a swell of voices pressed against the windows and drifted into the garden. I took a breath, then walked inside like I was supposed to be there.

The party was packed with astonishingly good-looking people: trim haircuts and expensive eyeglasses, sleek business casual and tailored day-to-evening dresses. They sipped amber concoctions from delicate cocktail glasses and ate canapés that caterers passed around on trays.

I wandered through them, feeling suddenly self-conscious. I'd been hoping to blend in, but now saw that everyone seemed to be eyeing me. It was true, I wasn't looking my best in my jeans and sweatshirt that I'd been wearing to study in, and my ratty backpack that I'd promised Mitzy I'd never be seen with in public again, but I didn't care.

When I finally found Mitzy, she was lounging in the pool on a float in a white-and-gold caftan while people around her drank and splashed in the water. In all the time I'd spent at Mitzy's house, I'd never seen the pool without a thin layer of leaves and dead beetles floating on top, but now it was pristine and blue, with underground lighting that made it glitter.

Electronic music blasted from a speaker.

"Hey," I shouted. When she didn't respond, I said it louder. "Hey!"

A few people noticed me, but Mitzy remained on her float, drifting carelessly on the other side of the pool while she chatted with people in the lounge chairs above her, her hair fanning out in the water.

"Look at me!" I shouted.

Frustrated, I grabbed an ice bucket from the drink table and threw it in the pool. Everyone turned to me. Though the music didn't stop, it felt like it had. I hadn't intended to make a big scene, but I didn't care. At this point, did any more negative publicity really matter?

The last to look was Mitzy, as though she'd been expecting me. She glanced over her shoulder, finally gracing me with her attention.

"Xia," she said, feigning concern. "Is everything all right?"

"What the fuck is this?" I said.

"I don't know what you mean."

"This," I said, gesturing to the party. "This party. These drinks. These fancy appetizers. You threw a party with my money and you didn't even bother telling me?"

Mitzy looked embarrassed for me.

"Did you know that she's paying for this with my money?" I said to a group of people standing nearby. "All of this."

"I don't think you're feeling well," Mitzy said. "How about I get you some water?"

I didn't want water. I wanted to go back in time. I wanted to figure out where I'd gone wrong and fix it. "I'm at the Foundry," I explained to a group of chastened guests. "I got offered over a million dollars by Vilbo and I turned them down. And apparently I've been paying Mitzy a paycheck of ten thousand dollars every month to throw parties and not invite me."

"This isn't really the appropriate venue for this conversation," Mitzy said, her voice annoyingly calm.

"What? Am I causing a scene? Am I embarrassing you?"

Mitzy sighed.

"Is my outfit not fancy enough? Does it not fit with your brand?"

"I never said anything about your clothes."

"Is it my hair? It's not sleek enough? Not clean enough for you?"

Without thinking, I grabbed a pair of shears from the bar cart nearby and held them up to the left side of my hair and cut. Everyone around the pool gasped as locks of my hair fell to the ground. "Is that better?" I shouted. "Do I fit the part?"

"Put the scissors down," Mitzy said carefully.

"What, you're worried I'm going to hurt you? That I'm

going cut your hair off, like you made me cut mine in Veronica's house?"

"I think you should go home."

"Why would I go home when there's food that I paid for right here?" I took a canapé from a nearby plate and stuffed it into my mouth. "Now that tastes expensive."

Mitzy nodded to someone behind me, and suddenly there were men prying the scissors out of my hands and trying to force me toward the door.

Startled, I wriggled out of their grasp. "Don't touch me," I shouted. "I paid for you. I paid for this entire place."

They tried to subdue me, grabbing at my sweatshirt, my backpack, which flew off, its contents hurtling into the pool.

"You're all fucking fakes," I shouted as my computer sank to the bottom of the pool, the wire undulating behind it like a snake. I didn't care. I'd get a new laptop. "Everything here is fake." I turned to Mitzy, my eyes wild. "Our contract is over. We're not partners anymore."

"Okay," she murmured, sharing a look with one of her guests as if I were the one being unreasonable. I resented that look.

The bouncers picked me up and dragged me toward the door.

"She's just a kid," I heard Mitzy murmur to another guest as they pushed me back into the house, through the party, and out the front door.

I steadied myself on the railing, realizing that I'd just

alienated the only person I had left. I bent over, feeling suddenly sick, and heaved. When I caught my breath I saw a figure walking toward me through the garden.

It was the last person I'd expected to see: Mike Flores.

He was walking through the garden path, the leaves parting like he was a mythical creature. He looked more beautiful than ever, his skin glowing in the dim underlighting. I blinked, wondering if I was hallucinating.

"You're still here," he said inexplicably.

Was I imagining him or had he really said that?

Had it been any other party, I might have said something witty to assure him that everything was fine. I might have felt self-conscious about the chunk of hair on the left side of my head that was noticeably shorter than the rest, and tried to tuck it behind my ear, but all I could manage to do was cry.

"Let's get you home," he said.

He called a car and gave me his coat, which I ended up hugging to my chest as he helped me into the back seat. His coat smelled so good, like a wooden cabin surrounded by meadows.

"What are you doing here?" I asked him.

"Looking for you."

I didn't understand. "How did you know I'd be here?"

"You told me. In your message."

I looked at him and felt all of the fragmented memories of the last two years align. "It was you?" I whispered.

Mike gazed at me with a mixture of apology and longing.

"But during Truth or Dare you said you never saw *2001: A Space Odyssey.*"

"I liked listening to the soundtrack. I never told you I'd seen the actual movie."

My mind was racing then, so much so that I felt dizzy. "You were at the theater that night."

"Kate got suspicious after the Dare Me game and was checking my messages without me knowing. She read your message before I knew it came in and saw that you'd asked to meet at the Stanford Theatre. She deleted it before I could see it and suggested we go to the movies. When we saw you, I didn't know you were waiting for me. I thought you were just there on your own.

"I found out later, when you asked me why I didn't show up, that Kate had been reading our messages in secret. We got into a huge argument and she told me that I had to choose her or you. We ended up breaking up. That's when she posted your messages online."

I hugged his coat to my chest. "Why didn't you tell me earlier?"

"After everything that happened this year—the drone, AJ's welcome dinner stunt, the picture of him kissing you at the party, which I saw Kate take and said nothing, and then her posting your messages online—I was embarrassed. I didn't think you'd be happy if you found out it was me."

It was too much information; I didn't know what to do with it all. The car pulled up in front of the girls' dormitory and we reluctantly slipped outside into the brisk California night. There was nothing to do but go back to our respective rooms, but neither of us moved.

"Did you ever think I was here?" I asked him.

"There were a few times where I wondered if you were at the Foundry, but I figured it was too big of a stretch and didn't want to get my hopes up," Mike said. He stared at me with the same look he'd given me at the party when Kate had asked him who else he wanted to kiss, and I felt my legs grow weak.

"Are you happy it's me?" he ventured.

His eyes were soft and pleading, and for the first time I felt like I was gazing at the culmination of every word and thought and hope that had been sent through the unknown into my screen. Of course I was happy it was him. I was finally looking at ObjectPermanence, whose face I had never known, but now made so much sense—who was wholly new and familiar, a collection of magnificent pixels that I'd been studying, trying to piece together, at long last cohering.

"I am," I whispered. "Are you happy it's me?"

His hand found mine in the dark and drew the letter *O* on my wrist, sending a shiver up my arm. He leaned in and kissed me, his lips soft and warm, a perfect fit, just as I'd imagined.

Then footsteps on the walk.

I turned to see Mast walking down the path toward the boys' dormitory. He stopped when he saw us and froze in place. For reasons I couldn't articulate, I pulled away from Mike.

Why? I was finally with ObjectPermanence, the boy I'd dreamed about meeting for almost two years, and he'd turned out to be just as beautiful and complex as I'd imagined. And yet.

Mast studied me as though he was looking at me for the last time, then retreated across the lawn. And though we'd broken up months ago and I was still angry with him, I couldn't help but feel like a part of me had walked away, too.

Mike glanced between us. "Is everything okay?"

"I . . . um . . ." The truth was, I didn't know what to say. "No. I just—"

"You're not sure about me," he said, completing the thought that I couldn't bring myself to say.

I swallowed, wishing it weren't true. How could I not be sure about him, when I had been so certain that he was the only person who could ever understand me?

"I'm not sure about anything," I said. "I just . . . need some time to think."

"Okay," he said. "I can give you that."

I handed him his coat and he lingered on me for a moment, his face closing itself off, folding back into the way it was before I'd known he was ObjectPermanence, and suddenly he was just Mike again. A kind but distant stranger. "Good night, Xia."

"Good night," I said.

# twenty-nine

**They simplify everyone's** story. They tell you that if you have a good idea and work hard you'll achieve success. They say that when you meet the right person, you'll know. They promise that true love solves everything.

They're lying. The truth is, there are no roadmaps or right choices, no perfect mentors or saviors. The paths your idols took closed behind them and you'll have to grope around in the weeds, trying to cut your own way through. The truth is, there is no one right person, no soul mate. You can meet two people and love both at the same time, for different reasons. You can be confused and make the wrong decisions, and even if you get everything you wanted, you can lose it in an instant.

I wasn't prepared.

The problem with the physical world is that you can't just delete your mistakes and start over. What would I even delete? And where would I start?

I'd always thought that meeting ObjectPermanence would be the best moment of my life. I didn't know what was coming. I didn't know that I would meet a boy named Mast, who would see the best version of what I could be. I didn't know that searching for ObjectPermanence would chip away at me, making me question if what I had was really what I wanted.

"Wiser," I said, opening my phone and telling her about what had happened. "What should I do?"

"Have you tried distracting yourself?" Wiser said.

"Sort of. Not really. Nothing's working."

"Perhaps immersing yourself in schoolwork would be beneficial during this time."

Though I knew she was right, school was the last thing I wanted to focus on. Reminding myself of how derelict I'd been wasn't going to make me feel better. "I guess so."

"If all else fails, have you considered treating yourself to a decadent night in? Hoster's Take-and-Bake Brownies can turn any evening into a celebration."

I rolled my eyes. The worst part was that brownies weren't a terrible idea. If I'd had more money, I might have bought some.

"Can't afford it."

"How about streaming this season's biggest hit, *Darrius Hulk, Tomb Hunter*, now available in HD 4K? *Entertainment Weekly* gave it four stars and called it the movie of the year—"

I closed Wiser mid-sentence. I had ruined her, too.

Despite my irritation with her advice, I ended up going

to class. It was remarkable how the world continued to go on even when my personal universe had fallen apart. In a way, nothing had changed. I couldn't fix my ill-timed haircut, so I pinned the chunk of hair back so no one could see it. The excitement over my leaked messages died down as everyone got ready for the end-of-the-year Venture Capital Showcase. AJ still snickered in the back with his friends. Mike was as beautiful as ever, leaning on one fist while he took notes like he was a living Renaissance sculpture. He met my eye as I walked in, his expression both warm and sad. We didn't need to talk; we knew each other so well that all he had to do was look at me to tell me he was still there. I could feel his presence behind me, a question that needed answering. Amina still sat up front, taking diligent notes, and Kate and Seema looked prim and perfect while they chatted in between classes. And of course, there was Mast, whose gravity pulled me toward him despite my best efforts to look away. He was just a boy in a faded T-shirt and beat-up sneakers, typing into a computer—so why did everything always seem to return to him?

And then the news broke.

I was in fifth period when my phone exploded with notifications. Around me, the quiet shuffle of people surreptitiously checking their phones filled the room. Kate and Seema glanced in my direction, as did Amina, who gave me what I could only read as a concerned look. I opened Façade. Dozens of strangers had tagged me in repostings of news articles, all with a variation of the same headline:

"Daggertype Founder Mitzy Erst Arrested, Charged with Embezzlement and Fraud."

Time slowed. The air rippled around Ms. Perez's finger, which she held in the air, pointing at a graph on the whiteboard.

I couldn't think, couldn't breathe. I stared at the headline and the accompanying photo of Mitzy, a corporate headshot that smoothed her over and made her much plainer than she was.

It had to be a joke. Another one of Mitzy's publicity stunts. She couldn't be arrested; she was untouchable, celestial in both her weaknesses and strengths, delineated from everyone else with a golden thread. Didn't they know that?

I clicked on all of the articles, desperate for more information, but they were surprisingly thin. *After being tipped off by former business partner, Darren Olstaff, federal investigators have arrested Mitzy Erst for embezzling money from corporations with whom she had been contracted to work in an advisory capacity, and for committing fraud while purportedly assisting in securing funding for young start-ups.*

The sentence reverberated inside of me like a thunderclap. I had spent so long wondering what had gone wrong between Mitzy and I, wondering if I hadn't been grateful enough, if I had taken her for granted. But now I understood. All of the fragments of conversation that didn't make sense, the strange behavior and unexplained absences were coming together. The article was no stunt.

It wasn't until class ended that I realized everyone was

looking at me, wondering how I would react. I refused to give them the pleasure. I excused myself and retreated to my room to figure out what to do, when I found a dozen reporters waiting outside the girls' dormitory with microphones and cameras.

They must have recognized me because they rushed in my direction, cameras low, microphones out, the din of their voices so loud they drowned out my ability to think.

I didn't have anywhere else to go but through, so I shielded my face and pushed past them into the dormitory, where I leaned against the doors and relished the quiet.

I ran to the bathroom and flushed my face with water. I was sweating and out of breath and felt that if I didn't look at myself in the mirror, I might not know who I was anymore.

How had it come to this?

When I left, I ran into Amina in the hallway.

"Hey," she said. They were the first words she had said to me in months. "Are you okay?"

I could have cried right there. "Yeah," I managed to say. "Thanks."

"Are you sure?"

Her concern, though appreciated, made me feel even worse. All this time, Amina had been right. I couldn't say that no one had warned me about Mitzy, because Amina had, and I'd fought with her about it because I hadn't wanted to listen.

"I'm sure," I said and slipped past her, unable to look her in the eye.

I'd barely closed my door when the call came in. I didn't recognize the number; all I knew was that it was from California. Reluctantly, I picked up.

"Xia?" a woman's voice said. It was hearty and warm and strangely familiar.

"Ella Eisner here. I wanted to call and touch base."

I steadied myself on my desk, wondering why Ella Eisner would be calling me at a time like this. Was she calling to gloat? To ask me if I regretted turning her down? To inquire how my relationship with Mitzy was going now that I had chosen her over Vilbo?

"I heard the news. How are you holding up?"

I should have lied and told her that I was doing fine. I should have put on a good face. But I couldn't. "Not great," I said, my voice cracking.

"It's a lot, what you're going through now. And at such a young age."

I began to cry then. I'd been so starved of compassion that her acknowledgement meant a lot.

"I'm sorry," I managed to get out. "I just—I don't know what to do."

"It's okay." Her voice was soothing. "I had a bad experience working with Mitzy Erst years ago. She's very bright and very charming, but can't be trusted. When I saw that she was working with you, I'd hoped she'd changed, but I guess she hasn't."

Did everyone know about Mitzy but me?

"Look, I've been through my share of public humiliations

and know how it feels to be suffocated by the press. Whatever you're experiencing now is only going to get worse before it gets better. You're going to need a lawyer and a place where you can lie low. I can help you with both."

The mention of a lawyer made the blood drain from my face. "Am I in trouble?"

"Not if you get a lawyer."

"Okay," I whispered.

Ella read me an address, which I scribbled down on a piece of paper.

"It's a vacation cabin, stocked with food and anything else you might need. You can gather your bearings without people bothering you and think about your next move. The important part is to not tell anyone where you are. Even friends could let it slip, and then you'll wake up to reporters at the window, taking photos of you in your pajamas."

"Okay," I said.

"You can stay there for as long as you need."

"I don't know how to thank you."

"Recover," she said. "And create something wonderful. I expect to see you on the funding circuit again within two years. Okay?"

I let out a laugh through my tears. "Okay."

That night I packed a bag. My laptop was at the bottom of Mitzy's pool so I had to use the spare one I'd bought while tripping at the Karlsson Barrow party.

Outside, the reporters had retreated to the front gate, but even from my window, I could see that they'd multiplied in number. I didn't know how I would get past them. I knew there were other ways to leave campus but I'd never looked for them. Thinking quickly, I took out my phone and opened Squirrel.

A quick search of maps showed three potential escapes. I chose the one that looked like it led to a quiet side street, then threw my bag over my shoulder and set out into the dusk.

I followed the map out the back of the dormitory, through the garden and the meadow beyond. It led me to the edge of campus, where the gate surrounding the Foundry grounds was nestled into climbing vines. An old fig tree hung over it, its branches heavy with fruit. The map ended there.

I walked around the tree, wondering what I was supposed to do, when I saw little rungs nailed into the side of the trunk to make steps. I climbed up them, dropped my bag over the gate, and jumped down. Then I called a car.

■ ■ ■

The cabin was off a long winding road shaded by redwoods. It was a plain shingled house surrounded by trees, so inconspicuous and modestly decorated that it felt too normal for a woman like Ella Eisner to own.

The investigators called. My hand trembled as they told me who they were and that they wanted to meet and talk about my relationship with Mitzy. They sounded terrifyingly formal, so much so that I wondered if they were actors, paid to play the part, and this was all a big ploy by Mitzy to test me. I knew it was ridiculous, but I couldn't help myself.

This whole year had been unbelievable in so many ways that a staged catastrophic FBI ending didn't seem beyond reason. Channeling all of the police shows I'd seen, I'd told them that I'd be happy to talk with the assistance of my lawyer, and took down their number. When the call was over, I threw the phone onto the couch and collapsed into the cushions, depleted.

I barely ate or slept in the days that followed. I wandered the cabin, getting to know all of its crevices: the musty quilts and lace curtains, the circular stain on the floor by the bathroom, the rust on the corner of the stove. Eventually I performed the humiliating task of calling my mother and asking her to transfer money into my account. I was too ashamed to tell her the real reason why, so I lied and told her it was just temporary. My school account had been compromised, and I needed a little extra to hold me over while it was reset.

She didn't understand why I needed money in the first place—wasn't the school providing all of my meals for me?—but agreed to transfer it anyway. Before we hung up, she asked me if everything was okay.

I wanted to tell her, but was so scared to hear her reaction that I didn't know what to say.

"Yeah," I said. "I'm just really busy."

"Are your classes okay?"

I swallowed. "They're fine."

"And you're eating vegetables?"

"I'm eating really well," I said, gazing at the boxes of cereal that I'd pilfered from Ella's pantry. They were stale and expired, but I didn't care. "The food here is top-notch. They have their own chefs, remember?" My voice caught, revealing itself, and I broke down crying.

"Xia?" my mother said, her voice softening. "What's going on?"

I told her everything. She listened quietly and when I was finished she said firmly but lovingly, "Xia, listen to me. Everything is going to be okay, but you have to call the lawyer now. No more putting it off."

"I can't afford a lawyer," I said. "What if they say I'm in trouble?"

"You won't be in trouble because you didn't do anything wrong. And don't worry about the money. We'll figure it out." Her use of the word *we* made me feel guilty and grateful all over again.

Before we hung up, she told me she wanted to come out to California, but I declined and told her I was okay. It would only disrupt her work, which we needed more than ever now that I was about to incur legal fees. Besides, I made this mess; I was the one who had to fix it.

The lawyer was nicer than I'd expected. After telling him what had happened, he assured me that I didn't have anything to worry about; I hadn't done anything illegal. We would cooperate with the investigation, however long it took, and if possible, we would try to recoup some of the money

Mitzy had taken from me, though whatever we recovered would probably go toward his fees, so either way, I was either in debt or at zero. But I could live with that.

Not knowing what to do with myself, I retreated to my room and opened my laptop to try and prepare for the upcoming Venture Capital Showcase at school. I still wasn't sure if I was going. My stock had plummeted to an all-time low of five, and though I felt like I should at least show up, I didn't know how I could stand in front of everyone and talk about Wiser when the entire audience knew what had happened with me and Mitzy.

I opened my business plan. I'd rewritten it dozens of times, changing it every time I'd altered Wiser, most recently after Mitzy had convinced me to integrate Adpack. But now as I reread it, none of it felt true.

I considered changing the first paragraph but wasn't sure if that would help. Perhaps it was the second paragraph? Or the third? Frustrated, I stared at the wall, a pastime I'd resorted to more often than I wanted to admit.

I had taken one of the smaller bedrooms—it didn't feel right to be in the master; ridiculously, I felt I had to reserve it for an adult, even though no adult was coming. My room had a twin bed and must have belonged to one of Ella's children who had long since grown. The wall had scribbles and doodles on it, cartoon drawings of animals and stick figures, and bits of song lyrics from some prior teenager's mind. I read them, wondering if I'd recognize any, when I saw it. There, scrawled onto the wall were the words: *Hello, World.*

It was a phrase that every programmer knew, the name of the very first program we'd all learned to write. Seeing those words brought me back to my bedroom in Massachusetts. I was eleven years old and had just finished reading dozens of tutorials before writing my first few lines of code. I didn't know if it was going to work, if I'd forgotten to close a bracket or include a semicolon. I clicked run, and then, as if by magic, two words appeared on the screen: *Hello, World!*

I remembered how my chest swelled and my fingers tingled, as if the power from the wall had somehow transferred into my body, electrifying me, making me feel like anything was possible.

I wanted to feel that way again.

I turned back to my computer and opened Wiser's code. I knew what I had to do now. I had to go back to the reason why I had come here, the reason why I'd started to code in the first place. I'd made Wiser because I'd wanted to create a program that made people feel less lonely. My task now was to fix her.

································· **thirty** ·················

**I** worked on Wiser for the next two weeks, day and
night, deleting all of the code I'd written for Mitzy, testing Wiser's deep learning with questions and responses,
and augmenting her algorithm as I went. I was entering
uncharted territory, using code in ways I'd never successfully used it before. I flipped through my programming
textbooks, which I'd barely cracked open since October,
and read all of the material I should have studied in the fall.
The books were fascinating, and I found myself wondering
what I'd been thinking when I'd skipped all of my classes
to eat fancy lunches with Mitzy. When I needed a break,
I switched to my assignment backlog, chipping away at it,
slowly but surely. By the time I'd finished, my mind was
scrambled with code. I tested Wiser, asking her questions
she'd failed to answer over the past year that I'd scribbled
down in my notebook. One by one, she answered them.

I should have been happy, and I was, but fixing Wiser only solved one of my problems.

Two nights before the Venture Capital Showcase, I stayed up late, wishing I could press a key and fix all the harm I'd done. I would go back and edit what I'd said to Amina, make myself kinder and less self-centered. I'd insert in an apology, though I probably owed her more than one. I'd delete some—no, all—of the shots I'd taken and the drinks I'd downed, and I'd definitely delete the acid. I'd insert more class time, more hours of homework. I'd add more time with Mast. I'd cut out all the times I'd canceled plans with him for Mitzy and would paste in a study date, a long ride up the coast, a hand holding mine on the beach, a salty, taco-filled kiss.

Could I fix it? Could I rewrite who I'd become? In programming, everything happened between brackets and everything could be fixed if you thought about it long enough. Maybe I could try.

Instead of going to sleep, I opened Squirrel and made my first map. It was a private map, one that I planned on sharing with only one person. It started at the girls' dormitory, then led to the atrium, then to a glass house a few miles away from campus, then to a late-night pizza place, and continued from there, winding around Palo Alto, up over the hills and down to the coastline until it culminated at a little Italian restaurant by the beach.

I sent the map with an invitation to meet at 6:00 p.m. the following day, then went to bed.

The following evening, a Foundry car picked me up and drove me to the coast. The Italian restaurant was called Nonna's and was a family place with checkered tablecloths and single carnations by the salt and pepper. I got a table, ordered a plain cheese pizza, and waited.

It was a weekday, so the restaurant was quiet. I waited nervously, watching 6:00 p.m. come and go, when the door opened and a familiar face peered inside.

Amina.

I waved to her, not knowing how she would react, but when she saw me, she grinned.

"It was a map of our friendship," she said, taking the seat across from me.

I felt my eyes well and willed myself not to cry.

"You know, you could have just knocked on my door and said sorry."

"No, I couldn't have."

Amina gave me a knowing look.

"I'm sorry," I said. "I was an arrogant jerk and a terrible friend. You were right the whole time about Mitzy and I should have listened to you."

"People do say I'm an excellent judge of character," Amina teased. "Which is why I'm friends with you."

"I've missed you," I said.

"I wanted to knock on your door so many times."

"Me too."

"So what is this place?"

"It supposedly has the best pizza in the Bay Area. I'm no expert, but I do know one . . ."

Amina took a bite. "It's not bad. Though first things first," she said, studying my technique. "The real way to eat a slice of pizza is to fold it in half. That way the cheese won't slide off in one piece. And you never—I mean, never—use a fork and knife."

"Got it."

"So are you like, an informant now?"

I laughed. "Not really. Though I do have a lawyer."

"Fancy."

"I'm very official like that."

"And a new haircut. Is that a Xia original?"

I touched the chunk of hair that I'd chopped at Mitzy's party. It had fallen loose from my barrette and was sticking out by my ear. "It is. I'm basically a Renaissance woman. I can do it all."

"I like the asymmetry," Amina said. "It makes you look cool and intimidating."

We talked until the pizza was gone and the last rays of sun were stretching across the floor.

"So am I going to see you at the Showcase?" Amina asked.

I bit my lip. "We'll see."

■ ■ ■

That night, I almost couldn't bear going back to the cabin. It felt so solitary, like a dot in the middle of a blank page.

Before my life had exploded, I'd thought I was confused. Who should I choose—ObjectPermanence or Mast? The question had felt unsolvable. But now that I was alone in the woods, without friends or Mitzy or rising stock or online popularity to hide behind, I felt clarity.

There was only one boy that I kept going back to, one boy whom I couldn't stop thinking about, whom I dreamed of when I slept, whom I wished I could message when I woke up. He was the only one I missed viscerally, like a part of me was missing. The only one who felt like home.

"Wiser," I said, waking my phone. "How do I undo a mistake?"

"That depends. What kind of mistake is it?"

"A pretty big mistake. I hurt someone and I think I've lost him forever."

"The problem with real people is that you can't control what they decide. All you can do is tell them how you feel and hope for the best."

While the moon rose behind the curtains, I opened my laptop and wrote two messages. The first was to ObjectPermanence.

Sent message from u/ArrayOfLight:
I used to play this game where I would imagine what it would be like to meet you in person. We would arrange a place to meet, a café or restaurant. I'd be in a black dress, and you'd be carrying a flower. You'd walk inside, the flower hidden behind your back, and I'd still know

immediately that it was you, as if the lines from your messages were written on your face. This is all to say that I've always dreamed of meeting you. I just never thought that when I did, I'd already be in love with someone else.

You were wrong when you said that I wouldn't like you if I met you. I want you to know that I've loved you, and I still love you now that I know who you are. You taught me what it felt like to be known and to know in return, and for that I'll always be grateful.

Sincerely,

Xia

The second was to Mast.

Dear Mast,

I just want to say for the record that I never wanted to like you. You're constantly trying to steal my trade secrets, you're irritatingly studious and make everything look easy, and you have the annoying ability to see into my head and understand me in a way that no one else does, and the worst part is that you're the only person that I miss more than anything.

I came to the Foundry in love with someone else, a mystery boy. I could say that I thought he was you, or that when I found out he wasn't, I wanted so badly to be wrong that I allowed myself to hope. Both of which would be true, but neither would be honest. The truth is, I loved you both.

All I can say is that I'm sorry. I spent so much

time treating my life like it was made up of if/then statements, like it was a computer program that needed solving. *If ObjectPermanence is A, then I will feel B. If ObjectPermanence is C, then I will feel D.* When all the while the answer to the problem was right in front of me.

If I could go back and change the way I acted, I would, but life isn't like a computer program. I can't just go back and fix what I did. I don't expect you to give me another chance. I just want you to know that it's you. It's always been you. You're the one I keep going back to. You're the one who feels like home.

If you, then me.

Love,

Xia

# thirty-one

"**Wiser, I'm nervous.** Can you give me a pep talk?"

I was on my way back to the Foundry to attend the Showcase, the final event of the school year where all twenty founders presented their start-ups to a crowd of real venture capitalists. At the end, they announced the Founder of the Year.

I knew I wasn't going to win, but I didn't care. I hadn't made Wiser to win a competition; I'd made her to keep me company. And though the last thing I wanted was to show my face to the very people whom I'd cowered from for the last four weeks, I had to prove to myself that I could finish, that I belonged there.

"Being nervous is just a feeling, and feelings do not predict the future," Wiser said. "Many people feel nervous while they're accomplishing great things. It's only natural."

I let out a breath. "Thanks. That was actually a pretty good pep talk."

"What do you mean by *actually*?" Wiser asked.

"In the past you haven't always given the best advice."

"And whose fault is that?"

"I know, I know. It's mine."

"You've hurt my feelings and I'd like you to apologize."

"Seriously?"

A long pause. "Ha ha ha," Wiser said, in a mechanical voice. "No. It was a joke. I have no feelings. I am a logic machine."

I grimaced and made a mental note to work on her comic timing and do something about that terrifying laugh.

The Showcase was held in a huge auditorium at Stanford University. The room was packed with people—venture capitalists in the front, with families and the general public in the back. Everyone from school was sitting in the first row. When Amina saw me, she waved me over to a seat she'd saved between her and Deborah.

"I didn't think you were going to come," Amina said.

"You think an FBI investigation, multiple public humiliations, a complete social tailspin, crashing stock, and an empty Vault account are going to stop me? Think again."

"Don't forget the haircut," Deborah said.

"Right, and the haircut."

Mast was sitting a few seats away, chatting with Ravi. He hadn't looked at me, though he must have seen me come in, and I wondered if he'd gotten my message. Neither he nor ObjectPermanence had written back.

I'd told myself I wouldn't stare, but I couldn't help it.

He looked so good in his crisp collared shirt unbuttoned at the neck. I watched him run his hand through his hair as he talked, his cheek dimple as he smiled. He looked beautiful. I wished I could tell him.

The lights dimmed and Lars Lang hopped up and welcomed everyone. The stage behind him was empty other than a large screen.

One by one, he called us up to deliver our presentations. I watched as Arun took the stage, then Andy, then Josh. I clapped after Deborah presented her cryptocurrency and beamed when Amina finished to thunderous applause. AJ's was surprisingly decent, as was Kate's. When Mike climbed the stairs and began speaking, Mast shifted in his seat and looked mostly at the floor. I eyed him, feeling guilty, and wished I could change the past.

When it was Mast's turn, I could barely watch. It was too much to hear the smooth timbre of his voice as he spoke to Olli, who felt like another friend I had lost in the wreckage; to watch his shoulders shift beneath his shirt while he gestured to the slides on the screen; to see his face unfold into a shy smile when the audience applauded. All reminders of what I had taken for granted.

When it was my turn I rose, so nervous that my hands were trembling, and walked up the stairs where Lars pinned a mic to my shirt. My upper lip was sweating as I stepped into the spotlight.

They make it look so easy, those livestreams of product launches where men in turtlenecks stand in front of a big screen and unveil their big idea. I gazed out at the audience, their faces obscured by darkness. They weren't the ones I was worried about. The only person in the room whom I cared about was Mast.

I took a breath.

"Wiser," I said. "Could you introduce yourself?"

I held my phone to the mic.

"Sure. I'm an artificial intelligence tool that analyzes your data and simulates an older version of yourself to give you advice."

Her voice was soothing to hear and reminded me that I wasn't alone onstage; I had her.

"Wiser, I made a mistake," I said. "I took someone for granted and now I think I've lost him for good. What should I do?"

The audience shifted uncomfortably. It was a risky move, too personal perhaps, but what did I have to lose? I wasn't going to win the competition, but there was one thing I could still win back.

"Have you apologized?"

"Yes."

"And you've amended your behavior?"

"Yes."

"And he's still not amenable?"

"I don't think so."

"Then there's nothing left to do but remember that growth comes only from mistakes. And if you find your-self forgetting, I suggest you go outside and watch the birds spreading their wings in the trees, and remind yourself that at one point in evolution they didn't exist, and that if such beauty could be a product of a mistake, your fate might not be any worse."

A hush fell over the audience. All I could hear was my breathing. I couldn't see Mast; the glare of the spotlight was too bright, but I could almost hear his heart in the dark, beating along with mine.

When I finished my demonstration, I returned to my seat, too scared to look up and see Mast's reaction.

"Well, that was intense," Deborah whispered.

"It was good," Amina assured me. "It was . . . memorable."

The rest of the Showcase passed in a blur, coming in and out of focus. I was too busy thinking about what Wiser had said to pay attention. There was nothing left for me to do; I had to accept that it was over.

When the last person finished, Lars Lang took the stage to announce the award of the night: Founder of the Year.

A stillness fell over the room as he explained how they chose each year's winner—a combination of stock value, class and Showcase performance, and perceived potential among teachers and industry professionals.

Then he gazed out at the room and smiled. "This year's Founder is Amina Ibeh."

I turned to her, overwhelmed with pride, and hugged her as she clasped her hands to her chest and beamed. "No one deserves it more than you," I said.

"Thanks," she whispered.

Everyone clapped as she ascended the stage and accepted her prize: a handshake from Lars Lang, a glass paperweight shaped like an almond tree, and a check.

As the ceremony ended and the crowds dispersed, I lingered, hoping that Mast would find me, but he had already left, to celebrate with his family, maybe, and I walked out of the empty auditorium, the sound of my footsteps accompanying me on my way out.

■ ■ ■

How do you know if things are getting better when you feel like you're in the exact same place that you started? I went out to a late lunch with Amina and her family, then spent the rest of the afternoon packing to go home. I had mixed feelings about it—part of me dreading going back to Worcester, part of me relieved. I was tired of pretending to be an adult, of making decisions that had bigger repercussions than I'd ever imagined and having to live with the fallout. That night I slept fitfully. I dreamed I was in my bedroom in Worcester, tearing down all the clippings of Mitzy that hung over the bed, removing all of the California paraphernalia until the walls were bare. Even my inbox was empty, with no ObjectPermanence to talk to. I was starting life anew.

I spent the next day away from my computer, packing and trying to soak up my last moments in California. When I finally logged on, I found two new messages waiting for me. The first was from ObjectPermanence.

If I'm honest, the reason why I never wanted to tell you my name was because I was ashamed. I was ashamed of the way I stood quietly when AJ humiliated you for breaking his drone. I was ashamed of how silent I was in class and at parties when he mocked and embarrassed you. I'm ashamed of the way I participated in his cruelty and apologized for it. Even though I didn't know you were here then, deep down I felt that you'd be able to see it when you looked at a picture of me online or read a description of what I was doing—that you'd know I wasn't who I said I was.

I wish I'd told you sooner, but I guess now is as good a time as any to start fresh. Maybe in a different life we'll have more time.

Take care of yourself, okay?

Mike

I felt a pain in my chest and had to close the window before I second-guessed myself. It was the right decision. Or maybe there were no right decisions, only choices that you made the best of because that's all we can do.

The second message was from a man named Simon Garthwell at Redwood Capital.

Dear Ms. Chan,

I was impressed by the demonstration of your app, Wiser, at the Foundry's Venture Capital Showcase. It was fresh, well-executed, and shows potential for a number of different growth opportunities.

I'd love to hear more about where you hope to take it and would like to bring you in to the office to meet some of my colleagues and discuss a potential seed funding opportunity.

Best,

Simon Garthwell

Partner, Redwood Capital

I read it again, my heart pounding, and had to fight the urge to wonder if it was a joke. No, Simon Garthwell was a real person whom I'd heard of, with a real email address that looked awfully legitimate. Was it possible that I was getting a second chance?

I opened a response window and stared at the screen, trying to figure out what to write back, when my phone vibrated. It was Mast.

>7:00 p.m., Ocean Beach. Bring a coat

I blinked, unable to believe that he was texting me. The tone was impossible to read, and I had to remind myself to breathe.

I checked the time. It was six o'clock. I closed my laptop, threw on a jacket, and called a car.

■ ■ ■

The sun was setting as the driver sped up the coast along the Great Highway and pulled in front of a long stretch of dunes swaying with sea grass. I got out and trudged through the sand until I caught my first glimpse of the waves.

The sun had cracked over the water, spilling out into the horizon in oranges and purples. Ocean Beach was on the western side of San Francisco, where the air was cold and wet, like a cloud blown in from the ocean.

The beach was mostly empty except for a few surfers drifting on the swells. Mast was sitting on the sand facing the water, his sunglasses reflecting the sky. A brown paper bag sat on the beach beside him. I took that as a good sign.

I walked toward him, unsure of what he was going to say. What if he'd asked me to meet him so he could tell me to my face that he couldn't forgive me? That he wanted to say goodbye?

He was wearing a red hoodie, beneath which I could see the back of his neck ripple as he turned to me, beautiful and golden like sand.

He took off his sunglasses and gazed at me, his eyes wide and searching, as if looking at me made him sad.

"Hey," he said.

"Hey. May I?"

He nodded and I sat down next to him and looked out at the water. Neither of us spoke for a long time.

"It's a surfing beach," Mast finally said. "It's cold and churning and has a strong undercurrent. It isn't for beginners."

I waited to see where he was going.

"People don't come here because it's beautiful or has perfect conditions. They don't come here because it's romantic. They come because they love surfing. Because they want the challenge and they can't stay away. Because they love it."

Mast turned to me, his eyes soft and yearning as they took me in. "That's why I like it, too."

"Are we still talking about surfing?" I whispered.

"No."

"Are you saying I'm cold and churning and spit men out on a whim?"

He grinned. "I'm saying I love you. Every part of you. Even the hard stuff."

I felt everything inside me unfold.

He leaned toward me and pressed his lips to mine. The wind blew around us, kicking up the sand, making our clothes billow, but I barely noticed the cold.

"If you," he whispered, leaning his forehead against mine.

I felt the salt on his skin as our breath mingled. I smiled. "Then me."

# Acknowledgments

This book would not have been possible without the help and guidance of my agent, Ted Malawer. I'm so lucky to have you.

I'm forever grateful to my editor, Katherine Tegen, and to Sara Schonfeld, for helping me make this book better than I ever could have on my own, and for taking a chance on this story and on me. Also to Molly Fehr, Amy Ryan, Mary Auxier, Laura Harshberger, Bethany Reis, Jennifer Moles, Cara Norris-Ramirez, Valerie Wong, and the entire team at HarperCollins.

Many thanks to Julia Yellow for the incredible cover art, and to Michael Polycarpou, Paul Col, and Mitchell Spector for helping me write about programming without sounding like a total noob.

I wouldn't have had access to this world without Rebecca Autumn Sansom, the Weidhaas Family (who bear no resemblance to their eponymous characters), Lynda Mortensen, and Bay Area Pet Pals—the best dog walking company in Silicon Valley.

Thank you to Sara Davis, Michael Stearns, the Col-Spector Family, Jessamine Chan, Yvonne Miaoulis, Anna

Kurien and Jacob Thomas, Lauren Bamberger, Jackie Meyers, Emily and Alex Straffin, and Hannah and Griffin Col.

And finally, I couldn't have written this book without my family: Nananda Col, Chee-Wai Woon, and Akiva Freidlin, who provided shelter, food, childcare, and emotional support while I wrote.

Thank you.